I SPOT HIM ACROSS THE ROOM AND REALIZE I HAVE ONLY MINUTES TO LIVE. THE PARTNER I BETRAYED SEVEN YEARS AGO. HOW PATIENTLY HE WAITED FOR HIS REVENGE. BUT THERE WAS NEVER REALLY ANY DOUBT HE WOULD RISE FROM THE DEAD TO COME FOR ME.

A master criminal who's also a passionate art lover.

A long-lost painting by Johannes Vermeer.

A completely green and very young private investigator hired to find a missing art professor by a wife whose motives are suspect.

And two police detectives investigating an unidentified corpse pulled up from the depths by a fisherman.

Near the shores of Lake George in upstate New York, a mystery is taking shape and the person trying to solve it, Harvey Grace, has no idea who he can trust.

Early Praise for A Patient Enemy

"Greco hooked me from page one. As a thriller addict, I will be on the lookout for all of his work. Reading his book was like watching a 3-D movie — as if you were right there with the characters. Take *A Patient Enemy* to the beach, you'll inhale it in a day!"—**Robin Lewis, publisher, author, former executive VP and executive editor at WWD, CEO of The Robin Report**

"... a classic noir from S.E. Greco that's true to the genre and doesn't disappoint....unfolds with all the suspense of a black and white thriller from 1940s Hollywood. ... pour yourself a drink, settle into a comfy chair, and enjoy this entertaining read. One you start down this road of twists and turns, you'll be hooked, as was I".—***Robert Sultan, author of The Vientiane Affair and Slaughtering Girl***

"Greco hooks you and *Patient Enemy* reels you in. The twisting plot kept me guessing and I could not put it down. I was taken in by the head-fakes, hidden clues and salty characters. I will never believe the attribution on a painting again. Overall, a great read."—***Robert Berne, author of Tuscan Son***

When Kane opened the drawer and his hand found the gun, he lifted it and instantly realized he was dead, as dead as if he already had a stake in his heart, or a bullet buried deep in his brain because he knew from the weight of the weapon that his friends were gone, those thirteen little guys who had been his steadfast buddies for all these years—the twelve bullets that had rested snugly in the clip, waiting so patiently to one day be called upon, and the loner that had loyally stood at attention in the chamber the whole time.

They had all been kidnapped by Zola.

Kane dropped the useless weapon.

And then he realized Zola was of course behind him already, after moving in dead silence from whatever spot in the room where he had invisibly crouched like the ghost he was, or on second thought maybe he hadn't moved because no one could move that quietly. He'd just materialized behind Kane. Teleported, maybe.

Zola spoke only two words: "Goodbye, Gaspard," as calmly and politely as if they were old friends parting after having a drink together at the neighborhood bar, and Kane's final thought was: Seven years. He waited that long to get me. If nothing else, he's a patient enemy.

A PATIENT ENEMY

S.E. Greco

Moonshine Cove Publishing, LLC
Abbeville, South Carolina U.S.A.
First Moonshine Cove Edition Aug 2022

ISBN: 9781952439377

To Steve and Erin -- thanks for all the love, encouragement, and inspiration

About the Author

S.E. (Stephen Edward) Greco grew up in the Philadelphia suburbs and studied science and engineering at Cornell University. After a career at a major tech company, he pivoted from writing patents and technical papers to penning fiction. His mystery, suspense, humor, and science fiction short stories have appeared recently in Suspense Magazine, The Dark City Crime and Mystery Magazine, Literary Hatchet, Scarlet Leaf Review, Commuter Lit, Bards and Sages Quarterly, Society of Misfit Stories, Suspense Unimagined, Strange Stories, and Going Down Swinging: Pigeonholed. His work has been nominated twice for the Pushcart Prize anthology and his story "I Called to Say You're Dead" was a runner-up for the Short Mystery Fiction Society's 2020 Derringer Award for best mystery novelette. He also received honorable mention for a writer's grant from the Speculative Literature Foundation for his dystopian sci-fi story, "As Good as My Brother." He resides in New York and divides his time between writing, reading, and oil painting. Visit him at:

segrecoauthor.com

A PATIENT ENEMY

Chapter 1
Wednesday, May 20, 7:02 p.m.
New York City

It was during his dinner, as he raised a forkful of Caesar salad to his lips, that Benjamin Kane saw a ghost.

The ghost of Alexander Zola.

It passed behind the maitre d' who stood at his podium as he decided with regal impunity which of the people on his long waiting list would dine in this fine New York City restaurant tonight, where the portions were slim and the prices were bloated. Whoever or whatever glided behind the preoccupied maitre d' in those brief seconds didn't attract even a wisp of his attention.

And probably most of the other diners didn't notice, and even if they did, they wouldn't have cared. Just another nobody going nowhere in a city of millions.

But Benjamin Kane noticed because he'd lived for seven years dreading the moment when Zola would finally come for him.

Despite the new identity Kane had manufactured for himself and his relocation from Europe to the States, Kane had kept his senses tuned for all this time, his antennae fully extended. And even as he lived his busy life, building a successful business, he was always waiting, listening, watching. He'd spent years glancing over his shoulder as he walked the streets. Years sitting with his back to the wall in restaurants or other public places, expecting that someday Alex would walk in.

But Alex died in that fire seven years ago.

Kane *knew* that.

So then why did he search the internet every day for any scraps of news about Zola? And why did Kane still, even after all these years, keep his gun at least near him, if not on him? Right now, it was in his hotel room upstairs, tucked behind some clothes in the back of a dresser drawer. Was it because some repressed, subconscious part of Kane knew there was a finite chance, however minuscule, that Zola had survived the fire, cheating death and evading capture again?

Kane put his fork down and wiped his lips. He willed himself to calm down. He'd experienced many of these sightings in the past seven years, probably twenty-five to thirty times in all. They were much less frequent now than in the beginning of his new life. But every incident turned out to be inconsequential. They always began with a momentary glance of someone who, in low light, bore a slight resemblance to Zola. The person was usually moving quickly and very often in a crowded area, where the senses can be fooled by distractions. When you walked through cities that held millions of people, the odds were good that sooner or later you would run into someone who looks like someone else, right?

Kane began to relax now. Of *course,* it was a false alarm, just like all the previous times. He knew it because Zola was dead.

Dead, **Dead, DEAD.**

And Kane didn't believe in ghosts.

So, FORGET IT.

Kane looked across the table at the lovely creature having dinner with him. She had flaming red hair that fell in luscious waves over her shoulders. His eyes traced the delicious curves of her twenty-six-year-old body. He was lucky. He had it all. A successful business, which had led to moderate wealth. A waistline under reasonable control for a man of fifty-five. A beautiful wife. Three beautiful kids, who weren't too badly behaved. At least his wife could manage to keep them under control. And a beautiful mistress.

There were days when he might work a bit late and then meet his wife for dinner, but not today.

Today was a mistress day, not a wife day, and that was the reason he had a hotel room upstairs. He would make good use of the room and then be home by midnight, from his "late night at work."

10

"Is anything wrong?" asked Christie. "You looked a little uneasy a moment ago."

"Uh, just thinking. About nothing in particular," Kane answered. "How's your salad?"

"The dressing's a little too vinegary." She wrinkled her nose and smiled. "Uh, is *vinegary* a word?"

Christie was very conscious of how she spoke because she came from a poor background. Like her brothers and sisters, she hadn't finished high school. But that didn't matter a bit to Kane. He had no interest in her mind.

"Yes, I think so," Kane replied politely. "Shall I order you another salad with a different dressing?"

"No, no. I wouldn't eat it anyway. I have to save room for my entree."

A well-groomed young waiter in a starched white shirt and black pants appeared next to Kane.

"Champagne, sir," said the waiter, showing the handsome green bottle to Kane, with the label facing him to allow for an inspection.

"I didn't order champagne," said Kane with a puzzled look.

"Compliments of the gentleman sitting at the bar," the waiter retorted.

"What gentleman?"

The waiter pointed. "In the trench-coat, sir. At the very end of the bar."

Several people obstructed Kane's view of the far side of the bar. He remained seated but bent his torso to the right to see around one particularly obese woman. He caught sight of a khaki trench-coat moving toward the exit adjacent to the bar.

Kane sprang out of his seat. The waiter started to say something, but Kane cut him off by saying tersely to Christie: "Wait here." Kane began to walk rapidly toward the disappearing coat. He deftly dodged chairs, tables, waiters, and waitresses, but when he reached the doorway there was no one in sight. He peered through the doorway and looked down an empty, softly lit hallway that led to the alley behind the building.

Kane scratched his chin and thought: *Was this the same man who walked behind the maitre d'? That one wore a khaki trench-coat, too, but so did a lot of other men in this room today because of the rain. And that one in profile looked something like Zola, but I didn't see the face of this one at the end of the bar, just the back of his head. The hair looked the same maybe, but he was pretty far away...*

Okay, I know a lot of people in this town, it's possible one of them spotted me and decided to buy me a bottle of champagne. A business associate. Sure, that's it. I've got lots of business friends in this town. Maybe one of them wanted to surprise me but remain anonymous. And hey, let's face it, I've got business enemies, too. Just last year I forced a competitor out of business. Maybe one of them saw me sitting here with Christie, realized she wasn't my wife, and just wanted to let me know I was seen, to play head games with me. Okay, I can handle it, if that's the case. Christie works for me, so what's the big deal? I had a meal with one of my employees, right? It's not like I was seen going into a hotel room with her...

Kane was much too cautious for that. They would, of course, go up to the room separately after they were finished with dinner.

Kane smoothed his hair with a stroke of his hand, straightened his tie, and began to walk casually back to his table. He saw that no one was staring at him, so he felt certain he didn't look worried or flustered, and that he hadn't done anything to draw attention to himself.

It had been, after all, seven years. The passage of that much time can certainly change a man's appearance, and the guy who had passed behind the maitre d' might have looked a little like Zola from seven years ago, but he would have changed quite a bit since then. Zola probably had gray hair by now, or maybe *no* hair, because you don't lead a life on the edge like his without having it take a toll on you physically.

And anyway, why am I even thinking about this, because the guy is dead.

DEAD.

Kane reached the table and saw Christie had already begun her entree, a small chicken breast stuffed with spinach, gorgonzola, and pine nuts. His entree of lamb chops waited for him, and it looked delicious. The champagne sat in an ice bucket next to the table, and two tall crystal glasses were filled with the cold, bubbly liquid.

"Did you see who it was that sent the champagne?" she asked.

"No," said Kane simply. He relaxed once again, and he wanted to forget the whole thing. He looked at Christie's shapely body, and his thoughts wandered to what they would do after dinner...

Christie sipped her champagne. "Well, whoever sent this must have made a mistake," she said. "The name on the card is wrong. But there's no point in letting it go to waste."

"What card?" asked Kane as he sat down.

"It was on the bottle," she answered, pointing to a tiny paper card, silver on one side and white on the other, that sat on the tablecloth near Kane's plate.

She said with indifference: "It's for somebody named Gaspard."

Gaspard!

Kane hadn't been called by his real name, Gaspard Boulle, in ... seven years...

A sudden hot flash engulfed him. He lunged for the card and read the short message, written in a beautifully legible script with a black fountain pen:

> My Dear Gaspard:
> Let's drink to old friendships.

The gun.

He had to get the gun immediately. Without it, he didn't stand a chance. He knew very well what Zola was capable of, and Kane couldn't count on anyone to protect him, not the security guards in the hotel, not the police. He absolutely needed his gun, with it maybe he had a slim chance, but without it, there was certainly no chance at all. Maybe if he was very lucky, Zola wouldn't suspect he carried a gun.

After all, he had never carried one when they worked with each other long ago.

But then, Zola wasn't his enemy back then.

Kane looked around in a panic, jerking and spinning his head to survey the entire dining room. Nowhere did he see the man he so terribly feared.

"What's wrong?" Christie asked.

He ignored her.

She would have to fend for herself. Zola had seen them sitting together. Kane knew if he somehow escaped Zola today, then Christie would be a target. If she were alone, Zola could take her with ridiculous ease. He could probably even kill her in the middle of this crowded dining room if he wished, and then walk out without being challenged. But that wasn't Kane's problem. Should he warn her? He thought about it for only the tiniest of moments. The answer was clear: No. If he did, she might get hysterical. And he couldn't have her come with him, she would slow him down if something happened. Besides, what did he really owe her? They had slept together three or four times. So what?

"Stay here," Kane ordered Christie, with no explanation. She gave him a puzzled look but obeyed without question.

Kane stood and walked quickly out of the dining room, past the *maitre d* and into the luxurious hotel lobby, all the while searching, scanning everyone in his field of vision as they went about their business. There was no sign of Zola. Kane finally reached the elevator, punched the up button, and then turned around. As he waited, he continued his cautious surveillance of everyone around him, his foot nervously tapping the Italian marble floor.

He silently cursed Zuckerman for having come up with the scheme to betray Zola seven years ago. Kane also wondered how Zola found him. Maybe Zola had gotten the information from that pig, Hobblewaithe? Kane realized it was incredibly stupid of him to have trusted Tristan Hobblewaithe in any way, and if the information had come from him, Kane sincerely hoped he was already dead.

A chime sounded, and Kane whirled around as the double doors opened. The elevator car was empty.

He stepped in and hit the button for the twenty-sixth floor. The doors closed and the car lurched slightly as it began to gently accelerate its cargo upward. He was alone now, and safe for the moment. He watched the numbers above the door.

Three.

Should I have taken the stairs instead of the elevator? he thought.

Nine.

No way. Although Kane didn't like the idea of stepping into any kind of confined space like an elevator, he had to get his gun as quickly as possible. Twenty-six floors of stairs would take too long, and he would probably even have had to stop and rest a few times on the way up the stairwell because he wasn't in great shape.

Thirteen.

At least with the elevator you could see who was in the car before stepping in yourself.

Nineteen.

Kane fumbled in his pocket for his room keycard and thought about the comforting feel of the gun's smooth steel surface. That feeling would soon be his again. Maybe he would even get out of this place alive.

Twenty-three.

But what if Zola was waiting right outside the elevator? With a knife maybe. Kane knew he would be a goner because there was nowhere to *...hey, wasn't there some movie where that happened, the elevator doors opened and...*

Twenty-five.

This was a bad idea. I should have taken the goddamn stairs.

Kane's heart raced. Sweating and panting, he moved instinctively to the back of the elevator. *Please dear God, just let him kill me quickly, that's all I ask, and...*

Ding.

The doors opened on the twenty-sixth floor. Kane stared out into the hallway.

Nobody.

Nothing but a vase of flowers on a polished burgundy table against the rose-colored wall.

He stuck his head out, just enough to look cautiously right and left. Nobody.

And then he ran for his room, ran like hell in fact, and a room service attendant turned the corner, walking toward him with a surprised look on his face because it was not often he saw adults running in the hallways. But Kane didn't break his pace, he turned the corner that the attendant had come around and he reached his room a few seconds later and tried the knob first, finding it was locked as he expected and there was no sign it had been forced. He slid the card with the magnetic stripe into the door slot. The green LED lit up and he stood back as far as he could, turned the knob and gently pushed the door open with his foot and held it open with his right arm fully extended.

Kane held his breath.

The door hit the stop with a gentle *clunk* and so there was certainly no one *behind* the door. He could see, because of the desk lamp he'd left on, that the room looked empty. The bathroom door on his right was closed, just as he'd left it, but even if Zola was hiding in the bathroom right now, Kane was confident he could make it to the dresser and get the gun, flick the safety off, and be ready to fire in seconds.

So, he ran for it.

But when he opened the drawer and his hand found the gun, he lifted it and instantly realized he was dead, as dead as if he already had a stake in his heart, or a bullet buried deep in his brain because he knew from the weight of the weapon that his friends were gone, those thirteen little guys who had been his steadfast buddies for all these years— the twelve bullets that had rested snugly in the clip, waiting so patiently to one day be called upon, and the loner that had loyally stood at attention in the chamber the whole time.

They had all been kidnapped by Zola.

Kane dropped the useless weapon.

And then he realized Zola was of course behind him already, after moving in dead silence from whatever spot in the room where he had invisibly crouched like the ghost he was, or on second thought maybe he hadn't moved because no one could move that quietly. He'd just materialized behind Kane. Teleported, maybe.

Zola spoke only two words: "Goodbye, Gaspard," as calmly and politely as if they were old friends parting after having a drink together at the neighborhood bar, and Kane's final thought was: *Seven years. He waited that long to get me. If nothing else, he's a patient enemy.*

Kane didn't have time to resist or even twitch before a powerful arm clamped around his neck and the long blade of the knife sliced into his back and punctured his heart.

Chapter 2
Thursday, May 21, 11:56 p.m.
The town of Port Kole by Lake George in upstate New York

Harvey opened the door and locked eyes with her. Sensationally attractive. Early forties. Light brown hair tied up in a bun.

"Good afternoon," he said.

She looked a bit uncertain.

Did my appearance startle her... because I look like a kid? thought Harvey. *Almost certainly she hasn't seen a picture of me.*

Harvey didn't have a picture of himself on his website. The omission was standard practice in his business since surveillance is one of the normal services of a private investigator, which made anonymity important. For the same reason, he did his best to keep pictures of himself off social media.

He said with as much maturity as he could muster: "You must be Mrs. Damler. I'm Harvey Grace. Please come in."

It took her only half a second to shake off any look of surprise at his appearance and regain her composure. She said, "Yes, forgive me, I guess I didn't expect someone quite so, uh ..."

Young? thought Harvey. *Inexperienced? Naive? Unworldly?*

Harvey waited for her to come up with the appropriate adjective, but she decided not to finish the sentence.

It was her freckles that drew Harvey's eyes — just a few here and there, playfully sprinkled across her cheeks and the bridge of her nose. They went well with her soft features and hazel eyes. She removed her trench coat, evidently having decided to stay for a while despite the dubious first impression. Harvey gestured toward the visitor's chair in front of his desk. She sat down, crossed her legs, and leaned forward. She was close enough for him to catch the scent of her perfume, and as she looked up at him, Harvey noticed the slight reddening around her eyes, as if she'd been crying. He'd said all of a dozen words to this woman, had known her for only sixty seconds, and yet somehow he wanted to console her, to tell her that everything was going to be all right.

Harvey sat down behind the desk and asked in his best professional manner, "What can I do for you, Mrs. Damler?"

She held her chin up as if she was summoning her courage and said, "My husband Grant is missing. I need you to find him."

Jackpot.

Even though Harvey already knew the nature of her problem from her call this morning, his brain bubbled with excitement to hear her say it in person. Finally, a chance to do some real PI stuff.

Harvey had used all of his meager savings to get his business started a few months ago. Much of it had gone toward the first and last month's rent and security deposit on his little cabin on the shore of Lake George, which served as both his home and office. He'd only had a handful of cases so far, if you could even call them real cases — mostly involving local students with relationship problems, like the co-ed who wanted to know if her boyfriend was cheating on her. Fortunately, at twenty-six, Harvey could easily still pass for a college student, and his plain looks made him inconspicuous if he had to loiter around the Lake George University campus; A skinny kid, about five feet seven inches tall, with a mop of straight blond hair and a dimpled smile just didn't come off as threatening or even suspicious. On the whole, Harvey thought he handled the surveillance stuff pretty well, except for that one time when a concerned father hired him to check on whether his daughter was misbehaving at school. Harvey got caught hanging around outside her sorority house by her football player boyfriend who assumed Harvey was a peeping Tom and proceeded to beat the snot out of him. But Harvey was a fast runner and escaped before any permanent damage was done. The risk of getting your head bashed in went with the job of private eye. He gladly accepted it.

But he needed to get some real business in a hurry, and clients weren't exactly standing in line to hire him. And then came the phone call a few hours ago from this woman who wanted to see him today around noon. He'd played it cool and said, "Just let me check my calendar please," and after staring into space for three seconds, his answer was: "Noon will be fine."

You bet it'll be fine. Midnight would be fine. Where to meet? She said she'd come to my office. That would be fine. Top of the Empire State Building would be fine as well. Anything for a real case.

Harvey calmed himself and got on with the interview: "And...how long has he been missing?"

"Since yesterday morning." Her tone wavered a bit, enough to signal Harvey that she was concerned but in control. "We decided to both take the day off from work, to get some things done around the house. We had a nice breakfast, then we started puttering. At about ten o'clock I was in the yard planting some flowers and Grant was in the house, getting ready to put up a shelf unit. He came outside and said he had to go to Blane's Hardware to buy a bolt or something to attach the shelf to the wall, and that he might stop at one or two other stores after that. He gave me a wave and a smile, jumped in his car and drove off in the direction of town. That was it. I haven't seen him since. About ninety minutes after he left, I called his cell and it went immediately to voicemail. I've tried many times since then, with the same result. I called our wireless company this morning and they said his phone hasn't been pinging cell towers since about eleven a.m. yesterday. The phone may be in an area with no service, or it's turned off, or the battery has run down."

"Okay. Did he look agitated in any way when he left? Worried, angry, upset?"

"No, not at all.

"And where do you live, Mrs. Damler?"

"Right here in Port Kole, about a mile from you."

"Have you been to the sheriff?"

She nodded. "Yes, of course. I went to the sheriff's office yesterday evening. They immediately searched some databases and came up with these, which were taken by front and rear-facing traffic cams about five hours after Grant left the house."

She pulled two pictures from her purse. One was a photograph of a New York license plate. The other was a front view of a small sports car. Its black cloth top was up. A man could be seen in the driver's seat but the face and torso of the driver were partially obscured by glare.

"Is this Grant?" asked Harvey.

She sighed. "It *might* be. But you can see how poor the picture is. It's his license plate and the car model and color are correct. He drives a 2010 BMW Z4. The pictures were taken at the intersection of routes two eighteen and fifty-seven, about twenty miles from here, in the town of Millbury. They said the driver apparently tried to beat the light and went through a little too late. The sheriff's office is convinced it's him, based on pictures of Grant that I gave them. I made copies for you." She produced an envelope that she'd been holding and placed it on the desk in front of Harvey before continuing. "And... there's something else you should know."

Pamela hesitated for a moment and looked down at the floor as if summoning strength. She took a calming breath. "Three times in the past few years he disappeared and each time I reported him missing. On the first occasion he came back to our home after being gone two days. On the second occasion he returned after four days, and the last time he was gone for nine days. It was evident on each occasion that he'd spent much of the time intoxicated. The sheriff knows about his drinking problem. The last time, he was found sleeping in his car by the side of a rural road in Connecticut, over a hundred miles from home. The sheriff's department called me to drive there and pick him up. So now they believe he's out drinking again and will eventually turn up. They want to wait at least a week before they even enter him into the state's missing persons database."

"But you apparently don't agree with the sheriff's view?"

"That's right. On each of those last three occasions, before he left we had a minor argument and he walked out in a very angry mood. But he's changed now, he's beaten his drinking problem. And this time we didn't have an argument of any kind before he left. He's been gone for over twenty-four hours. I *have* to start looking for him, he may be injured or in some kind of trouble. I'm monitoring our credit cards and bank accounts and our EZ-pass car toll account. There's been no activity on those since his disappearance."

She stood up and paced, but there wasn't room to cover much ground in Harvey's tiny place. When she turned around, Harvey saw that her blouse was closed in the back by a single cloth-covered button at the top, above a six-inch slit. There were more freckles visible within the slit, as well as an interesting mole.

"Are there any local diners ... or other places... that he frequents?" Harvey had almost slipped and said *bars*.

"Not that I'm aware of, Mr. Grace. I can't imagine him stopping alone at a diner or restaurant unless he's on a business trip. And he doesn't go to bars. He still takes a drink once in a while, on social occasions, but he doesn't have a drinking problem anymore."

"He's not an alcoholic, then?" Harvey felt he had to clarify that point.

She answered without hesitation, "He doesn't get drunk. Not anymore." She seemed certain about it, and that was that. Harvey changed his line of questioning.

"What was he wearing when he left?"

"A multicolored plaid shirt, blue jeans, and a light spring jacket, khaki color."

Harvey scribbled rapidly on a yellow note pad.

"Have you checked the house since he's been gone to see if anything's missing, like clothes, spare eyeglasses, contacts, toothbrush, anything like that?" Harvey wasn't sure how she'd react to that question. He assumed she knew what he was implying, but she answered calmly.

"Nothing is missing that I can see, Mr. Grace. He wears eyeglasses all the time, he's nearsighted. He has a spare pair that he keeps in the glove compartment of his car."

"I see. And you've been married to Grant for how long, Mrs. Damler?"

"Five years."

"Any children?"

"No."

Harvey was about to ask her a few blunt questions about the state of their marriage and the arguments that preceded the prior disappearances, but then he decided against it. He took a picture out of the envelope. It was a shot of her and Grant sitting at a table, possibly taken at a party, both of them smiling. He was a reasonably handsome fellow, late forties, clean-shaven, medium build, with a thick head of dark hair and a trim upper body.

"What does Grant do for a living?"

"He's...retired...from teaching." She paused for a few seconds as she shifted in her seat. When she began again there was a hint of disappointment in her manner. "He's well educated, with business, law, and art degrees. He practiced contract law before I met him, but became bored with it and went into the art field as a teacher. His last job was as a professor of art history at Lake George University. He taught there for years but recently lost interest in that too and quit a few months ago, about six weeks after the beginning of the spring semester. Now he does some writing for art magazines and journals, a little bit of art appraisal, and some consulting. His specialty is sculpture and he authenticates and dates some pieces for museums. He also sometimes buys and sells pieces to make a profit. Grant doesn't earn as much as he did when he taught, but then we don't really need the money. I work at the Pillar Foundation in Lake George, and we could live on my salary if we had to."

"That's a charitable organization if I'm not mistaken, is that right?"

"That's correct, Mr. Grace. We raise money for various causes — orphans, disaster relief, medical research, and so on. I'm the northeast regional manager."

"It must be rewarding work. And regarding Grant's work, does it take him out of town?"

"Yes, he drives to New York City at least once a week, and he often stays there in a hotel overnight. He deals with several auction houses and museums in the city."

"I see. Now, Mrs. Damler, even though the possibility that your husband may have been intentionally hurt or abducted by someone is remote, I have to ask this — does your husband have any enemies? Maybe a student enraged by receiving a bad grade from him?"

"If he does, I'm not aware of them."

Harvey sat back in his chair, put his pencil down, and said with as much professional authority as he could muster: "I'm going to start making inquiries today, Mrs. Damler. And I'll stop by your house tomorrow. I'd like to take a look through some of Grant's personal things if that's okay with you. And get a look at his cellphone call log if possible. And I'm sure I'll have more questions for you by then."

"Certainly. And ...there's something else that may be...well, relevant to this case. And it has to do with why I hired *you* in particular. It's difficult to talk about this, even more so than Grant's drinking. But it's important."

She took a deep breath and said: "A few years ago, Grant had an affair with one of his students. It almost ruined our marriage, but I decided to stick it out. He ended the affair, I'm certain of that, and he told me the name of the student. She now lives and works on the west coast and is married. I'm sure he doesn't see her anymore. But there are whispers...rumors of possibly another affair. I don't have any specific information. At a faculty party shortly before Grant retired, I picked up some chatter as I milled about, from people who apparently didn't know I was his wife. The chatter was about him still being too... friendly... with female students. Even though he's denied to me that he's had any involvement with another woman since that first incident, I can't completely discount the possibility that there may be ..."

She stopped and looked downward. It seemed to Harvey that every word had come painfully. "Having another affair with a student?" Harvey asked as gently as he could.

"It's possible," she conceded, wincing as she spoke. "And if true...we can't rule out that it might have something to do with his disappearance."

"Was there anything in his behavior that led you to suspect another affair?"

"Nothing...except perhaps...he makes a habit of turning off location services on his phone. I know because when he needs to use a navigation app, he has to turn them on."

"That could mean nothing," Harvey said. "Lots of people do that for privacy reasons because they don't want their internet provider or an app developer to have their location data, as opposed to their spouse."

"Yes, I know. Perhaps the explanation is as simple as that. In any case, I think it may be prudent for any investigator I would hire to look into the... *situation*...at school, even though Grant hasn't worked there in a few months. You attended the University, didn't you? I found your name on a list of graduates from five years ago."

"Yes, I did."

"Good. I thought it would be advantageous to have an investigator who can question students and make them feel at ease because you're of their generation. And you could conceivably pass as a student if you feel it's needed. Hopefully, you'll find no evidence of another affair, but it's something I think you must look into. I had no confidence the sheriff could conduct an investigation into this with the discretion I feel is needed. But I trust *you* can. Am I correct?"

"Yes, certainly."

Pamela's expression turned more businesslike. "Of course, the other thing to consider when hiring a rather young investigator is experience. So, I hope you won't be offended by my asking how much experience you have because your online ratings are... a bit thin."

Harvey knew she was being polite because there were only two online ratings he knew of. One was from the case where the football player had beaten him up and his client had probably given him a good review for that one out of sheer pity. The other was from an elderly lady who'd given him a rave review for finding her cat. Harvey silently thanked the cat lady for not mentioning the nature of the assignment in the review.

"Well, that's because I've had my own business for just a short time," Harvey noticed a barely perceptible frown form on her face.

You're losing her, Harvey. Think quick...

"But before that, I was an assistant to another private investigator for three years, and together we worked on a number of missing person cases. With successful conclusions to *all* those cases, I might add."

Harvey nodded while thinking: *Well, we had a total of two cases. Two is certainly a number, right? It turned out that both people had left willingly and eventually decided to come home on their own, which qualified as successful conclusions, right? And my participation consisted of calling their cells every two hours, in between my other office duties of filing papers, sweeping the floor, and unplugging the toilet, skills that I'm sure will be of great use in finding your husband...*

"And...and yes, you're completely right about me being able to easily question students, and I still have friends on campus who can help me. Oh, I might also mention that I have a photographic memory. For numbers."

Pamela appeared to be deep in thought for a few seconds, weighing the pros and cons before she finally asked: "Can you give the case your full attention immediately?"

Harvey's mind raced to think of a non-embarrassing way of telling her that on any random day, a potential client calling him to inquire about engaging his full-time services would have a rat's ass chance of finding him busy.

"Yes, I can," he simply said.

She paused a few seconds before saying, "All right then. Please start immediately."

"Great. And I assure you I'll do my best."

My best? That sounds pathetic.

Chapter 3
Friday, May 22, 1:46 a.m.
A cabin on the shore of Lake George, twenty-five miles north of Port Kole

Now, what the hell is that idiot doing out on the lake at this hour? thought Walter, who was old as dirt, but exactly how old even Walter himself wasn't sure. He couldn't quite remember his age, memory being one of the first things that goes for crabby old farts like Walter Koosey, who sat on the rotting porch of his shack, on a lakeside plot of land that was handed down to him from his grandaddy. One thing he still had though was damn good eyesight for someone his age, and he was sure that this was a guy or a gal in a rubber raft.

Maybe one of those college kids out there on a dare or something?

He had once seen two college kids, a boy and a girl, playin' bury the weasel in the bottom of a canoe, almost flipped it too. But this person was alone and he wasn't out there to jerk off. Walter had just watched the fool push some kind of bags or bundles out of the raft and into the water, one large and one small.

Probably the schmuck was just getting rid of some trash. They closed the local landfill three years ago and now you had to pay two bucks a bag to get rid of your trash, and some folks were just too damn cheap. They'd rather pollute the lake than pay.

Walter considered calling the cops. He loved the lake and hated asswipes like the one out there who used it as their toilet. It was bad enough just havin' the damn tourists take over the place every summer, sweeping all the good fish out of the lake with their goddamn high-tech sonar and fancy x-ray guided fish finders and gold-plated e-luminated lures. It was cheatin', plain n' simple, that's what it was. His grandaddy had taught Walter how to fish the real way, with just a wooden pole, a single hook, and a worm, and that's the way he still did it to this day, and if he didn't catch nothin' then he didn't eat. So, when he saw people dump their shit in the lake like this, it made him furious. And since he couldn't sleep anyway, probably because he hadn't been able to take much of a piss tonight, his prostate being the size of a cantaloupe and all, he might as well make the call. He went inside the shack, reached for the phone and began to dial — but then remembered they had disconnected it last month when he couldn't pay his bill. *Oh, the hell with it*, he thought, and he went back to lay in bed and count imaginary sheep, and if that didn't work, he'd try counting the non-imaginary cockroaches scurrying around his shack.

Chapter 4
Friday, May 22, 10:14 a.m.

Harvey walked out of Blane's Hardware feeling discouraged as he recalled his conversation with the clerk, an elderly, humorless fellow with skin as course as the sandpaper he stocked in aisle five. When Harvey had shown him the picture of Grant, the clerk immediately asked in a voice like a file on a wrought iron railing, "You a cop?" Harvey answered no and the man quickly said, "Nah, never seen him, now move along, bud, we got paying customers here." As soon as Harvey stepped aside, the clerk became immersed in a deep conversation with a customer regarding the merits of low water usage toilets.

Harvey considered whether he should stop by later and look for a different clerk, but he wasn't optimistic about his chances of getting any useful information.

After Pamela left his house, Harvey had done some internet research on both Grant and Pamela, and nothing unexpected turned up. Pamela was featured prominently on the Pillar Foundation's website, and there were also some complimentary local news articles covering her work and a few about charity events that she and Grant attended. Grant didn't have a business website and he was no longer on the University's faculty list, but his name was tagged in some articles from the past few years about the art department. No arrests or anything else unpleasant popped up in public records. Harvey read through every comment about Grant that was listed on a *Rate My Teacher* website and found that most labeled him as a "good" teacher. A few students had less flattering opinions, but nothing sounded even close to a threat of any kind.

"Mr. Grace?"

Harvey turned around to find, standing some ten feet away, a fit-looking man in his forties with a full head of neatly trimmed brown hair, wearing a white cotton shirt, khaki pants, and a comfortable looking tweed sport coat. The man took a few steps toward Harvey.

"Yes?" answered Harvey.

"Mr. Grace, could I speak with you for a few minutes?" He handed Harvey a card which read:

Peter Damler
Art Appraisal and Restoration

Damler? thought Harvey. *Related to Grant?*

The card also listed a website, telephone number, and an address in Paris, France. Trying hard to look unimpressed, Harvey lowered the card and asked: "Were you following me, Mr. Damler?"

"Call me Peter," said the man. "Everyone calls me Peter. The answer is yes and no, Mr. Grace. I drove to your home to see you and arrived as you were pulling out of your driveway, so I tagged along behind you. I assure you it wasn't my original intention to follow you, but I have some urgent matters to discuss with you regarding the work you're doing for my sister-in-law, Pamela Damler. I thought it best that we talk in person."

Harvey tried not to flinch or even blink. He considered everything about the Damler case to be no one's business except his and Pamela Damler's, including even the fact that he was *on* the case.

Peter continued: "I realize you're reluctant to violate your client's trust by speaking to me about the case. But all I ask for is that you hear me out. Would you like to go somewhere we can talk comfortably, Harvey? Get some coffee, maybe?"

"I can listen right here, thank you."

Peter exuded self-confidence, and he looked unfazed by Harvey's cautious attitude. He continued with enthusiasm. "Certainly, here is fine. You see, I'm Grant's brother. We share a love for art which developed in our late teens, and we eventually both ended up in art-related fields. I'm an appraiser and restorer, and Grant recently asked me to do some work for him. He and I were supposed to meet at a coffeehouse yesterday morning at nine o'clock, but he never showed and he hasn't answered my many phone calls or e-mails. But let me back up. A few months ago, Grant cleaned out our recently deceased aunt's house after her death. She left everything to Grant, and in her basement he found many unusual antique and vintage items. She apparently bought many things at estate sales. Among the items was a small painting, only eight by ten inches, depicting a young girl holding a basket of flowers. He suspected it might be quite valuable. Did Grant's wife tell you about the painting?"

Harvey's mind raced: *Painting? What painting? Okay, give him a non-answer and try not to look completely ignorant...*

"Why don't *you* tell me about it," Harvey suggested coolly.

Peter smiled. "She didn't tell you, did she? I'm not surprised. Perhaps you're familiar with the seventeenth century Dutch master Johannes Vermeer. One of his works, called *Maiden With a Basket*, has been lost since World War II. Grant suspected he might have found it in our aunt's basement. He hired a company based in New York to evaluate the painting. The results of their scientific tests verified the painting was indeed done in Europe about four hundred years ago, but their so-called experts declared it to be a very good copy done by a student of the era, perhaps an apprentice of Vermeer's. Grant doubted that conclusion and decided to bring the painting to my attention. He asked me to take a look at it because I'm an expert in the area of seventeenth-century European masters. I haven't seen the painting in person yet, but based on a series of high-resolution photos that Grant sent me, I told him it was very likely to be the real thing, the genuine *Maiden* done by Vermeer himself, in which case it would be worth at least thirty million dollars."

No way I could hide my surprise at that. Holy shit. Thirty million bucks? That kind of money could draw all sorts of crazies out of their holes.

Peter smiled.

"As you can imagine, Harvey, I'm quite anxious to examine up close the brushstrokes, the paint layering, texturing, the canvas and so forth, and to publish a very thorough review of my observations which I expect will lead to the work being accepted by the worldwide art community as the genuine Vermeer. I live in France but eagerly came here at Grant's request to examine the painting. I don't know if he was going to bring the painting to our meeting or take me somewhere to examine it. He mentioned something about it being stored in a safe deposit box. I freely admit it would be quite a career accomplishment for me and a boon to my business to author a scholarly study of this painting. But of course, I'm very concerned about Grant as well."

"Really? How often do you see Grant?" Harvey asked skeptically.

Peter sighed and shook his head. "Not as often as I should. Not for years, since I moved to Paris. Unfortunately, we've drifted apart. We talk on the phone occasionally."

"Did you contact his wife?"

"No, I didn't, and for a good reason. Grant confided in me, on the phone when we arranged the meeting, that he may end up divorcing her because he suspects she's been cheating on him. If there's a divorce there may be a legal fight over ownership of the painting. If it's the genuine Vermeer as I believe then it's by far their most valuable asset. I don't know what Grant has told her about the painting, but I feel that talking to her about it would be a betrayal of Grant's trust. And... I wouldn't rule out the possibility that she had something to do with his disappearance."

Harvey tried to remain stone-faced at the suggestion that Pamela might be... what? ...a cheater? Kidnapper? Murderer?

Peter continued: "I haven't seen Grant at all since I arrived from Paris three days ago. I declined his invitation to come to his home for dinner the evening of my arrival, and I'll be honest, it's because I didn't want to see Pamela, and she probably feels the same about me. She and I never really got along. So, the meeting at the diner would have been the first time Grant and I met face to face in years. After he missed our meeting and didn't answer my repeated calls, I drove to his home and parked on the street, in a spot where I was sure Pamela wouldn't notice me. I waited in the car. At about noon the garage door opened and Pamela drove out. I could see that Grant's car wasn't in the garage so I followed her to your place."

"You followed her?" Harvey asked, trying to exude a bit of outrage. "Why?"

"I suppose I was hoping to discover something that might lead me to Grant."

"Why didn't you just go to the police?"

"I did, this morning. When he still didn't answer his phone this morning, or the e-mails I'd sent yesterday, I went to the sheriff's office. They didn't seem alarmed at all. They said his wife had already reported him missing, and they sounded certain he was just out having a good time and would come home soon. I know Grant has a reputation as a drinker, but I just can't believe he would have gone on a drinking binge now, skipping our meeting when there's so much at stake monetarily. That makes no sense. I didn't mention the painting to the police out of concern that the information would get back to Pamela. So, I assume she must have hired you to look for him."

Harvey was polite but steadfast: "I can't talk about any of that, Mr. Damler. So... what do you want from me?"

"Assuming she hired you to find Grant, what I want is for you to *succeed.* That's all. I want you to find Grant. And the painting. And now I've given you information which I believe will help you, since it appears to me you didn't even know about the painting's existence. I strongly suggest you ask Pamela about it. If she says it's in a safe deposit box she has access to, you should ask to see it, to determine if Grant might have picked it up before he mysteriously disappeared. And remember, if she's connected to her husband's disappearance, then her employing you is just a smokescreen. If this turns out badly for Grant, it will certainly look better for Pamela to have hired you to look for him even before any police investigation started. And please take no offense at this, but if she really wanted him found, why wouldn't she have hired a more experienced investigator?"

Harvey opened his mouth to explain her decision to hire him, but stopped himself before he said anything.

Peter continued: "I'm going to stop following Pamela. I certainly hope Grant is safe. If he contacts me or if I happen to come upon any information regarding his whereabouts, I'll call you immediately. I hope you'll do the same for me. And also, please let me know if you're able to determine whether the painting is in that bank box, even though I might never get to see it until, and if, it someday hangs in a museum somewhere."

"No offense to *you*, Mr. Damler, but I wouldn't even consider contacting you without some proof to back your story."

"But I *do* have some proof. Grant insisted on paying me for my appraisal services. I've got a bank statement here showing he transferred two thousand dollars to an account I have at a New York bank."

Peter pulled out his cell, tapped it for fifteen seconds and then held it out toward Harvey. The screen showed what appeared to be a genuine bank statement containing the details of a two-thousand-dollar money transfer. Harvey memorized Grant's account number and the routing number of his bank.

Peter shook his head and said, "You don't look convinced, Harvey. But that's all the proof I have. I'll leave you now, but please believe me, it's in your best interests to consider what I've told you. You should question Pamela's motives." After taking a step toward his car, Peter stopped, pulled a photo from his wallet, turned around, and showed it to Harvey. It was a picture of two children playing on a swing set.

"This is Grant and me. We had a very happy childhood together. I regret that we drifted apart. I hope to hear from you soon."

Harvey was rattled. If it turned out, for his first big case he was simply being used by Pamela as a pawn, it could be horrible for his career, perhaps even send it completely down the crapper before it barely got going. Somehow, Harvey would have to check up on what Peter had told him. Finding out if she had a lover was a start. But the idea of asking Pamela directly about her alleged infidelities didn't appeal at all. She might become enraged and just fire him. Maybe he could follow her around for a day or two, to see if she meets up with a boyfriend. But following her in his car was a problem because his old sedan was not exactly inconspicuous, and she'd seen it parked in his driveway. He couldn't afford to rent a car out of his own pocket, and he didn't have the balls to ask Pamela to pay for a rental as a case expense so he could tail her.

As Peter's car exited the parking lot, Harvey took out his phone and entered into the note app the information he'd memorized from the bank statement.

Chapter 5
Friday, May 22, 11:14 a.m.

Harvey stepped out of his car and walked toward the front door of the Damlers' attractive colonial house. He stopped abruptly when someone from the yard next door yelled, "Nobody's home!"

Harvey looked in the direction the voice had come from, but saw only a deep green privet hedge about six feet high. "I said, nobody's home," he heard again, and this time Harvey was able to zero in on the voice and found it coming from a small woman standing where the hedge ended and a low white picket fence began. She looked to be in her mid-sixties, about five feet tall with a plump build, dressed in dark purple shorts and a lime green tank top which was a bit too revealing since her figure was well past its prime. But her face was handsome and well-scrubbed beneath her curly black locks. A cigarette dangled from her mouth.

Great, a nosy neighbor. And her nose probably spends a lot of time hanging over that fence.

"Hello. Did you happen to see Pamela leave the house?" Harvey asked the woman.

"Oh, you on a first name basis with Pamela, bud?" The cigarette remained in her mouth as she spoke, its glowing tip bouncing up and down with every word.

"Uh, not really, I've only known her for a short while. How about you?" He walked toward the woman and stopped about six feet short of the fence.

"Ah, she don't give me the time o' day. Neither of 'em do, they barely say hi to me. Like, they're so much better than me? I been livin' in this house a hell of a lot longer than *they've* been here. This was my neighborhood way before the professor types started movin' in.

Anyway, I see her outside in her yard. She does some flower gardening."

Harvey glanced over at the orderly beds of pansies that dotted the front and sides of Pamela's house. It was a beautiful yard, not a weed to be seen anywhere.

"She does a nice job," said Harvey. "Does she spend a lot of time at it?"

"This time of year she's out there for at least thirty minutes a day, weeding, watering, and such after she comes home from work. But she went out in her car about an hour ago."

"Do you know when she'll be back?"

"No idea. Were you supposed to meet her here?"

"No, not really." Harvey didn't want to say he'd been hired by Pamela. And he didn't want to lie to the woman either. He waited to see if she'd offer more information.

"Ohhh," the neighbor said in a knowing tone, nodding her head. The lit end of the cigarette bobbed up and down, and then her expression changed to one of surprise at Harvey's appearance. "Well, I'm Gloria. And whoever *you* are, you look a bit young to be hired by her to go lookin' for her husband. Even so, I'll bet that's why you're here. Either that or Grant maybe got himself involved with your sister? Or your girlfriend? And you came over to punch him out? Hmmmm?" She eyed Harvey up and down as if evaluating his ability to throw a punch or take one.

"Why do you think he's missing?"

"People talk. Like the local deputies. They're just people, and they probably had a good chuckle over Grant takin' off again to do some drinkin' and tail chasin'."

"You know about Mr. Damler's...umm... wanderings?" asked Harvey, trying to be delicate.

"I sure do. It's tough to keep secrets around here."

Yeah, I'll bet it is, when your busybody neighbor has her nose up your ass.

"When was the last time you saw him?" he asked.

"Wednesday morning when he left in his little car. What does *she* think happened to him?"

"Pamela has no idea," said Harvey, realizing he was implicitly admitting that Pamela had hired him, but at this point he wanted to see if the neighbor was willing to dish more dirt on Grant. "She doesn't feel he would've left willingly, so that leaves either an accident or foul play."

"Foul play?" She smirked. "Yeah, sure. Who does she think kidnapped him? Santa's elves? More likely, he ran away with one of his little honeys."

"You mean he's having an affair?"

"Most likely. And it ain't the first one."

"Can you tell me about the women he's had affairs with?"

She took a deep drag on the cigarette and began: "They were barely old enough to be called women. There had to be three or more, all with big boobs and tight buns. That's what he likes. Must have been a student/teacher infatuation thing. He used to be a professor, you know, and he's got sort of a distinguished look to him. It was only his latest that was an older woman." She grinned. "Hah, by older I mean she was at least in her twenties."

"If you knew about them, he couldn't have been very discreet about it."

"Oh, he was discreet enough. He ain't stupid. I'm just very observant, and I got a little lucky being at the right place at the right time. First, there was the gossip, which probably started at the school, and then spread to town. And then once, maybe a year ago, I saw him at a little Italian restaurant in the middle of nowhere — about fifty miles or so north of here. My husband and I were coming home from a weekend in Rochester and we stopped for dinner. And there's Grant Damler sitting with one of his little coeds. She couldn't have been more than nineteen. Barely legal, you know? I don't think he noticed me, 'cause we sat in a booth some distance behind him. But I could see he was having some trouble concentrating on his dish of spaghetti. She was wearing a tight little top with a deep V-neck, and his eyes were moving from her boobs to his pasta and then back to her boobs again."

"Tell me more about his latest girl, the one you said was at least in her twenties."

"Not much I can tell you, 'cause I didn't see her. But my friend Sadie saw her in a gas station, somewhere far outta town. She said the girl drove a sporty red car, with Grant in the passenger seat. And she said the girl was in her twenties, and blond with a good figure, like the one I saw. He has a thing for blondes, I guess."

"And when did Sadie see them?"

"A few weeks ago."

"It looks as if Mrs. Damler has quite a problem on her hands," said Harvey. "A cheating husband." He paused to see if the woman would offer more information.

"Yeah, but I'll bet she's no saint herself, pal." She took another long drag on the cigarette, smiling as she sucked.

"What do you mean?" asked Harvey, his interest heightened.

"I mean, I ain't got no proof or nothin', but it wouldn't surprise me at all if someone told me *she* was getting a little somethin' on the side, too. She's awful friendly with Louie. I caught him playin' peek-a-boo a couple of times at her window."

"Who's Louie?"

"The gardener. You don't think she takes care of all this ground by herself, do you? She does the flower beds and that's about it. And her husband seems to have no interest at all in outdoor work. So, they hire Louie to do all the harder work Pamela doesn't do, like grass cutting, hedge clipping, and so on. He's a big muscular guy, about thirty-five, and he comes over usually once a week, on Saturday or Sunday, but sometimes on weekdays. I'll see her talking with Louie outside sometimes. He has the hots for her, and she'll be sayin' in her sweetest little voice, 'Oh Louie, help me with this,' or 'Louie, would you lift that for me?' And when she gives an order, he jumps to it. And it's not like she's helpless, physically. She can handle a boat all by herself. Sometimes she rents a kayak or a small sailboat down at the marina. I've seen her out on the water a few times by herself when I was havin' lunch at Tilly's Pub. I don't think Grant's much interested in boating."

"What's this about peek-a-boo?" Harvey asked.

"Oh, you know, I caught Louie lookin' through her bedroom window. It's at ground level. I don't know if he saw anything. Maybe she forgets to close the drapes once in a while when she's changing. Or maybe he just *hopes* she'll forget. She sunbathes in the backyard sometimes too, in a bathing suit. She's got a nice figure, there's no denyin' that. Hell, I had a figure like that a long time ago. Anyway, Louie chats with her sometimes when she's sunbathing. I can see him leering at her body, salivatin' like an old hound dog when it hears the dinner bell. If she notices the attention, then it doesn't seem to bother her at all."

"Hmmm. I'd like to talk to Louie. Do you know his last name?"

"It's Parker. He doesn't have a website, but he's listed in the business directory under *Parker Landscaping*. He lives in a trailer. I hired him once, about a month ago, to trim some trees. He's a good hard worker when he's got nothin' to distract him. And I sure as hell ain't no distraction for him."

"And could you tell me how to get in touch with Sadie as well?"

Gloria recited Sadie's phone number and address, and Harvey entered the information into his cellphone. Gloria seemed very happy to help. Harvey figured that snitching on her neighbor was probably the highlight of her week.

She ended with: "Hey, kiddo, stick it to 'em. To *both* of 'em. Serves 'em right, far as I'm concerned. Maybe they'll get divorced, move outta here, and I'll get some *friendly* neighbors." She took one last mighty suck on the cigarette, flicked the butt onto her lawn, then turned away and headed back to her house.

Harvey decided he would come back later in the day to talk to Pamela. As he walked to his car, he turned his head so he could feel the sun on his face.

In his mind he pictured Pamela Damler in a bathing suit, sunning herself.

Chapter 6
Friday, May 22, 2:54 p.m.

When Harvey returned to the Damlers' house in the afternoon, Pamela opened the door and gave him a somber nod.

He stepped into the small foyer of the tastefully decorated home. The pictures on the walls of the foyer and the living room were mostly floral prints, brightly colored and cheery. The dark oak furniture had an elegant English country look to it and the upholstery and curtains were stylishly striped in earth tones. Wicker baskets filled with dried flowers were everywhere.

"How are you holding up, Mrs. Damler?" asked Harvey, trying to sound sympathetic.

"I'm...managing," she said. "Sorry I missed you this morning. I had to go to the drugstore to get something to help me sleep. Is there any news?" There was resignation in her voice as if she'd mentally prepared herself for the worst.

Harvey shook his head. "I wasn't able to find anyone at Blane's who remembered your husband coming in on Wednesday to buy something, but that doesn't mean he wasn't there. Unfortunately, they don't have any video cameras inside or outside the store. Maybe he went there and looked around without being noticed by the store clerks. And it's a very small store, so if they didn't have what he wanted, he might have gone to another place farther away. So, I'll be checking some other hardware stores as well. I also called all the police and sheriff's departments within a fifty-mile radius. Some wouldn't give me any information and just said I should file a missing person report. Others were more cooperative and told me his name hadn't turned up in any of their arrest or accident reports. I checked hospitals within the same radius, just to make sure they didn't have any patients brought in who might have been unconscious and without ID. I also drove every possible route he might have taken from your house to Blane's Hardware. I drove slowly and looked carefully along the edges of every road, especially areas which had steep embankments, but saw no signs of a car going off the road recently."

"Thank you, Harvey." He read the disappointment in her voice and decided to offer a word of encouragement.

"We're a long way from giving up, Mrs. Damler. I've really just started searching." *Careful, I don't want to make it sound like hiring me is going to be a money pit.* "I came over to look through some of his things if that's okay with you. Do you have a den? A place where your husband works, reads, and so forth?"

Pamela nodded and led Harvey through the center hall toward the back of the house.

"Why, by the way?" she asked.

"Why, what?" Harvey didn't understand her question.

"I mean, how will looking through his belongings help you find him? I'm just curious. I have no objection at all."

Should I tell you that looking through his things may turn up a reason for him skipping out on you? No, not a good idea.

"We may find something that will give us an indication of what he's been up to in the recent past. Maybe there's something you weren't aware of, something that might be connected to his disappearance. Something he didn't talk to you about because he thought it to be of no importance." She nodded, and to Harvey she seemed satisfied for now with that wishy-washy answer.

They entered the den, and Harvey was immediately impressed by the number of books visible. They were everywhere — on shelves, on top of tables, in piles on the floor. He glanced at a few titles and saw that many of them dealt with art and art history. There were texts on Egyptian tomb carvings, Mayan jewelry, Italian Renaissance sculpture, and scores of other subjects. A corner table and several wall shelves held an interesting collection of dozens of small wooden carvings of animals — everything from mice to elephants to fantasy creatures like dragons and unicorns. There were some tiny pieces the size of a thimble, and others the size of a grapefruit with an incredible amount of realistic detail.

"He collects these carved animals," Pamela said when she saw Harvey admiring them. "He traveled in Europe and Asia with his aunt for several years before I knew him. Grant bought most of these pieces during those travels. He still adds to the collection now and then, when he finds something he likes."

"They're very nice."

In a small space on the shelf between books, Harvey spotted the framed picture of two children playing that Peter had shown him. He decided not to mention anything about it to Pamela. He continued to silently scan the room's contents.

"Do you use this den too, Mrs. Damler?"

"No, I have a desk in our bedroom that I use. I don't really need much space because I don't collect as many things as Grant does."

Harvey's eyes wandered over to an old oak desk against the far wall with a top that was nearly hidden by clutter, mostly books and magazines. Spotting a small book with a black cover, he opened it and was pleased to see it was an appointment calendar. Paging through it, Harvey saw that Grant's entries for appointments usually had just a single letter and no details at all. They could have been face-to-face meetings or scheduled phone calls. He flipped to yesterday and saw an entry for nine a.m., marked with a simple *P*. The date and time agreed with the missed appointment Peter had told Harvey about.

"Mrs. Damler, may I borrow this appointment book?" he asked.

"Certainly."

Harvey slipped the book into his pocket, and then picked up two credit card receipts from the desk. The first was for gasoline, dated May fifteenth.

"Mrs. Damler, was your husband on a business trip on the fifteenth of May?"

Pamela thought for a moment. "Yes, he was. He stayed in New York the night before and came home on the fifteenth."

"Was he driving his Z4?"

"Yes."

"Does he always drive the Z4 on business trips...I mean, does he ever *rent* a car instead?"

"He always takes the Z4," she said with certainty. "He loves driving that car."

Harvey could tell the gas purchase was definitely for more gallons than could ever fit in the tank of Grant's sporty little roadster, even if it was bone dry. Which meant Grant may have been riding in his girlfriend's car that day and paid for gas.

The second receipt was for maintenance on the Z4 at a local car repair shop, and it was dated a week and a half before Grant's disappearance. It was probably a small shop because the receipt was handwritten and gave no details of the work that was done, except for itemizing the cost in terms of parts and labor.

Harvey pointed to the receipt and asked: "Was the Z4 having any problems recently?"

"I remember him saying he took it in to have the oil changed and the engine checked because the gauge that reads the battery charge was behaving strangely. He said that occasionally the needle would go down near the bottom like the battery was draining, then it would come up again. He thought maybe something was wrong with the alternator, that it was working intermittently or something. But when he brought it in, apparently the gauge was reading fine, the battery was fully charged, and they couldn't find anything wrong, so they just told him to bring the car back in immediately if it happened again."

Harvey nodded but said nothing more about the Z4. The labor expense on the receipt was definitely more than the cost of doing just an oil change, so they had charged him for checking out the alternator. He took out his smartphone and quickly took pictures of the repair shop and gas station receipts. It took him another few minutes to complete his quick inspection of the room. He tried his best to gain some sense of Grant's personality and habits without seeming overly nosy to Pamela.

Next, Pamela led Harvey to the master bedroom. It was pleasantly decorated in a way that made it appear neither feminine nor masculine. The dark cherry four-poster bed dominated the room. Several prints of Thomas Eakins gave the space a cozy and interesting appeal. A few of Grant's personal items were strewn on top of the dresser — a wristwatch, two combs, and a tiny pocketknife. No clothes were visible. Everything was apparently tucked away into drawers or closets. They walked into the master bathroom and Harvey saw two toothbrushes in the holder. On the sink top was a man's safety razor and a white mug that held a handsome black-handled shaving brush. Harvey didn't feel comfortable asking Pamela if he could rummage through the medicine cabinet. But he felt that he'd seen enough, at least for now.

Harvey said, "I'd better get going, I have a lot more things to check on. I'll be in touch, but call me anytime if you have more info for me."

As they walked toward the front door, Harvey said, "Mrs. Damler, I know you're checking on credit card activity since your husband's disappearance, but I'd like to see all his charges from the past month, if that's okay. And his cellphone call log for the same period. Oh, and the EZ pass toll activity for his car."

"Of course. I'll e-mail you PDFs of the information today. I went through them already and didn't find anything that looked unusual, but it's good that you check also."

They stopped in the foyer and Pamela quickly retrieved her purse from a side table and opened it to find her phone. Harvey caught a glance of something inside which startled him — a small, semi-automatic handgun. She found the phone and closed the purse quickly.

He thought, *Looks like Pamela is prepared to take care of herself.*

When Harvey's hand reached the doorknob, he turned back toward her. *Time to ask about the painting. Make it look smooth and casual...*

"One more thing, Mrs. Damler. Grant apparently found a painting recently, in his deceased aunt's house. You're aware of this, I assume?" Harvey noted there wasn't the slightest twitch of surprise or concern in her voice or mannerisms.

"Yes, of course. How did you know about that?" she asked in a tone that was curious but not accusative.

Harvey lied: "I started making inquiries at the University. Someone there mentioned it to me. Grant must have talked about it. What's it worth, do you know? I'm just wondering if its value could motivate someone to...well, take it from him."

She shook her head. "No. It's worth only about fifteen thousand dollars according to the company he hired to evaluate it — Tracer Analytics, based in Westchester. Their scientific analyses of the paint indicated it was done in the 1600s in Europe, but the company's art experts concluded it's a copy of a Vermeer painting, done by an unknown student. Grant had hoped it might be a genuine Vermeer, but he's not an authority on paintings, and to be honest with you, this isn't the first time he's been incorrect in that area. Over the past few years, he's spent thousands on several paintings that he thought might be unrecognized masterworks, only to be disproven in all cases. I'll e-mail you a copy of the report from Tracer Analytics. Grant also mentioned something about wanting to show it to his brother, Peter, who's in the painting appraisal business, but I'm confident that Tracer's experts drew the right conclusions. The thought that a genuine Vermeer worth a small fortune could have turned up in his aunt's house is ridiculous."

No point in telling her yet that I've already met Peter...

"Do you know Grant's brother well?"

She shrugged. "Well enough. We socialized with him before he moved to France. I haven't seen him since he moved, years ago."

"Is he good at appraising paintings?"

"I suppose so," she said, sounding dismissive. "I really have no idea. I was just...pleased... when he moved away."

"Oh? why is that?"

A look of distaste crossed her face momentarily. She said in a matter-of-fact manner, "I don't like him. He...he just wasn't the type of person I wanted Grant to hang around with. Peter is full of himself, always planning some big art score, looking for undiscovered art treasures. But nothing ever panned out. I think he influenced Grant to some extent to think in a similar manner."

"I see. And did Grant show the painting to his brother?"

"I don't know. To see it in person his brother would have had to come over here from France, and Grant didn't say anything about that and I didn't ask, perhaps because I hoped Peter wouldn't come. Maybe Grant just meant that he was going to e-mail some pictures of the painting to Peter. On Grant's phone log there were several overseas calls to Peter in the past month."

"And did you mention the painting to the sheriff?"

She shrugged and answered, "Well, no, why would I? Since it's worth only fifteen thousand, I didn't see how it could be relevant to Grant's disappearance."

"So, where is the painting now?"

"In a safe deposit box at our bank. Grant and I brought it there after the studies on it were completed at Tracer but before they issued their final report to us. Grant insisted on locking it up."

"What if someone else was truly *convinced* it was a real Vermeer? Then it could be a motive for...well, *something.* Do you have access to the safe deposit box?"

"Yes. Either of us can open it."

"Then I suggest we check to see if it's still there. Can you do that?"

She hesitated before saying, "Yes, of course. I can go first thing tomorrow morning. It's at the branch in Millbury, which is open on Saturday."

Harvey smiled innocently and asked as if it was an afterthought: "Mind if I go with you? You're probably right that it has nothing at all to do with Grant's disappearance, but even so, I'd like to get a look at it myself. Just covering all the bases, you know?"

Did that sound convincing enough? Does she suspect that I might not trust her?

Pamela looked puzzled by the request, but said: "No problem, we can go together."

They agreed to meet at the bank at nine a.m. tomorrow. As Harvey stepped out the front door, he turned his head to give her a tiny smile of encouragement before walking to his car.

Harvey rolled his car window down and enjoyed the breeze as he drove back to his house.

The one person that Harvey knew of who was apparently convinced that the painting was a real Vermeer was Peter Damler.

Harvey felt the urgent need to know everything Peter knew about the painting and also whatever he knew about Pamela's alleged lover, but without being pressured to give up any information in return. For that, Harvey would need some help from his friend Dexter.

But first, he wanted to pay Louie Parker a visit.

Chapter 7
Friday, May 22, 6:27 p.m.

Harvey peered out the open window as he drove slowly along the dirt road, straining to read the rusted street signs. He was a few miles from Port Kole, on the outskirts of the trailer park that was home to Louie Parker. Harvey had decided not to call first, expecting that Louie might just hang up on him. And in any case, Uncle Willie, who was Harvey's mentor, always preferred a face-to-face approach for a first contact, emphasizing to Harvey the importance of reading people's eyes and body language when you asked them questions.

Harvey spotted a street sign which looked promising — it read MELBOU, and the last few letters were obscured by rust. Close enough to the Melbourne Street that he was looking for, so he turned. Melbourne was another dirt road with some large protruding rocks, about the same as the other roads around here, and actually, it was a bit too generous to call it dirt. Mud was a more appropriate term. In addition to the rocks, there were pits in the road surface large enough to swallow a subcompact car, which made for hazardous driving even at five miles an hour. One of the tires hit a huge rut, and Harvey's teeth rattled as the car's chassis struck a boulder with a loud bang. It felt as if the impact was right beneath his seat, and he worried for a moment that the muffler or some other equally expensive part of the exhaust system might have been ripped off the car. He glanced in his rearview mirror and thankfully didn't see any parts lying in the road.

As Harvey slowly made his way up the street, he passed trailer after trailer and finally saw the name PARKER on a battered metal mailbox. There was no driveway in front of the small trailer to speak of, only two ruts in the dirt where tires had repeatedly smashed down the weeds. Harvey pulled in between the mailbox and an old pickup truck, which had *Parker Landscaping* and a phone number stenciled on the side.

The characters had the slightly crooked look of a do-it-yourself job done with cheap cardboard stencils and spray paint. Rusted dents in the truck's fenders showed evidence of at least three prior paint jobs, all with garishly different colors.

Harvey got out and walked the twenty paces to the door of the trailer, wondering how Louie would greet this intrusion. The trailer appeared to be decades old, with its mustard yellow aluminum siding peeling in numerous places. By the side of the trailer was a large pile of assorted debris — an old engine block, rusted lawnmower parts, busted lawn furniture, hand tools, and broken clay pots. Harvey ducked beneath a laundry line that held two threadbare tee-shirts and some grayish socks that were probably white long ago. He reached the trailer door and gave it several sharp raps with his fist, then took a step back to listen and wait. Through the door, he could hear the musical jingle of a television commercial, and then there was an abrupt reduction in the television's volume, followed by footsteps. The door opened a few inches and an eye appeared in the crack. Harvey noticed that the eye was a considerable distance off the ground, well over six feet. A gruff sound came through the crack, like a low-pitched bark.

"Yeah?"

"Mr. Parker?" asked Harvey.

"Who wants to know?"

Oh boy, this probably won't be easy.

"Mr. Parker, my name is Harvey Grace. I'm an investigator hired by Pamela Damler and I was wondering if I could ask you a few questions. Uh, you *are* Louie Parker, right?"

No response was offered. The eye continued to study Harvey through the crack. Beneath the eye was some heavily tanned skin. It was difficult for Harvey to gauge Louie's emotional state by looking at just one eye. Perhaps Louie was afraid, but Harvey doubted it. Judging by the size of him, he could probably squash Harvey like a ladybug.

The door began to open slowly until Louie's entire frame was visible. He stepped to the side for a moment and Harvey caught a glance of Louie's right hand moving away from his body. There was something in the hand and even though Harvey had seen it for only a fraction of a second, he knew what it was — a gun. And now Louie's hand came back to his side again and it was empty, so he must have put the gun down, but Harvey realized then that when Louie had first come to answer the knock, he must have been pointing the gun at Harvey right through the door. From Harvey's glance, it appeared to have been a large caliber revolver and he had no doubt it could have shot right through the cheap aluminum door.

So, Louie is a cautious fellow, Harvey thought. *Or paranoid, or maybe just crazy. Maybe he's been robbed before and wants to make sure it never happens again. Or maybe he just doesn't like salespeople. Or he might just hate everyone, except for Pamela. In any case, once Louie got a good look at me, he apparently decided there was absolutely nothing to fear because he tossed the gun aside.*

Harvey wasn't sure whether he should feel insulted or not.

Harvey of course was unarmed except for his hands, which were hardly lethal weapons. He dug down into his pants pockets and felt for anything he might use to help defend himself if the need arose, perhaps a stabbing implement like a pen or even a crummy paper clip. But there was nothing except for a big lint ball, which he supposed he could shove down Louie's throat in an attempt to clog his windpipe, but from the look of this guy, he could probably swallow golf balls without needing water to wash them down.

A few beads of sweat trickled down Harvey's left temple. *Watch this guy carefully. He owns a gun and even if it's not in his hand right now, he may have another one somewhere.*

Louie's tank top shirt showcased his brawny shoulders, arms, and upper chest. About two hundred pounds of muscle standing there, Harvey guessed. The shirt hung out over an old pair of blue jeans with heavily soiled knees. Louie's face was deeply tanned and ruggedly menacing, with dark stubble on his chin and cheeks. His black, disheveled hair hung well below his ears. The ends were uneven, like he'd cut it himself with a hunting knife.

Louie squinted with suspicion as Harvey opened his mouth to begin his first line of inquiry. But Louie didn't wait for Harvey to speak.

"Stay away from Pamela," said Louie in a deep, gravelly voice. Not a question, just a simple order.

Harvey was a bit startled by Louie's opening salvo. "Stay away from her?" Harvey said in a friendly and puzzled tone. "You don't seem to understand, Mr. Parker. She *hired* me. I'm a private investigator. Her husband is missing and she wants me to locate him."

Louie immediately stepped back into the trailer and walked over to the kitchenette area, which consisted of a few badly dented squares of linoleum, a tiny stove that was probably broken because there was an electric hot plate on top of it, a small sink with a chipped and rust-stained basin, and an old refrigerator that wheezed and rattled as if it was about to surrender and die at any moment. Harvey wasn't at all sure if Louie's movement was meant as an invitation for him to enter, but he chanced it and stepped into the trailer. Harvey glanced to his left, looking for the gun as inconspicuously as possible. There was a ripped sofa littered with laundry next to the door, but no gun was visible anywhere, and Harvey wondered if Louie had tossed it behind the clothing. For just a few panicky milliseconds, Harvey actually considered the wild prospect of diving headfirst onto the sofa, rummaging for the gun, and then pointing it at Louie in self-defense, but he decided against it mainly because he didn't know what in God's name he would do or say if he didn't find the gun.

"Stay away from her," repeated Louie, this time with more hostility. "She doesn't need her husband. He's no good for her, she's better off without him." Louie spoke as if he knew what was best for her and that was that. No room for argument.

"What makes you say that, Mr. Parker?" replied Harvey. "Does Mr. Damler mistreat his wife in some way?" As Harvey spoke, he took in the rest of the small trailer's cluttered and grimy interior. It was apparent that Louie didn't spend much time on housework, and he presumably lived alone. Piles of unwashed dishes, soiled clothing, and old magazines were strewn around the living area where Harvey stood.

The place had a musty smell, sort of a cross between old sneakers and overripe bananas.

"Yeah, he mistreated her. He was real mean to her," said Louie gruffly.

Harvey noted that Louie spoke of Grant in the past tense...*like he was out of the picture?*

"How was he mean to her?" asked Harvey. "Did he hit her? Did they have fights?"

Louie pulled down hard on the bent handle of the ancient refrigerator. Harvey took a glance inside and could see only aluminum cans. Louie draped an arm over the refrigerator door and soaked in the cold air for a moment. Even at dusk on a spring evening, it was stifling in the tiny, poorly ventilated trailer. Louie removed a beer and rubbed the ice-cold can across his forehead before opening it.

"That's none of your goddamn business," he snapped.

"Yes, it *is* my business, Mr. Parker. If I'm to find Mr. Damler, I need to know a lot about him. Do you have any idea where he might be? Where were you on Wednesday when he disappeared?" *And am I nuts for talking like this?*

Louie ignored the questions and replied in a threatening tone: "I told you, don't even bother looking for him. Pamela doesn't know it, but her husband's screwed up her life. I can tell just from the way she looks at him that she spends a lot of time worrying about their marriage. Maybe she thinks she's been a bad wife, but the truth is, he's the only bad thing in her life." Louie paused to take a long swallow of beer. "What makes *you* such an expert on what's good for Pamela? How long have *you* known her? A few lousy days? And you think you know how to look out for her? You know nothing about her, nothing!"

"You're jealous of Mr. Damler, aren't you?" said Harvey. "You don't want him to come back."

What? Uhh...did I say that? Then Harvey remembered one of Uncle Willie's golden rules: *The world is full of assholes, don't antagonize them, especially the big ones with guns,* and Harvey immediately regretted what he'd just said, not only because of the asshole and gun thing but because he'd now made an enemy of this guy before getting any useful information out of him.

Harvey nervously fingered the lint ball in his pocket.

Louie put down his beer can, looked at Harvey with fire in his eyes, and spoke with a final menacing slowness, his voice half an octave lower than before: "Get out. Get out of here now, you skinny little dipshit, before I rip your face off and wipe my ass with it." He began to move toward Harvey.

When a giant says go, you go. Harvey left the trailer quickly and walked back to his car, feeling fortunate to be leaving with both of his balls. Out of the corner of his eye, Harvey could see Louie coming out of the trailer, and then he heard Louie's boots crunch on the gravel in front of the door. *Jeez, is he going to follow me? Did he decide to beat the living shit out of me anyway?*

Please God, let the car start. Twenty-five Hail Marys if you let the car start on the first crank. Harvey turned the key and heard the satisfying whir of the starter turning. The engine sputtered and kicked into life.

As he began to accelerate away from Louie, Harvey wondered if a bullet was about to shatter the rear windshield and slam into the back of his skull. Then he listened for the sound of Louie's truck starting up, but heard nothing.

Safe for now.

Chapter 8
Saturday, May 23, 9:05 a.m.

The next morning, Harvey stood at Pamela's side as she spoke to a young bank employee named Derek about accessing the safe deposit box. She gave Derek a plastic bank card and he inserted it into a reader on his desk. Pamela then punched a password into the keypad attached to the reader. Derek looked at his computer screen and gave a satisfied, "Very good," in response. Pamela signed her name on a grey screen using a stylus and then Derek requested to see Harvey's ID, which he happily produced.

After recording Harvey's name and address and having him sign the screen, Derek led them into the vault where he and Pamela inserted their keys into double-wide box number 5644.

Before sliding the box out, Derek asked Pamela, "Would you like me to bring this to an alcove, Mrs. Damler?"

"No thank you, we just need a brief look."

The employee slid the box open. It was roughly at Pamela's eye height. Pamela and Harvey leaned in from either side to look at...

Nothing.

The box was empty.

Pamela looked startled. "She said, "I...I... don't understand." She regained her composure and turned to Derek. "I need to see the record of all the openings of this box, please."

"Certainly. Please follow me," Derek said as he closed the box and then exited the vault with Pamela and Harvey trailing. Harvey's mind raced with different possibilities and scenarios, but he said nothing as he struggled to stay tuned into Pamela's reactions.

After sitting down at his desk and tapping at his keyboard for half a minute, Derek solemnly announced, "There was only one opening after the initial one when you and your husband first rented the box. It was opened last Wednesday at about 3:30 p.m., by your husband."

* * *

Half an hour later as he was driving home, Harvey pondered the bank visit.

After he'd mentioned to the bank employee the possibility that someone had posed as Grant and removed the contents of the box, the man immediately said he couldn't discuss those concerns, they would have to talk to the bank security officer who had taken a vacation day and was unavailable. Harvey decided to call the man tomorrow.

To Harvey, it appeared Pamela had been shaken by the whole thing, like she'd taken a ride on an emotional rollercoaster. She seemed very relieved at the revelation that Grant was apparently alive about six hours after she last saw him, but at the same time, she expressed confusion and dismay at the fact that he had lied to her about going to the hardware store and had instead picked up the painting that same afternoon. Although she hadn't said so, Harvey thought she must be wondering if Grant still believed the painting was worth a fortune and was determined to have it all for himself. And when Harvey threw another curveball into the equation by suggesting it might not have been Grant who opened the box, it seemed to bring forth a fresh surge of mixed emotions in Pamela.

Or...was it all some kind of an act on her part? Did she know the painting wouldn't be there?

If so, she deserved the academy award.

Chapter 9
Saturday, May 23, 10:10 a.m.

"Hey, Harvey," said Peter. "Nice to see you again." He smiled as he sat at an outdoor table in front of a coffeehouse in Lake George, sipping his drink.

Harvey stopped and turned to face the greeting he'd heard. "Mr. Damler? Are you... following me again?" he said with a tone of disbelief.

"Of course not. I've been sitting here enjoying my coffee. I like this place, it's a short walk from my hotel. I come here every morning. *You're* the one who walked by *me*, eating your breakfast. Looks good. Onion bagel with creme cheese?"

"Uhh...yes. They... have good bagels at that place up the street."

"Why don't you sit down, Harvey. Let's chat a little more. I'll get you a coffee or tea."

Harvey hesitated before approaching. But maybe he could use the opportunity to get the information he wanted. The conversation would be tricky because Harvey wanted to give no information in return.

"Uh, no thanks on the coffee, I've had mine. But I'll sit for a minute." Harvey took the chair across from Peter.

"How is the case proceeding? I'm getting very anxious about my brother's well-being."

"It's...proceeding." *Give him nothing.*

"Did you mention the painting to Pamela? And did you go to the safe deposit box?"

"I didn't do either of those yet," Harvey lied. "I'd like more information from you first about the painting. I did some internet research. The real Vermeer painting has been missing since World War II. I'd like to know why you're convinced the painting in Grant's hands is the genuine Vermeer."

"Well, Harvey, yes, in fact I researched the painting's history extensively as soon as I heard from my brother about it. I contacted many dealers and collectors to assemble a dossier of unofficial information that's been circulating within the art world. As you may have seen on the internet, the real Vermeer's last known legal owner was the Lemaire family of Lyon, France. The Germans stole the painting from them when they occupied France during World War II. When the war ended, the *Maiden* remained missing. After that, there's no official information on the *Maiden*'s whereabouts, but it's rumored that the painting came up in an interrogation of a criminal named Jean Mabboud that was conducted by the Austrian police about ten years ago. Mabboud operated in Europe, mostly as a money launderer. At one point they were grilling him for any bits of information he might have about a wanted criminal named Alexander Zola. Mabboud said that on one occasion he'd acted as a go-between for Zola, purchasing for him a small Vermeer painting from a very elderly ex-Nazi colonel. It was almost certainly the *Maiden*, and it ended up in Zola's collection."

"Alexander Zola?" asked Harvey. "Never heard of him. What kind of criminal is he?"

"The very nasty kind. The first reports of his criminal activity were in southeast Asia almost twenty years ago, selling weapons to any rebel or terrorist groups, large or small, that had the cash to pay — firearms, grenades, mortars, fragmentation weapons, shoulder-fired missiles, whatever. Apparently, he did a very lucrative business in places like Indonesia, Brunei, Cambodia, East Timor, and the Philippines. U.S. Army Intelligence looked for him, but they were never able to catch up with him. He dropped out of sight for a while, then a few years later he surfaced in the Middle East and Eastern Europe, taking advantage of the chaos and rebellion there. He'd sell to any faction or government that had a cause and a bank account, and it's believed that during this time his operation got so large that he took on three partners to handle the monetary details of his arms deals. They were skilled in making the banking transactions either untraceable or legal in appearance, and the business flourished. But he also made tremendous amounts of money from a solo side business— carrying out bombings for any terrorists or rogue nations willing to pay his price. You may recall the bombing in the theatre in Manila nine years ago which killed the British ambassador? That was Zola's doing. He spent some time in Turkey, where he sold arms to the Kurds. Through sheer luck, the Turkish police stumbled onto his apartment in Ankara when they were conducting an unrelated drug raid in the building, and they found some bomb-making materials, including several partially constructed bombs similar to the Manila device and an assortment of sophisticated homemade triggering devices, and he was arrested. U.S. Army intelligence records suggested, based on a facial description, that it was the same Alexander Zola that had operated in southeast Asia. But two days after his arrest, he escaped. No one knows exactly how he managed it, he simply disappeared from his Turkish prison cell and left three dead guards behind, one with his neck broken, the other two with fatal stab wounds.

"Anyway, Zola was rumored to have an extremely valuable art collection, mostly made up of stolen paintings, some missing since World War II like the *Maiden*. He had a whispered reputation in the business as a very knowledgeable art enthusiast, and his main interest was European masters. But he's dead now. About seven years ago, when his three associates found out he was also in the bomb-making business, they apparently got scared and anonymously gave the authorities information which could lead to his capture— essentially the date, time, and location of a weapons sale business meeting. As a result, Austrian intelligence cornered him in an abandoned warehouse in Vienna. The building went up in flames during the pursuit, and they eventually pulled his corpse from the rubble. Zola's associates also gave law enforcement the location of his safe house in Belgium, where he kept some of his art collection. It's believed that the Belgian authorities seized all the artwork in the safe-house seven years ago. The paintings in the collection they judged to be genuine masterworks were offered to various museums or returned to their rightful owners. Those they believed to be copies were sold. I believe the Belgians made a serious error in deciding the *Maiden* they found in that safe-house was painted by an unknown student of Vermeer's era, but they auctioned it off as such. If I had been aware of it, I would have bid on it myself. I don't know who bought it since buyers' records at reputable auction houses are kept confidential. I'm guessing the buyer must have subsequently died and our aunt probably picked up the painting for a pittance at his estate sale after an ignorant relative disposed of his belongings. And so you see, it's quite plausible the true *Maiden* could have ended up in Grant's hands."

Harvey remarked, "That's all very interesting, but how could Grant profit from selling the painting? If it's the true Vermeer, wouldn't he have to return it to the French family it was stolen from? Or their heirs?"

"Possibly, but it's not that simple. The Lemaire family would have to prove the *Maiden* which once hung in their estate in France was the true Vermeer. The experts who authenticated it before the war are long dead, and any documentation was destroyed in the war. Grant will likely be free to sell it and make an enormous profit. Or to donate it to a museum if he wishes. So you can see, Harvey, how important it is that you question Pamela about the *Maiden*. Will you do it?"

Harvey hesitated a few seconds before saying, "Uh, yes. But first I have some other things I have to check on."

Quickly change the subject before he objects...

"Can you tell me more about Pamela's... infidelity?"

After a few seconds of silence, Peter replied, "I may have more information on that topic. But for me to give it to you, I must insist you reciprocate. Please tell me about any progress you've made in locating my brother, and what Pamela has to say about the painting when you ask her, and get a look in that safe deposit box. We *should* be sharing information, don't you agree? Remember, we still have a common goal of finding Grant."

Don't betray Pamela's trust...

He gave a terse reply: "Okay, I'll give it some thought, and I'll be in touch soon. I really have to go now. Bye."

As Harvey began to walk away, he heard Peter finish with, "Please make it soon, Harvey. Because I've given some thought to hiring my own investigator."

Another investigator on the case?

This could get complicated.

Chapter 10
Saturday, May 23, 12:30 p.m.

Harvey drove slowly down Birch Street through the half block-long commercial district of the tiny town of Port Kole. He felt discouraged after making more phone calls to hospitals and checking with more police and sheriff's departments, this time covering a wider radius. None of his efforts had yielded any useful information. And the phone log, credit card, and EZ pass toll files he'd gotten from Pamela had yielded zip. Pamela was right, there was nothing suspicious in those records at all. Harvey identified every number in the call log, and every single call, incoming or outgoing, was explainable and looked innocent. So, if Grant was calling a girlfriend, he was doing it with a different phone. Pamela had also pulled for Harvey the location history of Grant's phone and she was correct that there was essentially no data because he routinely had his location services turned off.

He pulled his car into the small parking lot of his favorite pub, *O'Malley's,* to join the Port Kole lunchtime crush, which was usually no more than twelve people. He went inside, dragged himself up to the bar, and plopped his tired frame onto a worn leather stool.

The most unpleasant job Harvey had tackled so far, other than the aborted attempt at interviewing Louie, was speaking to five friends and associates of Grant's, from a list Pamela had compiled for Harvey. Pamela had already talked briefly to each of them, as she explained to Harvey when she gave him the list over the phone early this morning. But even so, he decided to call them himself, in the hope he might be able to dig something up, perhaps some clue as to why Grant might have run off, if indeed that was the case. To Harvey's surprise, two of these "close" friends hadn't seen Grant in over two years. The others had seen him more recently, but most left Harvey with the distinct impression they didn't really give a hoot that Grant was missing. So apparently, good old Grant wasn't all that well-liked. Only one of them was willing to offer any information at all, a female art history professor at the University named Dolores Mulvey. She was elderly, blue-haired, and British, and she hadn't seen Grant much since the last "incident." When Harvey pressed her for details, she spoke of it briefly and haltingly, obviously appalled by the whole thing. It seems that Grant was involved with at least one, and possibly two, of his female students last year, and it was known within the ranks of the faculty. The school administration got involved, and even though they didn't have any hard evidence of sexual dalliances, they told Grant that even the look of possible impropriety was unacceptable and he must put a quick end to anything that might be going on. Grant apparently followed the administration's advice. It was clear to Harvey that Dolores was quite pleased and relieved with Grant's recent retirement, from her comments like, "That bloody wanker has caused his last cock-up around here."

Paul the bartender came over to Harvey and gave a cheerful hello. Paul was thirtyish and remarkably skinny. He reminded Harvey of a pencil standing on its end, with his blond hair moussed to stick up, almost coming to a point.

"Thanks for comin' down, pal," said Paul, as he poured a beer for Harvey.

"Good to see you, Paul. It's unusual for you to call me up and tell me to get my ass down here pronto. Well, my ass and I are both here, so let us in on what's so important."

"Work," Paul said simply.

"Work?"

"Yeah, work. An investigative job for you, and it's nothing illegal. Get this. My grandmother wants to hire you!" Paul beamed as he waited for Harvey to respond to the wonderful news.

Harvey paused for a moment, and then with an expressionless face replied: "Your grandmother? Your ninety-three-year-old grandmother?"

"Yup. You remember her, right? She's a real peach, isn't she?"

"Let me guess. She thinks your ninety-four-year-old grandfather is cheating on her, and she wants me to follow him."

"Nope, you're way off. My grandfather hasn't cheated on her in two years. No, this is more like a murder mystery sort of thing."

"Are you serious, your grandmother knew someone who was murdered? Who was it?"

"Well, it wasn't exactly a who. It was more like a dog. In fact, it *was* a dog. *Her* dog."

"A dog? You mean someone murdered her dog and she wants me to find out who did it?"

"Well, there's a slight possibility it just died of old age."

"Then what's the job about?"

"Well, the carcass is lyin' in her front yard, stinkin' up the place. She'll give you fifty bucks if you'll haul it to the dump."

"Haul it to the dump?" said Harvey with disbelief. "This is the big detective job you want me to tackle?"

"Well, if you really want to, you can do your detective stuff and look into the dog's cause of death. But when you get right down to it, who gives a shit what it died of? It's just a dumb old hound. I know Grandma doesn't care. She just wants the carcass off her lawn."

Harvey shook his head. "Unfortunately, I'll have to take a pass on your grandma's big assignment. I'm actually working on a case right now."

"A real case? You're pullin' my leg, right? What's it about?"

Harvey sipped his beer again and swiveled his barstool so he could stretch his legs. "Well, I can't really...," and then he stopped because he caught sight of a strikingly beautiful woman seated at a table on the far side of the room. She looked to be in her late twenties. She wore tan slacks, a white blouse with a pleated neckline, and a well-tailored tweed jacket. Her blond hair was stylishly short, giving her a professional look. In her hands were an iced tea and a notebook computer.

It was no secret to Paul or to anyone who knew Harvey how lousy he was at meeting women. Harvey had fumbled through high school and college having no relationships of any significance because he couldn't bring himself to even talk to the type of girls he was really attracted to -- the pretty ones, of course. They were essentially unattainable for Harvey. He felt that they existed on a higher plane, and he was not destined to interact with them. Most of his attempts to start an initial conversation with them fell somewhere between completely incompetent and pathetic.

Paul said, "Harvey, put your tongue back in your mouth and go talk to her. She told me she's looking for a place to rent, so what about that rich guy's cabin you're keeping an eye on, aren't you trying to find a tenant for a few months?"

Okay, so now I've got an excuse to talk to her. And there she is, looking heavenly, a mere ten paces across the sticky floor. All right, Harvey boy, you're a little older and wiser now than when you were last shot down by a beautiful woman, so do you have the balls to approach her? And then she stood up and walked to the end of the bar and faced Paul, paying no attention to Harvey.

"Excuse me," she said directly to Paul. "How do I get to Rider Lane? It's not on my navigation apps."

"It's just a dirt road, but it's not too far from here," answered Paul from behind the bar, as he wiped a stemmed glass and placed it carefully in an overhead rack. "When you leave here, turn left, go down to the stop sign, turn left again, go three blocks and you'll see it on the right."

"Thanks," she said, walking back to the table. She stuffed the notebook into her purse and then started toward the door at a quick pace, passing behind Harvey, who realized he must act now, he must speak *right now*, or he would probably never see her again.

She was about five steps from the front door when Harvey said, "Stop!" He just couldn't think of anything else. She stopped and turned, looking at Harvey inquisitively as if to say, *You talking to me, pal?* But after a second's pause, she turned back toward the door and continued on her way out until Harvey called: "Wait!"

Cripes. That was wonderfully inventive and it really showed off the depth of my social skills. I used two words so far in speaking to her, and they were totally different from each other.

"Yes?" she said to Harvey with some hint of annoyance in her voice. "Do you have a problem?"

"Do I have a problem?"

Congratulations! That was a five-word string, and all the words were different from each other, and while it was true that points should be deducted for the fact it was a rehash of her question, I think it broke the official record for the longest phrase or sentence I've ever spoken to a woman as striking as this one.

"That neighborhood, around Rider Lane, isn't all that great. Let me walk you there. The streets in that neighborhood are filled with, uh, strange men."

"*You're* a strange man."

"I mean even stranger than me."

"I can take care of myself."

Paul piped in, "He's perfectly harmless, miss." But apparently Paul's opinion of Harvey didn't carry much weight because she smiled, turned, opened the door, and left without saying another word.

Harvey followed her out onto the sidewalk like a lost puppy. He couldn't help himself.

"It's no trouble at all miss, really," Harvey said, speaking to the back of her head. "How 'bout if I walk a bit behind you, I can keep an eye on you that way."

Without stopping or turning around, she said, "If you touch me, you'll regret it."

"No problem. My name is Harvey."

"Hello, Harvey. Do you always follow women as they leave bars?"

"No, not always. You're my first one today." She walked briskly now, and Harvey struggled to stay a few paces behind her.

"And why did you pick me?"

"Well, you looked like you could use some help. Are you new in town?"

"Just arrived today."

"Well, we wouldn't want anything to happen to visitors to our fair town on their first day here."

"Fair?" she interjected. "I thought you said Rider Lane is in a crummy neighborhood."

"Well, yeah, I meant it's fairly crummy. Actually, only a couple of square blocks in this town are kind of seedy, and you're headed right into them. Mind if I ask why?"

She continued to walk briskly, but delayed her answer for a few seconds as if she were trying to decide whether she should continue the conversation or not. Finally, she said: "I'm starting a new job around here in a few days, and I'm looking for a place to live. There certainly isn't much for rent in this town — two apartments, one of which I'm headed to see right now, and a couple of vacation homes on the lake, which rent by the month and are way out of my price range. And why am I telling you this anyway because it's none of your business."

"Ah well, I'm sure you and your husband will be able to find a nice place." Harvey saw no wedding ring on her finger but he had to be sure.

She turned and shot Harvey a *gimme a break* look as if acknowledging his lame attempt to mask the fact that he wanted to know if she was married. But for some reason she decided to answer anyway: "I just need a place for one," she said while shaking her head and smiling slightly.

Harvey's heart leaped. It seemed inconceivable that a woman as gorgeous as this one would not be spoken for. Perhaps she had very high standards? Harvey's confidence surged, and he felt certain he could somehow get her to drastically lower those standards and go out with him. But he tried to remain cool and not show any emotion as he continued.

"But if you do have trouble finding a place, I live on the lakeshore not too far from here, and next to me is the very nice vacation home of a wealthy man who's in the Caribbean for an extended period. He'd like to have someone housesit and he's willing to let it go to a trustworthy person at a bargain price. He doesn't need the money."

"How do you know I'm trustworthy? You know nothing about me. Not even my name."

"I can read people pretty well."

"Oh, really? Well, Harvey, thanks for the tip, but I think I'll check out the two apartments. Gotta go." She picked up her walking pace.

"Good luck," Harvey said to her back. He stopped. Her "gotta go" sure sounded like the brush-off. In fact, he was sure of it. So that was that. At least he'd given it his best shot, pitiful though it was, and now he wouldn't be kicking himself in the ass for years, for being too chickenshit to even say hello to her.

She made a left at the next corner and never looked back. Harvey turned around and walked back to the bar, wondering if Paul would have thrown the beer away by now. Harvey didn't think he had enough cash in his pocket to buy a second one.

He walked through the door of the pub. Paul greeted him immediately and said: "Hey, Harvey, I saved your beer. I figured you'd strike out with her and come right back here."

Chapter 11
Saturday, May 23, 3:15 p.m.

Harvey walked quickly along the quad of the Lake George University campus, toward the Engineering complex. He needed some technical expertise, and there was only one person he'd consider asking — his friend Dexter, an inventive whiz who was a grad student in the School of Engineering. Dexter spent at least half of his time in his dingy basement office in the electrical engineering building, tinkering with the dozen or so electronic components he worked on at any one time.

Harvey reached Dexter's office, strolled through the open door, and said: "Hey, Dex, how's it going?"

Jammed into the tiny space were a desk, a workbench, and a small cot. The floor was littered with pizza boxes, hamburger wrappers, and Chinese takeout cartons. Such was Dexter's sustenance, usually eaten with his left hand as his right operated a pair of needle-nose pliers or a soldering iron, working as deftly as a surgeon performing a triple bypass.

Dexter raised his head from the cot, rubbed his eyes, and fumbled for his steel-rimmed eyeglasses which were lying on the floor. After putting them on, which seemed to make his eyeballs double in size, he focused his gaze on Harvey and said: "Grace, where on earth have you been? Must be two months since you last called me." Dexter sat up and scratched sleepily at his disheveled mop of curly blond hair and his four-day beard growth. He wore a grimy tie-dyed tee-shirt and a pair of jogging shorts. His frame was lean and wiry, and he had a few inches of height on Harvey.

"I've just been a bit busy, Dex."

"Too busy to call an old friend?".

"Well, you haven't called me lately either."

"Yeah, well I've been kinda busy. Hey, but I'm glad you came today, because I've got a girl for you Harvey, Sandy's her name, and we're gonna go on a double date. Me and Marlo and you and Sandy. I guarantee this girl is gonna take your lonely, depressing, miserable, unfulfilled life and turn it around. I'll bet that equipment between your legs is atrophied from non-use, probably looks like a shoestring hanging from two raisins by now."

Harvey frowned. "I don't like blind dates. After the last girl you set me up with, I swore off blind dates forever."

"That was Beth, right? Can't imagine why you didn't ask her out on a second date."

"She was a bundle of neuroses."

"Hey, you should have told me that having a non-neurotic girlfriend was so important to you. All right, we'll discuss it later. Want some breakfast?"

Dexter looked around and located a promising-looking pizza box. He opened it, picked up a cold slice, and took a large bite. With his other hand, he held out a half-eaten container of Lo Mein toward Harvey.

"I'll pass. I've already got heartburn just from breathing the air in here. But listen, I actually came over for a reason, and it's good news for you if you're low on funds. I need your help to do a little surveillance. I haven't gotten rich since I've seen you last, but I'll pay you what I can for your time and trouble, out of what *I* get paid."

"Secret agent stuff, right? Count me in. Who are you after? Cuban spies? South American drug smugglers?"

"I'm not a secret agent, Dex, just a private investigator. It's just a case of a wife possibly cheating on a husband, or vice versa. Same old story." Harvey decided not to discuss the details for now, not because he didn't trust Dexter, but why get him involved any more than necessary?

"And you want me to take some nudie pictures of them with their lovers, right? I'll do it. I'm your man."

"Wrong. I know how much you'd enjoy doing that, but it's not what I had in mind. I need surveillance on someone who's not the wife or the husband, but he's involved with the case."

"What kind of surveillance?"

"Well, it would be nice if I could hear all his cell phone calls," said Harvey.

"No problem. We'll just clone his phone. We'll buy an identical phone, and we'll make a copy of the memory card in *his* phone, which means you'll have to somehow get your hands on his phone, take out the card, and put it into a card reader I'd give you, which would download the information on it in about fifteen seconds. With our clone, we'll be able to listen in. Another way is to put a snoop program, written by me of course, on his phone. It's nothing but software, so the dollar cost is zero. Again, you'd have to get your hands on his phone and plug a little jump drive which I'd give you into the data port on the phone, and the download would take about thirty seconds or so, then you just pull it out and you're good to go. With the snoop program there, the phone could be made to transmit all calls to us."

Harvey shook his head with frustration. "Impossible. We can't do the clone *or* the snoop because there's no way I can get my hands on his phone. What else have you got?"

Undeterred, Dexter continued: "Okay, we could use an IMSI catcher. It's an electronic device that mimics a cell tower. We get it near him and his phone will communicate with our catcher and we'll be able to get his texts and listen to his calls. The catcher relays the call or text to the nearest real tower, so he'll never know. A catcher can be purchased on the dark web. They're expensive, maybe fifteen thousand bucks, depending on what kind of range is needed. Fortunately, your genius friend sitting right here in front of you made his own catcher months ago just to see if I could do it, and of course I succeeded, and now it's sitting right here in my office." Dex waved his hand toward a closet, its door half-opened, that appeared to Harvey to be jammed with miscellaneous junk.

"How close to him do you have to be to pick up his calls?" asked Harvey skeptically.

"Not too close. But kinda close. We could do it from your car, parked a bit down the block from his house. Or we could follow him when he's driving and intercept the calls made from his car."

"You can forget about following him. I'm not taking any chances he might spot us. And he's probably staying in a hotel, not a house."

"Perfect. If it's a large hotel, I'll need the room number so I can position myself close enough. If we're lucky, the hotel bar might be in range and I can hang out inconspicuously there and use the catcher."

"Dex, no offense, but I have my doubts about you being inconspicuous. If any women notice you hanging at the hotel bar for hours eating their free popcorn and nursing one ginger ale, they'll probably call the cops."

"So...how 'bout we get the room next to his?"

"Hmmm. Budgetary constraints might get in the way of that plan," Harvey explained.

"All right, don't worry, I'll find somewhere I can sit and get a good signal if he makes cellphone calls from his room. And if I can't, I'll just plant a bug in his room. If he uses the phone on speaker, you'll get both sides of any phone conversation. If not, then you'll hear just *him* speaking."

"Bug his room? How are you gonna get into his room?"

"Oh, please, are you kidding me? If the lock is electronic, it'll be child's play. We can even get video."

"What? Video? No way, too risky, he might spot the camera."

"Hey, the cameras these days are amazingly small, with no exposed wires." Dexter pulled a shoebox off the floor and pulled out a camera that looked like a tiny insect with one glass eye.

"Looks like a nice little toy," remarked Harvey.

"Yeah, the proverbial fly on the wall. I've got others you can stick on a bookshelf, in a light fixture, or on top of a curtain, and they're essentially unnoticeable."

Harvey pointed to something else in the shoebox that had a small antenna sticking out of it. "And what's that thing?"

"I call it a chatterbox. It scans all non-cell frequencies used for voice communications, like walkie-talkie, citizen's band, police, and satellite. It searches for signals and lets you listen in through a Bluetooth earpiece. I've got a lot of other cool stuff too, and I'm aching for a chance to have it tested in the field, so this is a great opportunity."

"These cameras are tiny like you said, Dex, but even so, let's forget anything that involves breaking into his room, it's just too risky. We'll just go with the catcher, and I'll trust you to figure out someplace where you can put it and not get caught. In the parking lot would be preferable."

"You're such a scaredy-cat, Harvey. But okay, you're running the show. I'll need his cell number."

Harvey took out the business card Peter Damler had given him, wrote down the two phone numbers from the card on the side of an old fried rice carton on the desk, then pushed it toward Dexter.

"Monitor calls on both of these phones, incoming or outgoing. I'll find out where he's staying as soon as I can and let you know."

"Got it. One tiny last little thing I should mention. Using an IMSI catcher is highly illegal. Even possessing one is illegal, unless you're law enforcement."

"Hmmm, guess I should have known that. Cripes, what if we get caught?"

"You don't have to tell *me* what to do if we get caught. I know exactly what *I'll* do: run like my ass is on fire. And I'm sure if *you're* captured you won't reveal a thing, even under torture. I'll bet a secret agent type like yourself has one of those suicide suppositories hidden in the heel of your shoe."

Harvey shook his head. "Maybe we should drop the whole thing. Maybe even the catcher is too risky."

"I thrive on risk, Harvey boy. Life is a risk. Eating this pizza is a risk. It's been out for two days. But even if I got caught using my catcher, it'll be okay. It's homemade, about the size of a desktop computer, and the design is so unusual the cops probably wouldn't even be able to figure out what it is. I'll tell them it's a tabletop pizza oven or something."

"Sounds like a plan. And of course, if you tell them you're doing it for me, I'll throw you under the bus by denying I even know you."

"Well, of course."

Harvey sat back in his chair and thought in silence for a few seconds about the fact that Peter Damler had mentioned hiring his own private eye. And if that person had the resources, they might decide to start their investigation by snooping on Harvey. He said, "Dex, I had no idea it was this easy to tap into somebody's phone if you have one of these catcher gizmos. I'm a little concerned someone might try it on me."

"You're worried Big Brother is watching you, huh? Yeah, me too. That's why I take precautions. I've got a *bunch* of phones, I'm on the family wireless plan." Dexter pulled a relatively small, unimpressive looking phone out of his desk drawer. "I made some hardware and software changes to this one so it won't connect to an IMSI catcher. It's programmed only to connect to the towers that serve about a seventy-mile radius from here. It won't work outside of that range, except if it finds free WIFI. I also keep location services off, of course. That way, the only method of tracking the location of this phone is by cell tower signal strength triangulation, which sucks. It can only pinpoint position to within about half a mile. So, I recommend you toss your phone for now and use this one."

"Dex, how did you get the connectivity information for the local cell towers? I'll bet that's protected."

"Don't ask questions you don't want to know the answers to, dude. Just be thankful that you have a genius for a friend. Now before you leave, I'll set this phone up so all your calls will be forwarded to it, but the people you talk to will only see they're connected to your regular phone number. Then you should leave your own cellphone at home, but you'll have to keep it powered on so the call forwarding works."

Harvey shifted in his chair with unease at the thought of giving up his phone. "Are you sure I'll be able to use yours just like my own phone?" Harvey asked with skepticism.

"Yeah, yeah, of course," Dexter assured him, waving away his friend's concerns with a swish of his hand. "Have complete faith in me. I'll even load all your silly apps and photos on it."

"Well, okay... assuming I test it out before I leave here and everything checks out. And I need something else from you," Harvey said as he pulled from his jacket pocket the picture of Grant's car taken by the traffic cam and placed it on the desk.

Dexter said, "Traffic cam picture, obviously. What a lousy shot. Sun bouncing off the windshield. Who is it?"

"That's the problem. I'm not certain. Can you enhance it?"

"I'll give it a try. I have the absolute best image enhancement software in the world."

"I assumed NASA had the best."

"Right. I use NASA's software."

"You stole it?"

"Heaven forbid. I merely borrowed it."

Harvey put his hand up, palm facing Dexter. "Stop right there. I don't want to know any more."

"You got the file?"

Harvey produced a memory stick from his pocket and handed it to Dexter who immediately plugged it into his laptop and began to type.

"Just a few easy keystrokes and...viola." Dexter turned his screen so that both he and Harvey could see it. They watched as a status bar moved to the right, and then the enhanced picture popped up.

Dexter blew up the image to maximum size and said: "Well, the picture of the guy still sucks. The facial features didn't get any clearer. I've used this software a lot, and I can tell the image of the driver won't get better even if I play with the parameters. Just too much glare for the software to pull out any more resolution. But look, dude. In the passenger seat."

Harvey leaned closer to the screen and saw the vague outline of someone in the passenger seat who hadn't been visible in the original photo.

As Harvey stared, Dexter continued: "That's definitely a person. A *smaller* person than the driver. A woman or child. Likely a woman, from the outline of the chest."

"Yeah, definitely a woman," Harvey repeated as he stared at the image for a few seconds longer. Then he looked at his friend and asked, "Can you get a list of the female University students currently enrolled in classes being taught by a guy named Grant Damler? What I mean is, he started teaching the classes this semester, then he retired, so now other teachers must have taken over. I need the class list from the beginning of the semester, even if a student dropped the class by now. I know the University doesn't make class lists publicly available, but you can probably figure out how to get them."

"Sure. People tend to get sloppy about guarding data like that."

"Great. One more thing. How can I check the validity of a bank account number? I mean, it's somebody else's account, and I want to be sure it's a real account."

"Simple, you just wire some money to the account, from a bank account of yours. If the transfer doesn't bounce, then the account is real."

"Well, I don't think I want to wire money from *my* account. I mean, I don't want to have anything traceable to me."

"Hey, pal, again I am the problem solver. I'll do it for you. I have a *bunch* of bank accounts. None of them have much money, unfortunately. But I'll wire the minimum amount of ten bucks from one of them. I'll use an account that doesn't even have my name on it, a business account from a failed venture."

"A failed business venture?"

"Yeah, dude. Get *this* for a great business idea: *organic* edible candy underwear. Made from certified organic sugar, organic fruit juice, the whole bit. I can't imagine why it didn't take off, 'cause nobody else was in this market space, and..."

With a weary nod, Harvey interrupted: "It sure sounds like an earth-shattering investment idea, Dex. The perfect gift for the health-conscious sex pervert. But I don't have time to listen to all the wonderful details right now. Can you just do the wire transfer, please?"

"You got it. I'll need all the account information."

Harvey spelled Grant's full name out for Dexter and then took out his phone and showed Dexter the account number, routing number, and bank name from the check Peter had produced. Dexter's fingers moved quickly over his keyboard, and in a few seconds the wire transfer was launched. After waiting for another thirty seconds, Dexter announced the transfer had gone through, and so the bank account was valid.

"So, what are you paying me for all these services I'm doing you?" asked Dexter.

"Well, I haven't gotten paid yet for this case, and I'm a bit low on funds at the moment, but for now... how about if I ask my Aunt Mabel to have you over for Sunday dinner again? You like Aunt Mabel, remember? She makes those nice big pork roasts. I'll bring you over there for a real pork fest, how's that?"

"Dude, the only payment I want is for you to go on this double date with me and Marlo and Sandy. But if you throw in the pork fest, that'd be gravy. *Pork* gravy."

Chapter 12
Saturday, May 23, 3:58 p.m.

Ralph Cobb sat in a comfortable chair on the deck of his twenty-eight-foot sport fisher powerboat, the *Wasted Seamen*, soaking up the sun and drinking beer. The anchored craft bobbed gently with the passing swells, and the rocking motion was lulling old Ralph to sleep like a baby in a bassinet. In fact, if it weren't for Ralph's beard stubble and brutal mug, he might even pass for a sleeping baby by virtue of the fact he was plump, bald, and nearly toothless.

Now that Ralph's small business had come into its own after nearly thirty years and was turning a tidy profit, he had the time to take the summers off, and he spent them cruising freshwater lakes. Today he was on Lake George and in a few days, he would have his boat towed to Lake Champlain. Ralph had tried saltwater boating but decided it wasn't for him. He wasn't much of a navigator and didn't like ocean swells; he was comforted by the knowledge that on a lake if he traveled in any direction, he would soon bump into land.

Ralph felt that he'd worked hard at making his wire coat hanger company a success, and so he figured his summers off were well deserved, the reward of a lifetime of toil. Actually, the competent office manager he'd hired many years ago almost ran the whole business now, and so these days Ralph's "work" was mostly limited to screaming at the office manager and the other employees, who were extremely relieved when Ralph took his vacations.

Ralph was quite pleased with his boat. He loved the throaty sound that the powerful twin outboards made. Three years ago, when he reached his sixtieth birthday and decided it was time to go out shopping for a boat, he actually considered buying a sailboat. But then he concluded, after just a few minutes of uninformed thought, that sailing was too much work and it was just for pussies; after all, he was a man's man and he wanted the stench of motor oil, gasoline, and exhaust in his nostrils. And so, knowing nothing at all about powerboats, he walked into a boat dealership and told the first salesman he saw that he wanted something big, fast, loud, and shaped like a prick. The salesman was most happy to oblige, and now Ralph liked the idea of letting other boaters aware of his presence by generating three hundred decibels of eardrum-bursting noise as he barreled by at top speed. He didn't even mind the little oil slick he left everywhere he went. It was his macho way of marking his territory, the way a wolf pisses on a tree trunk as it walks by.

Through long swallows of cold beer, Ralph looked down at his naked gut hanging over the top of his bathing suit. *I'll have to go on a diet*, he thought. *Yeah, maybe next year. I could stand to lose a pound or two. Maybe I'll start drinking one of those low-cal beers? Nah, on second thought, I tried one or two of those last year, didn't I? And it was like drinking squirrel piss. Give me the dark European beers, they put hair on your chest and...*

What was that?

Water. From the sky. A few drops had landed on Ralph's sunburned head.

Ralph looked up and saw not a single cloud. But he definitely heard something. A powerboat. And then he looked over and saw the water skier whiz by. About twenty years old, Ralph guessed, and no doubt the skier and his friend driving the boat were a real pair of wise-asses to have passed so close to Ralph's boat. Yep, truly a matched pair of buttocks. Ralph squinted at the skier, who turned around and gave Ralph what appeared to be a little smirk, but Ralph couldn't be sure because of the distance and the sunlight in his eyes. He returned to his chair, picked up the fishing rod again, and sat down. Ralph couldn't remember if he'd baited the hook, but what the hell, did it really matter if you were out here to relax? He wasn't really in the mood to struggle with a large fish, and anyway, he hated eating fish unless they came battered and fried and served with tartar sauce. So, he leaned back in the deck chair and with his left hand reached down and groped for the cooler, pulled up the lid, pulled out another cold beer, raised the bottle to his mouth, and...

SPLASH.

Yep, this time it wasn't just a few drops, but a real splash, yes indeed, and it wasn't the beer that had made the splash. Lake water ran down the side of Ralph's face. Even though the water was cool, Ralph started to boil as he looked to the left and saw, as plain as the fucking nose on your face, a huge shit-eating grin on the water skier as he whizzed close by.

He was laughing at Ralph.

The little pimply-faced asshole college kid had drenched Ralph on purpose and then yucked it up.

Ralph jumped to his feet and yelled a few choice obscenities which seemed to make the kid laugh even more. Maybe they couldn't hear him over the sound of their boat's engine, but he must have looked ridiculous as he impotently shook his fist at them. *I'll show 'em*, thought Ralph as he rushed over to the anchor. The first thing to do was get his boat underway. He was anchored at least two hundred yards offshore, but he certainly wasn't going to sit here and get drenched again. As soon as he was free, he'd start the engines and take off after them. He was certain his boat was faster than theirs. Then what would he do? Maybe crash right into them? Nah, no point in wrecking his own boat. He would just steer pretty close to the kid on the skis, close enough to make him real nervous, maybe even cross his tow rope and cut it somehow. Now *that* would make the kid shit his speedo.

Ralph ran to the bow and turned the handle to reel in the anchor but it was tough going; the boat began to move very slowly toward the spot where the anchor touched the lake bottom. After a minute or so of strenuous effort, the anchor chain pointed straight down into the water, but Ralph couldn't turn the reel handle anymore. The anchor was snagged on something.

Shit! Out of the corner of his eye, Ralph could see the kids make their wide turn as they headed back toward him, eager to play their little game again and taunt him once more. Ralph put on his leather gloves, grabbed the anchor chain in his hands, and pulled hard.

Nothing. The thing wouldn't budge.

He pulled harder, all the while watching the other boat. It was coming right at him this time, screaming toward him like a missile. He could clearly see the face of the kid driving, and he was laughing out loud at Ralph's predicament. They were about three hundred feet away now and closing at blinding speed — *Jeez, the kid must have the throttle all the way open,* Ralph thought, and in a heartbeat the gap closed to two hundred feet, one hundred feet, fifty feet...

The kid jerked the wheel and the boat and skier streaked right past Ralph in a blur as he struggled with the chain, and the wall of water that was intentionally kicked up by the skier hit Ralph in the face, knocking him back and drenching him and everything on deck. Ralph looked toward the skier again and saw, as he whizzed away, not a laughing face this time but instead a hairy ass. The kid was mooning Ralph! It was his little way of saying fuck you old man and thanks for the jollies.

Ralph was beyond rage now, his brain was on fire, but he struggled to stay calm so he could think, and then he remembered the spear gun. He'd bought it just for kicks. He didn't scuba dive, he just occasionally did a little spearfishing in shallow creeks. He ran to the foot locker, pulled out the spear gun, loaded it and then set it down on the deck, ready for when they made their next pass. Ralph started the twin engines, idled them for about twenty seconds, popped it into reverse and started backing away from where the anchor was caught. The boat stopped as the chain became taught again but the anchor wouldn't move. Cursing, Ralph put the throttle at full reverse and the water at the stern erupted savagely. The engines roared like caged dragons, but still the anchor wouldn't pull free.

Shit, he would cut the damn chain and to hell with the anchor!

He ran to his tool box and cursed again when he realized that he didn't have any kind of bolt cutter on board that could slice through the chain. Maybe there was a mechanism on the reel to release the entire chain? But then Ralph saw the boat and skier making their turn, heading in to toss Ralph one last insult. He ran over to the anchor reel and looked for a release mechanism but found nothing, so he grabbed the chain and pulled again. The veins on the side of his head and neck popped out and his hernia truss felt as if it would snap. He ignored the pain in his groin and continued to pull with every scrap of his strength as the engines continued to roar, but the anchor still wouldn't budge. And then, as Ralph glanced up in both panic and fury at the boat coming at him again at full speed, he felt a tiny movement of the anchor, almost imperceptible at first, but it gave him an adrenaline rush that increased his strength, and then he felt even more anchor movement, as if something down there had finally snapped. The freed boat began to move in reverse, but Ralph knew that to get any speed up he'd have to get whatever was attached to the chain out of the water, so he continued to pull with everything he had. The thing had way too much drag to be only a small metal anchor, but it was moving nicely now. Ralph didn't bother to wind the chain onto the reel, instead he let it fall onto the deck into a pile as he pulled and pulled like a maniac.

There was something attached to the rope nearing the surface now. As the murky outline of the object became visible, he could see it was enormous, certainly too big to be a fish. Ralph looked up at the approaching boat, which would have to make its swerve any second now, and when another two seconds passed and it hadn't turned, Ralph looked at the driver's face and thought: *Is he crazy, will he smash right into me?* And just as Ralph pulled the load up next to the hull of his boat, the guy finally swerved at the last possible millisecond and the huge wave of water slammed into Ralph, who held onto the chain. As the water drained away from his eyes, he opened them and nearly let out a girlie scream when he looked down at the huge thing that had broken the surface of the water and it was...

What?

The skier looked back and his grin vanished immediately, replaced by a dumbfounded look, the look of someone who is seeing something both shocking and stomach-turning...

Something which used to be alive but was now obviously very dead.

A body, wrapped in burlap.

The anchor had caught the burlap around the corpse's neck area and ripped it open, exposing a man's head, his flesh a mottled gray, his hair dabbled with brownish-green slime, his eyes wide open in a ghostly stare. There was a short length of rope tied around the man's neck, with its other end attached to a canvas bag.

Ralph held onto the anchor chain as the passing wake hit the corpse, making it bob up and down in the water, its disgusting head banging against the hull. As Ralph's shock started to fade, he thought, *Christ, I can't just cut the disgusting thing loose and let it sink again because the skier saw it and maybe he'll tell the cops,* which made Ralph even madder at the skier, who was still looking back as he whizzed away, straining to get a final glimpse of the nightmarish site of a fat man in a bathing suit holding onto a dead body. And so Ralph, deciding he'd have to haul the slimy thing on board now and call the cops, grabbed a fishing rod and whacked the corpse on top of the head with it because he knew the cops would probably keep him all day, questioning him over and over about where and how he snagged it. They'd probably poke around the boat, so he should dump the weed he had on board and maybe even the hard liquor, and before it was all finished, they'd surely run a background check on Ralph, strip search him, and peek up his ass with a flashlight, so all in all it was turning out to be a much crappier than average afternoon on the lake.

Chapter 13
Sunday, May 24, 6:02 a.m.
Albany, NY

When Beale's eyes snapped open from the sudden ringing of his cellphone on the bedside table, he was startled at the bizarre sight of his wife's face, which was all of two inches from his own. He had grown used to the curlers, but whatever she had smeared all over her mug last night was bright blue. She lifted her cheek from the pillow, gave him a scowl, then rolled over and went back to sleep. Beale gave his standard pissed-off look to the back of her head. He put the phone to his ear and said in a groggy voice: "Yeah, what is it?"

His captain yelled in a commanding voice. "Beale, wake up and haul your ass over to Homerton Springs. And bring your rubbers 'cause you'll be slogging through lake water."

"Over to *where*?" muttered Beale, as he tried to rub the sleep out of his eyes.

"Homerton Springs. C'mon, I'm sure you've heard of it. That little pimple of a town on the southwest shore of Lake George. There's a sign as you enter the town that reads *The Jewel on the Lake*. It was erected by the mayor to drum up some tourist business. The mayor is also the town's road commissioner, dog catcher, snowplow driver, garbage collector, and funeral director. There aren't many people in Homerton Springs, so they each have to do a lot. It seems that somebody there pulled a body out of the lake."

"So, why can't the locals handle it?"

"Because the Homerton Springs sheriff's department consists of three country bumpkin cops who spend most of their time scraping roadkill off Main Street. Murder is a little above their heads, and since they have no forensics capabilities at all, they asked for our help. But don't worry, you'll be working with their head man, the sheriff himself. I

84

think his name is Barney. Or maybe it's Gomer or Goober, I don't recall."

"How do they know it's murder?"

"The sheriff deduced it from the fact that the body was tied up with rope. He's a bright boy, this sheriff. Now get moving. And bring your barf bag too, 'cause I hear the corpse is really ripe."

His boss ended the call abruptly and Beale tossed his cell onto the bed.

"Christ on a ten-speed bike," Beale muttered to himself as he pulled his sixty-one-year-old, overweight frame onto his feet. He stumbled over to the bathroom, splashed cold water on his face, and rummaged through the medicine cabinet for his razor, but he couldn't find it. The one stinkin' little thing he kept in there other than his ulcer pills, and it was always getting lost among the cucumber face creams and miracle mango moisturizers his wife bought by the truckload. He reached under the cabinet for his electric razor and felt the familiar twinge in his thigh.

He couldn't call it a pain. It was really just a sensation ... one of cold metal rubbing against muscle and scar tissue. The bullet that remained in him served as his constant reminder of how he had stupidly placed himself in grave danger thirty-one years ago. It was his never-ending penance for not being adequately prepared. His motivation for always being ready for any hint of trouble.

Two hours and five cups of coffee later, Beale and his young partner, Russell Zoober, walked into the sheriff's office in Homerton Springs. It wasn't difficult to find since there was only one building in town that housed all municipal services, including law enforcement.

Detective Zoober was lean and energetic, with neatly trimmed and combed reddish hair. He spoke first, which was usually the case. In the ten months they had been partners, the baby-faced Zoober had taken over most of the social chores, which included introductions. This arrangement was fine with Beale. Being only twenty-eight years old, Zoober was still young and idealistic enough to care about the public's impression of the Albany police department. The captain on one occasion had told Zoober about his hope that perhaps a tiny bit of Zoober's social skill might rub off on Beale. But Zoober knew that affecting even that small change in Beale would be difficult, if only because people viewed his appearance as odd and standoffish. Zoober had never seen Beale without that old brimmed hat made of black felt, with the tiny red and tan feather sticking out of the band. It looked as if it might have been stylish back in the sixties. And every day Beale wore the same black tie with a white shirt, along with one of several dark, rumpled suits which spanned the color range from navy blue to black. And those dark steel-toed shoes were certainly the sensible thing to wear for kicking suspects in the groin. Between his looks and his attitude, Beale didn't exactly project a modern, favorable image of the Albany PD.

"Hello," said Zoober with enthusiasm to an elderly deputy who was seated at a desk. "I'm Detective Russell Zoober, and this is Detective Martin Beale. We're with the Albany PD."

Zoober extended a hand in the direction of the deputy, who slowly took his feet off the desk and rose from his polished hardwood swivel chair. Calling the deputy slow was an understatement, but Beale figured probably nothing moved very fast out here in Homerton Springs. The deputy pumped the young detective's hand, sizing him up as he did so. Beale stood a few steps back, waiting for the ceremony to end.

"Well, thanks for comin' over, boys. I'm Deputy Ben Spooner."

Spooner then gave a glance at Beale, but the deputy didn't feel any warmth coming from the veteran detective with the pudgy, pock-marked face and the funny hat, who was standing out of range, and so Spooner didn't bother to extend his hand.

The deputy was about seventy, with weathered features and a frame that was getting too large for his uniform. The buttonholes were under considerable stress on a shirt that may have fit him comfortably ten years ago. Beale could see from the buckle impressions left on Spooner's belt that he was letting it out by maybe one notch every year. But Beale was in no position to criticize since he was struggling with his own weight problem. What he wouldn't give to have a metabolism like

Zoober's; The kid ate huge amounts of food but he was skinny as an antenna. Beale also noticed the ancient thirty-eight caliber revolver nestled safely in the deputy's holster, and the gun belt that held about two dozen bullets tucked neatly into their perfect leather circles. Beale wondered if the deputies in this podunk town had *ever* shot at anything other than raccoons at the local dump.

Beale was about to ask where the body was, but Zoober felt the occasion called for a few social niceties first, and so he managed to get out a question before Beale could speak.

"So, Deputy Spooner, have you had many homicides in this town?"

"Nope," answered Spooner. "Last one was when Muriel Fleener killed her husband nine years ago. We never did find the body. She says she fed it to her parrot, little by little. *I* cracked that case. But I shoulda said *allegedly* killed, 'cause it never did go to trial since that ol' girl was nuts. But this time we got a body and no name to go with it, that's why we called you boys in. It may take a bit of doin' to find out who this poor bastard is. Or *was*, anyway. He ain't from Homerton Springs, 'cause we ain't missin' nobody."

The sheriff walked in, a much younger, tougher-looking man in his thirties who exuded the confidence that goes with leadership. He was dressed in the same manner as the Deputy, but his creases were an order of magnitude crisper and he wore a polished silver badge that displayed his rank for all to see. Without offering even the slightest of smiles, he quickly introduced himself as Sheriff John Moody. When Zoober in turn introduced himself and Beale, Moody gave only a quick nod. He tossed a large manila envelope onto Spooner's desk, pulled a report from it, and began to leaf through it as he described the body.

"What we have is a middle-aged Caucasian male," began Moody. "Looks like he died from a single shot to the left temple, no exit wound. He was pulled from Lake George Saturday afternoon when a tourist in a powerboat hooked him with his anchor. The corpse was tied up and stuffed inside a burlap bag, which got ripped open near the head, probably by the anchor, but the corpse's face is still in good shape. A twenty-five-foot length of white polyester rope was used to tie him, uncut. It's the kind you could buy at any hardware store for five bucks. The legs, feet, arms, and hands were bound. Hard to say how long the body was in the water. Probably a few days or less."

"How do you know the rope is twenty-five feet long?" asked Beale. "You didn't untie it yet, did you?"

"Well, yeah," Moody answered. "How else could we have measured the rope length?"

Beale made his annoyance clear. "I would have examined the knots closely," he said in a gruff tone. "You shouldn't have untied them." He spoke as an elementary teacher addresses a slow student. Beale loathed incompetence. He took an instant dislike to the sheriff.

"What are you gonna tell from the knots?" the sheriff asked with skepticism.

Beale answered sarcastically: "Whether the killer has his boy scout knot-tying merit badge or not. The knots also might have told us whether the killer is right or left-handed. But not anymore. So go on."

Moody shrugged and continued: "A separate length of the same kind of rope went from the victim's neck, tied around the burlap, to the mouth of a canvas sack that contained a rock weighing about fifty pounds. And get this: The corpse has got no fingertips. All ten of them were cut off at the second joint. And both hands had plastic bags over them, tied at the wrists with small lengths of rope. The killer must have used them to prevent blood spillage before he dumped the body in the lake. So, the victim's fingerprints were probably on file somewhere, and the killer didn't want the body to be easily identified."

This yahoo is wasting my time, Beale thought. *I want just the facts, not his opinions.*

"Think so, sheriff?" Beale asked. "I worked on a case once where the killer collected the big toes of his victims. He wasn't trying to foil the toe print identification experts. He just had some kind of toe fetish. Kept them in the freezer between his fish sticks and his ice cream sandwiches."

Sheriff Moody stared at Beale for a moment, unsure if the detective had just made fun of him. The sheriff shrugged it off and continued:

"There's no wallet or ID of course, hell, that'd be too damn easy. No rings or other jewelry either. He had a wristwatch on but it was not an expensive one, not engraved. The corpse was dressed in a light coat, long pants, a long-sleeve shirt, a belt, underwear, socks, leather shoes. Nothing unusual about any of his clothes; looks like department store stuff to me."

"What kind of rock was it?" asked Beale.

"Huh?"

"I said, what kind of rock was in the canvas bag? Is it common along the lakeshore?"

"Well, I don't know what the mineral is, but yeah, it's common all along the lake shore. It's a gray rock with some white streaks in it, fairly smooth. The murderer probably didn't have to look hard to find one."

"When was the last time it rained around here, Sheriff?" asked Beale.

Moody paused, wondering what Beale was getting at.

"About a week ago." Moody waited to see if Beale would explain why he'd asked the question.

But Beale never felt obliged to explain anything to anybody. "Go on, sheriff."

Moody shrugged and responded: "Well, there isn't much more to tell. It's likely the rock was enough weight to keep the body on the bottom."

Zoober had his pocket memo pad out and was furiously taking notes, even though he expected to get a copy of the report from the sheriff. Beale just sat and listened. He carried a pad and pen but seldom took notes. He preferred to listen carefully, studying every feature on the speaker's face. This was Beale's standard practice, regardless of whether the speaker was a witness, a suspect, or as in this case another cop relaying information.

"Sheriff, do you have the exact location where the boater hooked the body?" asked Beale.

"No. The boater's a moron, he pulled the body up and came into the marina with it, then he called us. He didn't save the GPS coordinates of the spot where he hooked it. He thinks he was a few hundred yards offshore. The lake is about thirty-five miles long, running north to south, but it's narrow, only about two and a half miles at the widest. We took him out on the lake and he narrowed his north-south location down to about a two-mile long stretch, but that's the best he could do. The stretch is marked on a map in the report. In that area, the shore is heavily wooded and very sparsely populated. There are *some* houses along there, but from that distance, he said pretty much all he could see was trees, and they come right down to the water."

"Okay, Sheriff. Zoober and I will need the clothes, the canvas bag, the rope, and the body. You'll need to keep the rock."

"Keep the rock? What for?"

"How many miles of coastline for the whole lake?"

"Well...about a hundred and twenty-five or so, I think," he answered with a puzzled look.

"A fifty-pound rock is a pretty heavy thing to be carrying around, sheriff. The chances are good that the killer got it right at the shore, close to where he launched. And a big rock like that probably left a depression in the ground. Since it hasn't rained in a week, the depression is likely to still be there, nice and sharp. So, all you have to do is search the entire shoreline to look for the depression, and take the rock along. If you see a depression that looks right, stick the rock in it and see if it fits. If you find the spot, maybe you'll find other evidence there — tire tracks, footprints, whatever. If I was dumping a body, I would dump it a very long way from where I launched my boat. If he had a powerboat, he could have come in from anywhere."

"Now wait a minute, we have to search all hundred and twenty-five miles of lakeshore?" protested the sheriff.

"You can start with that two-mile stretch if you want. Do you have any other information to narrow it down?"

Moody sputtered, "Well, no, but..."

"You want the Albany PD to conduct the whole investigation ourselves, Sheriff?"

"Well, no...."

"Well then, you've got plenty to keep you busy. This is your backyard, sheriff, your territory. So, it's best if *you* search it. And you better hurry, 'cause I hear it might rain tomorrow, which'll muck up any exposed evidence. And we'll need your help to get the body over to Albany Med. Where is it now?"

"At the County Hospital morgue. The autopsy is scheduled for tomorrow morning."

"Well, cancel it," ordered Beale. "We'll do it at Albany Med, and we'll use *our* forensics people. And I'll also need whatever personal belongings you took off the body, a copy of your report, and the photographs you took of the corpse when it was tied up. I assume you took photographs?"

Moody gave up trying to deal with Beale. With a look of disgust and frustration on his face, Moody handed Beale the report and the envelope which contained copies of the photos.

"Sheriff, we'll expect the body at Albany Med within four hours because we need to do the blood tests right away, and we'll do the autopsy tomorrow morning, while the thing is still relatively fresh." Beale pulled a card from the inside pocket of his jacket and tossed it onto Moody's desk. "That's it for now. Call us if you find anything."

Beale turned and began to walk out. Zoober quickly placed one of his cards next to Beale's and then almost opened his mouth to apologize for Beale's behavior. But he couldn't think of anything to say that would even come close to making up for Beale's rudeness. Zoober simply gave them a feeble thank you and walked out behind his partner.

Outside, Zoober trotted for a few seconds to catch up with Beale, who was walking at a brisk pace.

"You really think they'll find the rock depression?" asked Zoober.

"They've got about as much chance of finding it as my wife has of being the Playboy centerfold next month. But it'll keep 'em busy and off our backs until we can think of something else for them to do."

"Why did you have to treat them like that, Martin? They may not have much experience in homicide, but they're just trying to do their jobs."

"Hey, this is *our* case now. If they wanna help, we'll give 'em some chores where they can't do any harm, but *I'm* gonna run the show. I won't be taking orders from those country ass hayseeds."

Zoober just shook his head. He had grown to respect Beale's investigative abilities but Zoober doubted that Beale would ever change his attitude. Beale's instinct was to treat people like dirt regardless of whether they were criminals, victims, or co-workers.

And back inside the sheriff's office, Moody was pissed. He wasn't used to being treated like a doormat. He knew that he needed the help of a good forensics lab on this one, but he'd be damned if he or his deputies would spend their time trudging along all those miles of lakeshore lugging a fifty-pound rock. Forget *that*. If he pursued the case himself, failure was likely without the forensics help from Albany, so he'd just as soon turn the whole thing over to Beale and be done with it. If Albany succeeded in identifying the body and finding the killer, Moody would of course proclaim it a joint investigation and take some of the credit. Technically it was, because Moody's department had done the initial report. And at election time, the locals wouldn't remember or give a shit who had run the case, as long as it was solved. Okay, so Moody would contain the situation, but he was still steamed at the way he'd been treated by Beale. He turned to Deputy Spooner, mumbled to him in an angry tone that he should make arrangements to have the body sent to Albany Med immediately, and then stormed out of the room.

Deputy Spooner wasn't mad at all. In fact, he was chuckling with delight at the thought of someone handling Sheriff Moody like that. The same sheriff, Spooner recalled, who yesterday was talking like Mr. Bigshot, saying he was going to have them do DNA testing and search dental records and run this test and that test. And now it looked like the Albany PD would run the whole show. As far as Spooner was concerned, it was about time somebody put their foot up the sheriff's rump because Moody was getting too damn big for his gun belt. Thirty-five-years-old when he made sheriff, and Spooner himself had twenty years more experience! Spooner was certain the voters had their heads up their asses when they elected Moody as sheriff.

Oh well, thought Spooner, *It might take a while to ID this poor slob and find his loved ones, if he has any.* To Spooner it all seemed like a hell of a lot of trouble and expense, and he was wondering if the Albany police would have the balls to charge the Homerton Springs sheriff's department for the forensics work. Sure as shit it would cost an arm and a leg, enough to blow a huge hole in the town's meager law enforcement budget. It would all be a hell of a lot easier if they had some clue about who this bastard was, but there was no one in the regional missing persons report from this morning that even came close to this guy's description. But then Spooner remembered something: *Didn't a fella call the day before this body was found, lookin' for a man who was missing? Yeah, it was somebody whose wife reported him missing after he was gone for only a day or two but he wasn't officially listed as missing yet, so some private detective, who sounded like a kid on the phone, was sniffin' around, tryin' to find him. What was the young fella's name? Began with an H ... Henry somethin'? Or maybe it was Herman?*

Henry or Herman or Horace or Horseshit, it didn't really matter because Spooner couldn't remember the last name, and without that, it was hopeless. But he'd written the name and phone number down on a slip of paper and promised to call back if any new information turned up. Now, where the hell did he put the piece of paper? He checked his pockets and took a quick look around his cluttered desk but couldn't find it. Ah well, chances are the guy who was supposedly missing was probably out on a drunk or somethin', just out havin' some fun, and he'd stumble home sooner or later. Or maybe he was out cattin' around with some young filly. Spooner had seen it many times before in his job as a deputy, yes sir-ee indeed. Most people shared the same vices and lusts. Hell, even Spooner himself had done some wild things in his younger days, but his wife Agnes had never caught on. She was too dumb, he supposed.

Maybe the slip of paper was in the pocket of his other pants, the ones Agnes had to wash yesterday because Barney, their dog, had thrown up on them. What the hell was it Barney had eaten that had turned his stomach? And speaking of eating, Agnes was making an apple pie this morning, and so he surely had to go home for his lunch today because her pie was just about the best in the county. Oh well, if he didn't find the slip of paper, he certainly wasn't going to mention it to the sheriff, who would surely be pissed that Spooner had lost it, and the last thing Spooner needed today was any lip from the young sheriff.

And if it was really important, the young private detective fella would call back, right?

Chapter 14
Sunday, May 24, 11:35 a.m.

Harvey's eyes slowly opened as he woke from his unintentional nap. He had laid down on his couch intending to rest for just a few minutes after doing some online research and promptly dropped off to sleep. Glancing at his watch, he was relieved to see he'd only dozed for about fifteen minutes.

This morning Pamela gave him a list of Grant's associates in the art business that were known to her. Harvey was trying to determine if any of them had criminal backgrounds, but so far, he'd come up with zilch, and now he was thinking this was probably a complete waste of time.

It was interesting that she hadn't included Grant's brother Peter on the list. Apparently, he wasn't on her radar, but Harvey had already checked him out online shortly after they'd met, and found nothing unusual. He'd been living in France for years, and although Harvey was unable to access things like arrest records in Europe, Peter had never been arrested in the United States. He had a bare-bones website for his business, a single page with nothing but a paragraph describing his art restoration services, a few pictures of works he'd restored, and his contact information.

Harvey also mused about looking further into Louie Parker's possible involvement with Grant's disappearance. The guy obviously despised Grant. And Louie *did* have an arrest record. Starting from his late teens there was a string of minor offenses ranging from shoplifting to vandalism, and in his late twenties a much more serious one — he had served six months in jail for injuring a man in a bar fight. Harvey wondered if Pamela was aware of his record.

Harvey's phone buzzed with an incoming call from an unrecognized number. As he reached for it, he was momentarily startled when he noticed it wasn't his phone. It was the secure one he'd borrowed from

Dexter. But it was working perfectly and he was confident the novelty would shortly wear off and he'd be completely comfortable with it.

"Hello?" he said.

"Hi, I'm the person you followed out of the bar yesterday. My name is Jenny."

There was no immediate reply from Harvey, whose larynx was instantly paralyzed.

"Hello? Do you remember?"

Harvey fought off the shock of actually being called by an attractive woman, and managed to answer: "Jenny, yes, Jenny! How are you?" He quickly tucked his shirt into his pants and smoothed down his hair with his hand before he thought: *What am I doing? This isn't a video call, dufus.*

"I'm fine, but still homeless," said Jenny. "I struck out with the apartment. It was too small."

"Not enough room for one person?" asked Harvey.

"One?" she replied. "There would've been at least ten thousand of us if you included me plus all the roaches. So, I went back to the bar and got your name and number from the bartender. You mentioned I might be able to rent your neighbor's house. Is it still available?"

Harvey's heart was pounding. "Sure," he said. "It's a nice place, you'll really like it."

"Great, when can I see it?"

"How about..." *Make it soon before she changes her mind and finds another place...* "Well, we can do it today. How soon can you be here?"

"Well...that depends on the address. You didn't tell me yet."

"Oh, right. It's 88 Hawthorne Drive. Right on the lake."

"Just a sec...okay... I've got it on my navigation app. I could leave shortly and be there by noon."

"Sounds good."

"Okay. I'll see you soon, then. Bye."

Harvey sat in stunned silence. Two major life events in the course of a few days. First, a real case. Next, a date with an angel.

What date, putz? Who said anything about a date? She's meeting you to take a look at a house to rent, that's all.

He sat back on the couch, took a few deep breaths, and tried to calm himself. He had another call to make, and it couldn't wait.

Harvey called Peter Damler. As it rang, he went over what he would say, even though he'd already thoroughly rehearsed his few lines.

Two rings.

Three.

And then Harvey heard a hesitant, "Hello?"

"Hello, Mr. Damler?"

"Harvey? I'm very pleased you decided to call."

"I've given it some thought and I'd like to meet in person to discuss an exchange of information."

"That's excellent, Harvey. When?"

"Tomorrow morning will be good for me. Let's meet somewhere convenient for you. What hotel are you staying at? Maybe we could talk in the lobby."

"I'm at the Lakeside Inn right in the town of Lake George. And it does have a small but comfortable lobby, and a snack bar where we can get coffee if you like."

"Perfect. Shall we meet there tomorrow morning at nine-thirty?"

"That will be fine, Harvey. I'm looking forward to combining our efforts."

"Uh...me too. Okay, I have to be going. See you there tomorrow."

Harvey ended the call.

After spending more time checking out the public records of Louie's arrests, Harvey realized he had only a few minutes to go before he had to meet Jenny. He ran to his closet and began a mental struggle over which shirt to wear. Should it be the pale blue button-down or the dark green one with the tan stripe? But when he noticed there were stains on the sleeves of both shirts, he quickly pulled on a comfortable old rugby shirt and bolted for the door. He cut through the woods, running most of the way. Ninety seconds after leaving his house, he made it to the front step of the house next door, where he found her waiting patiently.

Chapter 15
Sunday, May 24, 12:01 p.m.

Jenny was dressed in jeans, white sneakers, and a rose v-neck sweater. She had a small soft leather purse on a long strap slung casually over her shoulder. Harvey couldn't decide whether she looked more beautiful today or yesterday.

"Hi, Harvey. This is a really nice place, at least on the outside."

Jenny stood in front of an attractive Cape Cod style home with gray cedar siding. The small front yard was professionally landscaped with rhododendrons, azaleas, and colorful perennials.

"Sorry I'm late," said Harvey. "It's just as nice on the inside, Jenny. And fully furnished, too." *Try not to sound too soberingly anxious to have her live next to you.* "Let me get the door open." Harvey pulled the keys from his pocket, fiddled with the doorknob lock and the deadbolt, and then pushed open the front door. They stepped into a comfortable-looking living room accented by many large green plants. It had a warm, New England style decor with some colorful modern touches.

"Beautiful," said Jenny cheerfully. "I love plants. They really brighten up a room."

"So does Dan... Dan Palmeroy, that's the owner's name. A real nice guy. He's sort of a fresh air freak, claims the plants purify the air. I come in every few days to water them and to check on the place. And then he has a service come in once a month to prune and fertilize them."

"He doesn't trust you to do that?"

"Nope. And he's right not to. I never was much of a gardener."

"Who cleans the place?" The entire house had hardwood floors that shined as if they had been freshly waxed.

98

"He has a service come in for that, too. It's just very light cleaning when no one is living here. If you rent it, though, he'll discontinue the cleaning service of course, and you'll have to keep the place clean yourself. Is that okay?" Harvey asked sheepishly, scared to death she might protest. *Does she realize I'd lick the floors clean every day if that's what it would take to get her to stay here?*

"No problem at all. Cleaning doesn't scare me. I cleaned up after four younger brothers when I was living at home."

Jenny took a few steps farther into the house and saw the furnishings in the living room— a couch with bold red stripes, a large leather chair and matching ottoman, and curtains in a bright floral print that made the room look spacious and inviting.

They walked down the hall to the well-equipped kitchen which was decorated with hanging wicker baskets, antique copper pots and pans, and bunches of dried flowers. Next to it was a dining area with an oak table and matching ladder-back chairs. Jenny and Harvey poked their heads into the main bedroom, the smaller guest bedroom, and the two bathrooms. They wandered out onto the deck, which afforded the same breathtaking lake view that Harvey's deck did, except it wrapped around three sides of the house, which made it about three times the area of Harvey's deck.

"Spectacular view," Jenny said. "Harvey, this place is great."

"The only disadvantage I can think of is that there's no cell service down here, but if you walk up to the road, you can get a signal. It's weird, I always have service in my house, at least one or two bars, but I think it's probably blocked by the rockface on the side of this house. There's cable and internet, though."

"That's fine, I'll get a wireless router. I'd love to live here, Harvey. I need a place to stay for at least three months or so. Are you going to be my landlord?"

"Well, yeah, I guess I'd be the acting landlord for Dan. He gave me the keys and asked me to see if I could find someone to stay here and take care of the place. He wants only one or two people and he said I should make sure not to rent it to party animals. The rent will be very reasonable. Dan's major concern was to find a reliable and responsible person to watch over the place."

"How do you know I'm reliable and responsible? We've just met."

"Well, I do need to get a few details on a form concerning your background, your employment, and so forth, so I can give the information to Dan. Just formalities. You don't look like you'll trash the place." Harvey took a deep breath and decided to go for it. "So, why don't we go and get some lunch and you can fill me in. I'll treat."

"Okay, let's go." She returned the smile.

"What kind of food do you like?"

"How about pizza?" she answered.

Harvey breathed a slight sigh of relief that it would be an inexpensive lunch. He would take her to Favio's Pizzeria.

"Pizza it is," said Harvey.

"I might as well drive, my car's right here," she said.

Harvey was silently thankful that he wouldn't have to drive her around in his rattletrap of a car. They left the house and stepped into Jenny's blue sports coupe, a Nissan 370Z.

Wow, nice car, he thought.

He described to her the quickest way to get to Favio's. The engine started with a throaty growl, and Jenny gunned it a few times in neutral. She pushed the stick shift into first and then let the clutch out without hesitation. The car shot forward and they moved rapidly toward the top of the driveway, which had nearly the same steep pitch as Harvey's driveway. Jenny reached the street and without slowing down she quickly glanced left and right to confirm there was no oncoming traffic. Turning left, she pushed firmly on the gas and Harvey's head went back against the headrest as he watched the speedometer climb at an amazing rate. It stopped at sixty, which was fifteen miles per hour over the speed limit. She handled the car like a pro, shifting through the gears effortlessly, her hands and feet working in unison with the powerful machine. As they approached a bend in the road which was marked by a sign indicating that thirty-five miles per hour was the maximum safe speed, Harvey waited for Jenny to downshift... but it never happened. She took the right-hand turn without slowing down, and Harvey's entire body lurched toward Jenny. She was silent as they drove, seemingly oblivious to his alarm. Harvey saw no evidence at all that would indicate she was trying to impress him with her driving. The impression he got was that this type of driving was nothing out of the ordinary for her.

At the restaurant, the waitress showed them to a booth and handed them each a menu. Harvey liked the way Jenny boldly suggested they get a pizza topped with everything.

"Favio's pizza with everything is pretty spicy," he said with a knowing smile. "Are you up for it?"

"Sure. Spicy food doesn't bother me at all. My mom used to say I have a cast-iron stomach. How's yours?"

"My stomach? I left it back at that last hairpin turn."

She smiled. "Sorry. Did I drive a little too fast?"

"No, not really. I guess I'm just not used to sitting in the passenger seat. It's a bit frustrating, speeding along the highway and not having a brake to push. Maybe I'm a control freak at heart."

"It's all that scenery streaking by you, Harvey. You notice the trees by the roadside when you're sitting in the passenger seat, and they're a blur. Ignore the trees. You should watch the road ahead as if you were driving."

"Actually, I didn't notice the trees at all today. Most of the time my life was flashing before my eyes."

She chuckled.

Hey, how about that, I made her smile.

As they ate the pizza and sipped their beers, Jenny told Harvey how she had come to end up in Port Kole.

"I'm an architect. My home is in Syracuse and I work for Brightwater Creek Properties, which is considering the purchase of a ninety-six-acre parcel of very nice lakeshore property about a mile north of Port Kole. Brightwater Creek may build a full-service luxury resort there. The company has kept the project very quiet, but we have permission to survey the land, and if the results of the surveying phase look good, we'll purchase the land and soon after begin the approval process for town and state permits. I'm one of the initial planners, and I expect I'll be working in this area for at least three months to firm up the proposal."

"Does Brightwater Creek have projects all over the country?"

"No, it's a recent start-up, privately owned. Up to now, the company has just been raising capital. This place will be its first property. It's a nice opportunity for me to get in on the ground floor of a big commercial project and I'm glad to be working in this area. I was born and raised in the Albany suburbs, not too far from here. I lived there until I went off to Northeastern University in Boston. I graduated with a bachelor's degree in architecture seven years ago."

"Architecture is a great career choice. I went to the State University in Albany, but I was one of those flaky people who change their major every two weeks in a frustrating and fruitless search to find something they're both good at and enjoy doing."

"You must have taken a lot of courses. What did you finally end up getting a degree in?"

"Well, after four years I had an argument with the administrators about whether I would graduate. I think they just wanted to get rid of me. They finally decided I had learned enough to graduate with a degree in liberal arts, whatever that means."

"I couldn't help but notice the sign in front of your place. How did you end up being a private detective?"

"I sort of fell into it ass backwards. After I graduated I didn't have any idea what I wanted to do. I had a few boring and meaningless jobs at first, then I sort of rebelled and decided I wanted to go to the west coast and live with my Uncle Willie for a while."

"What's so rebellious about wanting to spend some time with an uncle?"

"Oh, it was wanting to live with this particular uncle that made the notion kind of outlandish. He's treated like an eccentric weirdo by the others in the family. He's a private investigator, self-employed, and the rest of them have steady jobs with fairly large companies. Uncle Willie lives in near poverty, but not because he doesn't work hard. It's just that sometimes he doesn't get paid by his clients, who often don't have much money themselves. But he takes their cases anyway because he likes to help people. I spent three years out there working for him. Uncle Willie's a real gumshoe. He fancies himself a Philip Marlowe type. But he's a sweet guy, and he's excellent at what he does. Actually, excellent is not the right word. Amazing is a better way to describe him."

"He sounds interesting. Why do you call him amazing?"

"He's got this... talent, I guess you'd call it. He's relentless. Uncle Willie digs and digs, chipping away at a mystery until he solves it. One of the cases he worked on before I lived with him involved the disappearance of an eight-year-old girl. The police had worked on the case for a year and a half without coming up with any solid leads, and the trail was stone cold when the girl's parents hired Uncle Willie. So, he plodded along, questioning many of the same people the police had interviewed until he found the girl. She'd been abducted by a childless couple who had kept her as a working prisoner in their house."

"I remember reading something about that case in the news. It said a private investigator had participated in finding the girl."

"Uncle Willie did much more than participate. He led the cops by their noses right to her. And he didn't even get paid for it. The parents had used up their life savings paying the private eye who worked on it before Uncle Willie. And he knew the money situation but he took the case anyway."

"So, you want to be like your uncle?"

"Well, sure. I don't know if I'll ever develop his abilities, but I hope someday I'll be able to do even one thing as important as finding that missing child. Anyway, after working for Uncle Willie I decided to come here and start my own investigation business."

"So why did *you* choose this area?"

"I grew up about thirty miles west of here. My parents and I used to spend a lot of summer Saturdays and Sundays at Lake George. Those were some of the happiest times of my childhood."

Harvey looked into Jenny's inquisitive eyes as he sipped from his beer mug. She seemed genuinely interested in what he had to say.

"Do your parents still live around here?" she asked.

"No, my parents are dead now, but I have an Aunt Mabel and Uncle Roger that live right in Lake George."

They each reached for another slice of pizza. Jenny picked off all the mushrooms and anchovies before she started eating it.

Harvey noticed, and said, "You should have told me you don't like anchovies or mushrooms. We didn't have to order a pizza with everything."

"Oh, don't mind me. It's an old habit. My roommate in college and I used to share pizzas with everything. I'd scrape off the mushrooms and anchovies and give them to her, she would give me the olives and green peppers. And we had a friend down the hall who used to scrape off all the cheese and sauce — she said it wasn't good for you."

"Then I'm in some major trouble because I practically live on pizza. My two largest monthly expenses are my student loan payment and my tab at this place."

"Really? Do you think you're satisfying all your nutritional requirements with pizza every day?"

"Oh, I'm not too worried about that. I round out my diet with nachos and hot wings."

Jenny chuckled at Harvey's modest little joke, as she tried to negotiate a long string of hot cheese.

Hey, I made her laugh again. I guess I'm doing okay. A remarkable performance for me. Usually, halfway into the first date with me, girls are stealing glances at their watches. But then, is this really a date?

They chatted about college life while finishing their meal. As they left the restaurant and walked through the parking lot to Jenny's car, they briefly discussed the rent for the house, and then Jenny asked: "So when will I know if I'm acceptable as the new tenant?"

"Well, I'd say it's looking pretty good," he said with feigned seriousness. "Just one more thing I should ask, though. Do you have a criminal record?"

She winced. "Will it make a difference?"

Harvey replied with disbelief, "You're kidding, you don't really have a criminal record, do you?"

She nodded. "Yep. I won't try to hide anything."

"Let's see, you flattened somebody's cat with your car, right? Don't worry about it, I'm sure it wasn't intentional, and even if it was, it's just a misdemeanor."

"Well, it was a little more serious than that. I took part in a protest in college. A sit-in. They arrested a bunch of us. We were released about eight hours later. As you can imagine, my parents were horrified when they found out."

Harvey said: "Hmmm, let me see if I can guess the cause you felt was important enough to go to jail for. You look like a nature lover. Was it *Save the Whales?*"

"Nope," she answered.

"*Save the Snails?*"

"Nope."

"*Dismantle the nukes?*"

"Nope."

"*Nuke the snails?*"

"No, but you're getting warmer. "

"I am? So, it had something to do with nukes and snails?"

Jenny smiled. "I'd better tell you or we'll be out here all day. In Boston, not too far from campus, there was a shelter for homeless people. My girlfriends and I did some work there as part of a sociology class we were taking. The place didn't cost much to run. The labor was all volunteer. Anyway, they announced it would be shut down because of state budget cuts. So, we held a protest in front of the state capital building. We blocked the front steps until the police came and hauled us away. That was it. Nothing too exciting."

"Did they close the shelter?"

"Yes, they did, right on schedule. The protest made no difference at all." She shrugged her shoulders.

"You're wrong, it *did* make a difference. It showed people that someone cared. You're a good person, Jenny."

"Thank you, Harvey. But really, you hardly know me."

"Hey, we shared a pizza with everything. I know you now, better than you think. I'm a pretty good judge of character."

Here's where you sink or swim, Harvey boy. Do you have the balls to ask her out for dinner? And if you do, will she say yes?

Harvey concluded that their lunch couldn't be considered a real date, since it had been hastily arranged to complete the discussion of the house rental. But dinner, that would be a one hundred percent social occasion. He decided it was worth the risk. If she said yes, he would go into debt to take her out to a nice place. He could always sell his blood if he had to.

"Jenny, would you like to have dinner tonight?" *Of course, she'd like to have dinner tonight, dork, the point is, would she like to have it with you?*

"I mean, with me?"

She hesitated before saying, "Harvey, I ....."

Oh no, here it comes. Please let me down easy!

"Harvey, I really enjoyed having lunch with you. I can't see you tonight, I have some business to take care of. How about some other time? I'll be your neighbor for months, so I think we'll be able to find some time when we can get together for dinner. Okay?"

"Sure," he answered lamely, forcing a half-smile. *Well, all right, that wasn't too bad, at least I asked, and she didn't laugh hysterically. Since we'll be neighbors, I can wear her down. If I ask her to dinner sixty or seventy times, she'll eventually say yes just to shut me up.*

As they drove out of the parking lot she said, "If I've passed the prospective tenant exam, when can I move in, Harvey?"

"You did indeed pass, and you can move in today."

"Great. But, I'm a bit tied up today. Would tomorrow be okay?"

"Sure. Somewhere buried in my e-mail inbox is Dan's rental agreement. I'll print a copy for you to sign. Do you need help moving your stuff in?"

"Not really. My belongings on hand consist of two suitcases. I'll have more of my things shipped here in a week or so."

During the remainder of the ride, they talked more about pleasant memories of college and childhood summer vacations.

Jenny stopped to let Harvey out at the top of his driveway. After Harvey handed Jenny the house keys, she thanked him for lunch, gave him a *see you later* wave, and drove off.

God, she's so beautiful, thought Harvey as he stood there watching her car pull away with three times the acceleration he could ever get out of his old jalopy.

* * *

Late that evening, Harvey sat in Dexter's office after spending hours worrying over the plan to have Dexter commit what was essentially a criminal act of electronic spying. Harvey had finally convinced himself that Dexter could handle it without getting himself caught, if he didn't do anything really stupid.

Harvey said, "So, the guy whose phone I wanted you to bug is staying at the Lakeside Inn. I don't know the room number, but..."

"No problem. I shouldn't need it. That hotel is small, so I'll probably get a good signal from anywhere in the parking lot. But if I do need the room number, I'll schmooze it out of someone at the desk."

Harvey had texted Peter Damler an hour ago to cancel the morning meeting at the hotel, saying that he'd had an emergency come up. Peter had texted back his extreme disappointment and Harvey texted once more to assure him he would be in contact soon to reschedule it.

Harvey said to Dexter, "If you're going to sit in the parking lot for hours, be careful because I don't know if there are security cameras outside the building, and..."

Dexter put his hand up to stifle Harvey's concerns. "Hey, just trust me, I'll be careful, dude, nothing to worry about. I'll get on it first thing in the morning. I'm just gonna stay there until I'm sure the catcher is working, then I'll hide it somewhere outside the hotel in a tree or something, and it'll record his calls. Leave it all to me, dude. I'll take care of everything."

Harvey couldn't decide which phrase worried him more – "nothing to worry about" or "I'll take care of everything."

Chapter 16
Monday, May 25, 11:20 a.m.

Lieutenant Beale sat at his desk and tried his best to ignore the annoying sounds of people chatter, shuffling papers, and clicking keyboards that engulfed him as he stirred the tepid coffee in his Styrofoam cup. It was a few hours since he and Zoober had sat in on the autopsy of the floater and Beale's stomach still hadn't fully recovered. *Floater* was the department's generic term for bodies recovered from the water, and even though this particular corpse must have spent most of its time on the lake bottom, it was still referred to in this morning's station house chitchat as *Beale's floater.*

Beale's stomach churned as he remembered walking slowly into the autopsy room of Albany Med in the early morning, with Zoober following closely behind. The odor of dead flesh had mingled with the room's strong chemical smells. But this particular corpse wasn't so bad in the stink department, since it had probably only been submerged for a few days, and the lake water was quite cold. Beale had been present at three autopsies performed on bodies pulled out of the Hudson River after they had been in there for several weeks during the summer. He recalled vividly that the stench from those stiffs had been unbelievable, enough to choke a skunk.

During the procedure, Beale had glanced over at his twenty-eight-year-old partner and saw that Zoober was completely unfazed. Before the autopsy, Beale watched Zoober eat at his desk a big bowl of some kiddie cereal like *Chocolate Covered Sugar Bombs,* followed by two donuts stuffed with blood-colored raspberry jelly. And then the kid saunters into an autopsy room and calmly watches some guy's spleen and liver spill out all over the floor. Despite his young partner's inexperience, God had for some reason blessed this kid with a stomach that could handle anything, and for this ability, Beale felt he somehow owed Zoober a grudging respect. As for Beale's own stomach, these days he was always slightly nauseous in the morning, probably due to the three or four bourbon shots he downed almost every evening, and on most days his spastic colon wouldn't allow him to take any sustenance before noon other than caffeine and nicotine.

Beale stirred his coffee again and examined its color, a sickening shade of gray. God only knew when the asshole whose turn it was to make the coffee this week had last washed the pot out. He looked up at Zoober, who sat in a chair on the other side of Beale's desk.

"All right, kid, let's go over it all again," said Beale.

They had already been through the medical examiner's entire report once very quickly, but it was Beale's routine to go over any medical or scientific evidence repeatedly until he was sure no important detail had been missed.

Zoober stared at the computer screen and began to read the highlights out loud. "We've got a male Caucasian, age forty-three to fifty-five, dark hair, height five feet eleven inches, medium build. The cause of death is listed as severe laceration of the brain parenchyma caused by acute ballistic trauma. Unconsciousness should have been almost instantaneous, and death would have occurred within sixty seconds. It was a single small bullet, a .32 ACP hollow point. It entered the left temple, penetrating the very top of the os temporal bone. It traveled in a fairly straight path and lodged in the brain just behind the os frontal. The shot came from behind and to the left, so with the victim's eyes facing twelve o'clock, the gun would have been held at roughly the eight o'clock position. The bullet was too mangled to allow for any useful ballistic fingerprinting, and they don't think they can even determine the manufacturer with any degree of certainty. There were no powder burns evident on the body. And there were no other wounds except for the missing fingertips—all ten of them gone, snipped off at the second joint, post mortem; fairly neat cuts done with a double-edged tool like a branch pruner or something similar. As far as time of death, the ME's estimates are very imprecise. He says the body was probably dumped in the water within seventy-two hours of death, but that's assuming it was stored outside in the Lake George area. The nights have been very cool in the area for the past week, which slows decomposition considerably. And then it could have been in the water for up to an additional seventy-two hours. The ME can't narrow the time of death without knowing the exact water temperature, which we don't know because we can't determine the exact depth where the body rested. Even at this time of year, the water in the thermal layer at the lake bottom is very cold, but the temperature varies greatly as a function of depth, and the depth varies quite a bit along the two-mile long swath the boater identified as the place where he hooked the body. And the burlap bag apparently protected the corpse very well from being attacked by marine creatures, so the ME didn't have any information in that regard to help with the time of death estimate. As for identification, there was no DNA match to any of the available law enforcement databases, and no probable close relative hits either. And the DNA ancestry companies are not allowing us to access their databases anymore. The corpse's face is somewhat bloated from water absorption, but in good enough shape for a visual identification by a relative or friend."

"Did you check the regional missing persons database this morning?" asked Beale.

"Yes. There's no one on the list who resembles the corpse."

"What about the New York DMV's database of photos?"

Zoober frowned. "Martin, I'm sure you're aware that it's now illegal to use the DMV database in that manner. The recent court ruling on facial recognition programs and privacy..."

"Yeah, yeah," Beale cut him off with disgust. "What about comparing his mug to pictures in public social media databases? You're good at that social stuff."

"Well, Detective Bremer has used a program that does a comparison to Facebook profile pictures. The problem is so many of them are stylized to flatter the subject that they're almost useless. People have strange facial expressions, indistinct lighting is used to soften features, colors are not true, and so forth. I tried his program and on my first attempt, I got over ten thousand hits within just a hundred-mile radius of where the body was found. Then I tightened the parameters enough to give just a hundred hits. I looked at all of them this morning and I'm certain our corpse isn't among them. Some were not even the correct sex. I could do more work with the program, but I don't hold out much hope for success. The algorithm is—"

"Sounds like a total waste of time, All right, so what else have we got from the ME that might help us ID the body?"

"Basically, nothing. He's got no significant scars. No surgical pins, artificial joints, or anything like that showed up on x-rays. No tattoos. No surgical or significant non-surgical scars. No dentures or caps. The corpse's teeth are in excellent shape. He's got one cavity and a preliminary inspection of the filling indicates it's at least twenty years old. The guy appears to have been in very good general health. No apparent cancers or diseased organs. He wasn't a smoker. No signs of arthritis or other degenerative diseases."

Zoober clicked on the blood report. The corpse's blood had been drawn, upon Beale's insistence, yesterday as soon as the body arrived in Albany, and the blood work was expedited. "He's got blood type O positive, with normal cell counts, and no chronic bloodborne diseases. The standard blood screening for twelve classes of drugs or toxins picked up nothing at all. And no alcohol was detected."

"What about the stomach contents?" asked Beale.

"No luck there, either. The stomach was filled with lake water and pretty well flushed out. They found some traces of vegetable matter, but it was almost fully digested. They weren't able to identify the vegetable or vegetables."

"So basically, we've got almost nothing from the M.E. What about the clothes?"

"The sheriff was right, it was all mid-range department store stuff, nothing unusual about it."

The two men were silent for a few seconds. Beale finished the last of his sour coffee and then said with assertiveness: "Let's go."

"Where?" asked Zoober.

"Well, we can either join our friend Sheriff Moody in looking for a hole the rock fits in, or we can talk to some of the people that live along the lakeshore, ask them if they saw anything unusual. We'll start with the shoreline along that two-mile swath. The sheriff said it was pretty undeveloped, but let's see what's there, and then we can work our way along the shore. How much total lake shore did the sheriff say there is?"

"A hundred and twenty-five miles."

"Wonderful," said Beale with disgust. "So, let's go talk to some people. You're driving. I'm takin' a nap on the way there, I feel like shit."

Beale pulled from his pocket a roll of antacid tablets and started eating them like popcorn.

Chapter 17
Monday, May 25, 1:16 p.m.

Harvey looked at the number on the house and then double-checked the street address in the notes app on his phone. He quickly found the entry he'd made: *1137 Mason Ridge Road.* This was definitely where Sadie Gumm lived, according to Pamela's neighbor, Gloria. Harvey got out of his car and walked up the short gravel driveway to the front door of the tiny, well-maintained cottage. He pushed the doorbell but heard nothing, so he gave three hard raps on the door and it opened almost immediately. A small, tough-looking woman stood in front of Harvey, studying him critically from his toes to the top of his head.

"Hi," said Harvey in an overly friendly voice, attempting to win her over immediately. "Are you Ms. Sadie Gumm?"

"Yeah, I'm Sadie," she said in a tone suggesting she was not impressed at all. "You're Harvey Grace, aren't you? Gloria told me you'd be coming."

Harvey nodded in acknowledgment, as he stared at the sixty-something woman who could have passed for Gloria's sister. Sadie had the same spreading figure as her friend Gloria, one which spoke of past splendor, but which had inevitably surrendered to an abundance of sweets and a lack of exercise. Sadie's face had a weathered look. Her shock of steel grey, curly hair looked as stiff as a scouring pad. She was dressed in a comfortable-looking rumpled sweatsuit and well-worn tennis shoes. Sadie showed not even the slightest trace of fear or apprehension at greeting a stranger on her front doorstep. She leaned against the doorjamb with her arms folded and simply waited for Harvey to speak, unembarrassed by the few seconds of silence that ensued.

Harvey said, "I'd like to ask you a few questions about Grant Damler and his girlfriend. Gloria said you saw them in a red car at a gas station a few weeks ago. Is that right?"

"Sure is. At least, I saw Grant with some young girl. Gloria seems to think it must be his girlfriend. I got no reason to doubt her."

"Are you sure it was Grant?"

"Oh yeah, of that much I'm sure. I've seen him walkin' outside around his house a few times when I've been over to visit Gloria."

"What were they doing at the gas station?" asked Harvey.

"He was filling the tank. She was in the driver's seat, fixing her makeup. She used that little mirror on the back of the visor. I was on a day trip with my church group, and our driver gassed up our van at the opposite pump. If it *was* his girlfriend then I guess he thought they were a safe distance from home. It was at least seventy-five miles from here."

"Can you describe her to me?"

"Young, blond, slim, and pretty. She had a nice figure. In her twenties. I guess Grant likes 'em young, huh?" She gave Harvey a knowing wink as if they shared a little secret.

Harvey continued in a businesslike tone: "Could you identify her from a photograph?"

"Yeah, I think so. Got a photo?"

"No, not yet. Have you seen her anywhere other than with Grant?"

"Not that I recall."

"What about the car?"

"What about it?"

"I don't suppose you remember the license number, do you?"

She looked at him scornfully. "You gotta be kiddin', ace. I don't remember my *own* license number."

"So, I guess you wouldn't know the *make* of the car either?"

"Nope. It was a red car, not too big, and kinda sporty looking."

That much Harvey already knew from Gloria. "Your friend Gloria said you might know the make of the car."

"Well, Gloria's wrong. She doesn't know everything about everything. Maybe she *thinks* she does," said Sadie with a bit of scorn.

"How about if I were to show you pictures of different cars? Do you think you could identify it, then?"

"What I think is you'd be wastin' both your time and mine."

Harvey conceded. "Let's get back to the woman," he said. "Would you be willing to try to identify her if I were to bring in some photographs of different women?"

Sadie hesitated before asking skeptically, "Well, what do you mean by *some*? Are we talkin' about a month-long project here? I got a life *too*, ace."

"Well, it wouldn't be all that many. Let's say... about a hundred?" Harvey had already asked Dexter for the names of Grant's recent female students. He figured Dexter could somehow come up with pictures, too.

"About a hundred, huh?" Sadie repeated as she pondered. "Yeah, sure. I could go through that many pictures pretty quickly and pick her out. So why are you looking for her?"

Harvey hesitated for a moment as he considered giving her some type of watered-down half-truth, and he also wondered what Gloria might have already told her.

"That's all right, ace," she said with a smirk. "You don't have to answer me, 'cause I already *know* the answer. I'll bet even though you can't tell me all about it, his wife hired you to find him and hall his wandering ass home, so she can geld him. I'm right, huh?" She smiled again.

Harvey ignored the question and gave Sadie a polite little smile as if to congratulate her on how perceptive she was, and then decided to wrap it up.

"Ms. Gumm, I'll probably be back in the very near future to see you. I'll contact you as soon as I get the pictures."

Harvey thanked her and left. He stepped into his car, and then slowly pulled out onto the road, a wooded stretch of highway meandering through rolling hills. After driving for about two minutes, he saw an old blue station wagon parked on the shoulder of the road. The hood was up, and hanging from a closed window on the side of the car was a handwritten paper sign which read: NEED HELP. Harvey approached the car slowly and pulled onto the shoulder, leaving his car about fifteen feet behind the disabled car. He got out and quickly walked toward the station wagon to see if anyone was inside, wondering as he approached whether something gruesome awaited him, perhaps someone very sick or badly injured. As he came closer, he could see that the car had a good number of dents and rust spots. The red glass over one of the rear taillights was broken and partly held together with clear tape. Harvey looked in through the windows and was somewhat relieved to see no one inside. Maybe the driver had already been picked up by someone and a tow truck was on the way. Harvey decided to call the police anyway, just to make sure they were aware of the broken-down car. He reached for his cell phone.

Harvey never saw it coming.

The blow caught him squarely on the back of the head and sent him sprawling onto the hood of the car. Blinding pain engulfed him and he let out a reflexive shriek. At the same time, he managed to turn his head slightly to face his attacker, who stood behind him now. The second blow caught Harvey solidly on the side of the head, and somewhere within his tortured skull he instantly thought, *What the hell is he hitting me with, a lead pipe?* because the pain was explosive, as if he had run into a brick wall at ninety miles an hour. As Harvey's head snapped to the side from the force of the blow, he caught a glimpse of two huge fists with knuckles that looked rock-hard, and with the strange detachment of an outside observer, he thought, *Hey wow, this guy isn't even using a weapon so he must really be good with his hands...*

The third blow caught Harvey on the cheek, and as he began to sink into a stupor, his fogged mind retrieved the memory of the beating he'd received when he was seven years old, the most terrifying beating of his life. It had been even scarier than the recent one from the jealous college football player because even as that linebacker's fraternity ring was being smashed into Harvey's forehead, he just somehow knew that the guy had no intention of killing him. But when you were only seven years old you imagined the worst, the *very* worst, and when a bully named Mikey Slater who was twenty pounds heavier than you was sitting on top of you, pounding the snot out of you, you're thinking: *This is it, I'll never live to see eight.*

A stinging left hook connected on Harvey's right ear, and his legs buckled. He went down hard, hitting the ground with his elbow and then the side of his chest. Now he was essentially helpless. Nearly blinded by the pain, his arms flailed pitifully in front of his face and stomach, trying desperately to ward off another blow.

Cut it out Mikey, STOP IT, STOP IT! I'll tell my Mom and Dad and they'll fix you good!

When the attacker leaned down over Harvey's prone figure and aimed the next blow, the one that was supposed to come down solidly onto Harvey's nose with a sickening crunch, a hand reached out and stopped the swinging arm. It was a relatively small hand, and Harvey could see it even through the brain-fog that clouded his vision, and he thought, *Hey, what do you know, it's a* female *hand.* He knew because he saw painted nails and a delicate-looking ring with a small green stone.

Mom? Mom! You came to save me! Get Mikey off of me, Mommy, he's hurting me!

And then Harvey saw his Mommy pivot on her left foot and aim a perfect kick right into Mikey's groin. Ouch!

Yo mom, terrific! But where'd you learn how to do that?

And as Harvey's vision began to clear, he could see it was not his Mom, it was Jenny, and it wasn't Mikey she had kicked, it was somebody much, much bigger, a giant in fact.

Jeezuz, it was Louie Parker, all two hundred pounds of him! And Jenny looked so small next to him, so very tiny. What chance would she have?

Louie winced in pain when Jenny landed the savage kick, the heel of her shoe stabbing into his very private parts, and as Louie went down on the ground and collapsed, Jenny hoped that maybe the one perfectly placed kick was enough to defeat him. Her hope was short-lived though, because as Louie wallowed on the grass, Jenny could see the handgun come out from somewhere under his shirt.

Harvey saw it too and knew what it was, but he couldn't tell at the moment whether it was Mikey or Louie who was holding it.

Hey Mom, I hope you're packin' heat, cause this guy's serious! Harvey faded in and out of the real world, but he was rational enough to see that Mikey or Louie or whoever was raising a gun toward Jenny or Mommy, and in about a fraction of a second more, he expected to hear a deafening roar because the revolver was a huge one, maybe a three-five-seven magnum, all shiny with chrome plating, and if it was Louie's gun it must have cost him a month's salary, or if it was Mikey's then a million weeks of saved-up allowance.

Harvey watched the magnum's hammer go back, but miraculously, before the gun could fire, Jenny's heel caught the back of Louie's hand and Harvey heard the crack of bone snapping, and the gun went spinning wildly, the bright afternoon sun glinting and pulsing like a strobe light off the silvery barrel as it turned in the air.

Jenny had jumped an amazing distance to land that kick, and Harvey watched as she landed softly, rolled, and sprang back to her feet like a cat. *She's incredible*, thought Harvey. *Do all architects know how to do that?*

But it wasn't over yet. Even though Louie was injured, the guy had a bagful of surprises, because within a few seconds a knife appeared in his hands as if by magic, and this was no butter knife, it was a hunting knife with a blade about eight inches long, jagged on one side and smooth like a razor on the other.

Louie, still prone on the ground, was in too much pain to take careful aim with the knife. He simply swung it wildly in an arc. Jenny jumped, but not quite fast enough because the tip of the blade caught her left calf, slicing into her skin and grazing muscle tissue. She let out a brief gasp as the pain struck her, but she knew that she couldn't let it slow her down because the knife was on its way back now to strike a second blow. With a hard kick from her undamaged right leg, she stopped Louie's hand, and the force of the blow sent the knife flying.

Louie groaned in pain again and lay on his back on the grass, his wrist broken and bent sideways at an impossible angle.

Harvey tried and failed to lift himself up. *What next?*

He watched in horror as Louie somehow shook off the pain of the broken wrist and sat upright. His good hand closed around a large tree branch lying on the grass. It was about the size of a walking stick and had some nasty-looking broken branch spikes sticking out of it, and Harvey yelled, "Look out!" to Jenny because the branch was long and heavy enough so that if Louie swung it hard, he could take Jenny's legs out from under her. Harvey wanted very badly to help Jenny, he wanted to be able to run the ten feet over to Louie and Jenny so he could throw himself between the two of them if only to show Jenny he really wasn't helpless, he could take care of himself, and maybe even protect her. He commanded his legs to move, but they responded much too slowly. He knew that he would never make it over to Louie in time to disarm him so he couldn't hurt Jenny with the branch.

Disarm him? Who am I kidding? Would I stand a piss of a chance against him even on my best day, even with his broken wrist and squished balls? Even if I got over to her, the best I could hope for would be to place my head in the way, so the branch would crack my skull instead of smashing Jenny's legs...

But Jenny was able to jump back out of Louie's range. She pulled a handgun out of a belt holster. It was a shiny black nine-millimeter. Harvey hoped she knew how to use it.

She pointed the gun at Louie's face and said with resolve: "That's it, no more games. You have two choices, drop the stick or get shot. Which will it be? And you have three seconds to decide before I shoot anyway."

Louie froze, holding the stick in mid-air, uncertain what to do. Would she really fire?

He waited, testing her.

But Jenny didn't wait. When Louie's three seconds were up and he hadn't dropped the branch, she fired.

The stick exploded from the bullet's impact, stinging Louie's face and upper body with splinters. The point of contact was about eight inches from Louie's hand, and he was left holding a stub instead of a stick. Now he knew Jenny meant business. He dropped what was left of the branch, sat back on the grass where he had fallen, and raised his hands above his head.

Jenny stood ready to fire again. Keeping her eyes on Louie's face and her gun pointed at his chest, she unzipped the pocket of the light jacket she wore and removed a thick nylon cable tie.

Harvey drifted back into a stupor, but he felt a warm tranquility in the knowledge that he was safe.

At least for now.

Chapter 18
Monday, May 25, 2:19 p.m.

Beale and Zoober drove slowly along the lakeside road. Zoober was behind the wheel, straining his eyes to try and catch glimpses of houses behind the dense groves of trees that stood between the road and the lakeshore. Beale strained his eyes too, staring at a cellphone screen that displayed a map of the area. So far today, they had stopped at twelve lakefront homes. Most of them were upscale vacation homes and the residents were generally difficult to talk to. They were here to escape the rat race and the high crime rate in New York City or Boston or wherever, and the last thing they wanted was to get involved in some local police investigation. Most of the houses had decks overlooking the lake, but so far no one had admitted seeing anyone dump anything into the lake recently.

Beale turned his attention from the phone map and looked out the window. "Slow down," he said. "I see something down there. Looks like a shack."

"Is there a dwelling indicated on the map?"

"No, but there's definitely a building of some sort down there," Beale said with certainty. "If there's a driveway it has to be along here somewhere." Zoober slowed the car to scan the roadside for an opening.

"There," said Beale as he pointed. "Right there, a dirt driveway between those two big maples."

Zoober spotted the opening and looked worried.

"Uh, I don't know if I can get the car through there. Looks a bit tight, and it's overgrown. If it's a driveway, it isn't used very often. Do you think someone is really living down there?"

"We won't find out from up here. Besides, we've struck out at all the fancy houses up the road we visited today, and this dump is the only place in the immediate area. Might as well try it."

Zoober cautiously pulled the car into the opening between the maples. The high weeds scraped the undercarriage and the low-hanging maple branches swept the road grime from the hood of the car as Zoober slowly eased his way in. He stopped barely ten feet from the edge of the road.

"I can't go any farther," Zoober said. "The car might get stuck. I'd hate to have to wait here for a tow truck."

"Then we walk."

They stepped out of the car and made their way through the clearing. After thirty paces they saw a small, dilapidated wooden structure badly in need of repair. The white paint on the siding was peeling badly and the ancient roof shingles were curling up in many places and completely missing in others. The shack stood in a clearing about forty feet from the water's edge. It appeared that there used to be a small lawn surrounding the structure but it had long since surrendered to the knee-high weeds and scrub brush which now came right up to the foundation. Beale and Zoober took the narrow footpath up to the front porch, which was vacant except for a single cheap lawn chair with broken webbing.

"Careful, some of these floorboards look rotted," said Zoober.

"Someone's living in this dump. There's smoke coming from the chimney pipe."

Zoober stepped over a hole in the porch about the size of his foot. He gave four knocks on the old door which released some tiny flecks of white paint that fluttered to the ground. In a few seconds it opened with a rusty squeak and the detectives faced a man at least eighty-five years of age, with a deeply creased and weathered face and a snow-white stubbly beard. His flannel shirt, buttoned to the very top, was only half-tucked inside his oil-stained blue jeans. On his head was a fluorescent orange hunter's cap, with the ear flaps pulled down.

"Hello, I'm Detective Zoober, and this is Lieutenant Beale." Zoober flashed his badge, but the old man didn't give it a glance. His eyes went from Zoober to Beale and then back to Zoober, examining the two men with suspicion.

"So what?" the man said gruffly.

"We'd like to talk to you," Zoober said, his tone remaining courteous and calm.

"You're already talking."

"We'd like to ask you a few questions."

"So, ask."

"And you are...?" asked Zoober.

"Busy."

"I mean what is your name, sir?"

"Walter Koosey."

Zoober continued, undaunted: "Mr. Koosey, we're looking for someone who may have dumped something into the lake, maybe from a boat or watercraft of some kind, in the past week or so. The thing he dumped may have been a large burlap sack, with a second, smaller white cloth sack attached to the other sack by a rope. Now, is there any chance you may have witnessed anyone dumping something like that?"

Walter answered Zoober's question with a question: "What's in the sacks?"

"We're not at liberty to discuss that at present," replied Zoober.

"It's money, isn't it? I want half."

"You mean you saw something?"

"Maybe, maybe not. Depends on what kind of a deal we can work out."

Beale smirked as he waited to see how his young partner would handle the situation.

Zoober continued calmly: "Mr. Koosey, there was no money in the sacks. No treasure, no jewels. Nothing like that. As far as we know, it may have been garbage. Illegal dumping of garbage, that's all." Beale and Zoober had agreed on using some white lies if necessary. The news that a body had been found in the lake had not yet been made public because of the concern that it might hurt the local tourist industry.

"Garbage my ass," proclaimed the old man. "I thought maybe it was garbage when I saw him dump it, but now I'm sure as shit it wasn't. You guys are from Albany. Two detectives from Albany wouldn't be sent over here to find somebody who dumps garbage in the lake. I've seen people dump shit in this lake my whole life, and up to now no fancy pants detectives from Albany ever came here before to help. Always it's been just our own local department, which consists of exactly three jerkoffs — the sheriff, who has his head up his ass, and the two deputies, who have their heads up the sheriff's ass, so you can see why they'd have real trouble spotting illegal dumpers. Now, why don't you tell me what was in those goddamn sacks."

Zoober looked at Beale, and they nodded at each other.

Zoober said, "Well, there may have been a body in the brown sack you apparently saw being dumped, Mr. Koosey. And we'd appreciate it if you would keep this quiet for now because local officials are understandably concerned about how such an incident might upset the good people who come to this area to vacation."

"Shit," said Walter. "No money, then?"

"That's right, Mr. Koosey. No money. But we'd appreciate your help anyway."

Beale spoke for the first time, as he began to lose patience. "C'mon gramps, we don't have all day to haggle. What'd you see?"

Walter sighed. It looked like he wasn't going to get any money out of this, so he might as well tell them. "On Thursday night, or really it was Friday morning 'cause it was after midnight, I saw somebody in a rubber raft dump a bundle of some kind overboard, probably big enough to be a body. I couldn't tell if it was one or two bundles he dumped."

"How far out was the raft when he dumped it?" asked Beale.

"Maybe four hundred yards out from here."

Zoober began to take notes, as Beale took over the questioning.

"Did you see him row out the four hundred yards in the raft?"

"No. I came out onto the porch and there he was, that far out."

"What can you tell me about his appearance?" continued Beale.

"Dark clothing. That's all I can say for sure at that distance, and with just moonlight. Coulda been a man or a woman."

"So, you saw him dump something, then what?"

"Then I saw him using his oars. He started to row."

"Row toward you?"

"No. Not toward the opposite shore either. This lake is long and narrow, runs north to south, and it looked like he was just rowin' north. I guess he was takin' a long ride. But I didn't wait around after he started rowin.' I just went inside and went to bed."

"You didn't report it?" asked Beale. "Why not?"

"Oh, excuse me, officer sir," answered Walter sarcastically. "I musta forgot it's my job to police these waters twenty-four hours a day."

Beale managed to suppress for now his mounting anger at this guy's attitude. He sputtered, "You're telling me you saw something in the water four hundred yards out at night, and you're certain it was a rubber raft and you're certain someone in it threw a bag of some kind into the water?"

"You're damn right I'm certain. I got arthritis in both shoulders, bone spurs, back problems, and lately takin' a piss has been a real challenge, but there ain't a damn thing wrong with my eyes. And there was plenty of moonlight that night."

"Oh yeah? Well, what do you see out there now?"

Walter looked out at the open water and immediately said, "One person in a rowboat, straight out, about a third of a mile offshore. So what?"

Beale was surprised the old guy answered without hesitation after just a glance. Taking out the compact binoculars he always carried in his pocket, Beale focused on the distant speck. Sure enough, it was one person in a rowboat. But he was still skeptical. "It doesn't prove a thing," he said to Zoober. "At night, visibility is cut way down, even with the moonlight." Beale turned to Walter again. "How can you be sure what you saw the other night was a raft and not a rowboat?"

Now it was Walter who was getting disgusted with this cynical bastard.

"I know a raft when I see one. I was in the Navy, and I spent twelve hours in a rubber raft once on a survival trainin' exercise. So, I think I'm smart enough to tell the difference between a raft and a rowboat, ya shit fer brains."

Beale took an angry step toward Walter. "Now you listen here, grandpa, you..."

Zoober quickly jumped in to prevent a confrontation and asked, "Mr. Koosey, was the raft light or dark in color?"

Both Beale and the old man calmed down, but as Walter answered the question, he kept his eyes on Beale.

"Dark," said Walter. "Black, or maybe dark green."

Zoober continued, "You said he rowed it. But did you notice if it had a motor on it or not?"

"I didn't see or hear any motor, but he coulda had an electric one. They're really small and almost silent."

"Did you ever see that raft at any other time, before or since?" Zoober asked. "I mean, is it possible it belongs to one of your neighbors along the lake, or maybe it's a rental?"

"In answer to your first question, sonny, I ain't seen it at any other time since, but it sure as shit is possible it's a new one just bought by one of my neighbors. They sure as hell don't pass their purchases by *me* for approval. They don't even like me. Christ, it could belong to any vacationer around here, who the hell knows?"

The detectives asked Walter more questions about what he'd seen, but he wasn't able to offer any more helpful details.

Beale took a step back from the door sill. He asked: "You got a phone here if we need to talk to you again? Or a cellphone?"

Walter shook his head. "Got no phone. The damn phone company cut me off for gettin' behind on a few payments."

"Well, don't go on any trips," Beale said gruffly. "We may be back to ask more questions."

"Well, detectives," said Walter in his best sarcastic tone, "I was plannin' on jettin' off to Paris tonight, but I will be most happy to cancel that and sit here with my thumb up my ass waitin' for you to come back and ask me more stupid questions."

"You do that, grandpa," said Beale angrily as he began to walk away from the shack. "Stick it *way* up there."

Zoober gave Walter a quick thank you and hurried after Beale. Walter continued to stand in the doorway, staring with suspicion at the two officers as they headed back to their car.

"Look at him eyeing us," said Beale with disgust. "He must be afraid we'll steal some of the weeds in his yard. What a cranky old coot he is."

Zoober delicately admonished his partner: "Martin, you really shouldn't talk to citizens in that way. He *could* file a complaint against us."

Beale dismissed Zoober's worry with a wave of his hand. "Ahh, that old fart's not gonna file anything. He just wants to be left alone. Jesus Christ, four hundred yards away, and he's so certain about what he saw. Was the moon even out that night?"

"Yes, it was full and there was no cloud cover. Do you believe him?"

Beale didn't hesitate. "Yeah, I do. He saw somebody dump *something*. Can't be sure about any details though, 'cause we don't know how good his night vision is. But let's assume for the moment it *was* a raft. It's pretty unlikely it's a rental. I don't think rubber rafts are too popular with tourists on this lake. Not fast enough. Small powerboats, small sailboats, rowboats, jet-skis, and kayaks are the popular rentals, that's about it. And a rental would more likely be a bright color, too. Let's talk to the rest of the neighbors that live within a few miles of this shack. Keep going house to house. Maybe we can find someone who can corroborate his story. And we'll keep our eyes out for a rubber raft. Maybe somebody around here has one. If not, it might have been bought locally around the time of the murder. There can't be that many stores in the area that sell dark rubber rafts large enough for two men. If he's right about the color then it might be an army-navy surplus model rather than a sport model. We'll find out if one was purchased around here recently."

"What if the raft he saw wasn't recently purchased around here?" asked Zoober.

"Then finding it will be a lot harder. But what if it was?"

Chapter 19
Monday, May 25, 2:23 p.m.

The emergency room at St. Anthony's hospital smelled like a blend of chlorine bleach, lemon floor cleaner, and rubbing alcohol. The blank walls were an unbroken sea of sterile white except for a depressing gray stripe that ran along the ceiling line.

Jenny sat in the small, cramped waiting area, pressing a piece of gauze over the wound on her leg as she watched a young police officer pace before her, the taut new leather of his holster creaking with every step to signal his authority. Harvey sat beside Jenny, still dazed from the beating. He held an ice pack in his hand and moved it back and forth from one lump to the other. An ugly purplish bruise had formed on his cheek, and his left eye was blackened. Although his jaw was incredibly sore, it seemed to have the full range of motion and he guessed nothing was broken.

"You're lucky, you know," said the officer to Jenny. "That leg wound could've been a lot worse. That was a military knife he used, razor-sharp. I checked it myself. You could skin a bear with it."

Jenny knew exactly how sharp the knife was. Certainly sharp enough to kill easily. But it had merely grazed her leg and had left a wound that was bloody but fortunately not deep.

The officer paused while he looked over at the admitting desk. "I'm sure the nurse will be with you two in a minute," he said to Harvey and Jenny. There was only one nurse visible and at the moment she was attending to a middle-aged man who had come in with a rag tied around his right hand. The rag was soaked in blood, and the man was visibly shaken. He mumbled something about his finger and a lawnmower.

The officer turned back to Jenny. He took off his hat, carefully placed it on a chair, scratched at his scruffy blond hair, and then opened his small white notepad. "Now, your name is..."

"I already gave you my name," said Jenny. Her discomfort was obvious in her voice.

"I know, I know, just double-checking, little lady. Need to make sure I get the spelling right."

"It's Jennifer Tabor." She spelled it out for him, for the second time: "T-A-B-O-R."

"And your friend here?" replied the officer.

"I can speak for myself, officer. The name is Harvey Grace. That's G-R-A-C-E." Harvey rubbed his sore head and winced. Both of the lumps felt as if they were still growing, despite the ice bag.

"Well, those are some nasty bumps and bruises you've got there, Mr. Grace, but I think you'll be just fine. We arrested your friend."

"He's not my friend."

"He had no ID on him at all," said the officer, ignoring Harvey's comment. "And he hasn't said a word since we took him in. The car he was driving is unregistered and the plates are old, probably stolen or counterfeit. You said his name is Louie Parker?"

"Yes."

"Do you know where he lives?"

"Yes." Harvey gave the officer the location of the trailer park.

"And do you know why he attacked you?"

"No, I don't."

"And so, you've met him before, is that right?"

"Yes."

"Well, did you know that the great majority of people who get assaulted actually know their assailant? Looks like this case is no exception."

Jenny and Harvey showed no sign of being impressed by the officer's knowledge of law enforcement trivia. He looked slightly disappointed at not being congratulated for his insight. The officer shrugged and continued his questioning.

"Mr. Grace, under what circumstances were you acquainted with Mr. Parker?"

"I'm a private investigator," explained Harvey. "I went to his place a few days ago to ask him some questions."

"Questions about what?"

"About a case I'm working on. The nature of the case is confidential."

"Confidential, huh? And what about you, miss?" The officer turned his attention again to Jenny.

She lifted the gauze momentarily to check her wound. The bleeding had stopped for now. Before she could open her mouth to reply, Harvey answered for her.

"She's an architect," replied Harvey.

"Oh, yeah? Do all architects carry Beretta sidearms?"

Jenny gave a quick response. "I have a concealed carry license, officer," she said.

"The architecture business is real dangerous these days, is that it?" the young cop said sarcastically, obviously pleased with his wit.

The events of the last hour were a blur in Harvey's brain, but the mention of the Beretta triggered in him a strong image of Jenny confidently pointing the gun at Louie. Harvey could accept the fact that a single woman might want to carry a gun in her purse for protection, but he had a more pressing question for Jenny.

"Why were you following me?" he asked her.

The officer showed great interest in Harvey's question to Jenny. "You were following him? With a gun?" he asked Jenny in an accusative tone.

Jenny looked with resignation at Harvey and then she addressed the officer. "I'm also a licensed private investigator."

Harvey's mouth flopped open.

Jenny removed some documents from her purse to show the officer, who took them and sat down next to Jenny as he scrutinized them. And then Jenny turned to Harvey. "I can explain," she whispered to him, a stoic look on her face.

They were interrupted by the nurse, a middle-aged matron with a mean expression and a generous tuft of dark hair on her upper lip, who now stood in front of Harvey and Jenny and addressed both of them. "Come with me," she said tersely. She turned without waiting for replies, apparently never even considering her order might not be instantly obeyed.

The officer was still examining Jenny's private investigator license and gun permit. He looked up and said to Jenny and Harvey. "I'll wait for you here. I have a few more questions. I'll give these back to you later, Ms. Tabor. I need to write down a few things."

Harvey and Jenny followed the nurse into a tiny treatment room where Jenny sat down. There was an extra seat but Harvey remained standing. He was too agitated to allow himself to get comfortable. "The doctor will be with you in a minute," the nurse said. She left the room quickly and closed the door behind her. Jenny began speaking immediately.

"Harvey, please, don't look at me like that. You probably know all about the painting the Damlers have. I was hired by the Lemaires, the French family that owned the genuine Vermeer painting until the Nazis stole it from them during WWII. After Grant found the painting in his aunt's house, rumors began to circulate that it might be the genuine Vermeer. Someone brought this information to the attention of the Lemaire family, and now they're preparing a court case to try and recover the painting if it proves to be the one that used to be in their possession. They hired me simply to keep an eye on the painting and keep them informed. They want to know immediately if the Damlers try to do anything stupid, like attempt to sell the painting, or even keep it in their house without taking adequate security measures. My orders are only to keep aware of the painting's location, and of the Damlers' general whereabouts, and if possible, learn their intentions for the painting, and report back to my employers regularly. Actually, I expected this to be an easy job. But then I arrived in town on Friday to find that Grant Damler was missing."

Harvey was more hurt than angry. He felt betrayed.

"Why the deceit, Jenny? Why couldn't you have just told me the truth about why you came to Port Kole?"

"Because I'm working for someone who will likely face your client in court someday. Would you have trusted me?"

"The painting is the last thing on Pamela's mind right now. She's distraught over the disappearance of her husband. She just wants him back."

"You didn't answer my question," countered Jenny. "Would you have trusted me?"

Harvey paused before answering: "I don't know. And that's the truth. But why you? Why did a family from France hire *you*?"

"They wanted an American. Obviously, a French person wouldn't blend in very well in this area. So, they made some inquiries and looked for investigators working in New York State. Maybe the fact that I lived in France for a while and speak the language fluently appealed to them. Maybe they thought it would make me more loyal to their cause. And I'm also from this area, so I know my way around here."

Harvey's hurt started to give way to a general feeling of stupidity. He had been so easily duped. He was, after all, an investigator, supposedly capable of uncovering lies. *Am I completely blinded by my feelings toward her?*

"But you said you went to Northeastern as an architecture major," he asked anxiously. "So how did you end up as a private investigator?"

"Maybe for some of the same reasons *you* did. I tried my hand at a job with an architecture firm. It was boring. I wanted something more exciting, something that would challenge me and allow me to travel, to meet people. This is it. I like what I do."

"How long have you been in the business?"

"Almost seven years now."

Harvey raised his eyebrows in surprise. She answered his question before he spoke it.

"I'm perhaps...well, a little bit older than I look, Harvey."

"And where are you based? I mean, where do you live?"

"I told the truth when I said at lunch that I live in Syracuse, in a small house. I have an office in downtown Syracuse."

"And what about Brightwater Creek Properties?"

"It doesn't exist, I made it up," said Jenny, with a trace of shame in her voice.

"Weren't you afraid I might try to contact Brightwater Creek to check up on you?"

"The thought had crossed my mind. That's why I made a simple website for Brightwater Creek. As I said, I'm pretty good with computers, so it only took me a few hours. It even had a phone number and e-mail address for the company. If you had called, you would have been forwarded to a friend of mine, who knew what to say. By the way, did you check?"

"No," he answered defensively, and then he quickly fired off another question so as not to bring attention to the fact that he really should have verified her employment before he approved her to rent his neighbor's house. "And you came all the way here from Syracuse for this job?"

"Yes. They're paying me quite well, Harvey, I won't deny that."

"Have you ever met your employers, the Lemaire family?"

"No. I was hired by their American attorney. He gave me my instructions, and I make my reports to him."

"And meeting *me*, in the bar. That was all planned?" Harvey had been trying to keep a professional edge to his questions, but when this one came out, he wasn't able to hide his hurt and disappointment. The thought that Jenny had deliberately deceived him made him physically ill. *My God, the courage I had to summon up to speak to her in that bar for the first time! And to think she'd planned it, waited for it, wondered how long I would squirm on my barstool before I'd speak up.*

"Yes, Harvey. I'm sorry that I had to mislead you. After I got into town on Friday, I drove by the Damlers' house a few times. I saw you standing in their front yard talking to their neighbor. I followed you back to your place and saw the sign at the top of your driveway. I parked up on the road and waited there until you left the house, and then I followed you again. I tailed you most of Friday and I saw you go into that pub, O'Malley's, for lunch and dinner. From what I could see through the window, you seemed to be very good friends with the bartender. I knew I couldn't keep following you around continuously because eventually, you'd spot me. So, I decided I had to meet you. I took the chance you'd come back to O'Malley's the next day for lunch, and it paid off."

"You were following me on Friday? Uh, come to think of it, I thought I saw someone following me, in a sports car, but I just...wanted to see how long it would go on for, so I played along."

She can probably tell I didn't have a clue that anyone was following me. She could've driven a truck up my ass before a light bulb appeared over my head. Should I have noticed? I had no reason to expect that anyone would be following me. But then again, I should have been prepared for anything. Uncle Willie would have spotted the tail in minutes.

Or... is she really that good?

"Well, even if you didn't immediately spot me tailing you, don't feel bad, Harvey." She gave him a slight smile. "I'm really good at it." She sounded consoling rather than boastful. "Plus, I'm sure you noticed that I'm driving a different car today, my own car, which I also used when I followed you. I'd say it's a little less conspicuous than the 370Z we took to the pizza place, which is just a rental. I removed the rental company's stickers." Jenny let the gauze drop and looked at the wound. She seemed satisfied that the bleeding had truly stopped.

Harvey now felt doubly stupid because he had just implied that he spotted the 370Z following him on Saturday. Jenny sensed his embarrassment. She broke the awkward silence by asking: "So Harvey, why was this Louie Parker guy so upset with you?"

For a few seconds Harvey silently struggled over whether or not he should discuss the case, but then he decided to answer Jenny's question because she had a right to know about the person that had just tried to shoot, stab, and club her. And after all, Harvey owed her. Maybe he'd be dead if it weren't for Jenny.

"He's the Damlers' gardener. Works there maybe once a week. I don't know why he tried to kill me." *My God, did he really want me dead?*

Harvey continued: "Pamela's neighbor, Gloria, told me Louie has some kind of crush on Pamela. I went to his home and talked to him briefly. I didn't get much out of him, but I *did* get the distinct impression he hates Grant. He certainly wasn't very friendly to me. He told me to leave her alone. It had occurred to me he might want to take a swing at me. I left his place in a hurry. When I went to interview someone this afternoon, he must have followed me out there, then doubled back and waited for me, hoping I would take the same road back. Did you notice him when *you* were following me this afternoon?"

"No, I didn't. When you stopped at that house, I pulled over about half a block down the road and waited. I'm certain he didn't pull over too, I would've noticed. So, I think you're right. You said Parker has a crush on Pamela. Do you think there's any chance she feels the same way about him?"

"I have no reason to believe that. He's the mountain man type. Not very bright and not at all like her husband. I'd consider it very unlikely."

"I've seen my share of odd couples. Look, you haven't told me why Pamela hired you, but I can guess. She wants you to find Grant. What I don't know is whether she's genuinely worried about him missing, or if she thinks he may just skip off with the painting."

"Skip off with the painting? What makes you think that's even a possibility?"

Jenny didn't answer Harvey's question. She got up from her chair, paced the tiny room for a few seconds, and then turned toward Harvey as if she'd reached a decision.

"Harvey, maybe I was completely wrong when I decided to hide my real role in this from you. Let me make a suggestion I think will benefit us both, now that things are out in the open. Why don't we work together on this case? We can cover more territory. We can help each other."

"I'm not sure what good that'll do. We have different goals. I'm *not* after the painting. You *are*."

"I don't want to *steal* it. Remember, my job is just to let my employer know if the painting is kept safe or not. And your job is to find Grant. I think the painting has something to do with his disappearance."

"How do you know? And why is your employer so worried about the safety of the painting?"

"I think their concern is justified, don't you? Considering that Grant is missing and the painting is no longer in that safe deposit box."

Harvey had been looking away from Jenny, inspecting one of the bruises on his leg. But now he turned to face her and asked in an incredulous tone: "How did you know that?"

"Simple. I followed you to the bank. It only took one quick phone call to verify they have safe deposit boxes there, and that's a logical place to store the painting if you think it's extremely valuable. I couldn't think of another reason why you would be going in there with Pamela. And then when you both came out, she looked flustered, so I suspected she'd received something of a shock. I didn't know for *sure* until you admitted to it... just now." She gave Harvey another half-smile. "Grant's disappearance and the painting's disappearance occurred too close together to be a coincidence, wouldn't you say? If I were you, I'd be very anxious to find out if it was definitely Grant who took the painting out of the safe box."

"Well, of course I'm anxious about that. It's a top priority. That's why I'm seeing the bank security officer in the morning."

"Let's go together, Harvey. I need to find out what happened there, too. Are you okay with us working together?"

Harvey thought for a moment. *Is it a breach of confidentiality to work with Jenny? After all, she already knew, perhaps through my carelessness, that I'd been hired by Pamela to find Grant, and she had a good point when she said her objective wasn't at odds with mine. But I'm kidding myself here. Working with another private detective who's working for someone else who might eventually be an adversary of my client in court, would certainly be unconventional and maybe unethical. Can I trust her? She's admitted she lied to me. I hardly know her. No, it's just too weird. I shouldn't even consider it. Absolutely not. Case closed.*

"Yes, I'll work with you."

When you get right down to it, I'm just a weak person, and she's just so darn beautiful. Should I tell her everything now? About Peter Damler and his suspicions about Pamela?

No. There's no reason Jenny needs to know everything about everything. I'll have to be careful about what I tell her so I don't compromise Pamela's interests.

And... if Peter hired an investigator like he said he might, then there are three PIs involved in this case now.

How will we keep from tripping over each other?

Chapter 20
Monday, May 25, 7:28 p.m.

Back in his home, Harvey held to his head a few pieces of ice wrapped in a dishtowel as he called Pamela. He was relieved that the doctor in the emergency room had concluded there was no concussion, but it didn't change the fact that he had a searing headache, even after he'd spent the last few hours resting.

Pamela answered on the third ring. Harvey said a quick hello and then got right down to business.

"Mrs. Damler, I'll be going to the bank in the morning to talk with the security officer, a Mr. Avery O'Connor. Could you please call him as soon as the bank opens in the morning and explain I'm your representative and that I need his full cooperation?"

"Yes, of course."

"And do you know where Grant would have kept his bank card, the one he needed to get into the safe deposit box?"

She answered quickly: "Definitely in his wallet."

"And what about the password? Would he have memorized it? Or written it down?"

"He probably would have put it in the notes or reminders app on his phone. The card is the same one we use at the ATM, but for security reasons, the password had to be a different one than the password he uses to get cash. For the safe box, they require a ten character password with a mixture of numbers and letters, uppercase and lowercase. We each chose our own password, so I don't know his, but I think it's very unlikely he would remember it."

"And the actual key to the box?"

"Unfortunately, I wouldn't be surprised if he put it right on his keychain."

"Okay. And does Grant know anyone who works at that bank branch? Someone who would recognize him?"

"Yes. He knows the branch manager, Michael Tillman. They went to college together."

"Good. I'll try to talk to Mr. Tillman also. Maybe he saw Grant in the bank on Wednesday. Does Grant go into that branch often?"

"No. As I mentioned, we use the branch right in Port Kole, but it doesn't have any safe deposit boxes. We went to the Millbury branch together to sign the box rental agreement and put the painting in the box. That was after Tracer Analytics did their tests on the painting but before they issued their report to us. I can't remember ever going to that branch before, and I doubt Grant would have gone either, unless he had some reason to drop in to see Michael Tillman. But I think that's unlikely."

"Okay, thank you. And... something else happened to me today, that I need to ask you about. Your gardener, Louie Parker. He attacked me."

"Attacked you?" She sounded stunned and alarmed. "What do you mean?"

"He stopped his car by the side of the road when he knew I'd be driving by, and he put a help sign on it. When I pulled over, he was hiding behind his car. He jumped me."

"Oh my God, are you okay?" she gasped.

"Yes, I'm fine. A few bruises, but I fought him off." *Yeah, right, I totally crushed him.* "Er, with some help from somebody who stopped. Louie's in the county jail now. I don't think he'll be making bail soon. He should be arraigned in a few days. I went to his place on Friday, to see if he knew anything about your husband's disappearance. He wasn't very friendly at all to me, in fact, he told me to butt out. I guess he was angry I got involved."

There was silence on the other end for a few seconds, and then Pamela said, "Mentally, he's perhaps a bit slow, and he's kind of wild-looking, but I've always thought of him as harmless."

"I can believe he wouldn't harm *you*. But did you ever get the impression he might want to harm your husband?"

"What? Harm Grant? No, of course not. He hardly spoke to Grant at all. I'm the one who gives Louie his work instructions."

Harvey pressed the towel a little harder against his skull. He certainly couldn't agree with the "harmless" adjective Pamela had used. But he decided to drop the discussion about Louie for now, because he was embarrassed to ask Pamela any probing questions about her relationship with him. It was better anyway to ask questions of that type face-to-face, when you could read a person's reaction in their eyes.

After telling Pamela he would be in touch tomorrow, Harvey ended the call.

To Harvey, she'd seemed completely surprised by the incident with Louie, but also, she'd sounded emotionally exhausted.

She must be having sleepless nights. For that matter, will I be able to sleep at all, with this banging inside my head?

He dropped the towel from his head and felt the lumps. Despite the ice, they were still warm to the touch.

How could he console Pamela? If that card was in Grant's wallet, then either someone mugged him and stole the wallet, or someone took it off his dead body, or someone kidnapped him and forced him somehow to retrieve the painting.

Or... maybe Grant simply decided to take the painting and go.

But go who knows where, and with whom?

All these scenarios were bad news for Pamela.

Chapter 21
Monday, May 25, 8:41 p.m.

The sign outside the Olympia Movie Theater read in bold lettering: *Most Historic Theater in New York City.*

No one really knew what that statement meant, not even the owner of the theater, who had made it up. But the owner was shrewd and he'd decided it was vague enough such that no one would challenge it. The Olympia was, in fact, just a seventy-year-old dump in a bad neighborhood, and for the past ten years, it had been showing only porn because there weren't many upstanding citizens who would come into this sleazy neighborhood to see a first-run movie. But there were still some people, mostly businessmen, who came here because they preferred seeing their porn on an enormous screen, or they weren't willing to take the chance of getting caught by their wife or kids watching this stuff at home, or maybe they didn't want to watch it online if there was any chance of leaving a digital trail.

It was a rainy evening in the city, just a few minutes before showtime. The ticket taker behind the glass window looked completely bored. She had worked here for about twenty of her sixty-five years and had seen just about every kind of freak, jerkoff, and weirdo the city had to offer. But she didn't mind working tonight since the rainy weather made attendance light, and in a short while she would be able to take out her nail file and her romance novel to pass the time.

An obese man approached the window and she immediately lumped him into the jerkoff category. He had a pug nose and thin grayish hair which was carefully arranged to try and hide his balding area. There was a sweaty look to him, and he wore a dark suit that was too small and strained at every seam. He carried a leather briefcase. She had seen him before.

She took his money, passed him the ticket, and watched out of the corner of her eye as he went into the theater. The man passed through the seedy lobby with its shabby, stained carpet and its odor of greasy popcorn, and stepped into the darkened theater. The film started just as he settled into a seat near the back.

After a few minutes, a man in a khaki raincoat sat down next to the obese man. Out of politeness, the obese man didn't turn to stare at the man in the raincoat, but he thought it extremely odd that someone would sit right next to him when there were only a handful of people in the theater. In a few seconds, the man in the raincoat leaned toward the obese man and said in a whisper: "Hello, Tris. Remember me?"

The obese man turned immediately and the color drained from his face as he stared in horror and shock. "Zola! Dear God, I thought you were...." He stopped in mid-sentence.

"Ah, you *do* remember," said Zola. "How nice. Thought *what*, Tristan? That I was dead? No, I'm very much alive as you can see, and I plan to be around for a long, long time. Much longer than you. I missed you in Vienna seven years ago. Do you remember that? You were supposed to be there, but you never showed up. Zuckerman and Boulle didn't show up either. But the police showed up, *lots* of police, in fact. Why didn't you come, Tris?"

"Alex, please, I, I ..." Tristan stuttered. His eyes were wide with panic.

Zola leaned a few inches closer to him and continued: "Even though they were tipped off by you three scumbags, the Austrian police set a pitifully inadequate trap. And I heard they didn't bring in agencies from any other countries to help. What arrogance, thinking they could catch *me.*"

Zola paused for a few moments and watched the beads of sweat form on Tristan's forehead. They grew in size until they reached a critical mass, then they rolled down his face and eventually dropped from his chin onto the sticky floor.

"And so, Tris, I've finally come for you. Sorry it took so long, but I wanted you to squirm for years, to constantly wonder if I would return from the dead. I understand you're in the monetary exchange business these days, Tris. Is it lucrative? It certainly couldn't be as lucrative as the business you, Zuckerman, Boulle, and I used to enact. Those were great days, weren't they? There's much more competition now in the arms business. Lots of South Americans are trying to get in on my markets."

Tristan Hobblewaithe's eyes glanced left and right as he looked desperately for a way out. Zola noticed and immediately clamped his powerful hand over Tristan's wrist, pinning it to the arm of the chair. Tristan whimpered as he felt Zola's vise-like grip.

"You know what your big mistake was, Tris? You wronged me but left me alive, and so of course I had to come to pay you back, because I never forget. *Never.* You're probably surprised I waited all these years to come for you, is that it? Well, Tris, the bitter truth is that although killing you will give me pleasure, your death will be for me only a minor trophy. By yourself, you're hardly worth the price of round-trip airfare from Europe. I came to the states mainly to retrieve some property of mine. My beautiful *Maiden*. And I'm certain Zuckerman was the mastermind behind my betrayal. You and Boulle are just too stupid to have been the brains. You're just a bit of unfinished business to take care of while I'm here."

"Please," Tristan whimpered. "Please Alex, please ..."

"I'm a bit disappointed, though, to see how you've let your guard down completely, Tris. I guess you really did think I was killed in Vienna. Well, let me tell you about Vienna. They chased me into a condemned building. I found a vagrant in the basement, put him down quickly, then switched clothes with him. I also put my ring and watch on him, along with some coins and a few other items. Then I set the place on fire. The whole building went up, and it was easy for me to escape in all the confusion that followed. I'm sure the vagrant was incinerated thoroughly, his flesh vaporized. When it was all over and they were sifting through the rubble, they found the skeleton and drew their conclusions."

Zola sat back in his chair, easily keeping his iron grip on Tristan. He continued, "And you should *never* have let your guard down. In the days when we worked together, you used to watch your tail, Tris. But I followed you into this theater with ridiculous ease. You're completely oblivious, you didn't give so much as a glance behind you. Why, I'd bet an old lady could sneak up on you, whack you over the head with her umbrella, and steal your wallet and briefcase. Taking your miserable life will be about as simple as snuffing out a birthday candle. Now, are you ready to join your traitorous friends Zuckerman and Boulle in hell?"

The whimpers emanating from Tristan's mouth had turned into pathetic, weeping sobs now, but the few other people in the theater could not hear them over the sounds of the couple making passionate love on the big screen. Tristan's head was now turned completely away from Zola, in a feeble attempt to deny his existence. In his panic, Tristan's respiration was raspy and shallow. His putrid breath reeked of the chicken in garlic sauce he'd overindulged in for dinner.

Zola continued his verbal torture. "By the way, Tris, if you scream now, I guarantee you'll die a *horrible* death. Perhaps I'll cut your fingers off one by one while you watch."

Tristan Hobblewaithe knew it was true, if Zola wanted to kill him, he was as good as dead right now. Physical resistance on Tristan's part was useless. So, he took the one recourse left to him. He pleaded for mercy.

"Alex, for god's sake, I have a wife and two children now. Think of *them*, they *need* me. How will they survive without me?" Tristan's eyes turned red as the tears began to flow.

"Oh, so you're a family man now? And what would your wife and kids think if they knew you spend your time in places like this, while you say you're working late? I should have planned to gut you in front of them, and then kill *them* as well. Or maybe the other way around."

The sobbing became louder. "I never wanted to harm you. Zuckerman and Boulle, they came to me, threatened me. I was *forced* to go along!"

"They *forced* you? You mean they twisted your arm or broke your fingers one by one or something like that? I doubt it very much. Nobody forced you. You had a choice, and you chose to betray me. You sold me out, fully expecting I'd either be killed or rot in prison for the rest of my life. And after all I did for you, Tris. I made you rich."

"Anything wrong here?" said the large man who now leaned over Zola. The sobbing had apparently been a bit too loud and had caught someone's attention. Zola turned his head immediately at the inquiry, and now, with a professional's eye, he swiftly analyzed the situation.

The intruder was most likely a plainclothes security guard because he could see the outline of the shoulder holster beneath the man's sport coat. It made sense that places like this would hire at least one guard to hang around during screenings, in case some pervert got a little too excited and pulled out his wang. The guard had an impressive physique, probably a result of long hours lifting weights at the gym. His hair was cut short and moussed to stand almost straight up in a way that accentuated his youthful face. But the muscles and the gun didn't worry Zola in the least, because he knew the man would not get the chance to use either.

Zola glanced at Tris and could see him, out of the corner of his eye, inhaling in preparation for a scream. Tristan apparently saw in the security guard his one last chance at life. But Zola knew there was no chance, at least not for Tris, because less than a second after the word "here" had escaped the security guard's lips, Zola's right hand grabbed the man's tie, which dangled down as he leaned over.

To an adversary like Zola whose hands moved at lightning speed, the tie was half the work done and this idiot security guard had done it himself. This morning in the mirror, right after he had combed his hair and had dabbed on his aftershave, the guard had taken extra care to make a pretty knot in the colorful piece of cloth which would help bring about his death.

Zola moved in a blur, pulling down hard on the tie, which in turn brought the startled guard's head down about a foot. It was enough. By the time the man's right hand began its journey toward the handgun which was safely cradled in his shoulder holster, the heel of Zola's left hand was headed toward his opponent's head. As it struck, the man's head snapped back, and with a sickening crunch, the bone in the guard's nose was driven upward into his skull. Zola could see the light of life extinguished from the man's eyes. The guard immediately collapsed in the aisle and there was a loud *whump* as the massive body hit the floor. The fingers of both hands shuddered in a few final spasms. And then nothing.

Zola turned back now toward Tristan, and saw he was far beyond fear. Tristan's skin was nearly white, his eyes wide open in terror and shock as he stared at the dead man. His mouth was wide open as well, but the paralysis borne of shock and terror had caused the scream to be squelched at his lips.

Zola quickly scanned the dark theater to check on the six or seven other patrons. The closest person was about five rows away. No one was making any moves or sounds to indicate they had witnessed anything. Even so, Zola decided to finish his business quickly. Without hesitation, he chose the means of Tristan's death. Zola reached over and loosened Tristan's tie, then knotted the wide and narrow parts together. He then took his former friend's compact umbrella, pushed it through the tie loop behind his neck, and began to rotate it. As the makeshift tourniquet tightened with the first few turns of the umbrella, Tristan's arms began to thrash wildly. But with a few more turns the thrashing slowed. In his death throes, the whites of Tristan's bulging eyes stood in stark contrast to the bluish tint of his skin. Soon the resistance stopped completely and the obese body slumped down in the seat. His task done, Zola stood up and moved out into the aisle. He carefully stepped over the dead guard and headed toward the side exit.

Once outside, Zola tilted his head back to savor the coolness of the damp evening air. The rain had stopped, and the glistening streets were slowly drying. The clouds were moving off to reveal a brilliant moon.

It was turning out to be a beautiful spring evening.

Chapter 22
Tuesday, May 26, 8:46 a.m.

As Harvey drove to the bank in Millbury, he felt the familiar vibrations as he hit forty-five miles per hour. He eased up on the accelerator, wondering what Jenny, who sat next to him, thought about his old car. But she seemed to be totally absorbed in the scenery. Slices of bright blue lake water could be seen through breaks in the trees.

"It's so beautiful here," she said.

"Yes, it is. A great place to live, or visit. Do you have any friends or relatives out this way?"

"Yes, I have a relative who lives not too far from here. Occasionally I come to visit. But not often enough."

She paused for a few seconds as if considering whether to reveal more of her secrets. Harvey wanted to hear more. He leaned toward her just slightly, giving her the maximum amount of attention that the winding road would allow.

"It's my grandmother," Jenny continued, her tone serious now. "She's in a nursing home. She has Alzheimer's and needs twenty-four-hour care. She played a major role in my childhood, so I am ... or *was*, very close to her, before her personality slipped away."

Harvey didn't quite know what to say. To have a human being's mind taken away by disease is a tragedy. What kind of meaningful consolation could he possibly offer her? And he didn't want to sound completely patronizing either. So, he gave her a soft but insightful "Hmmmm," accompanied by an understanding nod of the head, all the while keeping his eyes on the road.

Jenny continued, "It's very difficult for me to see her as she is now. I'd like to remember her as the loving, caring, intelligent person I knew when I was very young. That person ... just doesn't exist anymore. When I visit her, she usually doesn't recognize me."

More silence. Harvey again groped for something to say. He never had a close relative suffer from a long, devastating illness. "It must be terrible," he said.

Brilliant, that's sure to make her feel tons better.

When she didn't respond, Harvey changed the subject.

"You didn't tell me much about how you ended up as a private detective."

She turned toward him, seeming to welcome the new topic.

"Well, I quit my job with the architecture firm after about ten months and took off for Europe. I stayed there for almost two years. I did some traveling at first, then I settled in France. To support myself I took jobs in shops and restaurants. It was quite a learning experience. When I came back to the States, I was looking for a job when a friend of my mother's contacted me. She'd heard I was good with computers, and she was interested in reuniting with a brother she'd lost touch with twenty-five years ago. He didn't show up in any of the usual online public directories, so she asked me if I could locate him. The problem was, unknown to her, he'd changed his name twice, so I had to do a lot of digging online but eventually I found him. I gave his address to my mother's friend, she paid me very well, and soon two other people who heard about it called me with similar requests. I decided I could make a decent living at it, so I went to work for a veteran PI and got my three years of experience."

"You can defend yourself too. Yesterday you held your own in hand-to-hand combat against a man who was about double your weight. Mind if I ask where you learned those moves?"

"Back in college. I took four years of self-defense training, starting in my freshman year. Tae Kwon Do. It was a great stress reliever and it really boosted my self-confidence."

"Did you start the class because you wanted to reduce your stress level?"

"No, actually, I started it for the self-confidence reason. Near the beginning of my freshman year, I had an incident right outside my dorm room. I was accosted by some creep. Luckily someone came along in time to scare him away before he hurt me. But it changed me as a person. I lived in fear for months after that, deathly afraid it might happen again, either by the same guy or somebody else. When I walked into a room, I'd immediately scan the place for the guy who attacked me, or for other creeps, and if I saw anyone that I was the least bit suspicious of, I'd leave. My friends must have thought I was nuts. I found it affecting my concentration in school, too. So, I guess what started me on Tae Kwon Do was a weariness of being afraid. After training for about a year, I finally realized I could take control of my life again." She paused as if she was worried she'd said too much. "I'm sorry I ran on like that, Harvey. I didn't mean to dump my past troubles on you."

"No problem at all, Jenny. I feel ... privileged that you chose to share those thoughts with me."

Okay, here we go, here's the part where you think of something equally private to share with her, and maybe this will go a long way toward starting some kind of relationship. I could share my extreme fear of something. Hard to choose exactly what, because I've been scared shitless of so many things since I was a little kid. What'll it be — rats? snakes? boogie men? aliens?... or...

"Harvey, isn't that the bank ahead?" asked Jenny.

Damn, I barely noticed we'd reached the town. Missed my chance at bonding. Back to business.

In a few minutes, they were seated in front of the desk of the bank's forty-something security officer, Mr. Avery O'Connor. He was tall and fit, with a head of neatly manicured black hair and a definite air of authority about him. He introduced himself and invited them to sit down.

"What can I do for you today?" he asked with a smile that to Harvey appeared pretentious. Harvey was certain the reason for their visit had already been conveyed to O'Connor.

Harvey began, "As you know, we're here as Pamela Damler's representatives. Her husband, Grant, has been missing since last week, and we're searching for him on her behalf. The person who helped

Mrs. Damler get into the safe deposit box on Saturday, which is registered to both of them, told us your records indicate Grant opened the box on Wednesday afternoon at about three-thirty, which was after he went missing. The box was opened only once prior to that, when both Mr. and Mrs. Damler were here to sign the box rental agreement. If Grant *did* open it on Wednesday, it would indicate he was alive and well at that time, which is important information. But we need to be certain, so we're here to discuss with you the possibility that it might *not* have been Grant who came to the bank on Wednesday."

O'Connor gave another fake smile to Harvey before turning politely defensive. He said in a lecturing manner, "I'm sure Mrs. Damler described our procedures to you, which are clearly explained in the contract they both signed. Our institution does *not* guarantee it will only allow the box to be opened by the Damlers. It simply states we will only give access to someone who has the card, password, and key. In this case, our logs clearly show that these conditions were met. The bank is therefore absolved of any liability, even if it was not Mr. Damler who opened the box. And I can assure you these security precautions are standard for the industry."

Jenny asked the security chief: "I notice you have quite a few security cameras in the building, and also a few outside. Do you save the video for a certain period of time?"

"Yes, Ms. Tabor. We retain the video for sixty days," he answered.

"Could we see the video of the person who opened the box on Friday?" asked Jenny.

"Unfortunately, no. It's our policy not to allow people other than a number of designated bank employees to view those recordings unless a subpoena is produced. I'm sure you understand that our legal department insists on this."

Jenny continued, "If you won't let us see them, can *you* view the recordings and tell us whether it was Grant Damler who opened the box, based on some pictures of him that we can provide?"

O'Connor said firmly, "I'm afraid I can't do that either. Even if I could, my determination would of course be subjective."

Jenny said, "Mr. O'Connor, my guess is that you probably already did it before this meeting, using some publicly available pictures of him, perhaps from his days as a teacher at the University."

"I can't comment on that one way or the other," O'Connor said with a stone face.

Harvey piped in, "We don't want you to violate bank policies, but we really need your help. Mrs. Damler is quite anxious to find her husband."

"I sympathize with your mission, I truly do. I'm only conveying to you the bank's long-standing policies."

Harvey asked, "Everyone who goes into the safe deposit vault has to sign the electronic pad, right? Can we see his signature?"

"Yes, that I can show you."

O'Connor pecked at his keyboard and in thirty seconds turned his monitor so Harvey and Jenny could see it. The signature was a scribble, almost completely illegible as far as letter identification. Harvey knew it was nearly useless. Even so, he asked O'Connor: "Mind if I take a picture of your screen? I'd like to compare it to Grant's signature."

"Go right ahead. But as I'm sure you'll agree, signing is a quaint but essentially useless formality. Signature comparison is a very inexact science, so we don't have our associates even attempt it, and we don't say anything in the rental contract about signature verification. And those done on a screen are even less reproducible than those on paper. We'll probably drop the signature requirement in the near future."

After snapping the picture with his phone, Harvey continued, "Pamela Damler told me her husband is acquainted with the branch manager here, a Mr. Michael Tillman. I'd like to ask him if he saw Grant in the bank on Wednesday."

O'Connor put his elbows on the table and crossed his fingers together before replying, "Unfortunately Mr. Tillman wasn't here on Wednesday during the hours when customers are allowed to access their boxes."

"Why not?" asked Harvey.

"He has a daughter in middle school. There was a school shooter threat phoned into the school on Wednesday morning. Parents were contacted to come and pick up their children. He went there immediately."

Harvey's eyes widened with alarm, and he said, "School shooting threat... yes, I heard about that...the local school." He turned to Jenny. "No one was hurt, thank God."

"That's correct," said O'Connor. "It was a false alarm. No gunman ever showed up. The school was searched but nothing was found. Mr. Tillman is still home with his daughter, he's a single father. They haven't re-opened the school yet, but I expect they will soon."

Harvey and Jenny thanked O'Connor for his time even though his cooperation was lacking, and left the building. As they leaned against Harvey's car in the bank parking lot, they mulled over the interview.

"What do you think?" Jenny asked.

"I think it's an amazing coincidence Tillman was gone that morning. The one person who could recognize Grant."

"I agree. What about the card, password, and key?"

"Maybe all a potential impostor needed was to get Grant's wallet and keys, assuming he put the box key on his chain like Pamela said. And if the password was in the notes or reminders app on his phone, a determined person could have gotten to it. A fingerprint or facial recognition can unlock many phones. Those things could be managed even if Grant was unwilling or incapacitated or ..."

Harvey paused, not wanting to say it.

"Dead?

"Right. So, do you really think O'Connor looked at those videos?"

"Yes. *I* would if I had his job. And maybe he already formed an opinion about whether it was Grant or not. But I couldn't read him on that. He's got a real poker face."

"Yeah. And if a man came in who was roughly Grant's height and weight, maybe wearing a baseball cap and glasses, the video might be inconclusive anyway."

Using his phone Harvey quickly searched the internet for the latest on the school shooting threat.

"I can't find any new details about the police investigation," he said. "All the news stories just say a threat was phoned in anonymously and the cops haven't been able to trace it back to the caller yet."

"I have a few contacts in law enforcement. Not with the police around here of course, but it's a buddy-buddy system. Cops tend to give each other information. I'll make a few calls, see what I can find out."

Chapter 23
Tuesday, May 26, 1:56 p.m.

Beale and Zoober stared at the large, patriotic-looking sign which hung over the store entrance. It read, in bold red, white, and blue lettering: *Huckman's Army Navy Store.*

"How far are we from the lake?" asked Beale.

"About two miles."

They opened the squeaky screen door of the old building and stepped inside. There was an incredible amount of merchandise crammed into the small establishment. About half of it was clothing and the other half was military equipment of all kinds. Every last bit of wall space was covered with shelves. A mixture of unpleasant odors hung in the stale air including the musty smell of battle fatigues and the greasy smell of the light machine oil on the dummy ammunition casings and other artillery souvenirs. Zoober spotted the proprietor at the centrally located checkout area, eating a slice of pizza and taking long swallows of soda from a quart-size paper cup that said *COLOSSAL* all over the outside. He appeared to be about fifty years old and had grayish-brown hair tied back in a long ponytail. A sliver of his pot belly was visible, hanging out from beneath his fishnet tank top shirt. He had the look of a street punk who had aged badly.

"Hello, I'm Detective Zoober and this is Lieutenant Beale. We're from the Albany police department." Zoober held up his badge and the man barely gave it a glance. "We'd like to ask you a few questions if you don't mind. Are you the owner?"

"That's right," answered the man with wariness. He placed what was left of the pizza slice onto a greasy paper plate by the cash register. "I'm Dale Huckman." He offered no hand to shake.

Zoober opened his mouth to continue, but Beale impatiently stepped up to Huckman and took over the questioning.

"Do you sell many of those rubber rafts?" Beale asked, pointing to a black raft hanging on the far wall.

"Not many, it's an expensive item," said Huckman without enthusiasm.

"Is that a two-man raft?" Beale continued.

"Yup. It could even handle three small adults."

"Tell me about that motor on it."

"It's an electric trolling motor, comes with the raft. It gets you a top speed of about five miles per hour. Most people buy oars, too."

"Do you carry any other types of rafts?"

"Nope, just the one model."

"Did you sell any recently—say in the last week or so? "

"I *did* sell one in the past week."

"On what day?"

"Thursday, I think— in the late afternoon."

"Thursday, you *think*?" said Beale with undisguised annoyance. "Well, was it Thursday, or wasn't it? Can you look it up in your sales records?"

Beale saw that Huckman's register was ancient, practically an antique, looking as old as some of the World War II surplus crap that lined the store shelves.

Huckman didn't answer immediately. Instead, he bent down to retrieve a shoebox from some secret cubby behind the counter. He opened the box, fished through it, and after about twenty seconds he pulled out a piece of paper and studied it.

"It was purchased Thursday at four thirty-three p.m.," said Huckman with disdain. He had no desire to waste his time today talking to cops.

"And who bought it?" asked Beale.

"A man. Never saw him before. He paid cash so I don't know his name."

"Did he touch that piece of paper you're holding?" Zoober interjected, with a trace of hope in his tone.

"No, this is my copy of the receipt. The register prints a copy of all the receipts, and at the end of every day, I throw the copies into this box. I give the customer the original."

"So, did he ask you a lot of questions about the raft, or did he just walk in and say I wanna buy a raft?"

Huckman downed the last of the colossal soda, and then answered slowly: "I sure don't remember his exact words. I was busy with another customer when he walked in. But I'd say he wasn't in the store for long, maybe ten minutes or so, and he seemed pretty much decided from the start that he was ready to buy. I remember him asking me how many men it would carry, how much weight, that sort of thing. And he asked me to explain to him how to inflate and deflate it. I pulled the display down off the wall and showed him."

"Yeah, well how about you explain it to *me*?"

Huckman shrugged his shoulders and said: "Not much to it. It's got a compressed gas cylinder on it. You just turn a valve to open the cylinder and the raft inflates pretty quickly. There's a button you press to deflate it."

"Did he buy anything else or ask about anything else?" continued Beale.

"He bought a set of oars. That's all."

"You got any surveillance cameras in the store, or outside in the parking lot?" asked Beale gruffly.

"No."

"Well then, now comes the real important question. What did he look like?"

Huckman frowned, knowing he was about to displease the detectives. "Middle-aged, average build, regular looking white guy, clean-shaven, hair trimmed neatly. That's about it."

"Just your average Joe, huh? Was he local or a tourist?"

"How should I know? I never saw him before, but that don't mean he's not local. There's lots of people around here I don't know."

"Do you remember him touching anything in the store when he came in?" asked Zoober as he wrote on his pad. "Anything you showed him, or maybe some other merchandise in the store?"

"Not that I recall. Other than the bills he handed me, I think all he touched was the stuff he bought and carried out."

Two young boys in the store caught Huckman's eye as they handled some old ammunition casings with wide-eyed amazement.

"Hey, don't play with that stuff unless you're buyin'," Huckman said to the boys, who quickly put the items back on a shelf. Two aisles over, a female customer stared at Huckman impatiently, making it obvious she needed his help. He was the only salesperson in the store. In the woman's arms were two leather bomber jackets. She apparently had some questions about them.

"Hey, c'mon guys," Huckman said. "Are we almost done here? I got a business to run."

Beale decided to make it clear that police business was top priority. "We can do it here, pal, or we can take you to the station house. My partner told you we're from Albany. It's over an hour driving time to get there, but it's a real pretty drive. Lots of nice scenery between here and there. You'll enjoy it. Now tell me, what color was his hair?"

Huckman shrugged his shoulders in surrender. "It was dark, what I could see of it. He had a hat on."

"What kind of hat?" asked Beale.

"A soft cloth hat with a little brim all around. Like a golfer might wear. It was a light color."

"Did he have glasses?"

"Yes."

"Clear or sunglasses?"

"Clear."

"Wire rims or plastic? Rectangular or round?"

"Maybe rectangular plastic ones. I can't be sure."

"What about his clothes?"

"What about 'em?"

Beale took a deep breath and said very slowly, as if trying to make a two-year-old understand: "Describe them."

"I don't remember specifics. I'd say his clothes weren't shabby or anything like that. And he wasn't all dressed up either. Just regular clothes."

Beale changed the line of questioning. "So, he said he wanted to buy the raft, and then what?"

"I went to the storage area in the back to get one. I knew I had at least two in stock, in addition to the one on the wall. They're shipped to me in cardboard cartons. I brought one of the cartons out, got one pair of oars to go with it, he paid for everything, then he took the stuff out to his car and left."

"Paid how?"

"Like I said before, with cash. It's over three hundred bucks, with tax. He gave me a bunch of twenties."

"Still have 'em?" asked Beale, not expecting Huckman to answer yes, but it never hurt to ask.

Huckman looked surprised at Beale's question. "You gotta be kidding. I probably gave some out in change, and if there were any left, I would have already deposited them into my bank account."

"Okay. So, did you see his car?"

"Nope. I was busy, I had other customers in the store. Like I do now." Huckman glanced over toward the woman with the bomber jackets. She began to put them back on the rack. Huckman winced as he thought of the one hundred fifty percent markup on those coats. He bought them dirt cheap from some sweatshop in Mexico. "Hey, I'll be right with you," he called over to her.

"Then how do you know he had a car?" asked Beale.

"You mean instead of a van or truck or somethin' like that? I guess I don't know for sure. But he must have driven *something* here. I just assumed he wasn't gonna walk home with that big cardboard box and the oars to carry."

Beale pressed on. "Did you hear the sound of a vehicle pulling away right after he left?"

"I really don't remember. Listen, guys, I know I'm not being much help to you but if he comes back, I'll let you know, okay?"

"And what makes you think he'll come back? Did he say he'd come back?" asked Beale with interest.

"No, but I think he may not have his raft anymore. Maybe he'll come back to buy another one."

"And would you let us in on why you think he doesn't have it anymore?"

"I don't know for sure whether he has it or not, but the day before yesterday three kids brought one of these rafts in here, almost good as new, asking me if I wanted to buy it. I get kids in here all the time and they know I sell the rafts because of the one hanging on the wall. I figure the raft got away from him. Maybe he didn't tie it up properly and it drifted away. These kids just said they found it."

Beale and Zoober looked at each other, astonished at their luck.

"Did you buy it?" Beale asked anxiously.

"I sure did. The kids sold it to me at a bargain price, way below my cost. I looked at it, and it doesn't have any big holes in it. I don't know if it has any tiny holes in it, but if it does, I should be able to patch them."

"All right, let's see it," ordered Beale, showing enthusiasm for the first time since he began his questioning.

Huckman gestured for them to follow. He led them through a door into a dingy storeroom littered with cardboard boxes. The deflated black raft sat in a lump on the peeling linoleum floor, shoved into a corner.

"The cylinder's been used," said Huckman. "It was inflated, then deflated. But that's no big deal, I can fit it with a new cylinder. The motor still works, I checked it."

"So, is this the one you sold on Thursday or not?"

"Impossible to say if this is the one. They don't have unique serial numbers, but it's the same model I sold on Thursday. And this looks to be in pretty good shape — not used for long, that's for sure."

"Did you wash it or wipe it down, brush it off, anything like that?" asked Zoober.

"No, not yet. I haven't had a chance yet to get it ready for sale."

Zoober bent down over the raft and probed at something inside it with the eraser end of a pencil.

"Whatcha got?" Beale asked his young partner.

"A white fiber. Maybe from a rope or cloth," answered Zoober, who carefully placed the fiber in a tiny plastic bag.

"Let's get the whole damn thing to the lab," said Beale. He turned to Huckman. "We'll have to borrow the raft for a while. Did the kids bring the oars to you too?"

"Nope." Huckman didn't look pleased at all. His thoughts were on when and if he would ever see a return on his money, plus the one or two bomber jackets that had gone unsold because by now the lady had probably left the store.

"Too bad. Better chance of getting a full set of prints from the oars. So, tell us about the kids now."

"What's to tell? They were boys, three of 'em. All around twelve maybe, all with their hair cut short, wearing dirty clothes. Just regular kids. They probably all came on bicycles 'cause I saw at least one of them sitting on his bike out front when the door was opened. This thing is kinda bulky to carry on a bike, but maybe one of them had a wagon of some kind attached to the back of his bike. I'll bet they've blown the money on comics and candy by now."

Zoober took notes at a furious pace. Beale just stood and stared at Huckman with skepticism.

Beale said to Huckman: "We're going to need you to come down to the local sheriff's station. We'll arrange to have a police artist there and we'll want you to do your best to describe to him the appearance of the man who bought the raft, and of the kids and the bikes you saw. We're anxious to talk to all of them."

"Police artist! I'm tellin' you guys, I have only a fuzzy recollection at best of what the guy and the kids looked like! How are we gonna get an accurate drawing? That'll be a complete waste of time."

Beale had been staring at the raft. He turned slowly now to look at Huckman and gave him an *I've had it up to here with your shit* look.

"Well, that's no problem at all, Mr. Huckman," said Beale with sarcastic cheeriness. "Because Detective Zoober and I, we're real patient people, and we'd be willing to take you back to that police artist two or three times a day, over and over, until you *do* remember what they look like. And if that don't work, hey, we can try hypnosis. We got this great gypsy lady who works with us, and she can put you so far under that you can remember everything and you'll tell us anything we want to know about these people who came into your store or even anything we need to know about *you*. Sound like fun?"

"Martin, *please,*"Zoober whispered to Beale, stepping between his partner and Huckman. He turned to Huckman and apologized: "My partner is kidding, of course, about the hypnosis. We're very sorry about inconveniencing you, Mr. Huckman, and—"

"Of *course,* I'm kidding," said Beale. "Now I'd like you to please give detective Zoober here all your telephone numbers and your home address."

Huckman obediently gave Zoober the information. Next, the young detective took a roll of yellow *Police Line* tape from his pocket and cordoned off a triangle of space around the raft by running a long piece of the tape at waist height between the two adjacent walls.

"Don't cross this tape for any reason," Beale said. "On second thought, don't even walk back here while we're gone. This room is a shithole as it is, there's no point in you stirring up more dust. Let's keep the evidence as clean as possible."

"But the bathroom is back here," Huckman said with a worried look on his face.

"No problem, my friend, the lab guys will be here very soon to pick up this raft and vacuum the floor under it. I'm sure you can hold your bladder till then. They'll need to take your fingerprints, too, since we'll probably pick them up on the raft."

"I close at six."

"We're gonna call them right now, and my partner and I will wait outside for them. We'll also find out when the police artist is available."

"Thank you for your cooperation, sir," said Zoober to Huckman in a feeble effort to restore some degree of civility. The two detectives left through the back door of the storage room.

As they walked toward their car, Zoober said: "Martin, you really shouldn't have been rude to him. He could file a complaint against us."

Beale waved the suggestion away. "Ah, you worry too much, kid. He's not gonna take the time to file anything. He just wants to sell his army surplus crap."

"What do you think, Martin? The man had glasses and a hat. Possibly to disguise his appearance?"

"Yeah, maybe. I think it's one very long shot that we'll get any useful drawings from that bozo. But maybe we'll get lucky with the raft."

Chapter 24
Tuesday, May 26, 4:46 p.m.

Harvey walked out of Dexter's office and looked up and down the dingy hallway. He'd been waiting for about half an hour for his friend to come back. The sign on his door, which looked as if it were written in crayon, read *Gone Fishin.*

Harvey turned in the doorway and faced the office again. He wondered if there was any chance Dexter just put the sign up because he was sleeping in here, under a pile of rubbish somewhere. Unlikely, but there was another door at the back of the office, maybe just a storage closet. Harvey tried the knob but it was locked. He leaned down to see if he could look through the sizable gap between the bottom of the door and the floor.

Someone touched Harvey's shoulder, and his body jerked reflexively. He shot upright and turned around in one swift motion, pulling a neck muscle in the process. Harvey winced in pain and slapped the palm of his right hand against the back of his neck.

"Geez, you scared me," he said to Dexter, who now stood above Harvey, looking down at him.

"Man, you look like crap, what the heck happened to your face?" asked Dexter.

"Nothing serious, I kinda got beat up a little bit."

"Yeah, well if you're gonna be a peeping tom like that, you're gonna get beat up once in a while. Why were you trying to peek into my storage closet? I keep my clothes and my valuables locked in there, but I don't undress in there, you know. I use the men's lavatory down the hall."

"Don't worry, I wasn't trying to see you naked."

Dexter tossed his tackle box and his fishing rod onto his desk. A wad of slimy greenish vegetation that was caught on the hook plopped onto the desk blotter and left an oily stain, but Dexter didn't seem to care. With a quick motion of his forearm, he pushed a pile of papers from his desk chair onto the floor and then plopped down into the seat.

"How much time do you spend fishing?" asked Harvey.

"Not much. Maybe twenty hours a week."

"Twenty? That's a lot, wouldn't you say?"

"It gives me time to think."

"Yeah, and what do you think about?"

"Fishing, mostly."

"And how much time do you spend on schoolwork?"

"Too much, sometimes more than three hours a week."

"Wow, sounds like you're really rocketing toward that degree. You're a talented guy, Dex. You could for sure get a good job designing better toasters or something if you ever graduate. So anyway, how did the highly illegal interception of that guy's phone calls go? Did you get caught and arrested? Spent the night in the county jail?"

"Ah, you should have more faith in me because of course it went perfectly. I planted my catcher and the data is rollin' in."

"Where'd you plant it?"

"I stuck it in a bush at the back end of the parking lot. It's well hidden and I put a weatherproof cover on it and it's got a battery that'll last at least three days. It's just sitting there happily sucking up data and sending it to my cell."

"Have you listened to any of the calls so far?"

"Yeah, everything. Nothing interesting. He doesn't talk much. He made some calls to auction houses and art galleries. And he corresponds with two people who seem to work for him, a man and a woman, but it's always by text. He checks on how their work is going. They're each cleaning the dirt off an old painting. Real exciting. And the man is also working on a contract to do some kind of restoration work on some mural on a wall, and he and the guy talk about the price they should charge. It's all boring stuff. This guy's life is a real snoozer. I'll send you the files so you can listen and read everything. Do it at bedtime 'cause it'll put you to sleep."

"Okay, will do. And do you have the class lists I asked you to scrounge up?"

"Not yet, but I'm close. Grant Damler started teaching three classes this semester before he quit, and my friend Dave is in two of them, and I have another friend Horace who's in the other one. The classes are still going on, but they've got replacement teachers now. Dave and Horace are making up lists of the female students in all three classes, and I should have them by tonight."

"That's great, but now I also need printed color pictures of all the female students. And I'd like their date of student enrollment and home city and state. Can you do that?"

Dexter frowned in consideration. "Well, they don't have student ID pictures on the University website or personal information because of privacy issues. But I should be able to get them from yearbooks. If that fails, I can troll social media websites. What kind of pictures do you need? I mean, do you need to see their whole bodies? In bikinis or something like that?"

"I'm sure you're an expert at tracking down near-naked pictures of women, but no, just headshots will be fine, Dex. Clear, color headshots. Say, how can Dave and Horace remember all the girls in these classes, anyway?"

"Well, I know these guys pretty well, and about half of their reason for going to college is to meet girls. So, when they make the lists for us, they may forget one or two of the girls, but chances are they'll be dogs. And I'll bet this co-ed you're looking for is good-looking and well built, right?"

"That's probably a good assumption. Okay, can you have everything by tonight, including the pictures?"

"Yeah, if Dave and Horace come through. But it's gonna cost you. Not money, of course. You just gotta go on this double date with me and Marlo and Sandy. I need you, dude, 'cause for some reason which I simply cannot fathom, Marlo won't go on a date with me unless it's a double date, with her friend Sandy."

"Maybe Marlo has a simple fear of being alone with a weirdo."

"Could be. At least think about it, dude. C'mon, it'll be fun."

"Fun? She probably won't even like me. I'm not very talkative."

"Sure, she will. Sandy likes the silent type. And the skinny type. Silent and skinny, that's you."

Chapter 25
Tuesday, May 26, 8:48 p.m.

Zola approached the woman from behind. She stood on the sidewalk, gaudily dressed in a very short leather skirt and a low-cut, pink blouse with ruffles.

"Miss, I'd like to hire you," he said.

The woman turned around and scanned him up and down. She observed that he was rather handsome and rugged-looking. Well dressed, too. He didn't look like the type of guy who had to pay for sex. But the world was full of all kinds of kinks with different needs and desires. Probably he wanted something his wife or girlfriend was unwilling or unable to give him.

"Well, you came to the right place. There's only a few working girls in this town, and I outclass the others. What's your pleasure, Jack?"

Zola calmly explained: "First, I want you to take this money and go into that store across the street and buy yourself some nice clothes, and shoes also." He handed her some cash. The woman's eyes grew brighter at the sight of the money and she quickly stuffed it into her skirt pocket before he could change his mind.

"Oh, we gonna do dress up?" she asked with encouragement. "I'm real good at that. Want me to be a nurse? A schoolteacher, maybe? Lots of guys go for teachers or librarians. I don't know what it is, probably they had a crush on one when they were in school."

"I'm just looking for a ... well, let's say a very respectable appearance, if you please. Purchase a longer skirt, cut from a dark blue or grey cloth, or perhaps a nice pants outfit if you prefer. Pay for the clothes and put them on in the dressing room. And tie your hair back, if you don't mind. Then I'll take you to a hotel. I'll tell you what I want when we get there."

"Well, I like that. You're obviously a gentleman. I like privacy and clean sheets. None of this back-alley sex for you, huh?" Her demeanor then turned businesslike. "It'll cost you four hundred, Jack. In advance, of course. And that's in addition to the new clothes, which I get to keep."

Without hesitating, Zola took a money clip from his pocket, peeled off four hundred-dollar bills, and handed them to her.

She thought, *Shit, he agreed way too quickly, I should have asked for five or six.* Her mind raced to think of ways she could get more money out of him.

"Want me to dye my hair, Jack? I can make it exactly the shade of your eighth-grade schoolteacher if you remember it, or whatever color you want. For just an extra two bills."

Zola smiled at her. It was a strange, almost evil grin, and it momentarily unnerved her.

"That won't be necessary," he answered.

Chapter 26
Wednesday, May 27, 7:25 a.m.

Harvey opened his eyes slowly. His neck was sore, and there was a sour, pasty taste in his mouth. He looked around through half-closed eyelids, and saw he was in his own little living room, stretched out on the couch, and in the same clothes he'd worn yesterday. He realized the sore neck was from sleeping with his head on the arm of the couch, but he was pleased that the pain from the beating he'd received had subsided.

The pictures of Grant's female students, over a hundred of them, were scattered on the floor in front of the couch. As soon as Harvey had received them from Dexter very late last night, he'd started sifting through them, looking for ... for what? He wasn't sure, but he felt compelled to look at the photos anyway before he showed them to Sadie. Most of the pictures were yearbook mugshots and the remainder were from social media. Some of the women were plain, some pretty, and several very striking.

He stood up and then remembered he had to hustle over to get Jenny so they could go together to show the pictures to Sadie Gumm. He was excited by the thought of seeing Jenny again. They were practically partners now. It was still hard for Harvey to believe he was even speaking to her, let alone working with her.

Thirty minutes later, Harvey took the one-minute walk through the woods to her place next door and started pumping the doorbell button like an overanxious little kid at Halloween.

Jenny opened the door. Her appearance stunned Harvey. *My God, she's so gorgeous*, he thought. She was dressed in jeans and a bright red pullover top. To be so radiant at eight o'clock in the morning. He didn't think he'd ever reach the point of *not* being knocked over by her appearance.

"Morning," said Harvey with a huge grin. "Time to get going."

"Sure, come on in while I get a few things, Harvey," she chirped, returning Harvey's smile. As he stepped into the small entryway, Jenny opened the drawer of an end table and took out the shoulder holster containing the Beretta. She put the holster on quickly, buckling the thin leather straps to secure it to her torso.

She's ready for anything now. And wow, that gun makes her look even sexier. Geez, listen to this, here I am getting aroused by looking at a woman strapping on a gun. What kind of sicko childhood experience caused me to have that reaction? Shrinks would have a ball analyzing me...

Harvey looked around the room while Jenny put on a tweed sport coat that nicely covered her gun, and then she began to check the contents of a small leather purse. Harvey thought about what she might be looking for: *lipstick, eye shadow, pepper spray, extra ammunition...*

"So, you *do* plan to stay here for a while?" Harvey asked with genuine interest. "Even though you're not an architect who needs a place to stay?"

Jenny gave Harvey another grin, half mischievous and half apologetic. "I'm a private investigator who needs a place to stay. My employer agreed to cover the lease for three months, same as we discussed when you thought I was an architect. I guess he thinks I'll be needed here for at least that long to look out for his interests. As for me, I can't complain about staying in this beautiful house for the summer. So, I'm planning to be here for a while if it's okay with you and the owner."

"Okay? Sure, it's okay. Why wouldn't it be okay?"

"Well, I *did* lie to you about what I was doing here in Port Kole."

Harvey said, "I had a feeling something was not quite right when you told me you were an architect." *And now I've lied to you because the truth is I was totally clueless.* "So, I see you've added a few nice personal touches to this place. You've brought in some of your books, a nice throw rug, stereo, a few more plants, ... and a half-naked man," said Harvey in disbelief, as he saw a handsome, muscular guy in his thirties walk into the kitchen clad only in a towel wrapped around his waist.

Jenny said, "Harvey, meet Mike."

"Hey, how's it going, Harvey? Beautiful day, isn't it?" Mike said with a cheerful smile. "This is a great area you live in, Harvey. Fantastic for camping and hiking. I just love the outdoors."

Harvey watched in stunned silence as Mike opened the refrigerator. He grabbed a carton, poured himself a glass of orange juice and began to drink. The taut muscles in his chest and stomach rippled as he raised the glass. Mike's wet skin and thick, dark hair glistened in the filtered sunlight that shone through the kitchen window.

Geez, the guy looks like Hercules' younger brother.

"Mike is a private detective, too," Jenny said. "He works in the Syracuse area like me, and things are a little slow for him right now. He's going to take over most of my other cases so I can spend more time on my case here."

"Jenny told me about your little scuffle," Mike added. "I see you got a few knocks, but it doesn't look too bad. Glad you were able to fight him off."

Harvey gave Mike a weak nod and said, "Uh, yeah, we were able to get the upper hand, fortunately." *Did I really just say WE? Last thing I recall about the fight was crying for my mommy to save me.*

Mike finished the contents of the glass and then poured himself another. He placed the glass on the countertop and walked back toward the bathroom, smiling at Jenny and Harvey as he left.

Jenny said, "Mike came here so we could go over my other cases in person. I initially thought the *Maiden* case would be a breeze, just some easy surveillance, but now that the painting is missing, I expect to be spending all my time on it. At least for now."

"Oh, I see, yeah," said Harvey.

He's her PI partner... and what else? Her boy-toy?

Mike walked back into the kitchen, still wearing only the towel. He opened the refrigerator again and bent down to look in. The glancing sunlight brought out the impressive definition in his back musculature.

All right, all right, no need to show off. Doesn't this guy own any clothes?

Jenny said, "I don't have much to eat, Mike, but there's a loaf of rye bread and some butter. Make yourself some toast."

"Thanks, I will a little later." He closed the refrigerator and picked up the glass of juice from the countertop.

Okay, he's probably not her boyfriend. She would have called him honey or baby or something by now, right? He loves the outdoors, so he probably didn't spend the night here. Maybe he just came over to shower. Yeah, that's it, he probably slept in a tent at the campground by Henstead beach. No running water there.

Mike said, "Wow, I feel really refreshed after a good night's rest. It's so peaceful sleeping in this cozy little cabin right next to the lake."

Okay, okay, so he slept here. But probably not in her bed.

"And that bed of yours is so comfortable, Jenny."

Cripes, he slept in her bed. That's it, then. It can't get any worse. Unless he's hung like a horse.

Mike went back to the bedroom and Jenny said to Harvey, "Mike came here to talk to me yesterday about my other cases and he needed a place to stay last night. My bed was the perfect spot since it's too soft for me — right now I'm quite happy in a sleeping bag on the floor. I don't know if I told you, but during that tussle with Louie Parker, I hurt my back a little, and sleeping on a firm surface helps."

"Oh, I see," said Harvey with some relief. "Then he's not your...uh...I mean...Mike is...single?" Harvey asked.

"Single?" she repeated, as if she couldn't imagine why Harvey would be asking this. Confusion came over Jenny's face, but then it was followed by a startled look.

She said: "Oh, I didn't realize ... I mean, I thought when we were having lunch the other day, that you were ... well, I'm *usually* a good judge of people. Well, anyway, Mike is single and unattached. So, I guess you want to meet him?" She smiled.

"Whaddya mean, meet him? I already met him."

"What I mean is, do you want to go out with him?"

"Out where?" Harvey asked with a completely dumb-ass look on his face.

"Out anywhere... I mean, do you want me to ask him if he wants to date you?"

"Date. *Date?* He's..uuh...I'm not...I mean, I don't like men!" Harvey said in a panicky voice. "What I mean is, I like men just fine, but...not as much as I like women... I mean, not at *all* like I like women..."

"Omigosh, Harvey, I'm so sorry," said Jenny. "Mike is gay, and I guess I assumed you knew somehow and that you were interested. Wow, I feel silly. This is very embarrassing."

"Tell me about it," said Harvey, his face six shades of red. *Well, Harvey, you numb nuts, you talk to a girl over the course of a few days, trying to flirt with her and impress her with witty conversation, and then she ends up concluding you prefer men. Way to go. Back to square one.*

After ten seconds of awkward dead air, Harvey broke the deafening silence.

"Umm...you said... you hurt your back? How bad is it?"

She politely brushed away Harvey's concern with a wave of her hand and answered, "Oh, don't worry, I'll be fine. Hey, we'd better be going, Harvey." She called into the bedroom: "We're going, Mike. Lock up when you leave."

Harvey heard a muffled response: "Okay, see you guys later."

They walked back to Harvey's driveway along the little dirt path through the trees, then got into Harvey's car. As they reached the top of his steep driveway, the car's transmission protested with an unhealthy grinding noise.

"Will the car make it?" asked Jenny.

"Sure," said Harvey, giving her the thumbs-up sign. "After this, it's downhill most of the way there. Getting back will be the tricky part."

She smiled. "Downhill, huh? How are your brakes?"

"I try not to use them as a matter of principle. I'm saving my remaining half millimeter of brake pad for a real emergency."

Fifteen minutes later, Harvey and Jenny sat on the couch in Sadie's living room as she relaxed in an easy chair and concentrated on the photographs.

There was nothing subtle about the decor surrounding them. Over the couch was a large framed painting of a lighthouse, which looked like a paint-by-number project that might have taken months for Sadie to finish. On the opposite wall were two portraits of big-eyed puppies, painted on black velvet. And in the corner was a shrine to Elvis, which consisted of a three-foot-high, pastel color portrait of the King in his early years, framed by white plastic lilies and burning cathedral candles. Harvey and Jenny sipped the coffee Sadie had graciously poured for them, which was perhaps the strongest and most bitter brew Harvey had ever tasted.

"What do you think, Sadie?" asked Harvey, after he was sure she had taken at least a brief look at every one of the hundred and twenty-three photographs.

Before speaking she took one more picture from the main group and set it on top of a smaller pile. Then she gave a half-smile and seemed satisfied at a job well done. She reached for the coffee pot and poured herself another half cup of the syrupy brew as a reward.

"There are fourteen pictures in this little pile. I think if the girl Grant's been cattin' around with is one of the hundred and twenty-three you brought over, then she's gotta be in this pile of fourteen unless she did somethin' drastic to change the way she looks since I seen her."

"Great," responded Harvey with a smile. "So, his girlfriend is one of these fourteen, then." Harvey spread them out on the table in front of him, so he and Jenny could have a look at Sadie's choices.

"Whoa, ace, I didn't say that. I said *if* she's definitely somewhere in the group you brought me to look at, then she's gotta be one of these fourteen I picked out. There's a big difference. I ain't givin' you any guarantee she's one of these. *You're* the one who said she's one of the bunch you brought here. So lemme ask you, how come you're so sure of that?"

"Well, I'm not. But let me ask you something else. It looks like you used hair color as one means of narrowing it down to these fourteen. Sometimes it's difficult to judge hair color from photos because of the lighting. And hair color is something that's easily changed. But all fourteen of the students you picked are blond, or have very light brown hair. Am I correct?"

"You're right on both counts, sport. I did select only light-haired girls, and yeah, hair color is easily changed. *In-person* I can tell a bleached blond from a real one, but not from these pictures." She turned toward Jenny. "Like you, Miss, you're a real blond, aren't you?"

"That's right, this is the real me," Jenny said. She looked down at the fourteen candidates on the table and remarked: "But you picked girls with other features in common. I'd say they all have the same general facial shape, with narrow noses and high cheekbones. The hair lengths are different, though."

"I didn't screen by hair length or hair style. Young girls change those things a lot."

"But suppose we were to include the ones with hair that isn't blond, but which have the correct facial features," suggested Jenny.

"Then I'd definitely add a few darker-haired girls to that pile."

Harvey thought for a moment, and then said in agreement: "Show us which ones, please."

Sadie picked out an additional seven pictures without hesitation, then scanned the remaining pictures one last time, and picked one more. She gathered up the eight new choices and handed them to Jenny, who held the original pile of fourteen.

Jenny and Harvey both thanked Sadie for her help and the coffee. She seemed very pleased she could be of assistance, and she asked them to stop by sometime and let her know how it all turned out.

They left the house and got into Harvey's car.

"Well, inspector, we've got twenty-two possibilities now," Jenny said.

"It's disappointing, isn't it? She picked twenty-two out of a hundred and twenty-three pictures. We know Grant has a weakness for attractive coeds. I think I could have done almost as well myself by just picking out the most attractive ones."

"Hmmm. Attractive is a relative term. But I'd have to agree with you, it's disappointing."

Jenny's cell rang. As Harvey pulled out onto the road, she answered, listened to the caller for about a minute, mumbled a quick thank you, and ended the call. She turned back to Harvey and said, "That was my contact in the NYPD. She found out from the local PD there's been almost no progress in tracking down the person who phoned in the bomb threat to the local middle school. It was actually just a short text sent to the principal's personal cellphone, not a call. They know a recently purchased burner phone was used, and so far, it's been used for just that one text. It originated from a cell tower in the Albany area. Right now, the phone must be powered off or in airplane mode because it's not pinging any towers. The phone was purchased with cash in the city of Saint Teresa, Florida. They know which store sold it but don't have a clue who made the purchase. It was a small store with no security cameras."

Harvey asked, "Did they get any useful information from the text itself? Idioms? Slang expressions?"

"No, nothing."

"Did the caller make any demands?"

"No. Just a threat to shoot up the school, no reason stated. What do you think?"

"I think whoever sent that text had no intention of shooting anybody."

Chapter 27
Wednesday, May 27, 1:02 p.m.

Harvey sat at his desk, waiting for his ancient laptop to boot up. Recently the hard drive had begun making a funny squealing and grinding sound, and he wondered if the thing was in its death throes. He always turned it off when he finished with it, to lessen the chance it might burst into flames. While he waited, he decided to give Dexter a call.

It rang once, twice, three times while Harvey impatiently drummed his fingers on the desk. *C'mon, pick up. No fishing trips today, please.*

"Hello?"

"Dex?"

"Yup. Harvey? How's it going?"

"Just great. Listen, out of those photos you gave me, I have twenty-two possibilities."

"Twenty-two?" Dexter responded with surprise. "Geez, your witness wasn't able to narrow it down any more than that? I thought you said she got a look at this girl."

"Well, that's the best the witness could do. Maybe one of these students took off with Grant. Can we ask your friends which of these twenty-two have not been to class lately?"

"We can ask. We may not get an answer. My friends are like me, they don't go to class much, remember?"

"Have they gone at *all* lately?"

"Well, let's see ... Horace probably hasn't, he's on vacation now, most likely out of the country somewhere."

"Vacation?" Harvey replied as he shook his head in disbelief. "He's a student. How can he take a vacation now?"

"Horace always takes a vacation shortly before the end of the semester, so he can rest up for finals."

Why do I even ask? "Okay, how about the other one, I think you said his name was Dave."

"Well now, Dave I know is at least in town. He may have been to class recently, but then again maybe not. He kinda goes now and then in the first half of the semester, which allows the teacher to associate his name with his face. But in the second half, as he becomes more familiar with what's needed to get a passing grade, he rapidly winds down his attendance."

"Sounds like you and he have the same methodology when it comes to class attendance," observed Harvey.

"Not really. Dave actually attends class more than I do."

"Well, if he's in town, can you ask him if he can go to the next class, and tell me who out of these twenty-two are no longer attending?"

"Sure, I can ask him. But he may consider that a tall order. Can you pay him anything?"

"Pay him? You want me to pay him to go to his class?"

"Well, yeah. Of course, I wouldn't dream of taking a cut for myself, even if I was offered one."

Alternatives ran through Harvey's mind. He could try doing the surveillance himself. He could certainly pass for a student, and maybe he could wait casually outside the classroom door, with the twenty-two pictures in his hands and try to spot some of them as they went into class, and...

Wait.

ST. TERESA?

St. Teresa. The name of the town where Jenny said the burner phone used by the caller who'd made the school shooting threat had been purchased. Like a lightning bolt, it flashed into Harvey's consciousness because he'd seen the name somewhere before. Where?

Concentrate, Harvey. Where?

"Harvey, you there?" asked Dexter. "Did you fall asleep? Wake up, boy ..."

"I'm here, Dex. I just..."

Yeah, that's it.

It came to Harvey. He had seen the name St. Teresa last night when he looked through the pile of student pictures. Each one was labeled with the student's name, date of enrollment, home city or town, and state.

"Dex, I've gotta check something. Just give me ten minutes and I'll call you back, okay?"

Harvey grabbed the stack of pictures of the twenty-two students Sadie had picked out. He started to flip through them and his efforts were rewarded when he reached the eleventh picture. There it was — hometown: St. Teresa, Florida.

Her name was Linda Johnson.

Harvey stared at Linda's photograph. She was stunning, with blond hair styled in a casual, shoulder-length cut, fair and unblemished skin, dazzling eyes with long lashes, a perfectly proportioned nose, and a mouth, framed by dark, full lips, that any sane man would describe as sensuous. It was easy to understand why Grant, with his reputation for going after youthful beauties, would be instantly attracted to her, assuming she had a nice body from the neck down since the picture showed nothing below her shoulders. But there were certainly some other beautiful girls in the group of twenty-two.

Am I getting excited about nothing?

It's worth a shot.

Harvey called Dexter back.

"Dex, you said Dave is in town. I've got a list of the twenty-two coeds. I'll send it to you by e-mail as soon as we hang up. Give the list to Dave and tell him to get back to you as soon as possible on which ones are no longer going to class. Some of them probably won't be in Dave's class, so you'll have to get in touch with Horace, too. Based on what you told me, we may have to convince the two of them to go to class to get the information I need. Could you please ask them first if they'll do it for free? And then if they insist on getting paid, let me know and maybe we can work something out. But there's one coed I have reason to suspect a little more than the others. Her name is Linda

Johnson. I want you to ask Dave and Horace about this particular girl as soon as you get hold of them, and then call me right away."

Dexter agreed to do his best to try and locate Dave and Horace immediately. Harvey ended the call and then typed the e-mail with the students' names to Dexter and hit the send key. Next, he typed *Maiden with a Basket* in the search engine field, and then clicked on a hit that had a symbol indicating pictures were included. An article came up which appeared to be a biography of Vermeer. The text was long, but he scanned through it quickly until he found what he was looking for -- an old photograph of the *Maiden*. He clicked on it and was able to enlarge it to fill the screen. Even though the photograph, taken sometime before World War II, was of poor quality by today's standards, Harvey was immediately stunned by the *Maiden*'s beauty. It was an exquisite painting in a sumptuous style that somehow imbued this young girl, who appeared to be about fifteen years old, with a striking energy and radiance. The *Maiden*'s head was turned to face the onlooker as if she was slightly surprised to catch someone admiring her. Her blue eyes were vibrant and penetrating, hinting at innocence and mischievous fun at the same time. One could easily imagine how it might feel to touch the girl's face and hair, her pale skin smooth, her brown locks silky. On her head was tied a simple triangle of blue cloth and propped up on her shoulder was a basket made of coarse reeds that was filled with colorful flowers. These two accouterments were splendidly fitting; they lent as much beauty to this young girl as a crown and a scepter might lend to a queen.

Maybe the Maiden's the key. If Jenny and I could just find the Maiden...

"Where are you right now?" he asked the image on the screen. "Maybe riding around in the trunk of somebody's car?" Harvey noted that her rose-colored lips were slightly parted, giving the impression she was about to answer him, about to say something in her native Dutch tongue.

Harvey then googled the name Linda Johnson and clicked on a site that appeared to offer free address information from public records.

But the search produced thousands of Linda Johnsons. Even when Harvey limited the search to women in their twenties, there were still over five hundred hits. He typed St. Teresa, Florida in the location field and searched again, but got nothing. He then cleared the location field and typed Lake George University into the education field, but again got no hits.

The sound of his cell phone ringing made Harvey jump off the seat. He tapped its face and stammered: "Hello?"

"Hey, Harvey," answered Dex. "You are one lucky bastard because I got hold of Dave on the very first try. I told him what you're after, and I forwarded him the list you sent me. But I also asked him about Linda Johnson. He remembered she only attended class for about the first month and a half of the semester. He hasn't seen her in class or anywhere on campus since then. And do you know why he's sure? It's because of her looks. She's got a face and a body *to die for*, in his words."

"I know. At least about her face. I saw the picture," replied Harvey, as his mind raced ahead to form a plan.

"As far as the other girls in his two classes, Dave said he'd remember whether some of them were recently attending or not, but for the rest, he'll have to go to his classes again to get the answer. And as for Horace, I haven't gotten hold of him yet."

"Thanks, Dex. Now I need something else from you — Linda Johnson's local address. I'm having trouble finding it on the internet. Can you get it for me?"

"Probably. Let me go work on it and I'll call you back soon."

"Okay, Dex, and leave a message if I don't answer. Thanks."

Harvey ended the call and thought, *Linda stopped going to class at about the same time Grant quit his job. A coincidence?*

Harvey's cell rang. It was Peter. Harvey decided not to answer it and after six rings it stopped. Harvey put the phone back in his pocket.

It chimed once, indicating he'd received a text.

He took the phone out again and there it was on the screen.

A picture of Pamela Damler.

Naked.

Making love to a man who was *not* her husband. And there was a brief message from Peter below the picture:

Harvey, we must talk in person. I have the information you asked for concerning Pamela's infidelity. Can you meet me at the Easy Time Diner at 2:00 this afternoon?

Harvey tapped on the picture and enlarged it. The facial features of the man weren't clear. Harvey moved around the field looking for detail.

He needed to see more. He at least had to be sure it was Pamela.

As his mind buzzed with questions, Harvey texted back:

I'll be there.

Chapter 28
Wednesday, May 27, 1:58 p.m.

Harvey pulled his car into the lot of the Easy Time Diner in Port Kole. It was almost two o'clock and the lunch crowd was thinning out.

He entered the diner and recognized Peter seated alone in a booth at the far end of the room, drinking coffee. He looked up and spotted Harvey, who walked to the table without hesitation.

Peter stood and said, "Harvey, thanks for coming. Looks as if you had a little accident? The bruises, I mean. Are you okay?"

"Huh? Oh, this? Sure, no problem, just had an airbag in a friend's car deploy in my face. He's a lousy driver, but no one was hurt."

"Wow, an airbag blow," said Peter, raising his eyebrows. "That must have shaken you up quite a bit. Have a seat, Harvey. What will you have to eat and drink?"

"Oh, uh, just a cola, please." Harvey sat down in the seat across from Peter and then thought, *Cripes, why did I order a soda? It'll make me feel like a kid, sitting next to him and drinking soda when he's drinking coffee. I need to project maturity...confidence...*

Peter waved his hand and the waitress appeared in seconds.

"A large cola for my friend," said Peter to the waitress, and then he turned to Harvey. "The Danish here are excellent, would you like one?"

"Oh, no thanks. I'm not hungry."

The waitress left and Peter remarked, "This is a nice, cozy little town you live in, Harvey. I grew up in a small town myself."

"Yes, I like it here a lot," said Harvey in a monotone, uninterested in exchanging pleasantries. "So, I thought you'd be done with me by now since I didn't get back to you. I assumed you'd be looking for Grant on your own, and I didn't expect to hear from you again. But your text..."

"Yes, indeed. My text." Peter said solemnly. "There's more. *Much* more."

The waitress returned with the soda and a pot of fresh coffee to top off Peter's cup. He thanked her as he added a few splashes of cream to his coffee. When she left, he inconspicuously took a look around to be certain no one could see or hear them. The booths around them were empty.

Peter took a large white envelope from the seat next to him and carefully removed from it a group of eight by ten-inch color photographs. He put the pile down on the table in front of Harvey.

The top picture was every bit as graphic as the one Peter had texted. It showed Pamela naked, lying on her back on a bed. The same man was on top of her. He sat upright, his knees forward, facing her, riding her, groin to groin. Pamela's hands were up above her head, both of them clutching the metal headrail of the bed as if holding on for a wild ride. Her mouth was open. If she was about to scream, then from the expression on her face, it would clearly be a scream of pleasure. The man was in good physical shape. His buttocks rested on Pamela's upper thighs and his hands were clamped onto Pamela's hips, ensuring the two naked bodies were locked together. The flowery bedspread and white sheets had been kicked onto the floor, leaving nothing to cover the lovers.

Harvey's mind was flooded with a mix of emotions. Shock and disappointment were foremost. He fought off feelings of lust at seeing Pamela's naked body, and then waves of shame for feeling the lust. There was no denying that her body was beautiful, smooth, white, supple. Harvey moved his hand onto the pile of pictures. He clutched the top one and moved it to the side, feeling further shame as he did so as if he were touching Pamela herself.

The second picture was every bit as graphic as the first, but this time she was on top, her full breasts hanging down over his face. The man was clutching her shoulders, the dark, hairy skin of his forearms standing out against Pamela's fair skin. His face was better seen in this picture; He was clean-shaven, his thick dark hair neatly combed back, and he appeared to be in his forties. Harvey felt almost nauseous now at the thought of her betraying Grant in this way, the husband she'd cried for in front of Harvey just days ago. He flipped quickly through more pictures, showing Pamela and her lover locked together in various positions, and then Harvey paused when he reached the close-ups of each of their faces. These shots were slightly more blurred than the other pictures because of the high degree of magnification, but Pamela was easily identifiable. The man's face was contorted by the pleasure he'd apparently been feeling at the moment the picture had been snapped. And then the very last picture showed Pamela's clothing strewn in disarray on the floor as if it had been taken off in a hurry, or *torn* off by the man in a frenzy.

Harvey noticed there was something white framing the picture's left and right edges. Curtains, maybe? *The photographer must have shot the pictures through a window,* he thought. Overall, the picture clarity was remarkably good. But ...could they be fakes? An attempt to smear Pamela? Harvey was aware, of course, that these days anyone can buy very powerful software to manipulate photographs. He thought, *Could I be looking at Pamela's head attached to someone else's body?*

Harvey scanned the pile of photos again, one by one, as Peter waited patiently and sipped his coffee. Harvey looked for the mole on her upper back, the one he'd seen within the slit of her blouse the first time they had met. He quickly leafed back through the photos until he found two with excellent views of Pamela's naked upper back ... and there it was, the mole, only a tiny dark speck in each photo, but in exactly the right place in each one, which left no doubt in Harvey's mind. These were not fakes.

"So... how... did you get these?"

"I hired a private investigator. She took them yesterday, through a motel window. She used a camera with a telephoto lens. Pamela and her lover made a silly mistake, Harvey. They left the drapes open. They were on the second floor and apparently they thought it was safe, but my PI was on a ridge shrouded by trees about two hundred feet away, at an elevation slightly higher than their window. So, does she look to you like a woman who's grieving for her missing husband?"

Harvey ignored the question and asked: "How long was the PI watching them?"

"About twenty minutes. It was an evening rendezvous."

"And where were these taken?"

"The Sherwood Motel. It's a very secluded place on route eighty-three, about thirty miles north of Lake George Village. When Pamela hired you, she may have looked and acted like a devoted and worried wife, but she's got the same lusts and failings as millions of other people." Peter sighed and added, "Welcome to the real world, Harvey."

The real world, Harvey thought. *That's it, then. Everybody lies. Everybody deceives. Pamela is no exception.*

Harvey felt crushed. Pamela had lied to him. Not by telling him something false, but at least by omission. She should have told him about this, even if it was a great embarrassment to her. Grant was missing, and Harvey had asked her about Grant's enemies. Well, this man in the pictures might be considered an enemy of Grant's, right? This man might be the one who would benefit most from Grant's death.

"What's the man's name?" asked Harvey.

"I'm not going to tell you, Harvey. Unless you play ball with me."

"But maybe this guy has something to do with Grant's disappearance."

"My PI is looking into that. What you need to find out for me is if the *Maiden* is in that safe deposit box. Or if not, where Pamela might be hiding it."

Harvey leaned back in his seat and said, "You don't really care much about your brother's well-being, do you?"

"Of course I do, Harvey. I love my brother. But I'm a realist. It may be too late for Grant. He might be dead already. If he is, and if Pamela or her lover had anything to do with it, they'll eventually get what's coming to them. Even if the cops in this town don't want to investigate his disappearance now, eventually they will. As for the painting, Grant certainly wouldn't have wanted Pamela to end up with it."

"Can I... have these prints?"

"No, you can't. I only showed them to you to convince you that Pamela is not being honest with you. If there was any doubt about it left in you, it should be gone now."

Harvey sighed and said, "Perhaps it is. I have to go now. Let's meet tonight at eight-thirty, right here, and we'll talk about working together on this. Okay?"

Peter leaned toward Harvey and said, "Harvey, if you confront Pamela about this affair, she'll lie to you. I'm not sure which lie she'll use. Maybe she'll say she had sex with him just one impetuous time. Or maybe she'll say it ended a long time ago. Maybe she'll even claim these pictures were taken before she and Grant were married."

"I have to go, Mr. Damler. I'll see you tonight. Thanks for the soda."

Peter responded sternly: "Remember, Harvey, Pamela is using you."

"I understand. Tonight, here." Harvey stood up and turned to leave. As he headed for the door, he wondered whether he should go see Pamela immediately and confront her about keeping information from him that clearly had a bearing on the case. But then he decided he had to put it out of his mind for now, so he could accomplish what he'd already planned to do this afternoon.

Find out more about Linda Johnson.

Chapter 29
Wednesday, May 27, 2:12 p.m.

"I hate this," said Beale to his young partner.

Zoober sat at his desk in Albany PD headquarters, staring with contentment at his computer screen. Behind him stood Beale, squinting as he tried to read the same screen. Beale's frustration was apparent.

"You see something in the report that you don't like?" asked Zoober as he continued to read.

"Hell, no. How could I not like the report when I can't even read the damn thing at all on this screen? The text is way too small and blurry. But what I *really* don't like is the fact that Hair and Fiber won't give us a written copy of their reports anymore. You gotta look it up in their computer database, and they've set the damn thing up so you have to be a computer hacker genius to find it," said Beale with disgust.

"It's not that difficult. I'll be happy to show you how to access it. And I think the main purpose behind not supplying written reports anymore is the drive to save paper, which translates into saving money or saving natural resources, depending on how you look at it. But if you really would like to have a hardcopy, I can send it to the printer and we should have it in about five minutes."

"You mean our twenty-year-old printer down the hall? You'll be waitin' longer than five minutes, 'cause it's in the middle of its daily breakdown," Beale said with disgust. "I saw the repairman start to work on it just a few minutes ago. The guy practically lives here now."

Beale leaned a little closer to the screen, and to steady himself he put his right foot on the handle of the bottom desk drawer. His pant leg rode up enough for Zoober to see the handgun in his ankle holster.

"Er, Martin, please don't feel offended, but since the barrel of that Walther is now pointed at my feet, I feel obligated to ask you whether you're certain the safety is on."

"Yeah, yeah, of course it is. I checked it this morning."

"Is there a round in the chamber?"

"Damn right there is. And the clip is full. What's the matter, does it make you nervous?"

Zoober ignored the question. He asked one of his own: "Why do you have to carry a backup gun anyway?" Zoober had never pulled his gun out of its holster in the line of duty, even during his time as a patrol officer. He believed a very large percentage of successful detective work involved talking to people, and the remaining percentage involved mostly data analysis. The use of a gun was a fluke, an anomaly, an absolute last resort in an unpredictable situation.

"I thought I told you, kid. When I was a snot-nosed rookie patrol officer I answered a domestic dispute call. I got shot in the leg, and then I stared down the barrel of a madman's gun, waiting for the second shot, the one that would kill me. I was goddamn helpless. My gun had been taken away from me. If I'd had a second gun, I would have used it to blow that psycho away. After that, I swore I'd never, ever, ever be caught in that situation again, where someone pointed a gun at me and I didn't have a gun to point back at them. It's as simple as that. So, who did the work on the raft anyway?"

Zoober directed his attention back to the screen and answered: "Wilson Treadle."

"Treadle? I know the guy, he's a real pinhead," Beale said, shaking his head with undisguised contempt.

Zoober bristled with discomfort as he always did when his partner flung an insult at someone. He said, "Well, Martin, I think if you take a close look at the quality of his work, you'll be pleasantly surprised."

Beale ignored Zoober's remark. "I saw Treadle's boss, the chief lab rat in Hair and Fiber, shaking Treadle's hand the other day, saying what a super wonderful job Treadle was doing and that he was going to put him on the special Pubic Hair Analysis Task Force. He said Treadle had a fantastic future in pubic hair. And there's Treadle, glowing with all this praise, probably thinking: *Wowee, I'm skyrocketing to the top, and what's next after pubic hair? Maybe nose hair or navel lint?"*

No response came from Zoober, who was busy digesting the report.

Beale continued. "All right, so what's the bottom line here, since we can't print it and I'm not gonna risk eyestrain standing here trying to read it."

"Looks like a good match on the rope fibers. The computer rated it at ninety-seven-point-five percent certainty. But it's a very common polyester fiber. There were also burlap fibers in the raft, and the match probability to the burlap shreds that were found on the body is also high at ninety-four percent. According to Treadle, the burlap fibers make better circumstantial evidence than the rope fibers since there are lots of different kinds of burlap — different thicknesses, densities, colors, and so forth. But the type of burlap in the raft is also common enough so that there's essentially no chance of determining where the killer got the rope *or* the burlap. They could have been purchased at many hardware or landscaping stores. As far as hair goes, they found a total of seven human hairs in the raft and dozens of animal hairs. Only two of the human hairs had follicles, and both of those were DNA matched to the owner of the Army-Navy store, Huckman. The other human hairs came from at least two different individuals."

"What about the animal hairs?" asked Beale.

"The DNA analysis indicated they came from the common Norway rat."

Beale thought for a moment. "Rats, huh? Okay, let's go to the fingerprint report."

Zoober clicked on another document icon and more text appeared on the screen.

"There were plenty of prints on the raft," Zoober said. "Huckman's were all over it. And there were three distinct sets of what are probably children's prints, judging by their size. And also at least five sets of adult prints. We're running them all through the FBI's database, but it's likely some of the prints are from the people that manufactured the raft. It was made at a plant in North Carolina, and Huckman's records indicate it was shipped from the plant to him about fourteen months ago, assuming this is the raft he recently sold. I've already spoken to the plant owner on the phone, and he identified fourteen employees that could have touched the raft. Nine of them have since quit. The local sheriff will fingerprint the five that still work at the plant, and we'll have the prints by this afternoon. Of the nine that quit, three are still in the area, and the sheriff should be able to get their prints today, too. Of the six that left the area, two have criminal records for minor offenses, so we have access to their prints. The remaining four have to be tracked down. It could take some time to locate them. On the electric motor, they just picked up prints from Huckman and the same three kids that touched the raft."

"Could anyone else at Huckman's store have touched it?" asked Beale.

"Huckman says no," Zoober replied. "He doesn't have any employees. He's a one-man show, does everything by himself. And the rafts are delivered in boxes."

"Good work, kid, sounds like you're right on top of the print situation."

"Do you think anything will come of the print work?"

"Hell, no. This killer is not gonna be leaving his prints all over the raft, unless he's some wacko who wants to get caught, and I doubt that's the case here. And as far as the kids go, their prints probably won't help us find them, not many twelve-year-old kids have their prints on file. But don't feel bad, we've gotta check out all this crap anyway. Was there any blood on the raft?"

"No, but there was something else. Some small smears of a bright yellow semi-solid material, composed mainly of gelatin, sucrose, food coloring, and citrus extract. There were also samples of a second semi-solid material, this one white with a very porous consistency, and it's composed mostly of water-soluble proteins and sucrose."

Beale thought for a moment, and said: "Bright yellow, huh? And there's table sugar in it, so it's definitely a food. Together with the white stuff ... sounds like it could be lemon meringue pie. Did the lab guys taste it?"

"I doubt it. As a rule, they don't taste evidence."

"Doesn't matter. I still think it's lemon meringue pie. So, Russell boy, tell me how we could have gotten a pie smear on the raft."

"Someone riding in the raft was eating pie?"

"Doubtful. Pie is not the kind of thing I'd take on a raft ride. Too messy. I'll bet it got on there by accident. Like maybe the raft was thrown in the trash with some leftover pie. But this raft is kinda big, even deflated. It's not heavy, but it's very bulky. Once you get it out of the original box and take the shrink-wrap off, it's hard to fold up tight again. Might take up a whole trash can. More likely it was dumped into a large container, like a dumpster where it wouldn't be so conspicuous. Now, what kind of places use dumpsters and have food trash?"

"Restaurants. Maybe the man spotted a restaurant with a dumpster behind it, drove around the back, and threw the raft in, probably making sure it wouldn't stick out the top and draw attention."

"Yeah, and if it wasn't sticking out the top, how did the kids spot it?" asked Beale, thinking out loud. "Would they have climbed into a garbage dumpster to rummage around for treasure? I doubt it. Even *I* wasn't nuts enough to jump into a pile of food garbage when I was twelve. So that raises a real interesting possibility. Like, maybe the kids saw somebody throw it in, and then they fished it out after he or she left."

They both thought for a few moments about the implications, and then Beale said: "When was the last time you spoke to Huckman?"

"I called him about two hours ago," answered Zoober.

"Did he come up with anything else on the kids?"

"No. He says they haven't shown up at his store again since they sold him the raft. And he still can't seem to remember enough to provide us with useful sketches of the man who bought the raft, or any of the kids."

"And we got nothing at all useful from the search of the lakeshore along where that old coot saw the guy in the raft, right?"

"That's correct, Martin. No fresh footprints, or anything that would suggest a raft was launched. They cataloged all the bits of trash they found in the area, over fifty items, but none of it looked particularly *fresh* according to the report. It's the same type of general refuse, lots of plastic and paper, found all along the lakeshore. Most of it probably washed in."

"Then you and I might as well start looking for this restaurant dumpster. So, if we assume the kids found the thing in a dumpster and they took it to the Army-Navy store on their bikes, maybe strapping it to the back of one of the bikes, or towing it in a wagon or something, how far could the store be from the restaurant? How far do twelve-year-old kids travel on their bikes?"

Beale was about to guess at the answer to his own question, but before he could, Zoober said, "Well, I used to cover some very long distances on my bike when I was that age. I think we should assume at least fifteen miles."

"That sounds reasonable. So, let's double it, just to be sure we've got it covered. We need to get a list of restaurants within a thirty-mile radius of the Army-Navy store. And a sub-list showing which of those serve lemon meringue pie."

"I'll get on it," said Zoober. "I can get the first list very quickly from the internet, but to find out which ones serve the pie, we may have to call them, unless their dessert menus are online."

"All right, then, let's get going. We'll make some calls from the car on the way up there."

"But what if Huckman got the pie smear on it?" asked Zoober.

"Unlikely. He doesn't look like a lemon meringue man to me. I'll bet his diet is mostly pizza, chili dogs, and fried pork rinds. Go ahead and ask him anyway, but if we assume for the moment it's a restaurant and we find it, maybe we'll find the kids. And maybe the kids saw something. When I was a kid, I used to hang out at the same places almost every day, and if I found something in a dumpster worth a lot of money, I would sure as hell go back there again hoping for another jackpot."

"Do you think twelve-year-old kids will be able to give an accurate description of this person?" asked Zoober.

"Hell, no. Even most *adults* can't do that. When I was a patrolman, I interviewed a group of people, one at a time, who said they witnessed a purse snatching. A guy made off with an old broad's purse in bright daylight, right in front of them. So, I talked to a dozen different people and got a dozen different descriptions, take your pick. One says he's six-foot-two, another says four-foot-nine. Complexion? Well, according to these folks, definitely somewhere between albino and black. Hair color? One witness said he had straight blond hair, another said curly black hair, a third thought he was shaved bald, and one old lady swore you couldn't see his hair because he was wearing a Mexican sombrero hat. But maybe we'll get something else concrete from the kids, like maybe they saw the car the suspect came in. Lots of twelve-year-olds know something about cars. Or maybe they noticed something else." Beale paused to light a cigarette. Zoober frowned, knowing Beale was well aware of the no-smoking policy in the building.

"Or maybe," Beale added after blowing a smoke ring, "We'll get nothing useful from them at all."

Chapter 30
Wednesday, May 27, 4:07 p.m.

"Hi, Jenny," Harvey said into his cellphone.

"Harvey, where are you?" she asked.

"I'm in the lobby of an old apartment building in downtown Albany." He recounted to Jenny how he'd noticed Linda Johnson was from St. Teresa, and how a friend got Linda's address by gaining access to a campus computer database with a relatively low level of security. When Harvey went to her address on Main street in Lake George, he found it was a small, two-story building a few blocks up from the tourist area. There was a single apartment on the top floor, and an insurance office on the bottom floor. After he knocked on the apartment door and no one answered, he tried the office door and met the man who owned the building. He told Harvey that Linda had apparently moved out of the furnished apartment last Wednesday evening with no explanation, taking all her possessions. She was paid up on her monthly lease but left no forwarding address. The owner gave Harvey what he believed to be the address and phone number of Linda's father. Being a cautious businessman, the owner had copied the information from a rent check he'd received some months ago. So, the father, on one occasion at least, had paid the rent for Linda. He lived in the run-down Albany apartment building Harvey had just entered.

"I'm about to go up to the father's apartment," Harvey explained to Jenny. "I tried calling him earlier, but I got a recorded message saying the number is no longer in service."

"Harvey, could you give me Linda's exact address, and her father's address, too?"

Harvey tapped his phone a few times to get to the notes app, and read all the address information to Linda.

"Thanks. And what kind of car does Linda drive?" asked Jenny.

"The apartment owner said it's a late model Nissan Maxima, red. That seems to fit the general description I got from Sadie Gumm. She saw Grant and his girlfriend in a car that was red and sporty. I'm sure it has a significantly larger gas tank than Grant's Z4, and so it could easily account for some gas receipts on Grant's credit card I saw in Pamela's house. But the apartment owner didn't know the Nissan's plate number."

"I'll work on getting that, Harvey. Call me after you talk to the father, would you? And Harvey... be careful."

"I always am. Bye," he said, hanging up the phone. *She asked me to be careful. She must be starting to like me.*

But it's still quite a way from her offering to bear my children.

Harvey couldn't deny to himself that he was totally infatuated with Jenny. So why didn't he trust her enough to confide in her completely? He didn't tell her about the naked photos of Pamela, or about Peter. At least not yet. Maybe it was because of the nagging little fact that Harvey worked for Pamela, and Jenny worked for someone who wanted to eventually take something which was possibly very valuable away from Pamela. And there was also the *lying right to his face* thing. She deceived him initially, and even though she apologized, it was difficult for Harvey to push that act of deception completely out of his mind. Can you be in love with somebody, but not trust them? Harvey supposed the answer was yes, if you were some kind of moral degenerate, devoid of principles. He tried to put this paradox out of his mind for the moment and concentrate on the task at hand.

Harvey walked toward the ancient-looking elevator, pushed the up button and waited. The building was old and seedy, badly in need of some repair work and a coat of fresh paint. With a *ding* announcing its arrival, the elevator door opened, bathing Harvey in the harsh illumination that came from an uncovered fluorescent tube light. He stepped in and caught a faint smell of urine. Harvey guessed an apartment dweller's pet had relieved itself in the elevator. At least, he *hoped* it was pet pee and not people pee.

Trying his best to ignore the odor and the sticky floor beneath his feet, Harvey took a step toward the button panel on the wall and punched number seven. The doors closed and then opened again, and he found himself looking into a dimly lit hallway. He turned left and began to walk slowly past each apartment door, looking for number 707. The cheap indoor/outdoor carpet beneath his feet was a garish red with swirls of black and dark green, a fine choice if the landlord's intent was to hide food spills or bloodstains. Harvey found apartment 707 and knocked twice on the white door, which was grubby with black heel marks and oily handprints.

After a wait of about twenty seconds, his knocks were answered by a few barely audible words: "Yeah? Who is it?"

"My name is Harvey Grace, I'm a private investigator. I'd like to talk to Douglas Johnson, please."

From right behind the door came a muffled response: "What are you investigating?"

"I'm looking for Linda Johnson."

Silence. Harvey listened carefully, unsure about whether there was still someone behind the door or not. But then after about twenty seconds of dead air, Harvey heard three distinct clicks in sequence, as each of three deadbolt locks were released, and then the door opened to reveal a man Harvey guessed was about fifty-five years old. He was overweight by at least forty pounds and was tall but with the beginnings of the type of posture problem that usually comes at an older age. His face had a three or four day growth of grayish stubble, and Harvey guessed it wasn't there to give him a stylishly masculine look, but rather because the man had no reason to shave every day. His salt and pepper hair was disheveled, and he had the swollen reddish/blueish nose of a hard drinker. The dark bags under his eyes completed his weary countenance. He was sloppily dressed in sweatpants, slippers, and a wrinkled corduroy shirt. The apartment reeked of stale cigarette smoke, and Harvey also caught the scent of cheap bourbon.

"I haven't heard anybody ask about her in a long time," said the man.

What does that mean? Maybe he's had a falling out with his daughter and they're not part of each other's lives anymore?

The man seemed sober at the moment to Harvey, who peeked into the apartment and saw a dismal, retro-slum living space that was barely furnished. A well-worn easy chair dominated the small room, its faded tan fabric stained in many places, and the depression in the seat indicated that it saw heavy use. Next to it were a messy pile of newspapers and a three-legged metal stand supporting a large gaudy ashtray of green glass that contained dozens of cigarette butts. Across from the chair was a small, very old tube television on a cheap plastic table. There were two tiny windows that provided hardly any illumination because they were less than ten feet away from the brick face of the adjoining building. The walls were completely bare, their depressing grayish-white color interrupted only by brown water stains in two corners of the room. Much of the remaining floor space was covered by cardboard boxes, and Harvey could see they were filled with a wide range of personal possessions, from garden equipment to kitchen gadgets, tools, and clothing. There was a thick layer of dust everywhere.

"So, why do you wanna see Linda?" His gravelly smoker's voice conveyed both curiosity and caution.

"She may have befriended a man I've been hired to look for. I wasn't able to find her at school. She recently vacated her apartment, and she hasn't been to classes lately. Would you know where she is?"

The man scratched his chin and shook his head as if he were just asked a difficult question on a game show. "Who knows? I was hoping you could tell *me* where she is."

Harvey was puzzled. "Aren't you her father, Douglas Johnson?"

"Her father? Is that what she told you?"

"I've never met her. But her landlord gave me this address. He assumed Douglas Johnson was her father."

"I'm Douglas Johnson." He paused for a few seconds, and then apparently decided that Harvey looked harmless enough. "C'mon in, kid," he said. "And shut the door, will ya?" Johnson turned and walked into the living room. After closing the door, Harvey followed. The bourbon smell became stronger as he walked in.

Harvey remembered a piece of Uncle Willie's common-sense advice about conducting interviews: *Try to become a little friendly with whoever you're about to question before you ask them anything they might be inclined not to answer.*

Harvey struggled for a moment to think of a suitable subject for small talk. *The weather? Baseball?*

"Nice place you have here, Mr. Johnson," Harvey began. *Well, that was really great, because this definitely isn't a nice place. It's a dingy, depressing little dump of a place, and this guy probably realizes it.*

Johnson seemed uninterested in exchanging pleasantries. "Where are you from, Mr. Harvey Grace?" he asked in a monotone.

"I'm from Port Kole. That's close to where Linda goes to school."

"And you didn't drive all the way over here to talk about how nice my apartment is. Does Linda owe you money or something? If she does, you might as well get in line."

"No, she doesn't owe me any money. Does she owe *you* money?"

"Yeah, I guess you could say she owes me money." He walked over to his easy chair and sat down. The television was tuned to some inane game show, but the volume was down all the way. Johnson looked up at Harvey, either waiting for more information or for Harvey to ask another question, Harvey wasn't sure which. Johnson seemed to be in no hurry at all.

"Mr. Johnson, as I said before, Linda's moved out of her apartment, and she hasn't been to classes lately either."

Johnson was silent. He gave Harvey an expressionless stare. Harvey needn't have worried about shocking Johnson. He took the news well. *Too* well. *Something's weird here,* Harvey thought. Johnson simply continued to eye Harvey with a nearly blank look.

"So, you *are* her father, then?" asked Harvey directly.

Johnson paused for a few seconds before answering: "No, I'm not her father. Do I look old enough to be her father?" Johnson asked sincerely, as if he was genuinely interested in how he looked to strangers. While he waited for Harvey's reply, Johnson pulled from his breast pocket a pack of cigarettes and lit one with a disposable lighter. His first drag was a long, slow, hard one. He held the smoke in his mouth and lungs, savoring it like a fine brandy, then reluctantly let it escape from his nostrils at the last possible moment. It was apparent that he enjoyed this simple vice, but his general appearance evoked a weariness and a sense of defeat. Harvey guessed that life had somehow run over this guy like an eighteen-wheeler, dragged him for a few hundred yards and then spit him out, or what was left of him, into a ditch by the side of the road.

To Harvey, this man certainly *did* look old enough to be Linda's father, but he didn't want to say as much to the man's face.

"I'm very bad at guessing ages."

"Well, I'm not her father."

"But you *are* Douglas Johnson, so you're somehow related to Linda?"

"Related? Yeah, we're related," he said with a self-deprecating chuckle that spoke of some deep regret. He paused and then said: "Who're you working for?"

"I'm working for a woman whose husband is missing. He was a teacher at Linda's school. She was in one of his classes."

Johnson thought for a moment. He flicked the long cigarette ash into the green ashtray, and then said: "Sit down, kid, and tell me about this teacher." He pointed to the lawn chair next to the small television.

Harvey sat and explained, "I never met him, so I don't really know what he's like. But before we talk about him, could we go back and talk about you and Linda? How are you two related?"

After another long pause accompanied by a deep drag, Johnson shrugged, sat back in the chair, and began to tell his story. "I first met her about eight years ago. We bumped shopping carts in a supermarket. What with me going through my mid-life crisis, and her being so beautiful, I was attracted to her right away. No big surprise there, right? About three months later we were married."

Married? Eight years ago, she would've been just a kid.

"Wasn't she a little young for marriage?"

"She said she was nineteen when we got married. And then two months later she decided she wanted out. She left."

Harvey thought: *Geez, she must be quite a bit older than your average undergraduate college student.*

"Did she say why she was leaving?" asked Harvey.

"No. She didn't have to say. I knew." Johnson hesitated. His words came slowly as he summoned painful memories. "I think it took her two months to do what she came to do."

"Which was?"

"Which was to become joint owner of my bank accounts. She was penniless when I married her. At least, that's what she told me. After we got married, we went through the process of giving her joint ownership of my assets. Routine stuff when two people get married, if they plan on being together for the rest of their lives, right?"

"I suppose so."

"And when she left, she took it all with her."

Ouch. This guy has good reason to be bitter. "Do you know much about her background, Mr. Johnson?"

"Only what she told me, which is probably all lies. She said she was an orphan, originally from Ohio, supporting herself now by selling cosmetics door to door for a small company. And she said she was renting a room in town."

"Did you ever see it?" Harvey asked. He took out his small pad and a pen, and started jotting down notes.

"No. It was in downtown Albany somewhere, but I don't know the address. She said she was too embarrassed to show me the place. We'd always meet at my house when we got together. Before we got married, she brought her clothes and her few possessions over to my house and moved in. Said she was glad to leave her place."

"You said she moved into your house," said Harvey. "You mean to this apartment?"

"No. I had a house then. I lost it."

Harvey waited, but there was no further explanation. *He lost it.* As simple as that, like losing your car keys or your wallet. A former homeowner, then. That would explain the gardening equipment lying unused in cardboard boxes for years.

"Did she have a car?" asked Harvey.

"Yes, an old Ford. A dark blue Taurus. She'd drive it to my house, but then we'd get into my car and go out."

"You don't remember the license number, do you?" Harvey asked hopefully.

"No."

"Do you know the name of the cosmetics company she worked for?" Harvey continued.

"No. She never told me. She was not very open about her life, or her background. I assumed it was because she was ashamed, so I didn't press it."

"Mr. Johnson, how did she make these bank transactions? How'd she withdraw all that money without you knowing?"

Johnson shifted in his seat for a few seconds, signaling his great discomfort in remembering. Nevertheless, he crushed out his cigarette butt in the ashtray, took a deep breath, and said: "I found out afterward she had everything wired to her private bank account. And then she withdrew everything from her account as soon as all the transfers went through, and left. I came home from my job at six o'clock one day like usual and she was gone, along with all her things. I checked our hiding place for emergency cash and that was all gone, too. She left a two-word note for me taped to the refrigerator; it just read: *I'm leaving. Linda.*"

"Did you tell the police?"

"Yeah, but they said they couldn't do anything because there was no crime involved. We were married, and she was co-owner of those accounts, and they said she had every right to take the money out."

She left the note so the police would stay out of it, thought Harvey.

"Did you ever see her or hear from her again?"

"Yeah, four months later, just by chance, as she walked out of a downtown store. At first, I couldn't believe she was still in Albany. Her hair was dyed red and styled differently. I ran across the street to confront her, expecting she would cry, plead for forgiveness, offer an explanation, something like that. But when I called her name and she turned and looked at me, what I saw in her eyes was ... disgust. She looked completely revolted by my presence, as if I were a piece of trash she'd thrown away and never expected to see again. I started to rant about how she'd destroyed my life and ruined me. But I didn't get far before she cut me off. She spoke to me in a voice I'd never heard before. When I'd known her she was ... so sweet. But this was a sinister voice. She said she'd broken no laws and I'd better leave her alone. She said if I had a disagreement with her, she would ask Elliot to handle it because he was good at that sort of thing. When she finished, I was so stunned, I couldn't speak. I just stood there in front of her, not knowing what to say. In a few short months, she had gone from sharing my bed... to *threatening* me."

Johnson paused. He stared through one of the pathetic little windows at the stark, soot-covered bricks of the building next door.

"Who's Elliot?" asked Harvey.

"Her cousin. At least, she told me he was her cousin. I met him once. A very loud guy with an abrasive manner. He looked dangerous. It's a pretty safe bet he's capable of violence. Her mention of getting him involved was a threat. She knew I'd see it that way. I don't know Elliot's last name, but at the time he worked as a mechanic at Stensen's garage on Hurst Street. That's where I met him. We took Linda's car there once for some maintenance work. He was a real jerk, braggin' about how he was gonna strike it rich someday soon and retire to his cabin in the woods, over near Hartwell."

"Did you ever see her again after she threatened you, Mr. Johnson?" Harvey scribbled in his notepad as he spoke.

Johnson hesitated for a few seconds, and then turned his head away from Harvey and said in a muffled voice: "Yeah, about three years after the threat, she came to this apartment. By that time the bank had taken my house. I couldn't keep up the payments without my savings, because I lost my job, too, after she left. I used to have a good job with

204

an accounting firm before I went on permanent disability. The doctors called it clinical depression. Then I developed phlebitis in my leg. Anyway, I moved to this place. And she found me here."

"What did she want?"

"She was very different than when she saw me the time before. She said she was wrong to leave me and she wanted to start over. Said she missed me and was sorry about the money, she'd used it to pay off old debts so she wouldn't go to jail."

"Start over? She wanted to start over after she'd threatened you? Did you refuse her?"

Johnson paused, as if he were ashamed. He stared down at the stained carpet. Finally, he said: "I don't think I want to talk about this anymore."

Harvey waited silently to see if Johnson would change his mind. So far, he'd been remarkably open with Harvey, who sensed there was more the man wanted to get off his chest.

After about ten seconds, Johnson continued. "That second time ... she and I spoke ... then we went to bed." His eyes were still on the floor.

Harvey understood now. Johnson had never really gotten over her. She had him under some kind of spell, and he hoped that someday he could be with her again. Maybe Johnson didn't care about the money. He just wanted the old Linda back, or the young Linda rather, the sweet young girl he'd married.

"And then she left again?" asked Harvey.

"Yeah, the next day. I gave her some money, whatever I had in my wallet. And my dead mother's sapphire ring. Linda said she really needed the money because she'd had a run of bad luck."

"And did you see her again after that?"

"No, but she called me a couple of times. I paid her rent that one time, a few months ago. Mailed her a check made out to cash, to her post office box. I haven't heard from her since then. She wouldn't give me her phone number or tell me where she lived."

Johnson shifted again in his chair. He fished in his pockets and came up with another cigarette. He lit it quickly, with the proficiency of a true chain smoker. After the first deep drag, he looked a bit more relaxed.

"Mr. Johnson, what was Linda's maiden name?"

"She told me that it was Sedgewick."

"Is that spelled S-E-D-G-E-W-I-C-K?"

"I think so. That sounds right."

Harvey wrote the name down on his pad. "And I assume she was able to produce a birth certificate when you went for the marriage license?"

"Yes. I don't know if it was real or not, but I guess it looked real enough to the person who gave us the license."

"If it was a false birth certificate, then perhaps you aren't legally married to her, and she doesn't have a claim on your money. Did you ever consider looking into that?"

He shook his head. "What the hell difference does it make? The money's gone anyway. If she was rich, she wouldn't have needed me to pay her rent that time. She's not the kind of person who would save her money. If she wants something, she buys it...or takes it."

"If she did use a false name, maybe you could at least have her arrested. I mean, if she ever shows up again."

"Yeah, well, what good will *that* do me? Are *you* going to put her in jail?"

"No, Mr. Johnson. I'm not a police officer. I just want to find the man I was hired to find. He might be with Linda now."

"Look, if she left her apartment and she's not in school, then I don't know where she'd go. I can't help you." He shrugged and slouched down into his chair.

"Last time you talked to her, did she say she'd come back to see you?"

"Yeah, of course she did. But it means nothing. The lies that she's capable of. The deceit. He turned toward Harvey, and said: "She has an IQ of a hundred and forty, did I tell you that? That's pretty high, isn't it?"

"Yes, that's very high. How did you find that out?"

"She took some college entrance exam shortly after we got married, and I saw the results when they came in the mail. And to think she told me she sold cosmetics because she couldn't get a better job," he said, shaking his head. "Hell, she's probably smart enough to do anything she wants."

Johnson paused long enough to brush away the ashes that had fallen on his pants, and then said, "You didn't answer my question."

"What question was that, Mr. Johnson?"

"This guy that she might be with now, the one you're looking for. What's he like?"

"Well, as I said before, I never met him, but he's probably pretty intelligent since he was a college teacher up until a short while ago. Why do you ask?"

"I just wanted to know...what he might have in common with me and Lee."

"Who's Lee?"

"Lee Brinkman. An old friend of mine. I introduced Lee to Linda after we got married. That was during the time I was showin' her off. Lee did pretty well for himself, he owned a bunch of dry-cleaning places in the Binghamton area. I'd lost touch with him for a long time, but then I tried calling him up about a month ago. I got his sister on the phone, and she said Linda came to see him shortly after she left me. And she and Lee had gotten ... involved. He co-signed a large loan for her, and bought her a car and a bunch of other stuff. And then one day, according to Lee's sister, she just took off. Sometimes I feel ... guilty about it, but what was I supposed to do, go and warn everybody I introduced her to? Warn them about what she was really like?"

"Hmmm, maybe I should give Lee a call and talk to him about Linda. He might have an idea of where she could be."

"You can't talk to him. He blew his brains out when she left him. A shotgun, inside his mouth, pointed up so it took the top of his head off.

They spent days cleaning his brains off the kitchen ceiling." Johnson paused, and his gaze went back to one of the tiny viewless windows before he continued. "So maybe, if I never see her again ... I got off *easy*. Maybe I was lucky."

"Maybe," repeated Harvey, as he pondered the trail of human misery that Linda had left behind her.

Harvey asked a few more questions about whether Linda had any close friends, but Johnson couldn't come up with any names. He thanked Johnson and stood to leave.

"You'll probably never find her, you know," said Johnson. "She's too smart. She'll always be a step ahead of you."

"Maybe you're right. But I think I should leave you my phone number, anyway. I'd appreciate it if you'd give me a call if there's anything else you can remember that might help me. Or if she contacts you."

"Sure, kid," said Johnson. He reached down by the side of the chair and grabbed a bottle of bourbon that had been sitting on the floor.

Harvey wrote his name and number on a piece of paper and tore it from his pad. He handed the paper to Johnson, who was in the process of pouring a shot into a grimy glass. Then Harvey remembered that Johnson's phone number from the rent check was no longer in service. He probably had no phone because of money problems.

"Uh, call me collect from anywhere," said Harvey.

Johnson was drinking the bourbon now, and he apparently didn't have the willpower to pull the glass away from his lips before it was drained, so that he could respond. He just gave Harvey a slight wave.

Harvey thanked Johnson again and left.

So, there it was. She'd sucked this guy dry, like a spider sucks the juice out of a fly caught in its web. She left him a shell of a person, and every now and then she came back for more, and he was willing to *give* more. He couldn't help himself. He was as hooked as a heroin addict.

When Harvey reached the lobby, he decided to call Jenny again. She answered on the first ring and he summarized for her what he'd learned from talking to Johnson. "She sounds like some kind of con woman," Harvey said.

"Maybe she has a criminal record," Jenny suggested. "We should look into that. But listen, I just got a lead on Grant's car from my NYPD contact. It's apparently at a junkyard in Saylorville. Or at least his license plate is there. Saylorville is a small town about twenty-five miles from Lake George. Have you been there before?"

"Yes, I've driven through it."

"Can you meet me there at about six? I just called the place, they said they'll be open 'till six-thirty. The junkyard is on the outskirts of the town. It's called Falco Salvage.

"Okay, I'll see you there."

* * *

Back in his apartment, Douglas Johnson considered what he'd just told that guy Harvey Grace. And he decided that he'd probably told him way too much. Why the hell did he spill his guts like that?

But he *knew* why. It felt good, therapeutic even, to talk to someone about it. Even a stranger.

But if it got back to Linda that he'd talked to this guy about her...

He didn't think Linda would hurt him, not physically at least. But that Elliot guy was crazy, probably capable of anything.

He decided it was best to leave his place for a few days. Or maybe a week.

Johnson stood up and began looking for his car keys.

Chapter 31
Wednesday, May 27, 4:48 p.m.

"I smell a rat," said Beale.

Beale and Zoober were at the third restaurant on their list. They stood in the parking lot behind the building, looking at a large trash dumpster that sat against the wall. Next to the dumpster were several wooden pallets, one of them leaning against the wall.

Zoober looked puzzled. "You mean you think there's been foul play here?" he asked.

"No, I mean I smell a rat. I was a cop in New York City thirty years ago, in a lousy neighborhood. There were rats, plenty of 'em. Used to see 'em all the time, big ones. I remember once going into a filthy shithole of an apartment after getting a call that some wild animal was loose. I walk into the place and I see a brown rat the size of an alley cat run out of the kitchen and right through my damn legs, with something that looked like strawberry jelly dripping from its mouth. Christ, *that's* a sight you'll never forget. Anyway, rats that live on food garbage have a peculiar smell. Hard to describe it. A funny, greasy smell. And it's here. But you can barely smell it over the stench of this rotten food. And these pallets here give an easy way for a rat to climb up and get in."

Beale stepped onto a pallet and looked down into the open dumpster. "It's less than a quarter full. Christ, what a stench! What kinda crap do they serve here?"

"Mexican. The name of the place is *Yucatan.*"

"Mexican? But they serve lemon meringue pie? Hell, that's an *American* dessert. My mother used to make it for every fourth of July barbecue we had when I was a kid."

Zoober shrugged his shoulders. "When I called, they said they serve it here. We can go inside and check the menu."

"We will. A rat could easily jump in here, eat its fill of lemon meringue pie or refried beans or whatever slop is in there, and then leave. It fits."

"But do you think the kids could have ridden their bikes here? This restaurant is on a very busy road for kids to be biking. Forty-five mile per hour speed limit, with barely any shoulder in many places."

"Twelve-year-old kids are pretty clever. Maybe they found another way." Beale turned and pointed to the back of the parking lot, which was bordered by tall trees. "Let's look back there," he said as he stepped down from the pallet.

As they reached the end of the parking lot, Beale looked left and right. "Over there," he said, pointing to a small gap in the dense foliage. They walked the twenty paces to the gap and found the beginning of a winding trail in the woods. The trail surface was bare dirt, and in some areas, it was covered with matted leaves. There were bicycle tire tracks in places that were muddy from recent rains. They entered the trail and walked the first fifty feet, then stopped. It was apparent that it went on for a great distance.

"There's your answer," said Beale. "They came here through this trail. Looks like great fun. Probably lots of bumps and jumps to test your skill. We'll have to follow it, see where it comes out."

"Should we walk it now?" Zoober asked.

"Nope. The kids travel it on their bikes, so it could go on for miles. A couple of the guys at the station house ride bikes to work. Maybe we can get one of them with a mountain bike to come and help us out. But let's go inside and talk to the owner first."

They walked to the front of the restaurant, which had a Spanish mission look to it. Beale opened the large front door, a huge oak panel with a massive wrought-iron handle. They stepped onto the bright red carpet in the foyer and looked at the menu posted on the wall.

"There it is," said Zoober, staring at the dessert section, and pointing. "It says, *Lemon Meringue Pie, a Mexican Specialty.*"

"Mexican Specialty? Yeah, right," Beale said. "Let's find the manager."

They stepped through the inner door and were surprised at the large size of the dining area. It was decorated like an outdoor verandah. The wrought iron tables and chairs were clustered under huge leafy ficus trees which grew through circular holes in the slate floor. There were only two tables occupied, both by young couples who were chatting happily and sipping white wine. A solitary waitress roamed the dining area, straightening the silverware on the tables. A few feet from Beale and Zoober was a hostess who stood behind a small metal podium. She was young and pretty, with the perky enthusiasm of an employee of the month.

"Table for two?" she asked.

Beale flashed his badge. "No thanks, honey. We just need to talk to the boss. Is he around?"

The hostess seemed both impressed and concerned. "Yes, I'll get him," she said in a serious tone. She disappeared into the kitchen and thirty seconds later an elderly man came out, looking concerned. He was short and stocky with dark skin, dark eyes, and a full head of thick grey hair. His face was lined and weathered, and his hands were rough from years of hard work in restaurant kitchens.

Zoober was about to politely introduce himself and his partner, but Beale quickly put his hand up to silence the younger man and then flashed a badge in front of the owner so quickly that it could have been a badge for anything: police, building inspector, fire chief, board of health, whatever.

Beale said: "You got vermin crawling around your parking lot, you know that? Rats. Maybe you got 'em in here, too, huh?"

"I'm Henry Marr, the owner," the man said, obviously very alarmed. He spoke rapidly, with a trace of a Spanish accent. "Please officers, keep your voices down. My customers, you know? Rats? Surely, we have no rats here, officers. Maybe a skunk or raccoon comes around the trash bin once in a while, looking for something to eat. But we have woods all around us, you know, so it can't be helped. I can't stand in the parking lot with a gun all the time waiting for skunks."

"Gun? You keep a gun here? Got a license for it?" asked Beale in a suspicious tone, intentionally rattling the man further.

"No, no!" answered the owner with alarm. "I have no gun, officer, I was only making a point."

Beale hesitated as if considering whether the owner should be believed. Zoober wanted to step in now to alleviate the owner's anxiety, but before he could, Beale started again.

"Well, it's definitely rats. And it wouldn't matter if it was a skunk, anyway. Rats, skunks, whatever. They're all vermin in my book. The top of that dumpster is open right now. You keep it open all the time?"

"Ah, my employees that bring out the trash, sometimes they forget to close the lid. I've told them over and over!"

"How often does the dumpster get emptied, sir?" asked Zoober calmly.

"Twice a week, on Monday and Thursday mornings. Please, officers, if I've done something wrong, I will pay the fine and correct the situation, of course. I'm very sorry, it was unintentional."

Beale decided not to tell the owner that he didn't give a shit about rats in the dumpster, but he figured the man's fear that he might have health code violations might motivate him to help quickly with the real request. Zoober began to open his mouth to explain to Marr that he wasn't in any trouble, but Beale saw it coming and raised a hand to stifle Zoober's comment.

Beale said: "Mr. Marr, we're looking for three boys that might ride their bikes around here, in your back parking lot, all of them around twelve-years-old. Maybe they come here a lot. We think they might have taken something out of your trash dumpster, sometime in the last week and a half. First, do you have any exterior security cameras?"

"No, sir. But what did these boys take?"

"A rubber raft."

"I never saw a raft in the dumpster, officers."

Beale continued: "Maybe the kids saw someone throw it in, and then they took it out right away. Maybe one of your employees saw these kids. How 'bout we ask 'em?"

"Sure, we can ask. There are only nine employees here right now. I think Robert is the only one that might have seen them. He takes his breaks behind the building, to smoke. Follow me, please, officers."

Within a few minutes, the employees were gathered together in the kitchen. As Marr predicted, only the teenage busboy named Robert had any useful information.

"Yeah, I've seen some kids on bikes in the parking lot. Not recently, though," said Robert.

"When?" asked Zoober.

The teenager scratched at the acne on his chin while he thought for a moment. "A month ago, maybe. Sometime in the afternoon, I think. Three boys came out of the woods on their bikes, near the back of the parking lot."

"Where did they go?"

"Nowhere. They just sat on their bikes for a while, maybe for a few minutes. Then I had to get back to work. They were still at the back of the parking lot when I left."

"And did you ever see them again?" asked Zoober.

"Nope. I only remember seeing them the one time, but that don't mean they haven't been here on other days. I take only two smoking breaks, ten minutes each, out of an eight-hour shift." The busboy glanced over at the owner to see if the remarks about his strict adherence to the break time limit of ten minutes might buy him some brownie points, but Marr remained silent, his eyes moving back and forth nervously between Beale and Zoober.

"Can you give us a description of them?" Zoober asked.

"I didn't see their faces well enough. They were a good distance away, and they kept toward the back of the parking lot when they saw me."

"How about their bikes? What color?"

Deep in thought, the busboy hesitated before answering: "Uhh, one of them had a red bike, I think. Sorry, but I don't remember the others."

Beale said, "One was red. Woweee, that sure helps."

214

Zoober asked, "What kind of handlebars did the bikes have? Were they curved downward?"

"Uhh...no," replied Robert. "I think they had the kind that are nearly flat, the kind you see on most mountain bikes."

"Do you remember anything more about the bikes?" pressed Zoober. "Were they one speed? Multiple speed? Did you see derailleurs on the bikes?"

"Sorry, I really didn't notice."

A few more questions drew Zoober and Beale to the conclusion that the busboy could offer no further useful information. Beale then pulled the owner aside, gave him his card, and made him understand the police department would be expecting a call from him right after he spoke to the employees that weren't present today, and an immediate call if he or anyone who worked for him saw the kids from now on. There was an unspoken threat that if Beale sensed the owner was not giving his full cooperation, Beale's buddies on the rat patrol might burst through the restaurant's front door during the busy dinner hours, chase all the customers out, and search every square inch of the establishment for rat poop.

Beale and Zoober left and walked back to the car.

"Where are the nearest houses on this road?" Beale asked.

Zoober looked at his cellphone screen and replied: "About a half-mile north."

"Any intersecting streets near here?"

"Not until after you go past those houses."

"Then it's unlikely the kids live around here. They probably start their ride at the other end of the trail. So, let's get someone to follow it, see where it leads."

"Should we stake out the parking lot, too? Or maybe set up a wireless camera pointed at the trailhead?"

Beale said, "You can go ahead if you want to and start to fill out the shitload of forms to requisition the camera. Maybe you'll get it approved and set up in a month. But they'll never approve a request to have a black and white sit in this parking lot and wait for those kids to show up to question them. Besides, the guy in the car would probably fall asleep waiting."

"We could do it ourselves, on two different shifts.".

"Our time can be better spent doing other things. Besides, what makes you think *I'd* stay awake?"

Chapter 32`
Wednesday, May 27, 6:08 p.m.

As evening approached, Harvey and Jenny walked through a car graveyard in the middle of a field, following a sandy-haired, skinny teenager. They were careful to avoid the inky black oil spills which dotted the muddy ground. The teenager walked quickly, guided only by the clipboard he carried and an occasional glance at the numbered stakes hammered into the ground at regular intervals. He went to the third row, fourth space, and then stopped in triumph, pointing to a twenty-year-old brown Chevy parked in front of him. The right side of the car was badly smashed in, and the right rear tire was pointed at an odd angle. The car's brown paint was blemished with white streaks from whatever white car it had collided with.

"Found it," said the teenager with pride." She's a beauty, huh? One of the newest ones in here."

"A beauty?" replied Jenny, with a puzzled expression. "Looks totaled to me. And it also looks decades old."

"Oh yeah, right," replied the young man. "What I mean is that it was brought in recently, yesterday, in fact. Totaled? Hah, no way, man. The insurance dudes might tell you that, but with some frame straightening, new rear axle and suspension, new door panel, rear panel, roof panel, chrome trim, some primer, ten coats of paint, and a little sweat this thing could be hummin' down the road in no time. Be a shame to crush it. They don't make engines like this no more. Today's engines, they got all this computerized crap on 'em to reduce emissions. And this engine don't look damaged to me."

Harvey walked to the front and then to the rear of the car and saw the matching New York plates with the number Pamela had given him for Grant's car.

Jenny turned to the teenager and asked: "When exactly did it come in?"

"Yesterday afternoon, about two o'clock. Towed in and dumped here. The tow truck owner said the cops gave him the call. This car was owned by a little old lady, lives right in town. I know her, Mrs. Coleman's her name. She must be around a hundred and twenty years old. She's a sweet old lady, but she don't have much reaction speed no more. Just last week I remember seein' her at the gas station, and I says to her, I says: 'Hey, Mrs. Coleman, you're about as old as King Tut. When are you gonna give up driving?' And she laughed and said she'd probably *never* give it up. Anyway, I hear she was backin' out of her driveway without lookin' behind her, you know, like old people do? And she backed right in front of some guy in a brand-new Volvo, and WHAM! It was over in a second. She's okay, just shook up, and her dentures flew out. I hear the Volvo got it bad."

Harry turned to Jenny and asked, "How'd you find out about this car?"

"My friend on the NYPD, I asked him to watch out for Grant's car. The cop on the accident scene yesterday found that the plate didn't match the woman's registration. He red-flagged it, and my friend picked it up in a database search."

The right rear window of the car was missing, having been completely shattered in the collision. Harvey looked inside the car through the missing window. He could see pieces of broken glass on the back seat. The glovebox was open and empty.

"Wanna buy it?" asked the teenager. "We bought it from the old lady. Now it's up for sale. So are all these cars. See *anything* you like?"

"I don't think so," answered Harvey. "I already own one wreck, I don't need another."

Jenny knelt as she examined the front license plate more closely. Harvey bent down beside her.

"Looks like a simple plate switch," she said to him.

The two screws holding the plate on were slightly rusted, and it was evident they had been turned recently. Some shiny metal was exposed in and around the notch on the screw heads.

They stood up and Jenny said to Harvey: "This woman's plates have been reported as stolen. The police or the DMV will try to contact Grant if they haven't already. If they call his cell, they'll of course get no answer. If they call his landline home number, I assume Pamela will tell them that both Grant and his car are gone. Nothing more will happen unless a car with this woman's plates is stopped for a traffic violation. Then when the police run the plate number, they'll probably take the driver into custody."

Harvey said, "Maybe they picked an older person's car on purpose. Could've been switched in a parking lot or something like that, after they saw the woman get out of the car and go into the store. Maybe they figured an elderly person who doesn't drive too much might be less likely to notice the plate switch immediately. Let's go over and talk to the woman who owned this car, anyway. It's a long shot, but she might have seen somebody sneaking around the car."

* * *

An hour later, Jenny and Harvey were leaving the small house of the elderly woman who had been in the accident. As they expected, the woman had seen nothing suspicious and didn't even notice her Chevy had someone else's plates on it until the officer at the accident scene pointed it out to her.

Harvey summed up the situation as he and Jenny stood in the woman's driveway. "Well, about all we've learned here is that Grant's plates somehow ended up on her car. And we can't even say for sure the Chevy's plates are on Grant's car now."

"Right," Jenny agreed. "My friend will call me if this woman's plate is picked up at a toll booth or traffic stop, but there could have been another plate switch by now. There's not much more you and I can do as far as the car is concerned. I think I should dig into Linda Johnson's past some more. Let's learn as much about her as we can. And then

219

maybe you and I should go to the University tomorrow and try to find some of her friends."

"Okay, but right now I'm going home to take a hot shower and get a little sleep. I'll come over to your place in the morning, at about eight o'clock."

They exchanged goodnights and got into their cars. Harvey pulled out of the parking area and turned toward home. Jenny was right behind him.

Chapter 33
Wednesday, May 27, 7:15 p.m.

When Harvey slowed his car and began to turn into his driveway, he glanced into his rearview mirror and saw Jenny was still trailing him. She passed him and pulled into her own driveway.

Harvey was out of his car first. He walked to the side door of his house and paused there, noting how beautiful the lake water looked, illuminated by the evening sun. The crystal surface of the lake shimmered with flecks of red, orange, and silver as a large pleasure boat left a wake like a crack in a stained-glass window. Harvey stepped through the door, reluctantly surrendering the serene view. A few hundred feet away, Jenny closed her car door and went into her house.

About fifty minutes later Harvey emerged, looking invigorated. He got into his car and headed in the direction of the Village of Lake George. In about ten minutes he reached the Village's bustling little tourist area and parked on Main Street. He started walking along Main in the direction of the steamboat dock. The sun was setting and the street was softly illuminated by the Victorian-style street lamps. There were many people milling about, enjoying the pleasant spring evening.

Harvey strolled for almost two blocks until he reached a T-shirt shop. He took out his phone, tapped it a few times, and saw he had a signal. He knew there were various cell service dead spots in the Village, but this was not one of them. He put the phone back in his pocket and walked in the same direction for three more blocks, then made a right turn and walked down a steeply sloping street for about a hundred yards until he reached a soup and sandwich shop. He took out the phone again and saw he had no signal here. Entering the deli, a Mom 'n Pop place with just a few tables, he looked at the daily specials on the dry erase board while he waited behind several other patrons. When he reached the counter, a middle-aged woman in a bright red baseball cap and a stained blue apron called out: "Whaddlyahaaave, dear?"

Harvey ordered a turkey sandwich on a hard roll with lettuce and tomato, and then watched while a well-practiced teenage girl slapped the sandwich together, wrapped it in white paper, and handed it to him, all in less than ninety seconds. She gestured toward the cash register, and Harvey moved down to pay. He then selected an empty table near the window, where he sat down to eat. Harvey took large bites and ate quickly, replenishing the energy expended during his workday, but then he stopped abruptly when he was about halfway through the sandwich. He quickly wrapped the remainder, put it back in the paper bag, then stood up and left the shop. He looked right and left as he stepped out onto the sidewalk, and then began to walk to his left in the same direction he'd come from. He walked all the way back to the T-shirt shop and then stopped on the sidewalk, took out his phone and tapped it to make a call. After about ten seconds, Harvey heard: "Hello, this is Peter Damler."

"It's me, Harvey. Yes, I know I'm supposed to be there with you right about now. Something unforeseen came up. I'm very sorry, but I can't make it tonight. How about tomorrow night, same place, same time? I need another twenty-four hours. I'm really sorry, I don't mean to be stringing you along over this... no, there's just no way I can see you tonight, and I don't blame you for being upset, but I'll be tied up the rest of the night... yes, I do realize how important this is, but I have to go. I'll see you tomorrow night."

Harvey squelched the protests he heard on the other end of the line by disconnecting and quickly put the phone back in his pocket. He headed with his half-eaten sandwich back to the little deli at the bottom of the hill. When he entered and saw that the table he'd been using a short while ago was now taken, he chose another close to the window, sat down, and unwrapped the remainder of his sandwich. One of the workers behind the counter, a twenty-something man with a shock of spiked black hair and a mosaic of religious tattoos on one arm, gave him an odd look, as if he might be bringing his own food from home to eat in here, or maybe something he'd bought at one of the other local takeout places. But then the worker shrugged his shoulders and went back to wiping the countertops. To placate him, Harvey went up to the counter and bought an iced tea.

He sat back down and began to eat again, with as much gusto as before. A toddler sitting at the table next to Harvey gave him a curious look. His stout mother munched on her sandwich and sipped her coffee while the boy stood in his chair, twisting around and leaning over the back.

"Look, Mommy," said the little boy excitedly as he pointed at Harvey. "That man has a big bug in his ear!"

"Shhh, Benny," admonished the mother. "That's not a bug, don't worry. Now don't bother him." With one powerful arm, the woman turned little Benny around and pulled him down so he sat correctly in his chair. Using a hand on top of the boy's mop of red hair, she pushed his nose down toward his sandwich. "Benny, eat," said the woman.

Harvey finished his sandwich and drink, and then left the deli. He quickly walked back to his car and drove back to his house.

During the drive, he mentally readied himself for a confrontation.

Chapter 34
Wednesday, May 27, 8:56 p.m.

As Jenny cut lettuce and tomatoes in the kitchen of her lakefront house, a salad took shape. She gathered together the oil, vinegar, and spices to make a simple dressing, and then she heard a soft knock at the back door. Puzzled, she quickly walked to the door and opened it to find Harvey standing there. He looked at her without smiling and she knew immediately something was wrong.

"Harvey?" she said in a surprised tone. "I thought you were going to bed early."

"You and Mike followed me into Lake George tonight. I want to know why." Harvey was stone-faced. He looked straight into Jenny's eyes to gauge her reaction.

Her face didn't show panic, but she hesitated for a moment and then asked in a near whisper: "What did you say?"

"You followed me. Why?"

"What are you...how..." She searched for words.

"I picked up radio transmissions... on this." He took Dexter's small handmade metallic chatterbox out of his jacket pocket and held it up to show Jenny. He then took the Bluetooth receiver out of his ear. "It scans all walkie-talkie, police, and CB frequencies, searching for chatter. Walkie-talkies aren't used much by the public anymore because pretty much everyone carries a cell phone now. But I heard transmissions on a walkie-talkie frequency, from two sources. They were very strong signals, meaning the transmitters were very close. It was scrambled, so I couldn't hear what you were saying, of course. It sounded the same way static would sound, but the timing gave you away as I walked around. There was a lot of chatter when I first went into the no cell service zone around the deli at the bottom of the hill, then it got quiet when I sat down to eat my sandwich. As soon as I stood up from my chair, you guys started again on the walkie-talkies. There was lots of chatter when I walked out of the deli, then it got quiet when I walked back to where there was cell service because you got back on your cellphones at that point. Then lots of chatter again when I went back to the deli, then it quieted down when I sat to eat in plain view through the window. Then more chatter the moment I stood up to leave. I was obviously under surveillance."

Jenny stared at Harvey with a guilty look, silent for the moment. She knew she'd been caught.

"You can deny it, but I know it's true. You can also be reasonable and tell me what this is really all about."

She thought for a few seconds as she looked at Harvey.

"And Jenny, tell Mike to come in. He's probably getting cold sitting in his car."

She stared at Harvey with a *how did you know that?* look.

Harvey answered her unspoken question: "I also picked up a strong walkie-talkie transmission as I pulled out of my driveway tonight," Harvey explained. "Since there's no cell service in this house, and since I can tell you haven't gotten a wireless router in here yet because my phone isn't picking it up, I knew it was Mike. He sat in his car watching, then he told you I was leaving my house and that he was going to follow me. I pulled out, he followed, then you followed in your car. Right?"

Jenny lowered her eyes to the floor as if admonishing herself for being careless.

She slowly turned and walked into the kitchen and Harvey followed her. Jenny opened a drawer and took out a small walkie-talkie which was covered in black leather, with a stubby black antenna. She pushed a button on its side and spoke into it.

"Mike, come in."

Mike responded: "Yeah, I'm here, what's up?"

"No, I really mean come in. Come inside. Harvey's here with me."

"What? Where exactly is he?" Mike asked in a near whisper.

"He's standing right next to me. He cut through the woods and came to the back door."

Silence from Mike.

"He knows, Mike. Just come inside now, okay?"

There was a muffled response from Mike, which sounded to Harvey like the single word SHIT, and then Jenny shut off the walkie talkie and put it back in the drawer.

"How did you know it was us following you?"

A wave of relief swept over Harvey. *Whew, I'm not just paranoid, they really were following me. Good thing, 'cause if not I would've just made a total ass of myself with these accusations...*

"You followed me before, Jenny, the day we had the scuffle with Louie Parker. I had to know if you were still doing it when we weren't together. I had to know if I should trust you completely. And you're the only one who'd have a reason to follow me." *Other than maybe Peter Damler, and I eliminated him as a possibility when I called him and verified he was sitting at the diner waiting for me.* "You lied to me about why Mike was here. I want to know what else you lied to me about. You need to tell me what's really going on here. Tell me, or I'm out of here right now."

"Sit down and I'll explain."

"I'll stand." He turned around when he heard the front door open. Mike entered the room and walked over to stand next to Jenny. Without smiling, he gave a nod of greeting to Harvey, and then shot an inquisitive look at Jenny.

"It was for your protection," Jenny said. "We had no idea where you'd be going. You told me you'd be in for the night. *You* lied. Or at least, you changed your mind."

Harvey tried to maintain his self-righteous posture. "You followed me for my protection? Are you cops?"

Jenny sighed and answered: "We're federal agents, FBI."

"FBI? Show me some identification."

Jenny walked over to the couch where her purse lay, but before she reached it, Harvey interrupted, raising his hand.

"On second thought, forget it. What does it mean anyway? I saw your phony PI license. It was just a forged piece of paper. Now you'll have a piece of plastic with the words FBI printed on it, plus a tin badge anyone could buy online. It's all meaningless." He turned to Mike and said, "Show me your gun."

Mike looked puzzled by the command, but he reached inside his jacket and removed his gun from his shoulder holster. He held it up in the air so Harvey could see it well.

Harvey said, "A Sig. And Jenny, you carry a Beretta. Neither of you have a Glock, which is FBI standard issue."

Jenny said, "We're allowed to carry a handgun of our choosing, as long as we pay for it ourselves, and of course it has to meet Bureau guidelines."

Harvey shook his head, clearly refusing to allow himself to be convinced. "So why is the FBI stalking me?"

Jenny sighed and paused for a few seconds. She looked as though she had a long story to tell and was searching for the right words to begin. "Have you ever heard of the FBI's Art Crime Team?"

Harvey remembered reading about it in a news article. It was a task force of some kind within the Bureau, but he couldn't remember details.

"Yes," Harvey replied simply. He waited for her to elaborate.

"It was established in 2004, a group of special agents that work on nothing but finding art thieves and recovering stolen art. Do you have any idea how much stolen art is in the States? Billions. Every year billions in stolen art is moved through the States, and at any given time billions in stolen art is also being stored in the States. Trading in stolen art is a huge underground industry, which in turn spawns a torrent of related criminal activity -- more theft, smuggling, tax evasion, and even murder. The FBI decided to get serious about combating it, and Mike and I are part of that effort. We're on the Art Crime Team. Grant came to our attention when rumors began circulating that he might be in possession of Vermeer's *Maiden*. There's a good chance the painting Grant has is the real thing."

"Even if it is, if there's billions out there, why are you guys spending so much effort tracking down one little painting?"

"Because we think it may lead us to much more. Do you know who last owned the *Maiden*?"

"Sure, a French family named Lemaire. The family you said hired you when you told me you were a PI."

"But we know of another owner since then, although not a *legal* owner. His name is Alexander Zola, a criminal who died seven years ago. Zola was no ordinary criminal. He was a very successful illegal weapons dealer, but also a bomb maker, essentially a terrorist for hire. His activities were very profitable, and over the years he earned a small fortune. He's rumored to have used his money to amass an impressive private collection of stolen paintings, some of them more valuable than the *Maiden*. Most of these paintings have been missing since World War II, and the rest were stolen from museums within the past fifty years. And most of his collection is still missing. It never turned up after Zola's death. About seven years ago, when Zola's weapons business was at its peak, he worked with three people who ran his operation as smoothly as a legal business might be run. They found buyers, arranged meetings, handled the money exchanges, and laundered the proceeds of sales. But Zola and his partners apparently had a falling out and they betrayed him by giving European authorities information that led to an attempt to arrest him. The arrest operation was botched and it ended with Zola dying in a fire. The partners were never arrested and the Bureau knows very little about them. We do know, however, that one of them was an American with a surname of Zuckerman, or maybe Zuchmann. Recently, we pieced together as much information as we could on Zola's whereabouts during the period when he worked with these partners, through knowledge of the arms deals he was involved in. And then we sifted through European and Asian hotel records, looking for an American who was at the same places at the same times as Zola. We found one. Guess who?"

Grant's visage flashed into Harvey's consciousness. *Pamela said he traveled in Europe for years...*

"I can see you have the answer, Harvey, even though you're not saying it. That's right, it's Grant. We think Grant Damler and

Zuckerman are one and the same. And now, Grant Damler turns up with a painting that used to be in Zola's possession. It can't be a coincidence. Here's what we think happened: Grant surely knew of Zola's reputation as an art collector. After Zola's death, Grant went to Zola's safehouse in Belgium before he told the authorities about it. There he found and took for himself Vermeer's *Maiden* and maybe some other paintings. Pamela told you Grant found the *Maiden* in his dead aunt's house, right? Pamela may believe that to be true, but it's just a cover story. We're hoping Grant will somehow lead us to the rest of the collection from the safehouse. We don't have enough evidence to arrest him yet. We can't prove he didn't find the painting in his aunt's house. All we have is a bunch of hotel receipts. But if he leads us to the rest of the collection, we'll not only be able to recover the paintings, we'll be able to indict him for possessing and dealing in stolen art, assuming he's still alive. So, you can understand why we're very disturbed that both Grant and the *Maiden* have disappeared."

There were a few seconds of silence, as Harvey considered what he'd just heard. He paced around the room for a dozen steps and then turned back to address Jenny.

"If he disappeared when the FBI was watching him, then your surveillance couldn't have been very good."

Now Mike spoke: "The surveillance was intentionally very low-key. We didn't follow him around. We figured that we might have to watch him for quite a long time, perhaps months, and if he spotted us, our chances of his leading us to Zola's other paintings would be zero."

"But how did you lose track of him completely? I'm sure you tapped his phone. Couldn't you keep tabs on him by tracking it?"

"Yes, we did tap his phone, starting a few days before he disappeared. We didn't learn anything useful. He keeps location services off, and he even powers the phone off for long periods. And he must use a burner phone to talk to his girlfriend and we don't know the number."

Harvey countered immediately: "Even if he turned it off, I'm sure you guys have the ability to track it anyway. The federal government has all kinds of surveillance tricks for keeping tabs on everybody."

Mike added, "He could defeat *any type* of phone tracking by simply putting the phone in a foil bag. So maybe he sometimes did that, if he thought the authorities might have some interest in his whereabouts."

Harvey thought, *Or maybe he was just really paranoid about keeping his whereabouts a secret from Pamela when he was with his girlfriend?*

Mike continued, "But we also put a GPS tracker in his car at the same time we started the phone tap. From the tracker, we know that on the day Grant disappeared, his car left his house in the late morning, and it went directly to Main Street in Lake George."

Main Street in Lake George. So, he didn't go to the hardware store in Port Kole, like Pamela assumed. He went to the street where Linda's apartment is.

Mike continued: "Grant's car was there for a few hours, then he or whoever drove his car went to his bank, the Millbury branch where the safe deposit box is, then back to Main Street in Lake George, then to Saylorville. We assume that's where the license plate was switched. Then the car went west and we lost the signal after about twenty minutes, as it was moving. The GPS unit just stopped working, and we haven't gotten any signal from it since. It must have malfunctioned."

Jenny said, "So right now, Harvey, we've got nothing. We can't find the *Maiden*, or Grant Damler, or Linda Johnson. There's no arrest record for a Linda Johnson who was previously named Linda Sedgewick, and we haven't even been able to find any background information on her. There are plenty of people in the U.S. who go by the name Linda Johnson but we've been able to eliminate every one of them as a suspect in this case either by description or circumstance. We've made inquiries in St. Teresa but we've not been able to turn up any information yet on her living there. We have an agent from the local office showing Linda's picture to people in St. Teresa, trying to see if anyone recognizes her, but we're not hopeful we'll get any useful information about where Linda is now, or where she's headed. We talked to her landlord on Main Street, and he's got no information that will help us find her.

"I'm truly sorry about the deception. But you must understand what's at stake here, and why it's so important to keep the details of this operation a secret. If Grant were to find out we're after him and Zola's art collection, this whole operation would collapse. Grant could just decide to live off what he'll make from selling the *Maiden*, and he'll probably get away with it. We'd never recover the other paintings, and we'd never be able to convict him of trading in stolen art. He would go free, and we'd have nothing."

"So, why do you need *me*?"

"For one thing, you apparently have Pamela's trust. She may know something that will help us find her husband."

"Why don't you go talk to her yourself?"

"And tell her what? That the FBI wants to throw her husband in jail, and we want her help? If she still loves her husband like you say, she won't cooperate with us."

"So, are you going to arrest me now for obstruction of justice, or something?"

"Of course not, Harvey. You've done nothing wrong. We just want your cooperation. We're still all in this together. We all want to find Grant and the painting."

"Wrong. I told you this before and I'll say it again. I work for Pamela, and she doesn't give a damn about the painting, therefore *I* don't give a damn about the painting. You two want to find Grant so you can throw him in jail for dealing in stolen art, assuming you can get your hands on enough evidence to convict him, and I want to find him because Pamela wants him back. Therefore, we don't have common goals."

"But, listen, Harvey...," said Mike. He took a step toward Harvey and attempted to put a reassuring hand on his shoulder.

Harvey took a quick step back, jerking his shoulder away so Mike couldn't make contact. "Look, special agent Mike, or whatever your real name is. If I'm not under arrest, leave me alone and let me do my job."

Harvey walked toward the front door. As he reached it, he stole a look back toward Jenny.

"Harvey, I'm sorry," Jenny said.

"Yeah, me too. It was a good act. I thought you were really a private eye, after I thought you were really an architect. I'm gullible. But I'm learning."

"You have to believe me, I just want..."

"Why should I believe anything you say, after all the lies? All I want from you two is to be left alone. Just stay out of my way." Harvey left and shut the door behind him.

Jenny and Mike looked at each other.

"This is just terrific," Mike said.

"Damn, I should have talked to him alone. I could have reasoned with him. He's hostile toward you for some reason."

"Jealousy. He's attracted to you. I saw it in the way he looked at you before. Or at least he *was* attracted, until now. How did he get on to us?"

"He had a small receiver that detected our walkie-talkie chatter. The timing of our transmissions tonight gave us away."

"Christ, what a cock-up. The boss will not be pleased. We should have been more careful. We underestimated Harvey."

"Yeah, we blew it," said Jenny. "I had his trust. We should have given him more leash. Now, what do we do?"

"I still think he knows something that will help him find Grant. Something he didn't tell you. It could be something Pamela told him, or maybe Douglas Johnson. We really need to interview Johnson ourselves. Has he turned up yet?"

"No. He must have taken off right after Harvey talked to him."

"Well, we know Harvey's up to something because we haven't been able to tap or track his cellphone. But at least we can still track his car."

"Probably not for long," said Jenny. "I'm betting that within a few hours, we'll lose that ability."

"Then we have no choice, we have to keep following him. But this time we'll do it the old-fashioned way. No radios, no tag team. Just me. We'll let him do what he wants tonight, and then I'll catch up with him in the morning. Even if he drives somewhere tonight, he's got to come back to his place to sleep. He doesn't have money to throw around on motel rooms."

Jenny shook her head and said, "I'm worried. Harvey is smart and observant."

"Yeah, like that point he brought up about the Sig and the Beretta. Does the FBI really allow agents to carry nonstandard issue firearms?"

Jenny looked at Mike and said, "I have no idea."

* * *

As he left Jenny's place and walked back toward his own house through the woods, Harvey's mind churned with emotions. He was angry at Jenny and Mike for being deceitful, and angry at himself for being stupid enough to be so easily deceived. And he felt hurt by the notion that Jenny, whom he had come to care for, had apparently found it so easy to lie to him. *Twice.*

Should he be afraid, as well? If Jenny and Mike wanted to detain or even harm him, they could have done so just a few minutes ago.

Who am I kidding? Either one of them alone, even without a gun, could have whipped my ass.

And even though Harvey had no illusions anymore of having a relationship with Jenny, he just couldn't believe she would willingly harm him. When he left, she seemed to be sincerely apologetic... but maybe it was just another act.

Instead of going into his house, Harvey walked right to his car, which was parked in his driveway. *Can Jenny and Mike see me right now?* He thought they probably *could* if they had night vision goggles. Harvey wouldn't be surprised if Mike had a pair in his car. But it was possible the trees were dense enough to obscure their view.

Harvey opened the car door. The interior dome light didn't go on to give him away, because it had quit working long ago. He started the engine, hoping the cranking noise wouldn't be loud enough to alert them. It started quickly because it was still warm. Easing the old car up the steep driveway without headlights, he pulled out onto the road. He drove slowly because there was barely enough moonlight to see the lines on the highway. After going about a hundred yards, he turned the headlights on. A quarter of a mile further on, he drove around a curve and then pulled onto the gravel shoulder and turned off the engine and lights. He was pretty certain he'd be able to recognize Jenny's or Mike's car from the side if it rounded the curve.

He waited for five minutes. During that time, four cars he didn't recognize passed him and went right on by. So apparently, they weren't following him. Maybe they'd given up.

He got back into his car, cautiously pulled back onto the road, and headed toward Pamela's house.

Harvey thought about what he'd say to her.

Chapter 35
Wednesday, May 27, 9:38 p.m.

Pamela opened the door to find Harvey standing on her front step. She looked startled to see him at this time of night. "Harvey... you have news... about Grant?" she asked, with a mixture of dread and hope in her voice.

Pamela waited as if she were scared about what terrible revelation might come next. On the drive over, as he'd thought about the lurid pictures of Pamela and her lover, Harvey had rehearsed in his mind a dozen scenarios, a score of speeches. But now he couldn't bring himself to use any of them.

"May I come in?" he managed to say, stalling the inevitable for a few more seconds. In any case, this was not something to be discussed on a doorstep.

"Of course." They stepped inside and she closed the door.

"Mrs. Damler...I saw some pictures today. They were...very graphic."

"Oh, dear God, no." She began to tremble. "Pictures of his body..."

"No, no, I haven't found him yet."

"Then what...?"

"Pictures of ... you...and a man... not your husband...making love at the Sherwood motel."

Pamela's eyes went wide open and her jaw dropped. She stared at Harvey for a few seconds and then turned, sobbing, and walked away into the living room. Harvey followed her, wondering if perhaps he had traumatized her to the point where they wouldn't be able to even converse. She sat down on the couch and clutched its arm as if to steady herself. Harvey sat down on the opposite end. Momentarily the sobbing stopped and she stared straight ahead as if she were in a trance.

Harvey said, "Grant's brother Peter is here in New York. He came from France at Grant's request to examine the painting, as you said he might. Peter found out you hired me and he contacted me. He showed me the pictures. He said Grant told him he was going to file for divorce because of your infidelity. Peter told me...well, not to trust you. He said, in so many words, that you might not really want Grant found."

Pamela was shaken out of her trance. "What?" She protested. "The notion that Grant wants to file for divorce *now* because of my infidelity is completely absurd! My affair was three years ago and it lasted just a few weeks. I didn't love the man. I told Grant about it shortly after it was over and he forgave me, as I forgave him. And it was Peter—"

"Three years ago?" Harvey interrupted. "But—"

"Yes. Grant has had... several affairs. At one point three years ago, I wanted to get back at him. I was hurt, and I wanted some sort of ...revenge, I guess. And so *I* had a brief affair. But I didn't love the man. I ended it when I realized that I still loved Grant despite what he'd done to me." Pamela lowered her eyes to the floor. "I did a stupid, horrible thing, and I did it just to hurt Grant in the same way he'd hurt me. What I did only made our marital problems worse."

She took a tissue from her pocket and wiped her eyes before taking a deep breath and continuing. "It was Peter who brought my infidelity to Grant's attention. Peter apparently suspected I was having an affair. He warned Grant, who didn't believe it. So, Peter hired someone to follow me, and they took those pictures. Grant confronted me with the pictures three years ago. We talked it through and we forgave each other for our infidelities and decided to stay together to work on our marriage. Grant asked Peter to delete or destroy the photos and forget about the whole thing. Peter assured Grant he would, and I thought that was the end of it. Certainly, I was wrong in having the affair, but even so, Peter shouldn't have intruded in our lives as he did. I just couldn't look at Peter after that. And that's why I didn't want him to come over from Paris to inspect the painting. I never wanted to see him again. And to think he kept those... awful pictures of me... for years!"

A small gray cat ambled over toward Harvey and brushed against his leg. Pamela took no notice, but Harvey welcomed the tiny distraction. He bent over to pet the cat for a few seconds while Pamela continued to sob. Her crying was nearly silent but sitting on the couch with her, Harvey could feel the vibrations as her body shook.

"Grant and I have gone through some very rough times. Not just his affairs, but his drinking, too." Tears were streaming down her cheeks.

Harvey asked in a near whisper, "Mrs. Damler, the man you had an affair with...what's his name?"

She shook her head and looked down at the floor. "I...I can't tell you. There's no reason to bring him into this. Enough people have been hurt. The affair is over. I need to respect *his* privacy, too. He's married and even though it happened years ago, I don't know if he ever told his wife. There's no need for you to contact him."

"Okay, but please understand I have to consider every possibility. Do you think there's any chance that the man you had an affair with might have harmed your husband?"

Pamela turned toward Harvey and didn't hesitate in answering through her tears: "There's no chance. If I thought there was *any* chance at all, I'd have told you about him when I hired you. I couldn't live with myself if I thought I had any part, even indirectly, in bringing harm to Grant. But this man is incapable of harming anyone. And anyway, it was three years ago. If he'd intended to do anything, it would have happened long ago." Her voice then turned resolute as she went back to discussing her brother-in-law. "Harvey, don't trust Peter. He's jealous of Grant. Their aunt, Helen Baker, left everything to Grant and nothing to Peter. She did well for herself working as a financial attorney for many years and accumulated an estate worth several million."

"Why did she cut out Peter?"

"Peter was never really in the picture for her. Grant and his aunt traveled together in Europe and Asia for several years and had a great time together. That was a decade ago, before I met Grant, and at the time his aunt was unmarried. She conducted her business dealings on those trips and she greatly appreciated Grant's companionship, so they grew very close. Grant made all the travel arrangements and enjoyed soaking in all the culture and the sights. He became like a son to her. She married for the first and only time very late in life, after she retired, but her husband died after just a few years of marriage. Having no children of her own, she left everything to Grant when she died from a heart attack last year."

Pamela turned her attention back to the business of finding her husband. She asked, "What about the person who opened the safe deposit box. Was it Grant?"

"I'm still working on that. I talked to the bank security officer, who only said that if it wasn't Grant, the bank wasn't liable for anything. They refused to show me the video from their surveillance cameras. By the way, does the name Johnson mean anything to you?" He held his breath, waiting to see if she would ask if it was a man or a woman.

She said simply: "No. Who's Johnson?"

Harvey couldn't bring himself to say: *A young woman your husband has probably been sleeping with.*

"Someone at the bank," he lied. "I'm looking into who at the bank may have seen the person who opened the safe deposit box on Saturday. Unfortunately, Grant's friend Michael Tillman wasn't there that day."

Harvey stood and said: "Mrs. Damler, if you want me to, I'm prepared to continue to look for Grant until I find him, or until you tell me to stop looking."

The tears had stopped now. Pamela stared straight forward and answered Harvey's question in a very soft, almost pleading voice: "Please find him. I hope he and I can somehow make things right again. And even if we can't... I'd still like to know he's safe."

"Okay, then, I'll call you tomorrow. Don't get up, Mrs. Damler. I'll let myself out."

Harvey got in his car and drove about two miles until he reached a roadside convenience store. He pulled over into a parking space, took out his phone, and did a search for the number of the Sherwood motel. He punched it in and someone answered immediately.

"Sherwood Motel, how may I help you?" asked the man.

"Hello," said Harvey in a whisper. "I stayed at the Sherwood last night."

"Could you speak up please, sir," said the desk clerk. "I can't hear you very well."

"I'm sorry, I've lost my voice," whispered Harvey, a little louder than before. "I've got a bad cold. I'll speak as loudly as I can. I was at your motel last night, and I think I may have left something there, my spare pair of eyeglasses. I don't remember what room I was in. My wife, Pamela Damler, paid for the room... can you look it up?"

"Certainly, sir. Yes, I remember a Pamela staying here last night, I was on duty. But could you spell the last name please?"

"D-A-M-L-E-R." Harvey wondered if Pamela had even made the reservation.

After a twenty second pause, the answer came: "I'm sorry sir, there was no one with that last name who stayed here last night."

Harvey's mind raced. *The guy just said someone named Pamela stayed there last night. It's not a very common first name. She probably wouldn't have used her real surname, anyway. But she hasn't been married for that long, maybe she has an old driver's license in her maiden name, maybe even a credit card?*

Harvey recalled her maiden name from his internet search. An article he'd browsed about her charity work had links to other articles that covered work she'd done before her marriage to Grant.

"Oh, I forgot, she probably registered in her maiden name, we're newlyweds and her ID and credit cards haven't been updated yet. Her maiden name is Raines, R-A-I-N-E-S. Could you check, please?"

After another brief pause, the clerk said: "Yes, I found it under Raines. You were in room 204, sir. But I have no notes about personal items left in that room. If you wish, I can double-check with the staff, but I'm afraid it's not likely..."

"No, don't bother, I'm sure if your cleaning staff had found them, they would have turned them in. I must have left them somewhere else.

Thank you, goodbye." Harvey ended the call. He decided that he needed one more piece of corroborating information.

Harvey called Dexter. Dispensing with his usual chummy greeting, Harvey got right to it.

"Dex, got a question for you. Can you tell the date when a photo was taken if you have the image file?"

"Sure can. The date is usually embedded in the file. Different cameras or phones can put the information in different places in the file, so you have to flatten it to just a bunch of ones and zeros, and then search for the date. I have a program that can find it."

"Great. I'm going to send you a picture file right now. Can you find the date for me?"

"Yeah, sure. You'll have your answer one minute after I get the file."

"Here it comes."

Harvey went to his text messages, found the picture that Peter had sent him of Pamela and her lover, and forwarded it to Dexter.

"Got it. Hang on, dude."

In about forty-five seconds Dexter said, "It was taken yesterday."

"Are you sure?"

"Sure, I'm sure. Nice picture, by the way."

"Yeah, well, don't add it to your porn collection. Delete it immediately."

"Aw, you're no fun."

Harvey thanked his friend and ended the call.

Pamela lied to me. She met her lover just yesterday.

Maybe Peter is right, maybe Pamela is just playing me, using me.

Harvey pulled up Peter Damler's number in his contact list.

Maybe she had a good reason for lying.

Maybe she was too ashamed to admit she slept with that guy even after her husband was missing.

Maybe, Maybe. Maybe I'm an idiot. I just wish I could read people like Uncle Willie.

Harvey hit the call button. In a few seconds, he heard Peter Damler's voice.

"Hello, Harvey?"

"Yes, it's me, Mr. Damler. I just wanted to let you know Pamela lied to me about the affair. She said it ended long ago. It's very possible you're right, that she's just using me. So... I don't really see any reason to continue on the case. I'm going to tell her I can't work for her anymore. I felt that I owed it to you to...to tell you about her dishonesty."

"Harvey, don't drop the case. You can work for *me*. I still want Grant found. And the *Maiden*. I want you to continue to work to locate both. I'll pay you, of course. Will you do it?"

"Work for *you*? Why *me*? You said that you already hired a private investigator and she took those pictures of Pamela and her lover."

"I hired her only to conduct surveillance on Pamela. You, Harvey, are in a unique position, working for Pamela. The first thing you must do, before you even tell her you're no longer in her employ, is get a look in that safe deposit box."

"So...you think I should deceive Pamela...for the time being...into thinking that I still work for her. That's... unethical."

"Is it? Pamela using you is quite unethical, I'm sure of that. And if she had something to do with my brother's disappearance, that's certainly well beyond unethical, isn't it?"

There was a long pause before Harvey responded: "I'll... think about it. I'll call you back tomorrow. I have to go. Talk to you soon."

After two minutes of silently agonizing over what to do, Harvey called Dexter back. "Dex, me again. I need you to do another thing for me, in person. I'll be there in about half an hour."

"I was just about to take my nap."

"Then I'll be waking you up." Harvey ended the call.

He pulled out of the parking area and headed for the University.

Chapter 36
Wednesday, May 27, 10:35 p.m.

Dexter slowly lifted his head from the dirty, rolled-up gym towel he used for a pillow. Harvey shook his friend's shoulder. "Dex, c'mon, wake up. I need your help. I'll pay you more."

Dexter sat up from the rickety wooden cot and rubbed his eyes. He looked at Harvey and said: "How much?"

"Nothing. I just said that to get you to wake up."

"Figures. Hey, your face is still a bruised mess, all black and blue and yellow, and you've got a nice shiner there. Geez, you and I have that double date with Marlo and Sandy coming up. Can you make all those bruises go away in a few days? You gotta look your best, I don't want you scaring them. You never really told me what happened."

"A guy jumped me. He beat the crap outta me, I had to go to the emergency room. I'm alive only because a woman fought him off and saved me."

"Well, there's no way we're telling Marlo and Sandy *that!* You gotta look very manly, so I appear manly too, by association. Okay, you tell 'em it was *two* guys who jumped you... no, make it *three* guys. And you fought two of them off before the third one got you with a lucky punch, but then you ignored the pain and took care of him too."

"It was just one guy, and actually he beat me senseless, I didn't even connect with a single punch. I'd be dead probably if it wasn't for the one-hundred-and-ten-pound woman who pulled him off me."

Dexter thought for a moment and said: "On second thought, let's drop the fight story, there'll be too many questions about who they were, their motives, and whether they got arrested and all that. Let's just make it a simple mountain climbing accident. You were climbing up a sheer rock face and your piton came loose... no, wait, forget the piton, you're one of those guys who climb with absolutely nothing but a little bag of rosin strapped to his shorts. What do they call that, free-styling or something like that? Yeah, that's it. Falling off a mountain is a very manly way to get injured."

"Forget about it. Let's get down to business, I've got a question for you. If someone were to put a GPS device in your car so they could track its position without you knowing it, one that would have to work for an extended period, would you be able to spot it?"

"Sure. It would work like the GPS system on a cellphone works. The position of the car, at least when it's in motion, would be sent out every ten seconds or so by cell or satellite phone. The unit needs power, so it would either have its own battery or it would have to be hooked up to the car's electrical system." Dexter yawned and rubbed the sleep from his eyes again. He looked in several pizza boxes that were strewn on the floor, hoping to find a forgotten slice or a stray piece of pepperoni. He found nothing except for some hardened cheese stuck to one of the boxes. He peeled some of it off and started chewing it.

"Would it be smaller than a cellphone?" asked Harvey.

"Yes, it could be a lot smaller. It doesn't need all the functionality of a cellphone, a screen and all that. It could be really small if it gets its power from the car. If it has its own battery, that adds bulk. In either case, I could spot it."

"So, you could conceivably hook this thing up to the car's battery, and if it was reliable, it should last forever, or at least for a very long time?"

"Right."

"Dex, I want you to check my car, now. If somebody's been tracking me, I want to know about it."

"Your old car? Piece o' cake. I have a meter that reads cell signal strengths. When we reach your car, we'll set the meter so it just picks up very close, strong signals and we look for the type of short and regular signal that a tracker would send. We might have to drive it around to get the tracker to start transmitting. If we see that signal, then we start looking all over your car. It's so old that any shiny new little thing will jump out and scream at me. We'd better go right now, it'll be getting pretty chilly tonight. It could take me about half an hour to do a thorough check. I'll look under the hood first but I may have to crawl under the car, too. Where'd you park?"

"Where I always park, the visitor's parking lot."

Dexter groaned. "Geez, that's like a half-mile from here. Okay, let's walk over there together. You can help carry the stuff I'll need." Dexter took two large battery-powered lanterns down from a shelf and then began to put on his sneakers.

"I gotta find my signal meter and tools," Dexter said.

"Okay. How can I help?"

"While I'm looking for my stuff you can go get me a mineral water from the frig in the faculty lounge. And if there are any doughnuts left, grab one. It's up on the second floor, down at the end of the hall."

"They let you take drinks and doughnuts from the faculty lounge?"

"No problemo. But just make sure the room is empty before you walk in, and if somebody catches you in there, just act mentally ill, like you wandered in by mistake and don't know where the hell you are."

* * *

An hour later, Harvey and Dexter leaned against the hood of Harvey's car. By the purplish light of the two lanterns, they stared at the little electronic device, about the size of a quarter.

Harvey asked, "You sure it's a locator?"

"Absolutely. A nice one too, very compact, and it sends a strong signal. Not some piece o' junk you buy at a spyware novelty store. Whoever's tracking you placed it under the dash and it was powered by the car's twelve-volt system."

"What would happen to this thing if the alternator went bad?"

"Well, it would run off the battery, like the other electrical systems in the car, until the battery went dead. Unless the alternator blows in a way that sends a voltage spike through the system, then it might burn out the GPS chip, because this thing had no surge protector on it."

"Okay. So, did they break into my car to place it?"

244

"They had to get the hood up. Either they jimmied the hood or broke into the passenger compartment to pull the hood release. Don't look so shocked, dude. I could break into your car with a toothpick."

* * *

As he drove home, Harvey felt exhausted. It had been a long and tiring day, both physically and emotionally. Now the most important thing for Harvey to do was get some rest because he decided *not* to quit the case. Not yet, at least. Tomorrow he would follow his one good lead.

He'd considered spending the night on the grimy floor in Dexter's office, but then decided he'd have to go back to his house because there was something there he needed.

The revolver.

A gift from Uncle Willie when Harvey started his business, the old revolver had sat all these months in Harvey's kitchen cabinet. Willie had finally upgraded to a nine-millimeter and figured Harvey could use the ancient but reliable .38 caliber wheel gun. Was there a chance he'd need it maybe tomorrow or the next day, or sometime before this thing was over? Harvey had such grand thoughts of being a tough guy private eye when he got the gun from Willie, but now the thought of even carrying it on a case made him nervous. When Harvey had apprenticed with his uncle, that revolver was *always* with Willie when he went out, tucked under his arm in a leather holster that was shiny from wear. Harvey remembered seeing the gun for the first time on his uncle's desk and being mesmerized by the old revolver's oily smell, its black metallic sheen, and the cold, hard feel of the barrel when he touched it in reverence. And now, incredibly, it belonged to Harvey.

But...did I really expect the gun to instantly make me like my uncle?

Maybe I'm kidding myself. Maybe I just don't have what it takes— whatever Uncle Willie has that makes him a great investigator.

Harvey thought through the implications of Jenny and Mike knowing where his car was at all times over the past week. Luckily when he visited Dexter, Harvey always parked in the campus visitor's lot.

From there it was a long walk to Dexter's building, which was situated within the dense cluster of all the science and engineering buildings. And since Harvey had switched phones before he ever called Dexter about this case, it was extremely unlikely they knew about Dexter's involvement.

But Harvey decided he shouldn't park in his driveway tonight because they might try to plant another tracker in his car while he slept.

When Harvey was within a half-mile of his house, he pulled over into the dirt parking lot of a boarded-up barbecue shack. He carefully pulled his car around the back of the building, then got out and walked to the front. Satisfied the car was invisible from the road, he began the walk back to his place.

Without streetlights, he walked in almost total darkness. There was no pavement and nothing but forest on both sides of the road. The shoulder he walked on was narrow, and although there weren't many cars out at this time of night, he felt a scary rush of wind as each one passed him. This was definitely not a stretch of road where a sane person would take a leisurely walk, which is why he should easily be able to spot anyone following him back to his car in the morning.

When Harvey reached his house, he entered without turning any lights on, slumped onto the couch, and was asleep within two minutes.

Chapter 37
Thursday, May 30, 9:12 a.m.

The next morning, Mike strolled the sidewalk in the village at a steady pace, wearing blue jeans, a dark blue windbreaker, a Yankees baseball cap, and a pair of eyeglasses with dark plastic rims. The lenses in his eyeglasses made no correction to his vision. He needed no help with his eyesight, for his vision was near perfect, but the glasses together with the cap changed his appearance just enough so that from a block away, it might make the difference between Harvey recognizing him or not.

Mike never wore fake beards or mustaches. They didn't look real enough unless they were put on by a professional make-up artist, and anything that didn't look real aroused suspicion, not necessarily in the person being pursued, who might be a block away, but instead in the people right around the pursuer. They might treat him differently, avoid getting too close to him, or walk away from him when they noticed something odd. And that kind of behavior might in turn be noticed by someone else much farther away. And fake facial hair wasn't the same as wearing a toupee. If you wore fake hair on top of your head and someone noticed, they might snicker at you, or maybe feel pity for you. But if they spotted you wearing a fake beard, they assumed it was part of a disguise and branded you as either a criminal, a cop, or a weirdo.

There were two additional changes Mike had made this morning to complete his transformation. He'd wrapped and securely tied a bedsheet around his midsection. It gave the appearance of an additional twenty pounds of weight. He couldn't go overboard and wear two sheets—it would look suspicious in comparison with the leanness of his face and limbs. The other thing he did was change the way he walked. It wasn't a limp he added, he never did limps, they were for amateurs, and a limp often attracted unwanted attention. Rather, he changed his gait so that he had a very slight bounce to his walk. He knew it was the added weight and the walk that would make the most difference to someone a block ahead who might give a casual glance backward, because the general outline of the body and how a person moved were the types of visual cues people relied on when trying to identify someone at a distance.

Harvey was ahead of Mike and on the other side of the street. There were plenty of people on the sidewalks despite the chill in the morning air. Main Street was already bustling with tourists who were window shopping or out getting some breakfast. Some were making quick takeout stops at one of the coffeehouses. But Mike noted that Harvey wasn't window shopping, and was probably not out to get breakfast either. He walked in a straight and steady manner as if he were on a mission.

Today it was just Mike doing the stalking. Using a drone, he had tracked Harvey early this morning as he walked to the spot where he parked his car last night. Mike was almost disappointed in Harvey because it was pretty dumb of him to assume he could give them the slip simply by parking a half-mile away. But here in the village with the crowds and the stores, the drone wasn't very useful, and anyway it was usually illegal to fly them over commercial areas, so it might have soon been brought to the attention of the local cops. Following on foot was the only way to do it here, and Mike would have to be very observant and very careful if he was going to keep Harvey in his sights without being spotted himself. It was easy to follow someone. The challenging part was to follow without being noticed. Mike would have to keep a safe distance away, and he knew Harvey would be on alert after the last incident. Fortunately, Harvey had not even glanced behind him yet.

Harvey abruptly stepped into a drugstore and Mike found himself facing his first tough decision of the day. Should he run to the back of the store and cover the rear door or should he wait here to keep an eye on the front door?

Mike moved farther down the street and reached a point where he could see ten or fifteen feet into the store through the open doorway.

Fortunately, the sun was low in the sky and shining through the door, which the proprietor had left open despite the chill, probably to let in some fresh morning air.

Mike was certain Harvey hadn't spotted him yet, so he quickly decided his best play would be to watch the front door instead of covering the back. But Mike couldn't just stand here on the sidewalk. If he could see partway into the store, then someone inside would have an excellent view of Mike as well, especially since he was standing out in the morning sun. Mike would have to go for some cover immediately. Fortunately, he was directly in front of a coffeehouse with an outdoor service counter and six tables on the sidewalk. Mike quickly went to the counter and stood behind a woman who was paying for her order. He faced sideways as he waited so he could see the door of the drugstore out of the corner of his eye.

In less than a minute, he was at the service counter. The aromas coming through the little opening were enticing— other than the earthy fragrance of darkly roasted coffee beans, he picked up hints of cinnamon, chocolate, and hazelnuts from the breakfast pastries. Mike paid for his coffee and then sat down at an unoccupied table well out of the foot traffic stream. From here, the only thing that would block his view of the drugstore's door, and only for about a second at a time, was the occasional bus that drove by. He took out his cellphone and lowered his head to pretend he was reading. He knew that a person sitting alone at a table was always conspicuous, but much less so if they were reading. His eyes were all the while on the drugstore.

Prepared to move at a second's notice, Mike waited for Harvey to reappear. He kept his eye out for Harvey's tan baseball cap and his dark blue jacket with the wide green stripes on the sleeves.

Mike looked at his watch every minute or so, sipping his coffee between glances.

Three minutes passed. Add to that the four minutes that had elapsed from the time Harvey went into the drugstore to when Mike got his coffee, and it totaled seven minutes. A long time to be in a drugstore? Maybe not. Mike had certainly waited in drugstores for longer than seven minutes when getting a prescription filled. Had he and Jenny come across any prescription medicine bottles in Harvey's place when they had searched it, bottles that might need refilling? Mike didn't think so.

Four more minutes passed. What did a young, healthy fellow like Harvey need in a drugstore anyway? Then again, drugstores today sold all sorts of junk.

After another three minutes, Mike was halfway through his cup of coffee. He watched more people enter and leave the drugstore but he didn't see Harvey. Now he was getting concerned. Maybe Harvey was leafing through magazine racks or something? No, he wasn't the type to waste his time like that. Harvey was on a case, the first big case of his life, and he was obsessed with it. He should be spending almost every waking moment on it.

Just then, Mike saw the blue jacket and tan baseball cap pass through the sunny area near the doorway, then disappear back into the store. He relaxed and took another sip of his coffee.

Okay, so he was walking around inside the store. Maybe he was looking for a birthday card for somebody. Some people take a long time to pick cards out. Mike sat back to wait it out. The breakfast pastry that the woman at the next table was eating smelled delicious. It looked like it had some kind of a honey and nut topping. He thought about buying one but decided against it. Harvey would probably be out any second, and Mike would have to move quickly.

But after another three minutes passed without Harvey appearing, Mike was concerned again. His instincts told him something wasn't right.

He's been in there too long.

Could he have left the store already? Unlikely. But it was possible. Harvey would have been watching for a tail, and if he'd spotted Mike over here, and if he'd waited near the door for a bus to come, and if there had been enough people on the sidewalk at the moment the bus came... but then again, maybe Harvey didn't even have to go to all that trouble. He might have left by the rear door. Proprietors almost always locked their rear doors to prevent shoplifters from sneaking out the back, but if Harvey knew the owner...and then Mike saw the blue jacket and tan baseball cap appear again for two seconds before they disappeared back into the store.

Is he jerking me around? The moment I get worried he's been out of sight too long, he appears, then disappears.

Mike stood up from the table, tossed his empty paper cup into a trash can, and walked about fifty feet to the nearest intersection. He didn't want to jaywalk in broad daylight, which might attract attention. There was no light at the intersection, so he waited a few seconds for a small break in the traffic, and then crossed the street with a few other people. When he reached the curb, he quickly turned left and walked to the drugstore, hugging the storefronts along the way. Just before reaching the door, Mike stopped. He didn't want to just barge in and take the chance he'd walk right into Harvey. Shielding his eyes from the sun, Mike leaned into the doorway so he could peek inside.

And then he froze.

He saw the coat and baseball cap. Harvey stood only five or six feet away but faced the inside of the store. Mike tensed his calves to make the turn so he could immediately put some distance between himself and Harvey, but in the fraction of a second before his leg muscles could respond, Mike saw something strange—strands of curly blond hair hanging out from under the cap. And Harvey didn't have curly hair.

"Hey," Mike said out loud, as he jumped into the doorway and grabbed the blue coat, spinning Harvey around, and ...

It wasn't Harvey.

"How's it goin', dude?" Dexter said.

"Goddammit!" Mike grabbed Dexter by the coat collar with both hands and pulled so their faces were only inches apart. "Where's your friend?"

"I have no friends. Will you be my friend?"

Mike spoke in a low, menacing voice. "Listen, you fuckin' geek, where's Harvey and who the fuck are you?"

"Well, I gotta be going now. It was real nice meeting you, and..."

251

"You're not going anywhere." Mike quickly turned so that he was side to side with Dexter, and with his right hand, he firmly gripped Dexter's left upper arm. Mike put his hand inside his jacket, pulled his gun from the shoulder holster, and jammed the barrel into Dexter's ribs. "Feel this?"

Dexter knew what it was. The goofy smile left his face.

Mike gave a hard tug on Dexter's arm and in seconds they were through the doorway and standing on the sidewalk, locked together like best buddies. Mike quickly looked up and down the street and spotted an alley between two stores, about twenty feet away.

"Move," he yelled, pushing Dexter toward the alley.

Dexter moved, but it was downward. He melted. Mike couldn't support him as he collapsed into a blob on the sidewalk. And then Dexter did something bizarre. He started to shake.

"Look, that guy is having a seizure!" cried a middle-aged woman, pointing to Dexter. Behind her was an older woman, who also stopped to look at the young man writhing on the sidewalk.

In seconds, two more people stopped to gawk, and then another group of four.

"Look, Mommy," said a little boy who had just come out of the hobby shop next to the drugstore. "There's spit coming out of his mouth." The mother looked with helplessness at Dexter who was flat on his back on the cold sidewalk, convulsing and drooling.

As more people gathered from all sides, Mike started taking slow backward steps, until he was out of the circle formed by the onlookers. An elderly man pulled a cell phone from his pocket and said, "I'll call an ambulance."

The woman who had first pointed to Dexter spoke again: "Is there a doctor or nurse here? Does anyone know what to do? Anybody know first aid?" The people in the crowd shook their heads. They could only stare at the spectacle and wait for the ambulance to come.

Mike started walking up the street. He didn't think anyone in the crowd had really taken notice of him and Dexter leaving the drugstore together.

He cursed his own stupidity. Fooled by a couple of bush leaguers. Harvey was surely long gone in his car by now. Mike quickly headed back to his own car.

He picked up his pace to a fast jog as he pulled his cell from his pocket to call Jenny.

Chapter 38
Thursday, May 28, 10:46 a.m.

Zoober drove slowly, his eyes moving between the road ahead, the odometer, and the rearview mirror. Beale gazed steadily out the passenger window at the treeline along the roadside, which was shrouded in fog.

Beale asked, "So, where is it? I don't see anything."

"Martinez said it was exactly one point eight miles north of the intersection of routes 4 and 78A, in the town of Port Kole. It's got to be right around here. We should be within two hundred feet of it."

"Then pull over. Let's get out and walk."

Zoober turned the wheel gently to the right and eased the car onto the gravel shoulder. The detectives got out and walked the ten feet through the grass to the treeline. A dense grove of maple trees shrouded the roadside. The new spring leaves formed a lush canopy that dripped with moisture from the brief rain that had just ended. Beale turned up his coat collar against the dampness.

"Right there," said Zoober, pointing. "Just north of that fallen tree."

They took thirty paces and found the small opening to the bike trail, between the thick trunks of two mature maple trees. The trail surface here had the same appearance as at the other end, behind the Mexican restaurant, bumpy from protruding rocks and tree roots. Beale took a few steps in until his left foot promptly sunk into a mud puddle. The ooze engulfed his shoe and reached his sock.

"Goddamn!" Beale cursed, pulling his foot from the muck with a great sucking sound. He backed away from the trail opening and then did his best to wipe the sludge from his shoe onto the grass.

"I think there are some rags in the trunk," Zoober said.

"Forget it," Beale snapped, pissed off at his carelessness. "I'll survive."

Beale turned around and surveyed the general area. The only buildings in sight were a gas station about a hundred yards south of the trail and the local sheriff's station a little farther down the road.

"What do you think the total length of the bike trail is?" asked Beale.

"Martinez measured it as almost two miles."

"Does the trail intersect any roads?"

"No. Martinez found it was totally wooded around the trail, no roads or houses. The only thing the trail crosses are a couple of shallow streams."

"And did you find out who owns the land?"

"A developer. Maybe someday it will be cleared for houses, but the latest versions of the county map, the internet map, and the satellite shots all agree with what Martinez saw. There are no dwellings or streets at all in this tract of land."

"So, the kids don't live anywhere in that land between the Mexican restaurant and here. We're close to the center of Port Kole, right? They could live somewhere in this town, or maybe on the outskirts. About how many houses are in Port Kole?"

"Several hundred," answered Zoober.

"Hmmmm. So, this area probably has lots of kids and I'll bet most of 'em have bikes." Beale paused for a moment and considered whether it was worth expending any more effort to find the kids.

"How far are we from Homerton Springs, where they found the body?" asked Beale.

"About twenty-five miles."

"Well, it's a long shot, but let's go down the road and talk to the gas station people and the local cops. You take the gas station. Maybe the kids stop in there to buy candy bars and sodas. I'll take the cops."

Zoober looked worried at the suggestion he and Beale split up, as he remembered how rudely Beale had treated the sheriff in Homerton Springs.

The two detectives got back into the car. Zoober pulled out onto the road, made a U-turn, and drove the short distance to the police station. He parked the car and then began to walk the two hundred feet along the road to the gas station while Beale walked toward the front door of the sheriff's station.

Beale looked at the tiny building in front of him, a simple box of cinderblocks painted white and covered with a flat tarred roof. The high radio antenna attached to the side of the building was its only distinguishing feature. In the parking lot there was a single sheriff's car which appeared to be about ten years old. The car's body was rusted around the fenders.

He knew what to expect. Beale figured this station probably had just one or two deputies. No one on duty at night. They most likely used call forwarding to send the off-hours calls to one of the deputies' houses. And God help you if you were in some real trouble in the middle of the night around here because by the time the bleary-eyed deputy picked up the phone to hear the emergency call, pulled himself out of bed, found the bullets for his gun, took a crap and finally got in his car to leave, you'd be dead or close to it.

Beale walked through the door and saw the deputy sitting behind his desk, gulping coffee from a grimy ceramic mug. He was about seventy years old, small and squat in stature, with a shock of snow-white hair buzzed flat on top. He wore a pair of thick glasses with heavy wire frames. The collar of his gray uniform was badly frayed, and the purple clip-on tie he wore sported stains from various lunches eaten over the last ten or twenty years.

Beale thought, *Probably this guy's nearing the end of an illustrious law enforcement career.* The deputy had a newspaper spread out in front of him, and he appeared to be surprised by the interruption.

Beale flashed his badge. "Lieutenant Beale, Albany PD," he said, acting as if he were the deputy's boss, expecting the man to snap to attention.

Beale looked around quickly at the dreary one-room station house which had three desks, a few file cabinets, a lavatory in the far corner, and a small lockup made from chain link fence. He didn't waste any time. "Deputy, I'm lookin' for some kids, three boys about twelve years old, who ride their bicycles on that path through the woods, the one that starts across the road, north of that gas station out there. You know 'em?"

"Kids," the deputy said with a country nasal twang. "Kids?"

"Yeah, that's right. Kids. People like you and me, but smaller." *This guy is slow as shit. Must have just got up from his mid-morning nap.*

"The deputy scratched at his forehead, stood up, and said: "Well, now, there's lots of kids ridin' bikes around here, that's for sure. Lots of kids in this town, and I'll bet almost all of 'em have bikes. So why do you wanna know?"

Beale thought for a moment about how much or how little he wanted to tell the deputy. He decided to give the basic story without details.

"At the other end of that bike trail is a Mexican restaurant with a trash dumpster in the back. We think three boys may have pulled a raft out of the dumpster, a raft that may have been used to dump a body in the lake. And so, we wanna talk to those boys. Simple as that." *So simple that even you can understand it, I hope.*

"Well, lots o' kids ride on that trail. Looks like fun to me."

"And you just let 'em go? Is it legal to ride a bicycle in there, deputy?"

"Well now, it *is* private property, but the owner don't seem to mind, or maybe he don't know about it. If he asked me to stop 'em, I would, you know. But I can't see it does any harm. Better'n havin' the little ones ridin' on one of these busy roads. And I don't let motorbikes go in there, no sir. Let's see, I'd say in the category of boys that could pass for twelve years old, we got at least fifty that bike on that trail, maybe even more. Yeah, I heard about the body pulled from the lake over by... where the hell was it? Oh yeah, over by Homerton Springs. But I didn't know they brought the city cops in on it." Beale noted the deputy seemed aghast at the idea of calling in outside help. The man was apparently convinced that he and the other local cops could handle everything from jaywalkers to nuclear terrorists. "So, why'd they need city cops to investigate?"

'Cause it seems like every local cop around here couldn't find his own prick by searching his pants? thought Beale, but he decided to give a less confrontational answer: "They tried to get one of those caped superheroes but they were all real busy, so they called us."

The deputy gave a blank stare, unfazed as the sarcasm sailed right over his head.

Beale decided it was time to leave. This guy was too stupid to be insulted, and this conversation was likely to be about as productive as looking for the impression of a displaced rock along a hundred miles of shoreline.

"Well, I think I'm done here, deputy," Beale said with a disgusted shake of his head. "Sounds like you can't help me."

"I guess not. We don't register bike owners. You'd have to go door to door asking about these twelve-year-old boys on bikes. Or hang around the trailhead and question kids as they go in and come out. And as far as the body in the lake, I can't offer any new information there, we've got no missing people in this town right now." The deputy paused and then added in a low voice: "Well, maybe except for..."

The deputy's voice trailed off, as he decided not to finish the sentence.

But Beale asked: "Except for who?"

The deputy looked sorry he'd mentioned it at all. He leaned back in the old wooden armchair, then said with apparent reluctance: "Well, there's a guy lives here in Port Kole, his wife came here about a week ago and said he was missing. It's more'n likely he's out on a drunk somewhere. It's happened with this guy a couple times before. She said she'd call us if he showed up, but I haven't heard from her yet. If he doesn't surface in a few more days, then we might have to treat it as a missing person."

Beale paused as he considered whether to take this new bit of information seriously. It was probably just one more dead-end.

"How long has he lived here?"

"He's been in Port Kole maybe, oh, between five and seven years."

"And how many times has this guy been 'out on a drunk' as you said, in his time here?"

"Maybe three times."

"And what's the missing guy's height and weight?"

"Hmmm. I'd say about... five-eleven, with an average build."

Beale nodded his head in consideration. "Close enough. Got a picture of him?"

The deputy pulled an envelope from his desk drawer, removed a photograph from it, and showed it to Beale, who took out his cell and brought up a picture of the corpse. He compared the two photos, frowned, and said, "There's enough of a resemblance that I think we should have his wife take a look at the body. Unless maybe you have his DNA profile?"

A dumb look came over the deputy's face as if he had no idea what DNA was.

Beale shook his head in disgust and said, "You know what deputy? Let's just have the wife take a look. The body's face is kinda bloated but a wife will know her husband. What did the wife say about the circumstances of his disappearance?"

"To the best of my recollection, she said he just got in his car and took off one day. I told her, as gently as I could, we'd have to wait a while before we listed him as missing, on account of his drunken reputation. And he's got another reputation, too, for runnin' around with young women, and he could have took off with one of 'em."

"Sounds like a real soap opera. Give me the address, my partner and I will go over and visit her."

"I could do it myself," said the deputy. "How 'bout if I go over and talk to her again, see if there's anything new, then I'll call you?"

Beale thought: *No way, I ain't waitin' another three weeks.*

"My partner will handle it," said Beale, trying to contain his anger at having his order questioned. "He's great at this stuff. Fantastic bedside manner. He'll talk to her, and then if he thinks it's appropriate, he'll be able to convince her to come down and take a look at the body." Beale figured he'd get a ride back to Albany by calling Martinez, who was probably still somewhere in the area with his mountain bike strapped to the back of his car, waiting to see if any more assistance was needed. Zoober would take their car to go see this woman.

"Well, geez-o-pete, you guys must be pretty slim on leads if you're gonna personally follow *this* one up. Like I said, I really think he's probably drunk somewhere, like before."

Beale thought about the raft fingerprint report, which had yielded no useful information at all because all the prints except for the children's were now accounted for. He also thought about his great *witnesses* like the Army-Navy store owner Dale Huckman, whose memory had proved to be too feeble to provide any physical descriptions, and the old coot by the lake who was much too far away to give any description of the person in the raft. Beale shook his head in disgust. "You're right about one thing, deputy, I *am* slim on leads, and I may have to sit out there waiting for those kids to show up at the beginning of this bike trail, or go door to door in your town and ask every kid around twelve years old if he has a bike and found a raft recently. And if me and my partner are gonna go to those lengths and spend some time in your fine town, then I think visiting one more house to see this woman might not be too much additional work."

The deputy paused for a few seconds, then shrugged his shoulders and said with resignation: "All right, but I'll go with your partner to see her. We don't want to give her the impression that city cops have to do our jobs for us, do we?" He snickered as if he'd made a hilarious joke.

Beale couldn't give a shit about what this woman thought of the local cops. But he'd tell Zoober to go and talk to her, and Beale figured his partner, who got along with everyone, wouldn't mind bringing the deputy along.

"What's her name?" asked Beale.

"Pamela Damler. Nice lady. Her husband's name is Grant."

Chapter 39
Thursday, May 28, 10:58 a.m.

Harvey drove slowly by the sign that read: *Entering the Town of MERIDIAN,* and beneath that: *A Little Bit of Paradise.* Little was right. Even though it was only about twenty-five miles from the bustle of Albany, the whole town consisted of about two dozen buildings scattered along either side of the state highway. Harvey could see that the combination service station and car repair shop he was looking for was ahead on the right. Just beyond it, there was a diner and a small general store that probably doubled as the post office. The remaining buildings that made up this tiny hamlet were all within three hundred yards of each other. Then nothing, for as far as Harvey could see down the highway, except for forest and green fields dotted with grazing cows.

He pulled into the gas station and parked right below a hanging sign that was rusted at the edges. It read, in bold blue letters: *Zeke's Fill 'er Up and Car Repair.* In slightly smaller print, the line below declared Zeke to be *The Car Doctor.* The building was stark but functional, a boxy-looking brick structure. There were two front-facing garage doors that were closed, and at the bottom of each was a small opening for a car exhaust hose, one of which was belching a plume of bluish-gray smoke. Harvey opened the building's front door and walked into the tiny customer service area. The smell of car exhaust was immediately evident, a result of the poor ventilation in the room, but it wasn't quite strong enough to completely mask the burnt and bitter odor of bad coffee. On top of the customer counter were a cash register and a tray with a dusty assortment of chewing gum and candy bars. The rest of the merchandise hung on the wall, the usual service station items including car air fresheners, combs, small packets of aspirin, and a very impressive assortment of multi-colored condoms. Next to the door leading to the garage was the tiny table that held the offending coffee maker; It sat within a puddle of spilled sugar that provided a feast for a colony of happy ants. There was a single wooden chair where a customer might wait while his car was getting fixed, passing the time by drinking the bad coffee and perhaps reading the one seven-year-old issue of National Geographic that rested in the magazine rack on the wall.

A girl of about fourteen stood behind the counter, with a look of total boredom on her face. Slightly stout, with reddish curls and bright red lipstick, she was too young to be wearing the gobs of eyeliner that Harvey could see had been applied with a hand that was obviously a bit unpracticed at the task. She'd surely be ready to blow this small town the minute she got her driver's license, or sooner if the opportunity arose. Harvey was uncertain whether he should declare himself a private detective and start questioning this adolescent.

He turned to her and asked in a voice which he made certain was loud enough to break any daydreaming spell: "Miss, can I talk to Mr. Zeke?"

She slowly looked up at Harvey and replied in an unenthusiastic voice: "Ain't no Zeke. It's just a name."

"A name?"

"Yeah, you know, just a catchy name to draw in the customers."

"Oh. Does it work?"

"Oh, yeah. We're turnin' them away."

A fourteen-year-old with an attitude. Harvey shrugged. "My name's Harvey Grace. I'm a private detective. I've been hired to look for someone and I have a couple of questions to ask." He waited to see if she would offer to answer. She eyed him suspiciously.

"I better get Mel," she said, and she walked to the door which led into the garage, opened it, and the smell of car exhaust immediately increased tenfold. Harvey turned his head away and coughed, but the girl didn't even flinch. *She must be used to it,* Harvey thought. *Not the greatest thing, for a teenage girl to be breathing in carbon monoxide all day.*

"Mel, somebody here to see you," she shouted, so she could be heard over the sound of the idling engine. "A detective."

In a few seconds, Mel came into the service area, wiping his hands on a greasy rag. The girl walked back behind the counter and leaned forward on it, her chin in her hand, waiting to listen to Harvey ask his questions. Maybe this would give her a tiny break from her boredom.

Mel was in his mid-thirties, wearing a one-piece blue coverall that had a huge grease spot on the chest. His face was rough but pleasant, and his hair was combed up in a moussed pompadour. *Maybe a James Dean fan?* thought Harvey. The long sideburns and the cigarette propped over his left ear completed Mel's retro visage.

"Detective? You a police officer?" Mel looked surprised, but not concerned.

"No, I'm a private detective, sir. My name is Harvey Grace, and I've been hired to look for a missing person. I'd just like to ask you a few questions."

Harvey went right into his first question, not bothering to first ask Mel if he'd be willing to answer, and not allowing Mel the time to even think about whether he wanted to talk to a PI or not. Uncle Willie had long ago given Harvey this little tip: *"You start asking questions with confidence, so the person you're talking to figures that you ask people questions fifty times a day and they all answer every question, so of course he will, too."*

"I'm trying to locate a man who drives a 2010 Z4. He may have had it worked on here. Did you service a Z4 recently?"

"About when?" asked Mel, as he continued to wipe his hands.

"Last Wednesday or sometime after that."

"Why do you think he came here?"

"The woman who hired me to look for her husband said he drove a Z4 with an alternator that might have been faulty. That's an expensive part that hardly ever goes bad, and no auto repair places keep it in stock, not even dealers. I contacted the BMW parts distribution center for the northeast. They shipped out only three of these alternators recently. One was shipped here." Harvey paused. Mel looked thoughtful and Harvey wondered if he would answer with yet another question. They were both a bit surprised when the next remark came from the girl behind the counter.

"So, what'd this guy do, anyway? Beat up his wife or something? Did he shoot her?" A cynical question coming from the lips of a fourteen-year-old. She leaned forward over the counter, perked up by the possibility of hearing some sordid story of love, betrayal, and violence, and about how life was dangerous and exciting outside the boundaries of this tiny, dull burg.

Harvey said, "No, nothing like that. His wife is worried about him. He's not a hundred percent mentally stable, you know?" Harvey tapped his head. A white lie that would make it seem to Mel that by giving Harvey the information, a good deed would be done. "Sometimes he goes away for days, this time he's gone longer than usual." The girl was disappointed at Harvey's mundane answer. She sunk back into her bored silence.

"Yeah, we had an alternator delivered here last week that I installed in a Z4. I did it Thursday morning, I think."

"What color was the car?"

"Green," replied Mel. "And I think it was a 2010."

Harvey's heart started to beat a bit faster.

"But it was brought in by a woman, not a man," added Mel.

"A woman? Uh, well, do you know the plate number and the woman's name and address?"

"I'll have to look it up." Mel walked behind the counter and the girl stepped aside as he bent down to pull a service log from a low shelf. He paged through it and quickly found the entry.

"It was last Wednesday the car came in, New York plate CRN1753. The woman was named Danielle Williams. She gave me a New York address."

Harvey's disappointment was evident. He wrote down the plate number but it wasn't even close to the one from the little old lady's car that had been totaled. "Do you know the car's vehicle identification number?" asked Harvey.

"Nope. We don't record 'em, just the plate number."

Harvey shrugged. *All right, so a green Z4 got a new alternator here last week. Just a coincidence, maybe. Green was probably one of the most popular colors for the sporty little roadster, anyway.*

He might have to visit the places where the other two alternators had been delivered, even though they were quite a distance from here. Of the three car repair shops, *Zeke's* had seemed to Harvey to offer the greatest chance of success, seeing that it was fairly close to Saylorville, and Mike had said that their tracking signal was lost when the car was heading west, away from Saylorville.

But of course, who knew if Mike and Jenny were telling the truth about the tracking device?

"This woman, did you *see* her name on the registration?" asked Harvey.

"No, we don't ask to see registrations unless we do a state inspection."

"Was the woman with anybody?"

"No. She came in alone."

"Is there any chance she was with someone, maybe a man who waited outside for her? This man, maybe?" Harvey pulled Grant's picture from his jacket pocket, and walked over to Mel, holding the picture in front of him.

"Is this the guy who's missing?" asked Mel.

"Yes."

"Well, I've never seen him before, and I'd say that it's pretty unlikely that she was with someone who waited outside because she was in here for some time. She waited in this room while I pulled her car in the garage to check it out."

"And about how long did it take you to check the car?"

"It took just a few minutes to figure out the alternator was dead. She was lucky to make it here, she said the warning light was on for a good many miles. When I told her she needed a new alternator, she waited right here while I called the parts distributor to ask them how fast they could get one to me, and they put me on hold for about five minutes.

Then they finally told me they could deliver one here the next morning. After I told the woman where she could go for something to eat and where she could get a room for the night, she took a shoulder bag out of the back seat of the car and left. Now if there was someone with her, I'm sure he would've come inside, too, unless he was hiding out there because he didn't want to be seen or something."

Harvey asked: "This woman, was she young and attractive?"

"Yes, she was young and *very* attractive." Mel glanced over at the teenager, and he saw she was smirking again.

"Is this her?" Harvey pulled the picture of Linda Johnson from his pocket and held it in front of Mel. Up to now, Mel had thought that Harvey's interrogation was a waste of time for both of them, but when he saw the picture, his eyes widened.

"Yeah, that's her all right"

Harvey thought, *Jackpot. She gave a false name, and she must have switched plates again.*

"Is this the missing guy's wife?" asked Mel.

"No. It's his... er ... friend ... that he was traveling with." Harvey didn't say it very convincingly. The teenager's eyes lit up at the renewed prospect of hearing about some sordid infidelity.

Harvey added, "And you said the name of the woman was Danielle Williams. How did she pay you?"

"Cash. I remember 'cause a new alternator for this car ain't cheap, and she had to pay extra for the overnight shipping, too. When I finished the job the next day and she came back to pick it up, she pulled out a nice stack of twenty-dollar bills. She ended up buying a new battery from me, too. I told her I could charge up the old battery for free, but she wanted a brand new one. She didn't want to take a chance with the old battery that was nearly drained from running with a bad alternator. And by the look of that stack of bills, I got the idea it was no big deal for her to drop another hundred and fifty bucks on a battery."

"Did she seem angry or upset about staying overnight in this town?"

"No, I wouldn't say angry or upset. She didn't seem real happy about it, but she accepted that she didn't have much choice. She asked about renting a car, but there's nothing to rent in this town. The closest rental place is in a town about eight miles from here, and she called them to see if they could get her a car, but it was closed. By that time, it was late, after six p.m. And then she called a few rental places in Albany, but they wouldn't deliver a car out here. We're a little too far out."

"So, she left here that night at about what time?"

"Around six-fifteen, I'd say."

"And you suggested someplace where she could get a meal?"

"Yeah, not a hard decision. There's only one place in town, the diner. It's just up the road, about a hundred yards north of here. And there's only one place to stay overnight, too -- The Shady Maple Motel. It's next to the diner."

"What time did she come back the next day?"

"The alternator arrived at about nine in the morning. I called her right away, told her I'd have it done in about an hour. She showed up here around ten. She paid and left."

"Did she say where she was headed?"

"Nope. And I didn't ask. None of my business. There was no small talk between us. She seemed anxious to get going."

"The day she brought the car in, did she talk about anything at all other than the repair and where to eat and spend the night?"

"No. Like I said, she was pleasant enough, but not talkative."

"Were you the only one here that she spoke to?"

Harvey turned his head toward the girl behind the counter, who was still listening. She made no attempt at all to respond.

"Yep, just me," was Mel's reply. "Rhonda there doesn't work on Wednesdays or Thursdays. And she hardly works the other days." He nodded his head toward the girl, and then looked at her with a smirk, in return for the one that she'd given him earlier.

"Could you give me the woman's cell number?" asked Harvey. Mel looked in the logbook again and obligingly read the number to Harvey, who recorded it in his cellphone.

"All right then, thanks, Mel...and Rhonda."

Harvey left, and in his car he called the number that Mel had just given him, not certain what he would say if Linda Johnson answered. He thought that he might pose as a person from Zeke's doing a customer satisfaction follow-up, and inquire about whether she was fully satisfied with the repair. But after one ring Harvey heard a recorded message saying that the person he called was unavailable and voice messaging was not enabled. He guessed she'd been using a prepaid cell phone and had probably tossed it by now.

Harvey eased the car out onto the highway and drove slowly until he reached the Imperial Diner. It was a small, fifties-style establishment, a flat-roofed, bus-shaped building with a sheet metal exterior, trimmed with hot pink and lime green stripes. A garish neon sign announced that it served the best food in New York State. This was undoubtedly the proper place to stop after you just received the best auto repair service at Zeke's.

Harvey parked his car in front, hopped out, and pushed at the heavy glass and metal double doors. He immediately caught the pleasant aromas of freshly baked blueberry muffins and apple pie. Inside, the fifties theme was unblemished. Chrome and red vinyl were everywhere. The shiny black and white checkerboard linoleum floor looked as if it had just been waxed. Patrons had a choice of taking either a booth or one of the shiny stools with padded red tops that lined the counter like soldiers at attention. The stools were vacant except for the two men who sat next to each other at the far end of the counter. They both appeared to be about ninety years old, and their backs faced the counter as they stared at everybody and everything. The waitress, an attractive woman with her brown hair efficiently tied back in a bun, was busy behind the counter, using the slack time to tidy up. Although she appeared to be in her fifties, she moved with the energy and the sprightly step of a twenty-year-old. She turned to greet Harvey and told him with a welcoming smile that he could have a seat anywhere at all.

"Thanks," he replied, and he plopped down on a stool right in front of her.

"Would you like a menu?" the waitress asked.

"I'll just have some orange juice, thanks. And a blueberry muffin." The wonderful aroma was too much for Harvey to resist.

She smiled again and within twenty seconds there was a glass of cold, fresh juice in front of Harvey. He began to sip it.

Harvey turned casually toward the two elderly men at the end of the counter. They both wore baseball caps, windbreakers, black socks, and bright white sneakers. Their caps were identical, both sky blue in color with a large patch on the front that said *Coopman's Manure Spreaders* in bold black lettering. They eyed Harvey with curiosity and suspicion, not flinching in the least when he stared back at their weathered, leathery faces. The two men mumbled to each other out the sides of their mouths as they gawked, and Harvey guessed they were talking about just what kind of an asshole had walked into the diner now. It was probably their business to know everyone else's business, sitting there like they owned the place, staring at people for hours at a clip, sucking down their free coffee refills, and maybe taking breaks to use the can, but never going at the same time to exclude the possibility of missing anything.

As the waitress put a plate in front of Harvey that held a warm muffin and several slices of butter, he said to her: "Ma'am, my name's Harvey Grace. I'm a private detective hired to look for a young woman who may have stayed in town last week, on Wednesday night while she was getting her car fixed. She may have come in here that night for some dinner, and maybe again the following morning for breakfast."

"Well, Wednesday and Thursday are my days off," the waitress said. "The waitress on duty those nights is Sarah, but she's off today. Why don't you try those two guys, they might've seen this person you're looking for." She nodded toward the two elderly men. Harvey looked at the men again, and the waitress saw the reservation in Harvey's eyes.

"Oh, don't worry. They're harmless."

"They don't look very friendly. Who are they?"

"They own the place."

"Huh?"

269

"They're the owners, the Tule brothers. That's Homer on the left, Gleason on the right. Homer and Gleason Tule."

"You mean they really own this diner?"

"That's right, and they hang out here a lot."

"Hmmm, yeah, I guessed as much. I'll give it a try."

Harvey slipped off the stool and walked slowly toward Homer and Gleason. They stared at him with as much expression as if they were looking at a dog turd that had been tracked in on the restaurant floor. Their cool flustered Harvey, and he forgot his usual opening line about being a private detective.

"Hi," began Harvey with a forced smile. "I'm not from around here..."

"No shit," said Gleason.

"And I need some information. I'm looking for a woman who may have come in here on Wednesday night of last week for dinner, and maybe the next morning for breakfast. Here's her picture." He held the picture of Linda Johnson steadily in front of them. They barely gave it a glance. He hoped that their vision was okay, or the whole interview was pointless. They both wore glasses with super heavy-duty steel frames, a style the army might issue that would probably survive a direct hit from a sniper rifle. Harvey added: "She stayed in town Wednesday night while her car was getting fixed, and—"

"She's your girlfriend, isn't she?"

"Huh? No, she's..."

"Run out on you, right?" Homer said in a matter-of-fact tone. "Cheated on you? And now you want her back real bad, don't you? So bad you can taste it."

"So bad it hurts like hell, doesn't it?" asked Gleason.

Harvey interceded: "No actually, she's just a ..."

"Heartbreaker, that's what she is."

These guys are whacked. It's all the caffeine, probably. Twenty-six cups a day, it fries your brain and ties your bowels in a knot. "Thank you, gentlemen," said Harvey politely as he gave up trying to get their cooperation. "I guess you haven't seen her or don't remember her." He turned and began to walk back to his muffin.

"She ordered a steak," Harvey heard from behind him.

He stopped and turned back toward them. "Pardon me?"

"A steak," said Homer. "Took one bite, then put her cigarette out on top of the rest, and pushed the plate aside. What a waste. If she didn't want it, I coulda given it to my dog, but she smeared cigarette ash all over it. A damn shame. A complete waste of good meat. We serve only the best here."

"That's right, only the best," Gleason repeated.

"Um, so she ate dinner here," said Harvey hopefully. "Or at least, one bite of her dinner. Did she also come back for breakfast the next morning?"

Homer's turn. "Nope. But then, some people don't even eat breakfast. *I* don't. I just have coffee in the morning."

"Where did she sit for dinner, by the way?"

"Right over there," Gleason answered, pointing to a booth that was only ten feet away from them.

At that distance, Homer and Gleason would have had their eyes on her the whole time.

"Did she sit with anybody?"

"Nope."

"Did she talk to anybody?"

"Nope. Just us."

"She talked to you? What did she say? Did she mention where she was headed?"

"No," answered Homer. "She seemed like a smart lady who knew what she wanted and where she was going. But she did ask us if route 64 floods when it rains a lot. That's somethin' you can't read on a map or learn from one of those fancy-ass smartphone direction gizmos. We've had a lot of rain around here lately. Some roads in this county were closed from the flooding, maybe she heard about that."

"And does route sixty-four flood?"

"Nope," said Gleason without hesitation. Harvey wasn't sure which brother to address. Ask one a question and the other would answer.

"Where exactly does route sixty-four run?"

"It runs south," answered Homer after downing the dregs in his cup. He gave a silent signal to the waitress and she walked over to them with the coffee pot. "You catch it from this road, about a mile west of here, that's where it starts... or ends, dependin' on which way you're headed."

"And you said she didn't say where she was headed. Well, what's the first town you'll come to if you take route sixty-four?"

"Graver's Falls," said Gleason, pointing over his brother's head. Harvey assumed he was pointing south.

"Graver's Falls. Never heard of it."

"Not surprised, unless you're from around here. It's no bigger than the town you're in now."

"What if you go farther on route sixty-four, what's the next town you'll come to after Graver's Falls?"

"Hartwell," Homer said after a sip of his freshly filled cup. "It's pretty big. That's where I go to buy shoes. They got a Walmart there."

Hartwell. Harvey had heard that name before, just recently. Was it a person's name? Or was it in reference to a place? Then he remembered: *He had a cabin in the woods, over near Hartwell.* Douglas Johnson had said that about Linda's cousin, Elliot.

Harvey flipped through the pages in his small notebook and found the entry. It read: *Elliot / Linda's cousin / Stensen's Garage, Hurst Street / cabin near Hartwell.*

And fortunately, Harvey was sure he hadn't told Jenny about Elliot when he'd briefed her on his interview with Douglas Johnson. Or, for that matter, about Grant's possibly faulty alternator.

"Excuse me, I need to make a call," Harvey said to the Tule brothers.

Harvey went back to his seat, tapped his phone to open the web browser and searched for Stensen's Garage. He found it quickly and called the listed phone number.

"Stensen's Garage, how can I help you?" a woman answered politely.

"Hello. Uh, does a mechanic named Elliot work there?" Harvey asked. "I'm not sure of his last name."

"Elliot?" the woman responded with surprise. "The only Elliot I know of was a guy who used to work here named Elliot McDowell. That must have been at least seven or eight years ago."

"Uh, yeah, that's probably the guy I'm trying to find, I just didn't know if he still worked there or not. Can you give me some information about him?"

"Why do you wanna know about him? What's he done?"

"He's done nothing, Miss. I'm just trying to locate a cousin of his. Maybe if I find Elliot, he can tell me where his cousin is. I'm a private investigator."

Harvey heard an unhappy sigh on the other end. "I'm the manager here, and I don't really think it's a good idea to give out any personal information like that over the phone."

Harvey thought quickly: *Uncle Willie used to say that most people don't like to answer a lot of questions over the phone. If they can't look you in the eye, they can't tell if they should trust you or not. Now think fast, or you'll lose her. Something simple. The truth is way too complicated. Uncle Willie could strike up a conversation about something that everybody had in common, something everybody loved or everybody hated.*

"This cousin of Elliot, she has a dormant bank account. And she's gone, and she left no forwarding address. She has a lot of money coming to her, *if* we can find her. But if we can't find her, the state will just take it. Well, I say it's a damn shame, you know? The state sucks so much money out of our paychecks now, as it is. I mean, they've got their sticky fingers everywhere, don't they? So, what do you think, can you help me?"

After a few seconds of dead air, she answered: "Well...I'm sure with you there. I get hammered by state taxes myself. But I didn't really know Elliot, I just handed him his paycheck every week, and we don't

273

keep personnel records that long anyway. If there's anybody here who could tell you about Elliot, it's probably Gordon. He's been around a long time. Hold on, I'll call him."

The hold music started, an orchestral rendition of an old Beatles tune. As Harvey stood waiting, he had a direct line of sight to Homer and Gleason, and they stared at him the entire time, mumbling to each other, shaking their heads, giving him that *what an asshole* look, grinning apparently at the thought of this lovesick jerk chasing some girl across New York state.

The music stopped abruptly and then Harvey heard a man's voice on the line: "Yeah, this is Gordon, what's up?" His tone was slightly impatient, like he had been pulled away from something he was anxious to get back to.

"My name is Harvey Grace, and I'm looking for Elliot McDowell. The manager said that you probably knew him?"

"Yeah, sure, he worked here a long time ago, for about a year. I remember him. Hard to completely forget someone who threatens you."

"He threatened you?"

"Yeah, with a crescent wrench. Waved it in my face and hinted that one day he might bash my head in with it. He was a real psycho. Capable of anything, I'd say."

"Why did he threaten you?"

"Because I got to work on time every day, and he didn't. He was always late for work, for one reason or another. He said that me being on time made him look bad in the boss's eyes. Told me to cut it out, to start coming in late some days. Finally, they fired him."

"For being late?"

"Well, I think it was more that he was a lousy mechanic. If he got frustrated, his usual approach to difficult repair problems was to whack the bad part with a hammer. I'd see him whacking away at the engines of very expensive cars. That kind of treatment doesn't do fuel injectors any good at all. So, they moved him off engines, and he was just doing tires, brakes, and mufflers for a while. But he couldn't even do a good job at that. So, they fired his ass. I don't blame 'em. I usually try to stick up for the guys around here, but in his case, I agreed with management."

"Do you know where he went after he was fired?"

"I have no idea, and I don't care. I thought he'd be in jail by now."

"Can you give me a physical description of him?"

"He's about five feet ten, dark hair, average build when I knew him, I mean not overweight or underweight, and he usually had a pissed off look, like he was always mad at someone or something. Kind of an average looking guy. Not too handsome, not too ugly, I guess. He'd be about forty years old now."

"Do you know where Elliot lived when he worked at the garage?"

"No. I sure as hell didn't socialize with him."

"Did he mention anything about having a cabin near Hartwell?"

"Oh, yeah, he was always bragging about this cabin he had in the woods. Talked about it all the time. We all got tired of hearin' about it. Said he was gonna move up there someday and live permanently, just him and his dogs."

"Dogs? Was he a breeder?"

"No, he just had four rottweilers he was always talkin' about, said they'd protect his property from anybody including the federal storm troopers. Said he and his dogs could fend off any kind of attack 'cause he trained em' to go after anybody with a gun. He was constantly talkin' bullshit like that. Fancied himself some kinda wilderness survival expert."

"Did he say exactly where the cabin was?"

"Well, the way he described it, this cabin was in the middle of nowhere. He seemed so proud of that, like he was a real he-man to be roughin' it. Christ, the way he talked about it, you'd think he was killin' bears on his front porch with a knife. Sure, the place is in a wooded area, but it's only a forty-five-minute drive from downtown Albany. Anyway, Hartwell is a big enough town that people recognize the name, but his cabin wasn't actually in Hartwell. The cabin's in a real small town that's a few miles away from Hartwell."

"Do you remember the name of this small town?"

"Yeah, Graver's Falls."

Harvey's mind raced. What else should he ask?

"Can you give me a better idea of how I can find the cabin, if I drive over there? Maybe you can remember more that Elliot might have said about his cabin's location?"

"Hmmm, no, that's really all I can remember. It's been a long time, you know? Is that it, then? I gotta get back to work. If you find him, don't tell him you talked to me, okay? I don't need that kind of trouble."

"No problem. Hey, did he say what size his property was?" Harvey asked.

"I think he said it was about five acres."

"Okay, then. Thanks for your help, Mister ...er, Gordon. Goodbye."

Harvey put his phone back into his pocket, walked over to the Tule brothers, and said: "Well, gentleman, thanks for the information. I'm headed to Graver's Falls."

Gleason looked up and down at Harvey and said: "You should give up on her, kid, she's way outta your league."

Chapter 40
Thursday, May 28, 1:24 p.m.

As Harvey left the Imperial Diner and walked to his car, he took out his cellphone and called Dexter.

"This is Dexter. Speak."

"So, how'd it go?"

"Fine. It worked. He grabbed me. Stuck his gun in my ribs."

"He *what?*" asked Harvey.

"He stuck his gun in my ribs."

"Oh, God. Was it just Mike, or did you see Jenny there, too?"

"Just a guy. I assume it was Mike, he matched the description you gave me."

"Did he threaten you?"

"Not really, but he definitely hurt my feelings. Called me a geek. Do I look like a geek to you?"

"I'll assume you didn't overpower him and rip the gun out of his hands. So, how'd you get away?"

"Easy. We were on the street. He tried to move me back into an alley, where I assume he was going to beat the shit out of me. So, I faked an epileptic seizure, fell down on the sidewalk. A crowd gathered and he panicked. I'm so good, I'll bet he thought I really had a seizure."

"Did he hang around?"

"No, he took off. An ambulance took me to the hospital. Once I got there it was easy to sneak out of the ER."

"Did the paramedics do anything to you in the ambulance? Give you an IV, or snake a tube up your ass or anything?"

"Nope. Once I got in the ambulance, I just pretended I felt all better. They gave me some juice and a cookie. It was a cool ride with the sirens and lights going."

"Wonderful. Dex, now I want you to get out of there. Please go fishing for a week, or whatever you do for relaxation."

"That's just what I had in mind. I'm gonna get my camping equipment together and go."

"I'm sorry I got you involved in all this."

"No problem, buddy. I can handle it. I've stared danger in the face before."

"Yeah, but this is a little more serious than watching your toilet overflow. Call me in a few days. Now go."

"When are you gonna tell me what this is all about?"

"When I figure it out myself. Now go."

"Wait, did you listen to the calls and read the texts that the catcher picked up?" asked Dexter.

"Yeah. You were right. All boring stuff about art restoration and bidding on paintings and such. Why do you ask?"

"Just wanted to make sure my efforts are appreciated."

"Did you catch any more conversations?"

"Yeah, a few more. All equally as boring as the first batch, trust me. I sent you the files."

"Did you check for the four keywords I gave you? Grant, Pamela, maiden, and brother?

"Of course. There was a phone conversation where Damler's assistant asked him if he found his brother yet. Damler said no, but he was hopeful the guy would turn up. That's it for the keyword search."

"Okay, thanks. Now go, have fun, and I promise to listen to your fish stories when you get back."

Chapter 41
Thursday, May 28, 1:46 p.m.

Zoober walked out of the rear entrance of Albany Med Hospital and was surprised to see Beale leaning against an unmarked police car. But the fact that Beale had parked it in a convenient five-minute loading zone very close to the entrance, even though there were plenty of empty spaces in the parking lot, didn't surprise Zoober at all. A burly security guard who had just noticed Beale and his car began to walk toward him. Without saying a word or even looking directly at the guard, Beale removed his badge from his pocket and waved it at the guard. It worked like a magic wand repelling an ogre. The guard immediately backed away. Zoober walked over to Beale and stood next to him.

"Did she see the body yet?" asked Beale.

"The police psychologist went in with Mrs. Damler just a few minutes ago. They're in the morgue now."

"You didn't go in with them?"

"No. As you probably know, the new department policy is that when a citizen visits a morgue to attempt to identify a body, they're escorted by the police psychologist. I thought the psychologist would let me tag along, but she asked me to wait outside. You must know the department psychologist, right? Angela Havright?"

Beale winced and shook his head in disgust.

"Oh yeah, I know Sergeant Havright all right. She came to see me when I shot that burglar three years ago. One of her jobs is to counsel anyone on the force who shoots somebody. She told me she was going to get me in touch with my 'inner self,' so that I could come to grips with the fact that I'd seriously harmed another human being. Told me to close my eyes and visualize myself as the burglar so I could empathize. What a load o' crap," Beale snorted, shaking his head again. "I hear she even went to talk to that dumb fuck patrolman who shot himself in the ass a few months ago. Probably told him to visualize himself as his own colon."

"And how did your session with her go?"

"Oh, it was just wonderful. We spoke for at least half an hour. She wanted to know everything about me, like if my parents used positive or negative reinforcement for my toilet training, if I was a chronic bed wetter and shitter, how often I tug on my johnson, all that sort of stuff."

Zoober chuckled slightly to himself as he pictured the petite female psychologist trying to analyze this crusty, hardened, insensitive, boorish police veteran.

"And did she help you find your inner self?"

Beale took a long, deep drag on his cigarette. "Nope. She finally gave up. Told me I was the most uncooperative cop she'd ever interviewed, and my inner self was hidden so far up my ass, she'd need a telescope to get a look at it."

Beale took a few more drags on the cigarette, and then asked. "So, did Havright tell you why they insist on having the police shrink present now, every time a citizen comes in to look at a stiff? Is it just to hold their hands in case they lose it?"

"That's part of it, I'm sure. But another thing is that the psychologist is there to gauge the reaction on the person's face when they see the body. In the event that the person was somehow involved in a murder plot, they might unintentionally betray themselves. Do you remember the Pellman case two years ago?"

"Yup. A guy reports his wife missing, says she never came home from work, the body's found in a shallow grave a week later, turns out the husband whacked her. But as I recall, they solved the case by good old-fashioned detective work. I don't remember hearing that the husband had any unusual reaction when he ID'd the body."

"You're correct, Martin. Nothing unusual about the husband's reaction was reported. In fact, they didn't even seriously consider the husband a suspect until two months into the investigation. But perhaps if they had employed a trained observer to look at Mr. Pellman's facial expressions and body language when he had identified the body, they might have started investigating him as their prime suspect immediately."

"So, Angela Havright is our trained observer, huh? She's the one with the crystal balls? Well, I've been observing people for thirty years, and I think I'm damn good at it, even though I don't have a psych degree. And besides, anyone who's working on a murder case and doesn't immediately investigate or rule out the spouse isn't doin' their job. Speaking of spouses killing spouses, what do you think about this Damler woman? What's she like, and did you talk to her about her husband on the drive over here?"

"Yes, we spoke about her husband. All I can say is that she seems genuinely upset about the fact that her husband is missing. Her grief seems very deep. And she's a very refined lady, eloquent and well educated."

"How old is she?"

"A little over forty, I'd say." Zoober paused before asking, "So, why'd you stop here, Martin? You said this was probably another dead end."

Beale lit another cigarette. Only two people in the world called him Martin: his ninety-four-year-old mother and Zoober. Everyone else called him Beale, except for his wife, who had a variety of colorful names for him. Zoober wasn't the kind of person who was comfortable calling an associate by his last name. During the first few months they worked together, Beale kept correcting him to use his surname, but Zoober somehow innocently persisted in calling his partner Martin, until at last Beale let it drop.

"What I said was that there was only a slim chance this woman's husband is the guy we pulled out of the lake, but right now all we have are slim chances. Somebody had it out for that stiff, to go to all that trouble of tying him up, weighing him down, and dumping him in the lake. Looks well thought out. Did the wife mention to you if her husband had any enemies?"

"She said she has no knowledge of any enemies, but she implied that he deals with a lot of wealthy people in his line of work, which is restoring and appraising art, some of it *very valuable* art. Money is always a motive for crime, of course. Oh, and she also told me she hired a private investigator to try and find him."

"And has her private investigator come up with anything yet?" asked Beale.

"Apparently not. She wasn't very forthcoming with details of the investigation, but I got the general impression that so far it hasn't produced any substantial clues regarding her husband's whereabouts."

"You mean he's got jack shit. I swear kid, sometimes you take two dozen words to say something when it just takes four. Well, we might as well wait outside here and relax for a few minutes. If I don't chain smoke at least four times a day I get cranky as hell. These damn liberal anti-smoking laws are a pain. And they don't even let us smoke in department-owned cars anymore."

The topic turned to baseball as they waited for Pamela Damler to come out. For five minutes they discussed the Yankees' batting averages. Before they got too deeply into a discussion of the ERAs of the Red Sox pitchers, Beale said: "Christ, we really need to get going, we should talk to that old coot on the lake again before he croaks. What are they doing in there? Hell, I'm going in. I'm sure my old friend Sergeant Angela will be *so* glad to see me. You better wait here in case they show up, they might walk out a different door."

Without waiting for any comment from Zoober, Beale threw his half-finished cigarette onto the ground and walked into the hospital.

Zoober waited patiently, leaning against the car and enjoying the cool breeze. Five minutes later he looked up and saw Beale walking quickly out of the hospital and directly toward him. Beale's face was serious and businesslike.

"Did she ID the body?"

"She sure as hell did, kid. Christ, we totally lucked out."

Chapter 42
Thursday, May 28, 2:02 p.m.

Harvey drove slowly on the bumpy dirt road, looking for a driveway among the dense groves of maple trees. A paper road map was opened on the passenger seat, and he occasionally glanced down at it and worried he might be completely lost. He had no cell signal at all but it didn't really matter because his navigation app indicated he wasn't even on a road.

About two and a half hours ago, Harvey had left the parking lot of the Shady Maple Motel where he'd stopped to see if he could get any more information about Linda. Other than confirming she had indeed stayed there on Wednesday night of last week, the proprietor wasn't helpful. Apparently, no more words passed between them than were necessary to rent the room. Linda left the next morning after paying her bill in cash.

From there, Harvey had driven to the tiny town of Graver's Falls. Since a quick internet search on his phone hadn't turned up any online record of an Elliot McDowell owning property in the town, Harvey stopped at the post office to inquire where the local records of property ownership were kept, and he ended up in the house of a pleasant old woman named Mavis Tucker who kept mountains of paper records in apple boxes in her basement. As she explained to Harvey, Graver's Falls had no town hall and so her dining room served as the town office. The town had not yet entered the digital age, but fortunately Mavis was a remarkably well-organized paper record keeper, with everything efficiently alphabetized. While Harvey sipped tea and ate the oatmeal cookies she graciously offered him and which he felt obliged to accept, she quickly located a record of Elliot's ownership of a plot of land approximately five acres in size, complete with a survey that showed the position of the small cabin. To help Harvey find it she made him a copy of a map of the area with the plot outlined. There was a snaking line on the map indicating a dirt road simply called rural route one fifty-seven. It skirted the property and intersected a driveway about a hundred yards long that led to the cabin. That driveway was now the object of Harvey's search.

He stepped on the gas again, drove slowly for another half a minute, and then hit the brakes as he caught sight of a narrow opening in the trees. As he turned in, Harvey saw the NO TRESPASSING signs that were posted on either side of the opening. He wondered if, at the other end of the driveway, he might find the mean-tempered Elliot himself, holding a loaded shotgun. Harvey thought with regret about the revolver. He'd decided, at the last moment, to leave it behind. Even now he wasn't sure why he'd made that decision, but could he ever take a shot at someone, even if they were shooting at him? Maybe he didn't have the balls to even *point* it at a person. But he'd come this far. Gun or no gun, he'd have to take his chances now. If he got caught by someone, he could feign ignorance about the trespassing. *I got lost... didn't notice the signs ... thought this was a public road...*

Sure, with a map outlining McDowell's property opened on the seat next to me? Yeah, right, they'll believe me...as long as I eat the map before it's noticed.

Harvey eased his car down the driveway, which was shrouded by tall evergreens. The surface was dry and covered with a thick layer of pine needles, so it was impossible to determine if any cars had passed here recently. He spotted the outline of a structure up ahead in a small clearing and pulled off the driveway into a space between two large trees, cringing as he felt some fallen twigs scrape the underside of the car. The heat shield for his catalytic converter had fallen off long ago. Hopefully, the hot metal parts of the exhaust system wouldn't ignite the underbrush. It's hard to be stealthy if you torch the forest on your way in.

Harvey opened the car door and listened. He heard nothing but the serene sound of the wind rustling through the trees and the occasional bird chirping in celebration of spring. The air was thick with the sweet smell of pine sap. He stepped out of the car and peered around a large tree trunk at the house. It was still partly shrouded by greenery, but through the gaps he saw no signs of activity. He began to zig-zag from one tree trunk to another, peeking out at the house after reaching each one and feeling sort of stupid about it, like he was a little kid playing a game of spy. Harvey recalled that Uncle Willie always said this business was for people who never grew up.

About a hundred feet short of the house now, Harvey could clearly see the front. It was a small, A-frame style structure, with dark wood siding that was overdue for a fresh coat of stain, and a rickety-looking front deck. There were no cars parked in the driveway and no garage. So far as Harvey could discern from this distance, there was nobody home.

It was time for him to make a decision. A direct or indirect approach? Knock or snoop around? What if he knocked and Linda answered? He had no idea what he'd say, and he was amazed that he stupidly hadn't prepared some questions or some great speech during the drive here.

And what if Elliot answered? The guy was supposedly hot-tempered, and probably outweighed Harvey by a lot. Not a good combination. He certainly didn't want a repeat of the incident with Louie Parker.

Okay, so I'll snoop first. Just don't get caught.

As he moved closer and out from the shelter of the trees, any hope of his presence remaining a secret evaporated when he heard several dogs whining and yelping with excitement. The noise came from the backyard.

Elliot's Rottweilers?

They're here...

And of course, they have to be fed, which meant that Elliot is here, or if not, he'd be returning today.

Harvey walked to the backyard and immediately saw it was completely surrounded by a vinyl stockade fence about nine feet tall, apparently to keep the dogs penned in. They were still whimpering but

Harvey could tell they weren't running around in the yard freely right now, or they would have had their noses right up to the crack between the gate and the fence. He flipped up the latch on the gate and cautiously opened it, then leaned forward to peer in.

The four dogs, all handsome and regal-looking animals, were in a chain-link pen in the far corner of the yard, away from the house. Once the dogs saw Harvey, they stopped making noise and simply sat and watched him. Harvey wondered if they'd previously thought they were about to get a meal, but now they saw this was not the usual guy who brought the food.

Harvey took a quick look around the yard. The fenced-in area was large, at least sixty by sixty feet. There was a storage shed just a few feet from the back fence and next to the shed was another gate that led out to the woods. The fenced-in green space could hardly be called a lawn because the weeds were much more prolific than the grass. The perimeter of the yard was a mess, with an assortment of crap lining the fence — decrepit lawn furniture, rusted garden tools, broken pots. An old rusted lawnmower, half-hidden by weeds that towered above it, appeared to have given up on its assigned task long ago and gone to sleep. A rotting wooden table near the back door supported a large patio umbrella that consisted of shreds of moldy green cloth hanging from an exposed metal skeleton.

Harvey made a snap decision and went back to the front door, closing the gate behind him. Now that his presence had probably been revealed by the dogs, he decided it would be better to confront Elliot if he was home rather than sneak around and get shot as an intruder.

Just in case, get your story ready about being lost.

Harvey walked up the three wooden steps onto the front deck, raised his hand, and after a final hesitation he gave the door three cautious taps. He waited anxiously for half a minute, then gave three very hard raps. Still nothing. Then he shouted: "HELLO, HELLO. Anyone home? I'm lost. I need some help."

No response.

Harvey thought, *Okay, that's it, nobody's here. The knocking and shouting would have woken anyone who wasn't dead.*

Now what? I have to get in. I should check all the doors.

Harvey tried the front doorknob, but it was locked. Next, he tried the sliding glass door on the side of the house. He pulled the handle to the right and at first it didn't budge, but after a little more urging the cheap lock slipped and the door moved. He let go of the handle in surprise and stepped back. After listening for a few seconds, he pushed the door aside and pulled back the cheap, dusty curtain. Putting one foot on the sill, he paused.

If I go inside, will I be committing a crime? This isn't breaking and entering, is it? I wouldn't call what I just did breaking. No need to break. The lock was already broken.

And if I'm caught, I can always say I was injured and was desperate for medical attention, right? Or ravenously thirsty? Or I was so very certain that this was my Aunt Minnie's place and she wouldn't mind me walking right in?

Every excuse sounds phony...

Despite his strong reservations, Harvey commanded his feet to move again and in seconds he stood in the middle of what he assumed was the living area.

The interior of the house instantly reminded him of Louie Parker's place. In other words, a shithole, but a slightly bigger shithole than Louie's. Newspapers, blankets, clothes, and other assorted debris were everywhere.

He walked past a couch that looked a century old, its puke green upholstery badly frayed. As he turned slowly to take in his surroundings, his eye caught something that sat on a cheap bookshelf sagging under the weight of random clutter. From a crevice between two stacks of magazines, a young girl peered out from the darkness. Maybe he'd noticed her because her cherubic face was the only thing on the shelf not covered by dust.

And then Harvey's alarm bells went off because he realized it was her.

The *Maiden.*

The image appeared to be about eight by ten inches, the right size. And it looked like a painting as opposed to a photo because Harvey could see the edges of the image were frayed, like it was done on canvas or some type of cloth. It was attached to a backing made of a flat piece of wood. Harvey moved his fingers toward it slowly, then gently gripped the wooden backing and pulled it slowly toward him, hoping that his prints wouldn't be left on the rough wood. He stopped pulling when the painting hung a few inches off the shelf. He could see the whole picture now and mentally compared it to the images he'd seen online.

This was it. The real thing.

Or was it?

If it was genuine, it must have been stolen from Grant, who apparently believed it was a real Vermeer and never would have willingly left it on a shelf in this unguarded dump.

Harvey toyed with the idea of taking it and leaving immediately. But if it was really worth thirty million then he'd be committing a crime that was a bit more serious than his prior worst crime, which was snitching candy bars as a kid from a convenience store on a dare.

He looked at it more closely but was afraid to get too close, scared that the moisture from his breath might have some bad effect on it. Was it the real thing, the painting Grant had found? It certainly looked like an authentic masterwork, right down to the tensile cracks in the paint which he assumed were there because of its four-hundred-year age.

Harvey knew of one person who could tell for sure. And he couldn't just stand here forever and mentally debate his next move. He had to do something before Elliot came home to feed those dogs.

Harvey pulled out his phone and found Peter Damler in his contacts. He tapped the icon to make the call but he immediately heard a beep and looked down at the message on the screen: NO SERVICE. The signal strength indicator flipped back and forth between zero and one bar.

He decided to try texting, which he knew took less bandwidth and might work with a weak cell signal. He carefully tapped out a message:

Peter, when we spoke yesterday you said you wanted me to continue on the case, and I'd be working for you. I'm agreeable to that. I looked in the safe deposit box myself, the Maiden is not there. But I'm at a house, vacant at the moment, in a town outside Albany, and I think I've found it. Don't know if it's the real thing. Would you be willing to come immediately to authenticate it?

Harvey then texted the address and his GPS coordinates and hit send.

A sending status bar appeared. It advanced to the right at an agonizingly slow pace.

Two minutes.

Three minutes.

Time crawled as Harvey waited anxiously. Finally, a "message sent" banner appeared.

Now, there would be more waiting.

Harvey looked around the seedy interior of the house. He wandered into the kitchen and saw dishes piled everywhere—in the sink, on the countertop, even on the floor. A battalion of ants was feasting on some type of black slop encrusted on an old pot, possibly month-old refried beans. All the while he listened for any sounds of Elliot approaching the house, well aware that he could get the shit beat out of him or worse if Elliot surprised him.

Should I hide? I can run fast. But if he's got a gun, I can't dodge bullets.

After six minutes Harvey was about to go outside to wait, thinking it would be safer. But before leaving the house he took out his phone again, checked the contact information for Peter, and saw that he'd also saved Peter's overseas number. Harvey copied and pasted the message he'd just sent to Peter's domestic line and sent it to the overseas number, just in case he was monitoring that phone. Now Harvey felt he'd done everything possible to get in touch with Peter, short of getting in his car and driving around to find a spot where he could get a decent cell signal. He'd wait at least ten minutes more before resorting to that, but he would do the waiting outside.

Harvey's hand reached for the sliding door. His phone chirped as a text came in from Peter's domestic line.

Harvey, how did you find the Maiden? I'm not able to call you, it goes right to your voice mail. Can you take a high-res picture and send it to me?

Being careful to touch only the wooden backing, Harvey carefully pulled the *Maiden* off the shelf and placed it on the coffee table. He opened the camera app on his phone, snapped a picture, and immediately attempted to send it to Peter. The sending status bar appeared but after a minute with nearly no movement, it vanished, replaced by a *FAILED TO SEND* banner. Harvey tried once more, with the same result.

He texted back:

I'm in an area with bad cell service. Can only text and it's very slow. Followed a lead that had to do with a student who may be having an affair with Grant. I took a picture of the Maiden but it won't send. Likely too much data for weak cell coverage.

He hit send and the status bar appeared. Harvey carefully put the painting back on the shelf and then left the house through the sliding door and went into the woods. He crouched behind a large fallen tree trunk where he had a good view of the house and driveway. While he waited for a response from Peter, Harvey watched the driveway and strained to hear any sounds of a vehicle coming down toward the house.

The dogs had quieted down. He could hear birds, the rustle of a squirrel's tiny feet against dry leaves, and a toad chirping its springtime mating call.

After four minutes of crouching, his message finally went. After another four minutes he received Peter's reply:

There must be a link between this student and Pamela. You should take the painting and leave immediately. I'll meet you at your place.

Harvey texted back:

I can't do that. If it's the real Vermeer we'll have to get the police involved.

Harvey figured that if he had to call the cops, he'd leave the painting on the table and tell them he saw it through the window or something like that, which would limit his admission of guilt to only trespassing on Elliot's land. Harvey was pretty sure he'd left no evidence of his having entered the house.

Nine minutes after Harvey had pushed the button to send his last text, he received Peter's reply:

I'll be there in 45 mins. I'm in Albany now.

Harvey thought, *Okay, he's probably on the road already.*

Harvey sent one more text:

House hard to find. On an unpaved road. I'll wait for you at top of driveway.

He decided that while he waited for Peter it would be best to move his car off Elliot's property, in case the guy showed up.

Harvey trotted over to his car, started it up and pulled up the driveway. At the top, he turned left and drove only a few hundred feet until he spotted what appeared to be a logging trail intersecting the road. Obviously, it was meant for four-wheel drive vehicles but its surface looked dry and smooth enough. He turned onto it and went about a hundred feet until the trail made a sharp turn. Harvey parked the car just past the turn and walked back to the road. He was satisfied his car wouldn't be visible to anyone driving by.

He walked back to the top of the driveway and started looking for a spot to hide and wait for Peter. The mature tree with the first NO TRESPASSING sign attached to it had a very wide trunk and was surrounded by dense foliage. Hiding behind it while he waited seemed like a safe bet.

But something bothered him.

Something about the signs.

The cabin was how old? Decades at least? Harvey didn't know, but it definitely wasn't new. The yellow NO TRESPASSING signs, on the other hand, *did* look new. *Brand new.* He walked over to the sign closest to him and examined it carefully. It was stapled to the tree at eye level. The sign was made of some kind of durable-looking paper. At the bottom, in tiny print, were the words *weather resistant.* To Harvey, this meant the signs would degrade very slowly over time, but they didn't look weathered or discolored at all. And the staples looked shiny and new. So why did someone who owned this place for years wait until recently to put up these signs?

Maybe Elliot used to have signs up and they wore out, and he just got around to replacing them? If so, it was a stunning coincidence that he'd decided to do it shortly before Harvey decided to trespass. But if he'd replaced old ones, it was a fastidiously neat job, because there wasn't a sign of an old rusted staple or nail in this tree, or any tree around here. It was more likely that these were the first signs Elliot had ever put up. Maybe he'd recently seen people wandering around here and wanted to keep them away... a sudden urge for peace and quiet?

Or maybe it's because he's got something new to hide.

I have to go back down to the house and take another look around.

Peter wouldn't be here for at least another twenty-five minutes, so there was time to go take a closer look for...for what? He had no idea.

In two minutes, he was back at the house. The dogs whimpered as he approached, but when he poked his head through the front gate and looked at them, they went silent as they stared back, perhaps recognizing his scent as that of a previous docile visitor.

He stepped out of the yard and closed the gate behind him. He had to give it a slight push with his foot at the bottom where the gate rubbed against the post. And as he looked down, he noticed something on the ground right in front of the gate.

It was a little speck of red, out of place against the earth tones that surrounded it. Moving some leaves away from it, he uncovered another bit of whatever it was, an area about the size of a penny, and this part wasn't red. Harvey could see from the new area that the thing was a piece of cloth, with a pattern on it. A fine plaid pattern.

The last thing that Pamela saw Grant wearing was a plaid shirt.

Jolted to attention, Harvey stood up quickly and pulled his small notebook out of his coat pocket. Paging far back to the beginning of his case notes, he looked for information about the shirt, but he had nothing other than the word *plaid*. Nothing at all about the color. Why hadn't he asked her about the color? Maybe he had, but Harvey remembered that when Pamela had initially come to see him, he had taken his case notes on a yellow legal pad, which was back at his house, and then he'd transferred some details to the notes app on his phone and to his small notepad, things that he felt were very important. Maybe he hadn't considered the color of the shirt to be critical. And the lines on this plaid pattern in front of him were so thin, would Pamela even call it a plaid? It consisted of fine brown, black, and olive lines on a tan background, but from not too far away, the pattern looked like just a solid color — kind of a dark tan.

He bent down again to have another look.

The red spot on the cloth was a very dark red. Beet juice? Strawberry jelly? Marker? Paint? Okay, so what about the obvious choice, the one screaming inside Harvey's head right now?

Blood.

Harvey moved his face even closer now, squatting down on his hands and knees to examine the scrap of cloth. Yes, the red color could indeed be blood. He brushed more leaves aside but didn't find any more of the cloth. Leaving it where he'd found it, Harvey stood up and decided to check the area around the house and also the fenced-in yard, but this time he'd look down at the ground carefully as he walked.

Harvey slowly circled the house but he saw nothing unusual on the ground. When he reached the back gate he opened it, walked through it, and then closed it behind him. He stood in the small space, about four by six feet, between the shed and the side fence.

And he could feel something was different about this spot.

He felt it with his feet. The ground was softer here, although not muddy. And the dirt was just slightly mounded up.

And there was something else.

There were leaves all over Elliot's yard — last autumn's fallen leaves, never raked up, and now rotting and matted together. And there were leaves on the mound too, but Harvey could tell that they had been recently disturbed and replaced.

Had Elliot buried something right here?

There was an old rusted shovel leaning against the shed. Harvey grabbed it and tested it quickly by striking the metal part against the ground, and he declared it sound. His mind raced, churning through the possibilities as he pushed the shovel into the softened earth at the peak of the mound. It went in easily. There was no way this soil could have been undisturbed for years.

Would he find the grave of a dead Rottweiler? Or maybe just an old hot water heater that Elliot had buried?

There was no point in speculating now, for he was committed to digging. The answer was only minutes away.

With each push on the shovel, he dug a little faster, energized by a rush of adrenaline. The digging went quickly because there were no tree roots or other obstacles here. The hole grew wider and deeper, and he continued to prod the soil at the bottom.

After a few minutes of strenuous effort, he impatiently brought the tip of the shovel down with a hard thrust.

CLANG.

The jarring impact of metal against metal sent a shock wave up through Harvey's forearm. He scraped more of the loose soil away with the shovel, rapidly uncovering the manmade object. It was flat and white. But he saw very plainly that it was certainly not an old water heater.

It was... an old oven.

A stinking oven. Cripes!

He had consumed a great deal of energy digging up a piece of junk. Frustrated and angered at himself, he raised the shovel and with all his strength brought it down vertically onto the window in the oven door, a glass rectangle that was jet black from whatever greasy slop had been cooked in this thing long ago. It shattered with a pop that was nearly as loud as a gunshot and pieces of glass dropped into the oven.

And a plaid shirt shone through the hole in the door.

Harvey dropped the shovel and bent down to stare at the cloth. It was the same fine plaid pattern that was on the tiny piece of cloth on the ground, and it was dotted with the same red substance.

He frantically cleared more soil away, shaking all the while, until he saw that he'd uncovered a large double oven. He pulled on both doors, but neither would open. He decided to concentrate his efforts on the door with the newly broken window. Positioning one foot on the frame below the door and the other above it, he grabbed the handle and pulled until his arms ached, but the door wouldn't budge. It felt as if it were wired or screwed shut. He relaxed his grip for a few seconds and then pulled even harder, this time until his back hurt, but still the door wouldn't open. Reaching for the shovel now, Harvey jammed its wooden handle under the oven door's metal handle and pulled up as hard as he could on the shovel's head, taking advantage of every bit of leverage available.

Harvey grimaced from the exertion and he expected the shovel handle to snap under the strain. Then he heard a tearing sound, and with a violent release the door sprang open.

And Grant Damler stared up at him.

Bile rose in Harvey's throat and he felt sick to his stomach. This grotesque thing wearing a ripped plaid shirt and with a smear of dried blood under its nose was unmistakably Grant Damler, once a living, breathing person. Even though the metal wall between the two oven chambers had apparently been removed to make a single coffin, Grant's lifeless body was twisted, its arms dislocated, broken, bent at impossible angles to fit into the compact space. The palms of both of Grant's hands faced forward—one by the side of his face, the other one over his stomach. The corpse's eyes were hollow and blackened. It spoke to Harvey.

"Harvey!"

Harvey screamed. He spun around to see Peter Damler, his eyes fixed on the corpse.

"Oh, my God, no," said Peter in a soft, disbelieving voice. "No." Peter stood transfixed by the ghoulish sight of Grant stuffed into the absurdly small chamber. "My brother murdered...over a painting." Peter put his head down and dropped to his knees next to Harvey.

"I'm...I'm so...so sorry," Harvey said.

Tears began to stream down Peter's cheeks. They knelt side by side, staring at the corpse. Harvey didn't know what else to say. He simply waited for Peter to speak.

Peter eventually wiped his eyes with the back of his hand and said with remorse, "I wish... I just wish Grant and I had been closer in recent years. I feel like I abandoned him by moving to Paris."

Peter stood up and a look of determination came over him as he said, "Whoever did this to my brother will pay. I'll make sure of it. Let's move out of this area now. We shouldn't disturb the body anymore, we've already contaminated the crime scene. We have to contact the police. And I want to hear how you found this place."

Harvey nodded his head, but he wasn't yet able to rise from his knees. He tried breathing deeply to calm himself but he still felt nauseous and prayed that he wouldn't barf.

All right now Harvey boy, you can't throw up here, not now, and not in front of Peter. I'll bet I'm already in a shitload of trouble for messing up this crime scene, so I don't want to make it any worse by spewing my DNA all over the corpse.

Peter saw the expression of distress on Harvey's face and offered some encouragement. "Let's go, Harvey," he said gently. "You'll be fine."

Peter walked somberly through the yard toward the front gate. As Harvey struggled to stand, he felt his cell buzz with an incoming text. He took it out of his jacket pocket and looked at the screen.

It was from Jenny.

Harvey, we've been monitoring your texts. If you found the Maiden, you're in grave danger. Mike and I are U.S. Marshalls. We didn't come for the Maiden or for Grant. We came for Zola. He's alive. Get out of there NOW.

Harvey shook his head, trying to clear the fog that engulfed him.
Zola.
Zola?
Zola's alive? He...

As Peter approached the gate, his back still to Harvey, he pointed to an old wooden bench sitting in the tall grass near the gate and said, "Harvey, let's sit here for a moment and decide what to do."

"No, don't sit. Don't even fucking breathe," said someone in a commanding voice that was unfamiliar to Harvey.

Who... said that? thought Harvey. And then one more emphatic word in the unfamiliar voice: "Police!"

Harvey was still on his knees. He turned around, looked upward, and saw the obese police detective standing right behind him, wearing a funny-looking brimmed hat, pointing a gun at Peter. He'd come in quietly through the back gate.

Beale said to Peter, very calmly but with unmistakable menace, "Get your hands up NOW."

His back still toward Harvey and Beale, Peter raised his hands very slowly. He stopped when they were slightly below shoulder height.

The cop spoke again, this time with a voice that was low, determined, and even more menacing. "Mister, I want you to turn around very slowly right now and keep those fucking hands of yours raised or I'll decorate the fence with your brains."

Harvey stared at Peter and said, "Officer, this man... this man is..."

"Shut up and stay down on the ground, kid. I've been listening long enough to hear this guy is pretending to be Peter Damler. Somebody pulled Peter's body out of Lake George and he was just ID'd by his sister-in-law. The Paris police have had him listed as missing for a few days and they've been monitoring his phone. We all thought it was damn peculiar you met with a dead guy yesterday."

Beale's finger tightened on the gun's trigger.

Harvey looked at the man he'd known as Peter and finished his sentence in a whisper: "Zola."

And then Alexander Zola obeyed the cop's order and began to rotate counterclockwise so slowly, keeping his hands raised but below shoulder level. Soon his right hand disappeared from the cop's view, hidden by his torso.

BOOM! BOOM!

Two shots in quick succession and Harvey saw a gaping hole blown in the side of Zola's coat down by his hip. Harvey figured the cop must have seen Zola making some suspicious move, and Harvey expected that in another split-second Zola's blood would come gushing out from the hole. But when the blood didn't appear, Harvey knew that something was very wrong and then he realized the gunshots weren't nearly loud enough to have come from the cop's weapon just behind and above him. In another half-second Harvey turned his head to glance up at Beale and was horrified to see him clutching his stomach, blood oozing between his fingers.

Beale's frame crumpled and he fell face forward with a WHUMP, right in front of Harvey, who was still on his knees. The cop's collapsed body lay between Harvey and Zola.

A wave of sheer panic ripped through Harvey's body as he realized that when Zola's hand was hidden behind his torso, he'd reached into his open trench coat for his gun and fired twice, right through the coat, all in under a second. Aimed from the hip while facing sideways, both shots had struck Beale....an *incredible* feat.

Holy shit, this guy Zola is really good.

The cop had never even seen Zola's gun. And now it was up to Harvey alone to deal with Zola. Good ol' Harvey, who had left his own gun at home because he was afraid he might accidentally shoot himself in the prick with it, and even if he had it right now, all loaded and ready, he had never even pointed the thing at a human being before, especially one who was firing back.

Zola smiled at Harvey and said, "Call me Alex. We should be on a first-name basis. Teammates, right?" Zola held his gun at waist height, pointed at Harvey's chest, and he began a very slow and deliberate walk toward Harvey, who glanced at Beale's gun on the ground. It had flown out of Beale's hand and was now about six feet in front of Harvey, between him and Zola.

If he went for it, Zola would easily pick him off.

And then, at the very edge of his field of vision, Harvey saw the cop's hand twitch.

Beale wasn't dead just yet. His body was curled into a fetal position facing Zola and his right hand was behind him, down near his ankle. His pant leg was up enough for Harvey to see a patch of leather against his skin. Beale's hand crawled slowly along the ground, its movement hidden behind his legs. The hand crept along like a spider, scratching at the soil, closing in on the ankle, narrowing the gap.

Harvey was stunned that the cop was even alive.

Don't look! Not at the cop's crawling hand, not at the ankle holster. Or Zola will notice.

Harvey summoned all his willpower to force his gaze back toward Zola. He guessed that the cop's eyes were closed, faking death. But even if the cop's hand was somehow able to reach the gun, did he have the strength to aim and fire the weapon? Harvey wondered if he should lunge for the gun himself. He was an excellent shot, at least when he was shooting at paper targets. But it was probably a suicidal move, and...

Too late now because Beale's hand reached his ankle. He unclipped the snap that secured the weapon and eased it out of the holster. So slowly, quietly...

Without realizing it, Harvey held his breath. He waited for Beale to make his move...

And then with no warning, Beale used every last bit of his waning energy in one superhuman effort. He quickly rotated his body and swung the weapon up to the firing position, moving with amazing speed for a man who'd been shot twice.

But the effort wasn't amazing enough. Not even close.

BOOM!

At the same time the shot reverberated through the damp air, Harvey made his leap, from his knees to the area behind the shed. He hit the ground hard with his hands and pushed his body into a roll, ending up with his butt on the ground and his back against the shed, facing Beale and now out of Zola's sight. The dogs looked at Harvey with curiosity from their pen in the other corner of the yard.

As he hyperventilated, Harvey felt something drip down his face and neck. He opened his eyes and saw that the top of Beale's head was gone and pinkish brain matter was splattered everywhere. The backup gun that Beale had drawn rested on the grass in front of him.

Beale never had a chance to fire either of his weapons.

As he resumed his slow walk toward Harvey, Zola said, "Did you think this man would save you? Only in the movies, Harvey. Don't feel sorry for him, or for the Damler brothers. I never met Grant, but Peter was a fool who deserved to die. Two weeks ago, he bragged to anyone who would listen about his brother having found Vermeer's *Maiden*. *My* lovely *Maiden*. And how he was going to prove it to the world. When I arrived in Port Kole last Thursday afternoon and found Peter sitting in his car outside his brother's house, I had a chat with him. He told me Grant was missing and Pamela had hired you. He didn't know if the *Maiden* was in that safe deposit box or if Grant had taken off with it, or if Pamela might have hidden it somewhere. I certainly wasn't going to attempt to retrieve it from that box myself, in case there was a trap set for me. So, I decided to send Peter to rest on the lake bottom and take his place for a few days, to gain your trust. You were in a unique position to help me. I'm sure it was the salacious pictures of Pamela that swung you over to my side. They were on Peter's phone, taken three years ago. Did you go to the trouble of scrutinizing the JPEG file I sent you? I hope so because *I* went to the trouble of changing the date in it. I also hired a woman to rent a room at the Sherwood hotel in Pamela's maiden name. I guessed that you'd be smart enough to uncover that.

"And you're probably also wondering about your pitiful attempt at surveillance. I have software on my phone to detect when it connects to IMSI catchers. Any technological surveillance measures can be foiled by countermeasures. A few calls and texts staged with the help of some friends back in Europe left you convinced of my sincerity. I've survived this long because I'm careful. Deception is my tradecraft. Law enforcement agencies around the world have tried to capture me. And you, Harvey my young friend, are *so* out of your league.

"I know you're not armed. I would have smelled the machine oil, the holster leather. I would have detected any slight bulge in your clothing. You now have two minutes to tell me everything. There's no point in me giving you assurances that you'll live if you cooperate. You know who I am. You know I have to kill you. But you'll die a quick death if you comply. A bullet to the head will be your reward."

Harvey's hands shook as he tapped out a text to Jenny on his cell:

zola's here he killed a cop he's coming for me i'm trapped where
r u ?

He hit the send button and the status bar appeared. It crawled to the right.

The text might take three or four minutes to reach Jenny. I'll likely be dead in two.

Zola was about twenty feet from the shed now, still walking slowly.

"Unfortunately, Peter's body was found, despite the trouble I took to buy a raft and drop it in deep water. And so, we have very little time now. The painting in the house is a giclee, a digital reproduction done on canvas using an inkjet printer. Whoever had it made had access to a high-resolution photo of my *Maiden*. It was done, no doubt, to fool someone. So now I want to know how you found this place, I want to know who killed Grant — I want to know everything you've uncovered."

Harvey was trapped in the space between the shed and the fence. It was pointless to try and run out the back gate that Beale entered from, it was in Zola's sightline. The fence itself was about nine feet tall, high enough to prevent the Rottweilers with their powerful rear legs from leaping over. And it was made of smooth vinyl, with no places to get hand or foot holds.

Harvey needed a weapon. Both of the cop's guns were on the grass, out of Harvey's reach, and within Zola's sights. If Harvey went for either of them, he was certain he'd die instantly.

The shovel? Maybe if Zola got close enough Harvey could swing it wildly, throw him off balance, maybe even knock the gun out of his hand, or...

I'm kidding myself. That'll never work against this guy. But at least I'll die fighting.

Harvey reached for the shovel. His knee brushed the cop's hat on the ground, which had violently flown off his head when the first two shots hit him.

And Harvey sensed something very strange about the hat.

Its weight.

It was simply too heavy for a hat. There must be something hidden inside. A knife, maybe?

Harvey turned the hat over and was stunned to see a tiny gun held securely in place with a Velcro strap.

He undid the strap and removed the weapon, which he recognized as a Baby Browning. Only four inches long, the thing looked so small in his hand. Harvey guessed it had a six-round magazine. He pulled the slide back and saw there was a round in the chamber. Assuming the clip was full, he probably had seven shots.

He pushed the safety lever down. Now he was ready for... for what? Just jump out and start firing? He knew that as soon as he poked his head even an inch out from the cover of the shed, Zola could put a bullet in his temple. He also knew the little weapon in his hand had only a pitiful amount of stopping power compared to Zola's gun.

Should I just stick my hand out from behind the shed and fire without looking? No, with this little pistol I'll have to go for a headshot, which means I'll have to actually aim the thing.

Even though Harvey was now armed, it was *still* hopeless...

Zola stopped ten feet short of the shed, and said, "Harvey, it will be easier for you if you just come out now. Remember, your choices are a slow death or a quick, painless one. If you still have some hope of escaping, you are quite misguided. Do you really think that on your best day you have even a wisp of a chance of defeating *me*?"

Harvey answered: "No... no, I don't. I've heard about you, and now I've seen what you can do. I know that I have no chance against you, none at all.... but maybe *they* do."

From his sitting position behind the shed, hidden from Zola, Harvey took careful aim and fired.

The .25 ACP bullet from the little gun shattered the rusted hasp on the dog cage's door and it sprang open. Harvey threw the gun toward the cage as hard as he could and held his hands up to show they were empty.

The four dogs instantly burst out from their confinement like a cannonball. They moved as one huge dark mass, a black and brown blur hurtling toward the only person now holding a gun.

Zola's first bullet slammed into the lead dog's skull and it went down, skidding along the grass as its tremendous momentum continued to propel it toward Zola even as it collapsed in death. The remaining three animals flew over the fallen one without breaking stride, accelerating toward Zola, who unleashed his second round as quickly as the mechanics of his gun would allow. The bullet hit the new leader in the right eye, but not before the creature had already begun an incredible leap at Zola, who fired a third shot that was intended for the next closest attacker. But the animal hit by the second shot was still airborne and in the way; it saved its companion by intercepting the third.

There was no time for a fourth shot.

The remaining two Rottweilers were screaming like missiles toward their target when they collided with Zola. The lead dog's snout hit the barrel of the gun, easily pushing it aside, and then its teeth found flesh. Its jaws clamped around Zola's wrist, crushing his radial artery.

The fourth dog went for Zola's neck.

Zola screamed in agony and flailed wildly, but the vise-like jaws of the two animals were relentless, as they savagely tore at arteries and more. Harvey heard the sickening sound of teeth grinding against bone.

"HARVEY!" yelled Jenny from a few feet outside the front gate.

Harvey looked around the side of the shed. He could see the gate beginning to open. In a microsecond, she'd be visible to the dogs.

Harvey screamed, "JENNY, STOP! HOLSTER YOUR WEAPON RIGHT NOW! TRUST ME!"

The gate stopped moving, but only for a second. Then it opened all the way.

Jenny stood in the opening, unarmed, her hands empty. She looked at Zola's lifeless body in astonishment, his throat ripped open, his torso a bloody mess. The two dogs glanced up at her, but ignored her and went back to feasting on their prey.

"You're late," Harvey said.

Chapter 43
Thursday, May 28, 6:22 p.m.

Harvey sat in the back of an ambulance while a medical technician wiped Beale's blood and brain matter from his neck. As the technician worked, Harvey watched a small army of federal agents swarming around the property.

He said, "It's not my blood. I'm fine."

"Right. But we have to check," the technician said.

"Really, I'm fine."

"Okay, all done. I agree, you're fine."

"Thanks."

Harvey stepped out of the ambulance to find Jenny waiting for him by the side of the vehicle.

"You okay?" she asked, smiling with encouragement.

"Yeah, sure," said Harvey, trying to sound invincible.

"Hey, you probably saved my life back there. From the dogs. Thanks."

"Uh, well, thanks for trying to warn me. The text, I mean. How'd you get the number of the phone I carry now?"

"Mike followed the ambulance to the hospital. Your friend skipped out, but not before they got his name. He had four phones registered to him. We tapped all of them. Didn't know you'd actually be using one of them."

"But Dexter said his phone wouldn't connect to an IMSI catcher."

"We didn't need one. Just the patriot act and the awesome power of the U.S. Government."

"And that poor cop," Harry said somberly. "I'd be dead if it wasn't for him. I need to...know more about him."

"His partner will be here soon. He was with Pamela, getting her statement."

"And there's something else I have to know— was Grant a criminal? Was he really Zola's third partner?"

She said sheepishly, "Uh, no. We made that up, to try and vilify Grant and Pamela in your eyes, and get you on our side. Sorry."

"So...Grant was *innocent.* He did nothing wrong other than being an adulterer, same as probably fifty million other people in this country. And now he's dead." Harvey shook his head in disgust.

"Well, he—"

"And Pamela's innocent, too. Just a woman scared that her marriage was crumbling. She tried to pull her life back together, and she asked me for help. And I was duped. I didn't even stay loyal to her." Harvey winced at the thought of how he was so easily fooled.

"Don't be too hard on yourself, Harvey. You couldn't have saved Grant, he died before Pamela hired you. This case was—"

"Is your name even really Jenny?"

"Yes, it is."

"And your last name, is it Tabor?"

"Uh, no, actually it's not." She gave him a guilty half-smile. "Well, 'cmon, I *was* undercover. My real last name is Cippolini. That's right, I'm Italian, and named after an onion."

"Somehow, I don't see you as agent Jenny Cippolini. You're a U.S. Marshall?"

"Yes. Part of our mission is to apprehend federal fugitives. Zola was indicted on federal charges of weapons trafficking when he was arrested in Turkey. He would have been extradited to the U.S. after his trial there if he hadn't escaped. My superiors never believed that he died in that fire in Vienna seven years ago. The body they found was incinerated, every trace of DNA destroyed. All that was left were bones and an expensive ring and watch. It was all too convenient. So, when we heard the *Maiden* was apparently found by Grant, we figured that if Zola was alive, there was an excellent chance he'd come for it. Mike and I were assigned to come and wait for him."

"The bait drew *two* rats," Harvey noted. "Zola... and also a con woman, Linda Johnson."

"That's right. Linda appears to be long gone, but Elliot's in custody now. Before I got here Mike picked him up at the auto repair shop where he works. Elliot is just a thug, a follower. He's Linda's muscle and gofer. He spilled his guts to us because she apparently gave him the shaft. He told us about Linda's career as a con woman. She's no doubt an intelligent and talented person. Back in December, she was looking for her next mark and she caught wind of a local art professor who'd supposedly stumbled onto a very valuable painting. So, she enrolled to audit one of Grant's classes and began her seduction. She would have very quickly gotten Grant addicted to having sex with her, all the while pumping him for information about the painting. Elliot told us about the events of last week. When Grant left the house for the final time last Wednesday he went to Linda's apartment, they hopped into bed, and when he was drunk with pleasure, she suggested they run away together. She said they should pick up the painting immediately at the bank, sell it on the black market, and then just go off to an island somewhere and live happily ever after. But Grant didn't bite. Maybe he realized money was all she was really after. Linda's plan, according to Elliot, was that after she and Grant got the painting, she would sneak off in the middle of the night with it, leaving in its place that copy she made from one of Grant's photos, which she would attach to the original wooden backing. It would buy her some extra time to get away if Grant gave it only a casual look after she left, to verify that she didn't steal it. After Grant declined Linda's suggestion, she must have been convinced that Grant would never run away with her willingly, because she called Elliot to come over and basically threaten Grant into getting the *Maiden* from the bank. But Elliot is hot-tempered and impatient. Things got out of hand. Elliot claimed he choked Grant a little bit too aggressively, but didn't mean to kill him. In any case, when they couldn't revive Grant, Linda had to do some quick thinking to prevent the whole thing from collapsing. In Grant's wallet, Linda found the card that gave access to the safe deposit box and the key was on his keychain. She unlocked his phone with his fingerprint and found the password in the notes app. Linda and Elliot made the gutsy decision to retrieve the painting from the bank themselves that same day, before Grant could even be reported missing. Or rather, Linda made the decision and convinced Elliot that it was their best play. Why shouldn't she be in favor of it? Elliot would take all the risk. So, she made Elliot practice Grant's signature while she went to a store to get him some plain glass lenses in frames similar to Grant's, and a hat to obscure his appearance a bit. And according to Elliot, she remembered seeing a news story about a charity event when she researched his background months ago. It featured a picture of Grant and Pamela with some friends, one of whom managed the bank branch that housed the safe deposit box. She quickly did some online research on the guy and discovered that he was a single dad. She called in that shooter threat to the school that the guy's daughter attends, so he'd leave the bank. Within just a few hours of Grant's death, they went to the bank to get the painting. Elliot drove the roadster with Linda in the passenger seat. He dropped her at a coffeehouse some distance from the bank and then he drove the roadster into the bank's parking lot so that everything would look normal in video captured by the parking lot cameras. And Elliot was able to pull it off. He walked out of there with the *Maiden*."

"Amazing," observed Harvey. "With a combination of planning and some luck, they did it."

"Yes. After they got the painting, they had to go back to Linda's place and get rid of Grant's body. They had two cars, Linda's Maxima and Grant's roadster. The body wouldn't fit into the tiny trunk of the roadster, so Elliot put it into the Maxima's trunk. They left in the two cars late Wednesday afternoon and planned to meet here at Elliot's property, where they would bury the body. Not surprisingly, Linda drove the roadster this time and stuck Elliot with hauling the dead body in the Maxima. But being a cautious person, Linda stopped in Saylorville to switch license plates, in case the police were looking for Grant's car. Shortly after that, Grant's car broke down. She didn't realize it, but it was actually *good* luck for her since the faulty alternator sent a voltage spike through the car's electrical system that burned out our tracking device. So, she didn't make it here until the next day,

Thursday. Elliot said she left here Thursday evening in the roadster with the painting, to sell it. She was going to first ditch the car somewhere. She told Elliot she'd contact him within a few days. But she hasn't, and that's why Elliot was pissed enough to spill his guts. He said he'd testify against Linda if we catch up with her, in exchange for some leniency."

Harvey shook his head. "Wow. So, she drove away scot-free. Will you look for her?"

"Of course. She's an accomplice to murder. If I were Linda, I would've gone straight to Canada. The border is close, and leaving the U.S. would immediately reduce the heat. Being in possession of that painting is strong evidence of her crime, so she might have made arrangements to sell it as soon as possible. We're still questioning Elliot, but I doubt he'll have any information that will help us find Linda. Sounds like she's too smart to have told him anything, or to have let him see anything that could be used to find her. Unfortunately, she's got a good head start now."

They leaned against the ambulance, silent for a few moments until Harvey said, "Jenny, the things you told me about yourself... your grandmother with Alzheimer's... the protest over the closing of the homeless shelter... and you being accosted by the creep in college and how it changed you. All lies?"

"All those things are true, Harvey. I gave you at least *some* of the real me."

Harvey took some tiny consolation from the fact that in spite of all the lies, she had shared these small personal truths with him.

Harvey said, "Well...it sucks that Linda got away. But maybe the painting that she has isn't a real Vermeer. Hopefully, it's just a copy done by a student, worth only about fifteen thousand dollars."

Jenny looked surprised. "But it definitely *is* the Vermeer, because we know that Zola was in possession of the real one. That's why we were almost certain he'd come after Grant to get it back."

Now it was Harvey's turn to look puzzled. "But Grant was a nobody who found a painting in his aunt's house. So what? Why were you so sure it was the one Zola owned?"

"Remember I told you Zola had three partners who sold him out? Two of them were murdered within the past two weeks. Pamela told you that Grant's aunt was a financial attorney and he traveled with her for a few years when she did business in Europe and Asia, right? Her name was Helen Baker. She married late in life. Her maiden name was Helen Zuckerman. Zola thought government authorities had confiscated the *Maiden* along with his other paintings, but he was wrong. When Helen Zuckerman heard Zola had died in that fire, she took the *Maiden* from his safehouse before the authorities came in and took the remaining works. Zola didn't know she took it until she died from natural causes recently and the painting was found by Grant and its discovery leaked by his brother. Zola waited all these years to take his revenge because his former partners' murders would prove he'd survived that fire and the authorities would be out actively hunting for him again. But there was no point in delaying his revenge on the remaining two partners any longer when the painting surfaced. He just couldn't resist coming for his beautiful *Maiden.*"

Harvey's eyes were wide. "Holy crap. So, the aunt was Zola's third partner...and that means the painting is real...and Linda Johnson is now *filthy rich.*"

Epilogue

There was supposedly a breeze here on the beaches of Aruba all the time, at least that's what the locals told him when he arrived on the island yesterday. A trade wind, some called it. But he hardly felt it today. It was oppressively hot, and he forgot to wear a hat. He was wary of getting a bad sunburn because this was only the second day of his seven-day vacation.

Why had he chosen Aruba? He definitely needed a break from running his software company, and when he stepped into the travel agent's office three weeks ago with a beach vacation in mind, the colorful brochure on Aruba was probably the first one that caught his eye. Once the agent saw that he was interested, it wasn't difficult to sell him on the idea of spending a week here. What was the point in making loads of money if he couldn't stop to enjoy some of it?

He turned his head so that he faced away from the afternoon sun, and that's when he saw her. An incredible body, lean and shapely. Lying on her back in the sand, wearing dark glasses. She looked as if she were somewhere in her twenties. Just lounging there all alone, drinking in the Caribbean sun. Someone like that must surely have a husband or a boyfriend ... but what if ...? He decided quickly that he must try. This might be his only chance. Perhaps he wouldn't see her tomorrow, or ever again. If she told him to get lost, so what? He'd just leave. But if he didn't approach her, he'd wonder for months afterward, or maybe for the rest of his life, about what might have been.

He walked over to her, crossing thirty yards of sand as fine and pure as sugar. He was close now, and she looked stunning.

He summoned all his courage and said: "Hello. My name is Bob. It's a hot day, and you're lying here without an umbrella. I thought maybe you could use a cold drink. I'm about to get one for myself, and

I was wondering if you would like to join me. May I buy you a drink?"
Bob involuntarily held his breath as he waited anxiously for her reply.

Linda Johnson lifted her head from the blanket and then raised an arm and removed her sunglasses. She looked at the man who had spoken to her, taking a few seconds to form her first impression. Not too bad looking, actually. About forty-five years old. Not much hair, but that didn't matter very much to her. His overall look was adequate. Even though a man's physical appearance wasn't a primary consideration, she *did* have to keep in mind that if she took up with one who was exceptionally repulsive, it would make her the target of people's suspicions (*What could she see in him... other than his money?*). But this one didn't present any problem in that regard. She was pleased to see he wasn't too overweight. She had learned in the past that faking passion with a man who outweighed her by a hundred and fifty pounds was difficult for her, no matter how rich he was. The middle-aged man who stood before her carried perhaps a surplus ten pounds around the waist, but that was all.

Her eyes quickly scanned his hands in her usual practiced but casual manner. The hands told so much about a person. His were smooth and not calloused, his fingernails manicured. Diamond ring on the little finger, a showy but masculine-looking piece, black and gold, with three fair-sized stones. No wedding ring, although his marital status was of no particular interest to her, she could deal with it either way. By his speech, he was definitely an American, perhaps from California. There was a spark of sophistication in his voice. She noticed the gold money clip attached to his bathing suit waistband. Bold of him to display it, most men would have tucked it safely inside their bathing suit. There was a distinct possibility that he was very well off. Maybe a dot com tycoon? It should take her only a few drinks and probably less than half an hour of conversation to find out just *how* well off.

In her mind, she quickly played out the next thirty minutes. She would lean over just a bit when she talked to him, and she knew that his eyes would wander down to her cleavage now and then as they conversed. She would gaze into his eyes, seemingly transfixed as he spoke, and laugh shyly at his pathetic little jokes.

And after all, it was about time she stopped lounging around and got motivated because even though she'd made a killing selling the *Maiden* to that Canadian black-market dealer, she would have no trouble quickly blowing through it. When she scored big, she spent big. The dealer had expressed his grave doubts to her about its authenticity, but she knew how to read people. She was certain he felt it was a genuine Vermeer but voiced his skepticism only as a bargaining chip. Even so, she had to accept a black-market price for the painting that was far below its auction value. The risk to her of getting involved in a legitimate sale was out of the question. This was how she survived. A quick scheme, a quick profit, and on to the next thing.

Her mind wandered momentarily to Grant Damler. What a shame. He hadn't been unpleasant to be with. Too bad it had to end as it did. But when there was a painting worth many millions at stake, you didn't let anything stand in your way, not even murder. Especially when you had a psychotic cousin like Elliot to do all the unpleasant work. She'd been furious at Elliot for freaking out at her apartment and strangling Grant. But she kept her cool and regained control over Elliot, convincing him to take all the risks, including the biggest one — strolling into the bank to get the painting. She had thought, while waiting for him safely at that coffee house, that Elliot would almost surely get caught, and so she was ready to flee if he failed, and to write the whole operation off as a complete waste of effort. She was almost shocked to see him as he walked in with that dumb grin on his face, happily clutching the package in his hands.

After it was all over, she read the news coverage of Grant's murder. Not surprisingly, it was very thin on details, and was basically just a mess of unsubstantiated information, probably because no one was interested in saying much about it — certainly not the police who hadn't even put him on a missing person's list when his wife first reported him gone. One news story had included rumors of the involvement of some criminal named Zola. Who the hell was Zola? For that matter, who cared? *She* was the one who had ended up with the *Maiden*. And they'd also reported something about a private detective who was supposedly involved, some local jerkoff named Harvey or Henry something. Whoever he was, she'd beaten him, too. She'd beaten them all.

"Yes, a drink sounds like a wonderful idea," she said in a throaty voice that dripped with seduction. Her mind raced through her colorful palette of favorite names. Should she be Danielle Williams today? Or maybe Donna, Rita, or Bridget? She considered the fact that she was far away from the States, and from anyone who might be pursuing her. She felt comfortable enough to use her real name. At least her real *first* name.

"My name's Linda," she added with a sensuous smile.

The man was doubly stunned, first by the sexiness of her voice, and second by the fact that she'd said yes.

As she slowly stood up, she threw the man another seductive smile, and she could sense his excitement building. With her looks and her body, it was as if men were throwing money in her path as she walked, and all she had to do was bend down to pick it up.

It was all so easy.

www.ingramcontent.com/pod-product-compliance
Lightning Source LLC
Chambersburg PA
CBHW030643020726
47493CB00006B/1841